Renowned Be Thy Grave

Renowned Be Thy Grave

or The Murderous Miss Mooney

by

P. M. Carlson

Crippen & Landru Publishers
Norfolk, Virginia
1998

Cover painting and design by Deborah Miller

ISBN (limited edition) 1-885941-22-6

ISBN (trade edition) 1-885941-23-4

FIRST EDITION

10 9 8 7 6 5 4 3 2 1

Crippen & Landru, Publishers
P. O. Box 9315
Norfolk, VA 23505

E-Mail: CrippenL@Pilot.Infi.Net

TABLE OF CONTENTS

INTRODUCTION

Writing fiction about famous historical figures is challenging. The story has to be tucked in around so many facts.

Facts like how Jesse James was killed. There are detailed eyewitness newspaper accounts that tell us, moment to moment, what occurred. For example, the *Chicago Daily Tribune* quotes his killer, Bob Ford, on page 1, column 2 of their April 4, 1882 issue:

" '. . . Jesse was in the front room, where he slept. I never knew him to be so careless. He commenced brushing the dust off some picture-frames, but stopped and took off his weapons, and laid them on the bed. There was a Colt's revolver and a Smith & Wesson, each forty-five calibre. He also had in the room a Winchester repeating rifle, fourteen shots, and a breach-loading shot-gun. As he turned away from the bed we stepped between him and his weapons and pulled on him.' "

Clear enough. But here is the *Daily Tribune*'s report of the testimony at the inquest, on page 1, column 1 of the same issue, right next to the quote above:

"He [Jesse] said 'I guess I'll take off my pistols, for fear somebody will see them if I walk in the yard.' He unbuckled the belt in which he carried two forty-five calibre revolvers, one a Smith & Wesson, and the other a Colt, and laid them on the bed with his coat and vest. He then picked up a dusting-brush, with the intention of dusting some pictures which hung on the wall. To do this he got on a chair. His back was now turned to the brothers, who silently stepped between Jesse and his revolvers, and at a motion from Charlie, both drew their guns."

Oops. On a chair, or by the bed? Which eyewitness report do you believe?

(And was he really such a fastidious housekeeper?)

Beyond historical "facts" it gets worse. Was Jesse a hero, a Robin Hood who stole from the rich to give to the poor, as his neighbors said? Or was he a cold-blooded murderer, as railroad passengers and officers of the law believed? O. J. Simpson isn't the first to be judged not guilty by some, guilty by others. The tales that make up history, like trial verdicts and detective story clues, depend a bit on the facts, when we can figure out what the facts are, and a lot on who tells the story, and on who's listening, and on when it's told and why.

So yes, historical fiction is challenging. I love the research, finding all those "facts" and all those conflicts, and wondering if they can somehow be explained. Bridget Mooney's opinions would probably have been ignored in her time; but today, I like to think she makes a lot of sense.

P. M. Carlson
Brooklyn, NY
February 19, 1998

THE FATHER OF THE BRIDE; or,
A Fate Worse than Death!

"Hush, Bridget Mooney!" Aunt Mollie hissed at me. "Do you want them to hear us?"

"Oh, bother them all! I'm freezing here," I grumbled. "And my bustle keeps snagging in these damn branches."

"Enough sass! You'll never be rich and famous if you can't be a proper lady!" Aunt Mollie began, then broke off. "Lordy! They're coming!"

I peered over her cloaked shoulder and through the needles of the evergreen shrub where we had been huddling for—how long? An hour? A year? Till the last syllable of recorded time?

Beyond the new fence I finally saw them, cloaked and bundled like us against the chill and leaden sky. A frisky boy in his teens led the way, followed by a stout lively woman on the arm of a dapper man with a trim pointed imperial beard. Then, escorting a lovely girl with eyes as luminous as a fawn's, came the man we had been waiting for—a short muscular man with brown beard and kind thoughtful gaze. President Grant! I'll admit it, yes indeed: I was thrilled! I wanted to wrap myself in bunting and sing the "Battle Hymn of the Republic." He paused to light a cigar, and I noticed more people emerging from the White House behind him: a thickset young man with a dark mustache, a restless middle-aged man with reddish hair and pockmarked skin, a handsome, large, fleshy man. Then the entire party strolled toward our edge of the lawn.

"Papa, tell me!" I heard the fawn-eyed girl ask. "Why is a telegram like a blushing maiden?"

"Why, I don't know, Nellie." The president smiled at her. "Why?"

"Because they are both red quickly!"

They laughed. Aunt Mollie tensed as they approached, surreptitiously gathered up her skirt and cloak, and flung herself out of our hiding place and up against the fence just as the president reached the nearest point to us in the trajectory of his walk. But hurling myself after her, I found my head suddenly snapped backwards as though someone had slipped a noose around my throat.

Bridget Mooney foiled again! Always the comic relief. My bonnet had caught on an evergreen branch and I was snared like a rabbit.

Muttering unladylike words, I set myself to untangling my bonnet as Aunt Mollie called sweetly through the fence, "Mr. President! I have important news for you!"

The president glanced in her direction. Aunt Mollie was an earnest, pleasant-faced woman, her hair no longer red like mine but streaked with gray like a last year's peppermint candy. Her face was rosy with cold. He asked kindly, "What is it?"

"People are cheating you," she explained. "Thousands of dollars. I've got a friend, you see, works at Inverness in St. Louis . . ."

The president sighed and made a gesture of dismissal. "Thank you, madam. Consult my staff, please." He turned back to the girl on his arm and moved on.

"But I've got proof, Mr. President!" Aunt Mollie skittered crablike alongside the fence to keep pace.

The men with the president moved toward her in a leisurely way that made me think of big hounds that had spied a luckless turtle. The reddish-haired one said, "Move along, now, madam."

"But I must show him!" Aunt Mollie, waving a green-ribboned packet, was on the verge of tears.

The dapper man took pity and said, "Look, madam, write your name and address here. We'll try to get you an appointment."

"But this is important!"

The reddish-haired one was lean, excitable, and brusque. "Hundreds of people petition the president every week. Every day! He can't listen to everyone, now, can he?"

The big fleshy man had a thick beard and a kindly smile. "He needs time with his family, madam. Now, run along. We'll contact you."

They strode away to rescue President Grant from an onslaught of curiosity-seekers at the next turning. Aunt Mollie came storming back but didn't pause for me. I had finally disentangled my bonnet strings from the shrubbery but still hadn't tied them. She swept past and across the clean, satin-smooth breadth of Pennsylvania Avenue.

"Wait! Wait for me!" I exclaimed, darting after her and narrowly escaping the wheels of a speeding carriage.

She was still in a pout. "Look who's here! Precious little help you were, Bridget Mooney! And it's your prospects we're trying to improve!"

"My bonnet caught," I explained meekly.

"It's always something. Well, come along. Back to the boardinghouse to decide what to do. Maybe I should just hand them over to that newspaper editor. Fishback. But confound him, he won't pay."

"Back to the boardinghouse?" I squawked. "But you promised we'd go shopping after this! I didn't come all the way from St. Louis to hide in bushes!"

"Oh, Bridget, you are such a cross to bear! If I hadn't promised your dear mama—" That was only partly true, I knew. I was the bright hope of Aunt Mollie's life, her ticket to a moneyed life far beyond the means of a government copyist. But I'd never earn my way—and hers—to those flowery beds of ease if I couldn't get the training I needed.

I said, "I'm twenty-one, Aunt Mollie. Almost. You needn't treat me like a child. You won't even tell me what you're trying to do!"

She sighed, seeing the justice of my argument. "I reckon I could tell you. Here!"

She pulled the flat little bundle tied in green ribbon from the side placket of her skirt. I opened it: merely papers.

"These are from Mr. McDonald's office! Is that all?" I was bitterly disappointed. I had expected the Crown Jewels, at least.

"It's proof, silly goose! He's been cheating the government, and . . ."

Maybe it was the *silly goose* that got my dander up. I was tired of her bossiness, tired of standing around shivering in the cold when the nation's capital cried out for exploration. What a capital it was, new-minted now ten years after the exhausting war. Buildings were rising everywhere; streets were a chaos from the laying of gas lines and new pavement; noble young trees had been planted everywhere. Pennsylvania Avenue, an amazing broad ribbon of silky asphalt instead of St. Louis's broken cobblestones, beckoned me. I was young, pretty—well, pretty if you didn't mind freckles and low-class Irish red hair. I was on holiday, supposed to be having a splendid time. I stuffed her papers into my muff and skedaddled. "Come on, Aunt Mollie," I cried, "I'm going shopping!"

I know, I know, a proper lady doesn't go galloping through the streets of the national metropolis. But my tomboy years, shooting squirrels with my big brother in the Missouri hills, had taught me some useful skills. Yes indeed. Aunt Mollie chased me stoutly a block or two, then huffed despairingly, "And you wonder why I treat you like a child! Mark my words, Bridget Mooney, you'll come to a bad end!"

I had a splendid time, especially in the dry-goods stores. St. Louis had nothing to compare with the fine imported goods available here. Shopping without much money can be delightful—no need to make decisions about any of the glorious possibilities that present themselves, as they are all equally unattainable. In imagination, I costumed myself lavishly in fine velvets and French lace—as Juliet, as Cleopatra, as Rosalind, even as Lady Macbeth. But by two o'clock I began to feel guilty. A clerk had left a nice bit of Lyons velvet ribbon unattended on a counter. I hooked it as a peace offering for Aunt Mollie and turned back toward our boarding-house.

I know, I know, Aunt Mollie would scold too, but she knew value when she saw it. She'd keep it. And shouldn't clerks learn to be more careful?

There were two or three elegant taverns near the turn into my street. As I passed the first, a young man, well-dressed and devilishly handsome, tumbled out the door and against me. He clutched at my cloak to keep himself from falling, then hauled himself upright, blinking and swaying. "Oh, I shay, I'm terribly shorry," he exclaimed. An Englishman. A real swell. Reeking of drink.

I straightened my cloak with dignity. "Sir, you are rather rough. Please let me pass."

"Rough? Shorry. Really." But he didn't move, just swayed a moment as though collecting his woolly thoughts. He had a neat mustache, soft appreciative eyes, and a long, handsome, and somehow familiar, nose. He said carefully, "My lips, two blushing pilgrims, ready stand/To smooth that rough touch with a tender kish—um, kiss."

"O villain!" I retorted, "thy lips are scarce wiped since thou drunkest last!"

His velvety eyes glowed and he fell to his knees before me. "Shakespeare! On this benighted shore! Loveliest of sylphs, I shall be your slave forever! Come live with me! Or," he added more practically, standing and brushing off his elegant knees, "at least share a glash of wine?"

I put on my most ferocious Lady Macbeth glare. He shrugged, bowed, and disappeared into the next tavern while I stalked righteously around the corner into our street before I began giggling.

I waved gaily to the landlady from the stair hall. Mrs. Carter was fat as a walrus and almost as whiskery, and she seldom moved from her capacious rocking chair. She didn't respond, and I didn't know if she'd not seen me or merely needed more time to lift her plump arm. I ran up the stairs. Aunt Mollie and I had one of the two rear rooms on the second floor. The steps led up directly to our door. It was ajar an inch or two, and I was groping for the ribbon I'd found for her as I pushed the door open with my foot. It was jammed against something. I peered around the edge and saw Aunt Mollie sprawled on the floor with a great bloody gash in her throat.

A proper lady would have felt for her pulse, or wept, or shrieked. A proper lady would not have thought first of her own throat and how very much she preferred it ungashed. A proper lady would not have turned away from that partly-opened door and marched calmly down the stairs, still waving cheerfully at Mrs. Carter. Or walked straight back to that second tavern with a brazen smile for the young Englishman.

His sweet drunken eyes glowed welcome as he stumbled to meet me. "O joy! I thought you'd left my life forever!"

My hands were trembling in my muff and I couldn't even remember my Shakespeare. Aunt Mollie's image still shuddered at the back of my cowardly mind. I said simply, "Can't a girl change her mind?"

My favorite melodramas would claim that I was asking for a fate worse than death. But frankly, after seeing Aunt Mollie, I reckoned any other fate would do.

2

I woke the next morning in a splendid velvet and brocatelle bedroom amidst silken sheets wildly tumbled from my nighttime thrashings and exertions. Not that my handsome Englishman had been in any way involved. Whatever his original intentions, he'd been sound asleep long before his man and I had lifted him into bed, and while I'd flailed about in the throes of hideous dreams, he'd lain there lead-like and stinking all night long. In any case, I didn't fret much about my virtue any more. I'd been late to fill out, and Aunt Mollie, always clever in business, had taken advantage of my long time in the bud to sell my virginity. For a good price. Four times. The takers were St. Louis businessmen, proper gentlemen every one. Yes indeed.

During the sleepless intervals between nightmares last night, I had come to some conclusions. Without Aunt Mollie as guide and adversary, I was effectively alone in the world. Mama had died of a fever shortly after my birth; my older brother, after teaching me to shoot squirrels, had in turn been shot in the Civil War. Papa, though he adored me, had lost a precarious livelihood playing stage Irishmen because his love of the bottle caused him to miss too many cues, and he now spent his hours tippling at Uncle Mike's saloon. Uncle Mike would take me in, I knew, as a barmaid—his word for tart. Aunt Mollie had warned me away from that. To get on, she'd explained, a girl had to please people with money—in other words, men. Without a rich father, my choices were few: to be a servant or a tart, and remain poor; to marry a poor man, and remain poor; or to develop my talent for the stage and improve my chances. So I studied my Shakespeare, while

Aunt Mollie put out my virginity money at six percent and schemed to amass the remaining sum necessary to achieve the finer future she envisioned: rich, famous, even proper. I resolved now to aim for that future.

But first I would find the person who had killed her. Perhaps it was guilt for leaving her at the crucial moment; perhaps fury at the injustice of it. In any case, I'd go right back to that boarding-house, talk to the walrussy Mrs. Carter and her servants, look for clues like Hawkshaw himself. Oh, I know, I know, a proper lady doesn't go hunting cutthroats. She weeps prettily, and clever servants and heroes appear to fight for her cause. But weeping prettily did not seem to be a very practical strategy. For one thing, I was rather short of clever servants at the moment. And as for heroes—

I looked across the room at the only hero who had yet happened by. He was sitting ashen-faced in the armchair furthest from the light of the window, wearing slippers and a satiny maroon dressing-gown, his head bowed, seemingly studying the handsome top hat that stood nearby. His man was preparing some Seidlitz powders for him. But when I sat up his great pain-fogged eyes met mine and he attempted a smile.

"How is't with you, my lady?"

"I suspect my head feels better than yours," I observed. I tossed the sheet about me Grecian style and went to the washbasin.

"I hope so. Look here, sylph, who are you?"

"You wish an introduction, at this late juncture?" I wasn't sure I wanted this drunk and foreign stranger to know my horrid situation. What if he talked indiscreetly? There were people in this town who cut other people's throats.

"I know that you are either Mollie O'Rourke or Bridget Mooney from St. Louis," he said, swallowing the Seidlitz powders. "It would seem appropriate to know which."

He must have been reading my papers. I concentrated on my goddess-like attire and looked at him, heavy-lidded, with what I hoped was aplomb. "And you, in turn, are either John Bull, or else not."

He smiled. "Fair enough. My name is Algernon Charles Frederick Sartoris." He pronounced it Sar-triss.

"How grand!" I exclaimed. "With all those names you must be related to a duchess."

"Merely a countess. Oh, and this is my man, Littimer. Immortalized by Mama's late friend Dickens."

I bowed my head to Littimer, a highly respectable stiff-necked fellow with smooth short hair, and then looked back to my elegant host. Perhaps he was telling the truth. "Delighted to meet you, Algy," I said. "I'm Bridget. Do you usually ransack a lady's papers on first acquaintance?"

"I must confess to a certain curiosity about you," Algy admitted. "Generally speaking, tarts do not quote Shakespeare."

"Nor do they stay long to assist gentlemen numbed by drink."

Algy looked uncomfortable. Littimer smirked and said, "There's tarts and there's tarts," with as much innuendo as he could muster.

I whirled on him imperiously, nostrils flaring. "You block! You stone! You worse than senseless thing!"

"Littimer, leave us a moment. The lady is not a tart," said Algy with a weary wave of his hand, and Littimer sidled out, still smirking the smirk of the respectable. Algy turned back to me. "Littimer believes you hope to trap me into marriage."

"Marriage? Of course not!" I was appalled. "Then I'd have to leave the stage!"

"An actress! I should have guessed! What parts do you play?"

"Oh—the Colleen Bawn," I said, trotting out the best.

"Ah yes—the pretty girl milking her cow," mused Algy, then threw back his head and sang in a surprisingly strong, trained voice, "Brian O'Linn had no breeches to wear, so he bought him a sheepskin to make him a pair."

I couldn't help joining the spirited air: "The skinny side out, and the woolly side in, 'They are cool and convenient,' said Brian O'Linn."

We grinned at each other, then Algy asked shrewdly, "And nothing else but comic relief parts, right? Your voice is attractive but rather untutored, you know."

"Yes, I know! Aunt Mollie was going to get me voice lessons!" This was something of a sore point. The fourth St. Louis businessman had paid for my virginity by giving me a role in the theatre he managed. The laughter and applause that the audience had lavished upon me confirmed the passion for the stage I had harbored since seeing the greatest actress of the century when I was thirteen. But I had not been retained, because my St. Louis speech habits were suitable for too few roles, and in spite of Aunt Mollie's efforts, we had not yet accumulated enough for first-rate elocution lessons. I reported none of this to Algy, of course; I still felt it unwise to tell him the full extent of my difficulties. I concluded bravely, "In any case, most people think my voice is fine."

"Philistines," he declared. "Though perhaps my judgment is better trained than theirs. My mother sang opera before she married. My aunt was an actress, and my maternal grandparents. Perhaps you've heard of the

Kembles?"

I could not have been more astonished if he'd suddenly sprouted a halo and risen on a cloud of cherubim. But on the heels of my shock came recognition. I fell to my knees before him, reached up timidly to touch his face. "The nose!" I breathed. "The Kemble nose!"

Algy drew back impatiently. "Look, colleen, Kembles are no more than ordinary mortals like the rest of us."

"Algy, you're just wrong!" I sat back on my heels in indignation. "Papa took me to hear your Aunt Fanny when I was thirteen. Her midwestern tour. She read *Richard III* and took every role. I was enraptured! She was an army of people! No ordinary mortal can do that. She is the idol of my life!"

"Well," said Algy cruelly, "she does at least have a trained voice."

Clearly, kneeling before him was not advancing my case. I gathered my sheet about me regally and went behind the little screen. Someone, probably Littimer, had neatly arranged the items of clothing, Algy's and mine, on benches and hooks. It took time to don all the camisoles and petticoats and bustles required. When almost done I picked up my bonnet. Underneath was the ribbon I was going to give Aunt Mollie. The unexpected sight triggered a wild fit of tears.

"Here, here!" Algy was around the screen in a flash. "I say, what's the matter?"

His dressing-gown was embroidered satin, and I fear that I snivelled all over one side. He patted my shoulder awkwardly, and said, "There, there," and other equally useful things, and finally inquired, "Look, colleen, what have I done? Ruined your reputation? Insulted your voice? Forgotten to offer you a glass of wine? Tell me my sin, so that I may atone!"

I realized that I'd have to explain my tears. "My aunt's dead," I sobbed. "And I'm angry and miserable."

"Yes, yes, I see. Your aunt. Was this recent?"

"Just after we collided yesterday, I found her dead. That's why I came back to you. I was frightened. And alone."

"Ah." He nodded. "I suspected there was more to it than my noble Kemble nose. My poor Bridget!"

"You've been kind, Algy." I pulled a handkerchief from my muff, noting uneasily that my papers were gone.

"I understand. My older brother died a year ago. One is naturally sad. Tell me, how did she die?"

"She was—knifed." The mere thought of it made me quail.

"Knifed! On the street?"

"In our room."

"Well, ah, did you do it?"

"Me?" I stepped back indignantly. "What do you mean?"

"Look, colleen, at the facts. Your aunt is killed, in your room at Mrs. Carter's boarding-house, correct?"

He had definitely been reading my papers. I nodded.

"And you disappear at the same time. What would any reasonable person conclude?"

Thus challenged, I realized that there had been a logic to my thoroughly improper behavior. "Look, Mr. Sar-triss, sir, we only just arrived yesterday. And the only people we've met are Mrs. Carter and her servants. We went there because friends in St. Louis recommended her establishment. Said it was decent and would accept ladies traveling alone." I plunked my bonnet on my head and tied the strings. "But it can't be all that decent, can it, if the ladies are murdered?"

"You weren't followed from St. Louis? You met no one on the journey?"

"I wanted to, but Aunt Mollie made sure we kept to ourselves."

"And Mrs. Carter is the only person you met here?"

"Unless you want to count the president of the United States."

Algy's soft gaze became suddenly intense. "The president? You met him?"

"Oh, Algy, for heaven's sake! The president doesn't go about knifing people!" I remembered Shiloh and Petersburg, and added, "Well, except maybe Rebels. And anyway, we didn't really meet him. Aunt Mollie just had this silly idea. Thought she had proof that someone in St. Louis was cheating the government, and—"

I broke off. A new train of thought had suddenly presented itself. I had to go back to that boardinghouse, I realized. Not only to make sure poor Aunt Mollie was properly taken care of, but also to establish that I didn't do it. And to collect my things, and to see if Aunt Mollie had left anything that might tell me who her killer was. I'd been sure he was in Mrs. Carter's employ; now I saw that perhaps he was not. But whoever he was, I resolved, he was going to suffer a fate worse than death.

Algy, waiting for me to finish my sentence, prompted, "And what?"

"Nothing. She wouldn't tell me any details." I picked up my cloak.

"Did she tell the president?"

"No. We only saw him through the fence. He wouldn't listen. He was taking a walk, and just told her to get an appointment and then went on his way."

"Was anyone with him?"

"Several people. Family, I suppose, and four men."

"A girl? Your age, or a bit younger?" he asked eagerly.

"Yes. Dark hair, pretty. His daughter?"

"Nellie," sighed Algy. "Those eyes!"

Philanderer. I was vexed; how could he sigh over Nellie Grant's eyes when he'd just spent the night with me? Well, it hadn't been truly romantic for either of us, I'm bound to admit. And if he was acquainted with Nellie's eyes, he might be able to tell me about those people. I followed him into the room and said, "There was a young man. Thickset, mustache."

"That would be Nellie's brother, Lieutenant Colonel Fred. Fine young scamp. Went to West Point, you know. In discipline, he graduated forty-first in a class of forty-one." Algy seemed to approve.

"Even so," I said, "he seemed more disciplined than the middle-aged, nervous fellow with reddish hair and bad skin."

"Ah, yes, the terrifying General William 'Cump' Sherman."

"Also a well-dressed fellow with an elegant imperial beard. And a large, handsome man. Very genial."

"Grant's personal secretary, General Babcock. The large man had a beard?" I nodded and he said, "General Belknap. Secretary of War."

"Do any of them go about knifing people?"

He looked at me thoughtfully. "Did your aunt mention that she had proof?"

"No more than mention. You didn't answer my question."

He seemed a little distracted, fiddling with his stylish curly-brimmed top hat. "The answer is no. They are all close to the president, of course, and honorable men."

Like Brutus, I wondered? I was sorry now I hadn't pressed Aunt Mollie more about what she knew. It had all seemed just another of her blame-fool ideas to get me on stage. She'd planned to sell her knowledge to the president, then get me voice lessons from a professional in New York, and live off the fabulous earnings that would eventually ensue. I was in favor of all that, of course, but did not believe in it as fervently as Aunt Mollie. All I'd really expected from this plan was a trip to Washington. But Aunt Mollie had always been able to spot a good business deal, and if the papers she had hooked from her most recent employer's office were in fact of value—or danger—to someone . . .

I addressed Algy again. "Do you know of a man named McDonald?

Collector of internal revenue for the St. Louis district?"

"No, I don't know of him." Algy left his top hat where it stood and walked over to the great velvet-draped window. There were now some papers in his hand. With a sudden sense of horror, I recognized my boarding-house card and Aunt Mollie's green-ribboned packet.

"You wretch!" I cried, lunging for the papers.

He laughed and held them high, out of my reach. "Come, colleen, allow me to finish inspecting your most interesting collection."

I hauled up my skirts, kneed him where it would do the most good, snatched the papers from him as he doubled over moaning, and ran out, slamming the door behind me. It was becoming more and more difficult to be a proper lady these days.

Littimer had repaired to a respectable position by the staircase. "Your master is having a bad morning," I told him. "Better go see to him." He bowed without comment and was striding back to Algy's aid as I sailed downstairs and out the tavern door.

Today Mrs. Carter's entry was locked. I rang the bell and set my face in carefree lines. "Oh, Mrs. Carter," I bubbled brightly as she wheezingly opened the door, "I have so much news for Aunt Mollie! Did she tell you I met my father's cousin Emily, and went to stay with her last night? Oh, there are so many . . ."

"Poor child!" Mrs. Carter's small puffy eyes were brimming. "You don't know! Oh, a terrible thing happened to your aunt yesterday. I never knew of such a thing! A robber, it was."

"A robber? What do you mean? Everything was fine when I ran in yesterday to ask permission to stay with Emily."

"Yes, I thought I saw you. Oh, my poor Miss Mooney, she's dead."

"What? I don't believe you!" That was my cue to run up the stairs. Still, it was an effort to take the dreaded next step. I told myself that Mrs. Carter had the place firmly locked, that she and the servants were near and probably innocent. I reassured myself that if I saw a man with a knife I could scream for help. But it was hard to keep my heaving stomach under control because I wasn't sure I could face Aunt Mollie again. As I pushed the door slowly open, I prayed that they'd taken her away.

They had. But I didn't bother to scream for Mrs. Carter, because the same moment that the cold blade touched my throat, a hand clamped across my nose and mouth.

3

"No noise, now," murmured the voice in my ear as the door closed behind me. "Yer little windpipe slits as easy as the rest. If ye understand, whisper yes."

I understood, yes indeed. Voice lessons couldn't do much for a slit windpipe. As he released my mouth I whispered, "Yes."

"Good. Sit down, now. I have need of a quiet conversation with ye." He pushed the door closed while the knife nudged me into a chair.

"All right," I whispered, and added for good measure, "*sir.*"

"Who are ye? Why are ye here?"

I could see him now. He had a Union soldier's cap pulled low on his brow and a soiled scarf about his bristly chin, but the warty nose and pale eyes and listing posture reminded me of someone. St. Louis, I thought. At General McDonald's office where Aunt Mollie did copying. She had pointed at this man once across the courtyard, wondering why he was hanging about. But it didn't seem wise to let him know I recognized him. "Whisht, I am but the housemaid, sir," I said, sounding as low and Irish as I possibly could in a whisper. Papa would have been proud of me.

"Oh, ye are, are ye?" The knife point pressed a little closer. "And why the fine bonnet and muff, then?"

He was right; my meet-the-president costume was woefully inappropriate to this role. I improvised. "Sure and haven't I been visiting my fine cousin Emily? But it's a bit late I am getting back. I thought to start in, sir, before the old lady Carter missed me."

The knife point eased a little. "Aye, she's a bit slow, that one. So ye're the one who does up this room?"

"Yes, sir, that I am. And a fine jumble it is today, sir." It was true; drawers, carpetbags, wardrobes, all were open and the contents strewn about. I tried not to look at the dark stain on the carpet near the door.

The pale eyes glinted with something like craftiness. "Perhaps the two of us can make a little agreement, me girl. I've been sent to find some papers in this room, the rightful belongings of me master. Give me a little help and I'll let ye be."

"Of course, sir, being as the papers are rightfully his."

"That they are. Now, me girl, I've searched this room and found nothing. With yer practiced eyes perhaps ye'll have more success. But remember, if ye make any difficulties, the knife will put an end to them quick."

"Yes, sir." He had been talking softly; but I still whispered. It seemed to me that the muff was giving off sparks from the presence of the packet tucked inside. I was fortunate, I supposed, that this fellow hadn't seen me with Aunt Mollie. While I did not realistically expect to be in this world much longer, his ignorance had granted me a few more terrified moments of life while I searched for an escape from this dilemma. "How many papers, sir?" I asked.

"He didn't say. They're done up in a packet, he said, with a green ribbon."

Suddenly we both became aware of a commotion in the hall.

"'Shcuse me, madam! Just looking for my cousin!" There was a crash, and our door sprang open. Algy lurched into the room, clinging to the doorknob for balance. "Cousin!" He beamed.

"Who's this?" My pale-eyed companion was again grasping me tightly, knife at my throat.

Algy giggled. "Pirates! What a jolly idea! I shay, let's shail away on the bounding main!" He snatched the counterpane from Aunt Mollie's bed, waved it in the air, and dropped it neatly over the warty-nosed head. I jerked away at the same moment, so fast that I stumbled back over the chair.

The knife came slashing out through the counterpane, but Algy lifted the oil lamp and thumped it soundly down on my unpleasant companion's head. The counterpane-wrapped rogue collapsed at my feet. I snatched the knife from the limp folds, tucked it into my boot, and sat down on the bundle.

Algy, breathing hard, surveyed the situation and sat on the other end.

For a moment we both were motionless. I waited for my pounding heart to slow before I said shakily, "So now you're my cousin?"

"From across the billowing sea. Or so I told your rotund hostess when she asked if I were the cousin."

"Unfortunately for your clever story, I told her my cousin's name was Emily."

"Easily remedied. Poor Emily married a drunken Englishman."

"Yes, she's so impetuous. Should have held out for a better match."

We grinned at each other, but I was uneasy. We had not exactly parted friends, yet Algy made no reference to his recent discomfort. I fidgeted on my lumpy seat. "Warty-nose here is rather bony," I said. "Why don't we drop him on the back porch roof outside the window?"

We rolled him unceremoniously onto the roof. Then I locked the window and turned back to the chaotic room. "Terrible mess," Algy observed.

"Well, I'll just throw it all into our carpetbags," I said, and began to do so.

"Would you mind settling with Mrs. Carter about the lamp and counterpane? She's been through rather a lot, and I'll have to find what she's done with Aunt Mollie."

"You're afraid she won't tell you what she's done if she hasn't been paid for the damage?"

I shrugged. "*I* wouldn't."

"Mm. All right." Algy hesitated a moment, then asked, "Bridget, what is it you want?"

"At the present moment? I want a decent burial for Aunt Mollie, and a place to stay, and breakfast, and a good cry."

He nodded. "Right. But I meant—from life."

"From life?"

"Well, you're a deucedly odd sort of girl. For example, you seem in no hurry to contact your family in St. Louis."

"Aunt Mollie was all the family I had." Papa and Uncle Mike weren't worth mentioning.

"I see. And unlike your mythical cousin Emily, you don't seem bent on marriage. Rather the opposite."

"I love acting. And even your Aunt Fanny, the idol of my life, found that marriage and the stage don't combine easily."

"That's true enough. And the stage is what you really want?"

"Yes. Eventually. But first two other things. I need voice lessons, so people don't laugh at my Shakespeare."

"Good idea. And the second thing?"

I pulled the knife from my boot and tested the edge with my fingertip. "I want to find the man who killed Aunt Mollie."

Algy looked surprised. "Weren't we just sitting on him?"

"Oh, yes, Warty-nose. A hired hand. I want to find who hired him." My rage was very near the surface again, but I dissembled: Patience on a monument, smiling at grief. I said, "I've seen Warty-nose in St. Louis, Algy. Near the place Aunt Mollie worked."

"Connected with this McDonald you mentioned?"

"Perhaps."

His beautiful brow furrowed. "But your aunt was killed here, in Washington."

"Yes, that's part of the problem. Who is Warty-nose's master? And what's his interest in St. Louis?"

"If my ear at the keyhole didn't deceive me, Warty-nose wanted your aunt's papers."

"Yes." I looked straight into his disarming velvety eyes. "And so do you. Right?"

"Well—" He smiled boyishly. A good trick; if I hadn't understood him so well I might have been on my knees instantly, begging him to accept the packet as a small token of my esteem.

Instead, I said coolly, "You didn't follow me here out of love, Algy, not after what I did to you. I do appreciate the heroic rescue, but perhaps we could manage our business more efficiently if you told me what *you* want from life."

He hesitated, and seemed to decide on the truth. He said, "Nellie Grant."

I was startled. "The president's daughter? Truly?"

"I met her on an Atlantic crossing a year ago. We—well, I want to marry her." The man was actually blushing.

I turned away to slide Warty-nose's knife into my muff. "How sweet of you. I fancy that her fortune and connections don't repulse you either. An American princess. I take it there is opposition to this marriage? Your illustrious family, perhaps?"

"Well, they profess to be shocked, thinking all you Americans rather wild and uneducated. Aunt Fanny had a bit of bad luck with an American husband, you recall."

"He was a damn Rebel."

"Well, yes. But my family will consent if I press matters. And Nellie's mother is pleased enough with my connections. No, the real difficulty is the president. He dotes on Nellie, as well he might. And people close to him are advising against the match. So he makes excuses. First he said she should marry a countryman. I offered to become an American citizen. That was before my brother died, of course. Then he said she was too young. His advisors say—well, he finds countless excuses."

"Including, no doubt, that his daughter should not marry a drunken man who takes strange young ladies to his room at night?"

He looked disconcerted. "Bridget, you can't prove that! Littimer is incorruptible!"

I slid my fingers into the muff, next to the knife, and pulled out an extremely distinctive shirt-stud.

He said angrily, "You'll ruin your own reputation too!"

"Algy, Algy, what do you take me for? Of course I don't mean to do anything with this shirt-stud. But perhaps we can help each other."

"Ah. Yes."

I extracted the green-ribboned packet from my muff. "No, no, I'll hold it," I warned him, jerking it away from his eager grasp. "You may look, but must agree to tell me what it means. Then we'll discuss the price."

He nodded his consent. I undid the ribbon, rather rumpled from its strenuous adventures, and unfolded the enclosed paper.

It was only a short note. It said, "Tell J. the case against Inverness is now strong enough to ensure cooperation." It was signed "Robert E. Lee."

I watched Algy read it, saw the flash of excitement, quickly veiled. He said guardedly, "Actually, I'm not sure what it means."

"Well, then," I said regretfully, "I suppose I'd best sell it to a newspaper." I folded the note.

"No, no, wait! It's not from Robert E. Lee!"

"I don't need you to tell me that, Algy." My voice dripped scorn: Katharina the shrew.

He blurted, "Inverness is a distiller. In St. Louis."

"I knew that too. But you do tell me one thing of interest. I take it you have an idea what to do with this note."

"An inkling," Algy admitted. "Whereas you have no idea at all."

I reflected a moment. He was right: although I had an idea, it was far too vague. I knew only that the place to ask questions was the White House. Warty-nose had instructions about the green- ribboned packet. Therefore, my quarry was one of the men with the president who had seen the packet. Algy had recognized the writer of the note at a glance, obviously from the handwriting. So I decided to use Algy. A blunder could easily result in death for an unimportant St. Louis visitor. Algy, on the other hand, had the backing of the entire British Empire. If he were murdered, there would be a spectacular investigation.

There was a groan from outside the window. I picked up a piece of Aunt Mollie's scattered stationery and copied the words from the note in a schoolgirl's block printing. Then I tied the copy into the green-ribboned package, opened the window, and tucked it into the moaning man's pocket. He was still too fuddled to notice. I hoped he wouldn't roll off the roof before he woke up. I was depending on him to take the note to his superior, in the hopes he'd leave me alone. I relocked the window, turned back to Algy, and held up the real note.

"The price," I said, "is a situation and a letter."

"A situation?"

"In the White House. Housemaid, perhaps."

Algy frowned. "Not much chance of that. But—tell me, how are you at flowers?"

"I can learn anything."

"I believe you, Bridget Mooney. For now, I'll get Sir Edward Thornton to give you a temporary position."

"Who?"

"My host. Her Majesty's impeccable minister to this former colony. With his reference you can move on to the White House as soon as I convince Mrs. Grant to hire you."

Well, I wasn't likely to get a better offer. Besides, Sir Edward's would offer a safe harbor from which to observe both Algy and Warty-nose before plunging into the deeper eddies of the White House proper. I said, "All right."

"And the letter you mentioned?"

"A letter of introduction to your illustrious Aunt Fanny, explaining my desire for voice lessons and touching upon my many virtues, et cetera."

"Done!" He in turn grabbed up Aunt Mollie's stationery and, with great alacrity, wrote a laudatory note and presented it to me for my approval. The address was near Philadelphia.

I took the note and handed him the one from the purported Robert E. Lee. "It's a bargain, then."

"You give this to me now?" he asked warily.

I picked up my muff and smiled. "I trust you, Algy. As long as I have your shirt-stud. And a knife."

He smiled back and gave me a little salute. We understood each other, we two. What a shame that he'd already succumbed to the beauteous Nellie's fawn-like eyes.

4

I arranged for Aunt Mollie to be sent home to St. Louis to be buried, promising her shade that Warty-nose would be punished as soon as he'd led me to his master. I felt guilty for running off to the shops at just the wrong time; I was infuriated at Warty-nose and his phantom superior for cutting short her life just when she was so full of hope and excitement about both our futures. And, despite the demands of the lowly position Algy had obtained for me at Sir Edward Thornton's, I missed her sorely. For a while the world seemed to wear a black border. My every thought had a margin of sorrow. So I spent my last pennies on mourning crepe and plotted revenge.

But Warty-nose had disappeared. Although I spent weeks expecting him to leap out from every dark corner and chop me to flinders, he was nowhere to be seen. Perhaps he was still nursing his broken head.

Algy presented activities of more immediate interest. He in fact spent most of his nights in the beautiful rooms at Sir Edward's, rooms forbidden to kitchen-and-cellar creatures like me. Occasionally he would not come in at all. "Away on business," the respectable Littimer would tell me when they returned. I could guess the kind of business from Algy's bloodshot eyes, yes indeed. But most of the time he was a proper swell, bantering with Sir Edward and ignoring the servants. Including me.

But one day he came out into the yard as I was drawing water from the old-fashioned well by the kitchen garden. My arms were muddied to the elbows and there were smudges on my face and clothes, but I was declaiming "Now is the winter of our discontent" as I remembered the great Mrs. Kemble performing it. Algy said unkindly, "Ah, Bridget! Rehearsing for the wicked red-haired Lady Audley, I see."

I looked at him coldly. "Lady Audley, as I recall, pushed her enemies into the well."

"So she did," he smiled, stepping back out of reach. "I just thought you might like to know that Nellie and I have received the president's consent at last."

"Aunt Mollie's note?" I asked eagerly. "Who did you show it to?"

He held a finger to his elegant lips. "Shh! Telling you that is not part of the bargain."

"Getting me into the White House is."

He nodded. "I don't want to arouse suspicions. But I'll seize the first opportunity."

"Just don't forget who has your shirt-stud."

"I shan't, my dear Miss Mooney."

He wandered out the carriage driveway. I debated throwing the pail after him; but he had such a handsome nose.

It was clear that Algy would tell me no more than he had to. The wedding date was chosen; he had what he wanted, or would soon. But the news made me even more eager to get into the White House. I could understand why Nellie would find Algy's dashing ways attractive. But her famous father ought to know better. He'd been the victorious commanding general of a gigantic army of men; he'd maneuvered his way into the Presidency. He was a man of the world. Doubtless he understood Algy's character far better than the naive Nellie did. And yet Aunt Mollie's note had persuaded someone who could in turn persuade the most powerful doting father in the United States to allow this unsuitable match. My regard for Aunt Mollie rose.

I fitted another string to my bow by writing a guarded letter to the St. Louis newspaper editor Aunt Mollie had mentioned, Mr. Fishback. If he wanted interesting information about Inverness, I suggested, he should write to me as though from a cousin, Emily, and send the letter to me at Sir Edward Thornton's. Despite my attempt to shelter in Queen Victoria's capacious arms, and my furtive posting of this missive, I worried that it might be intercepted. For days afterward I sensed Warty-noses behind every tree; but no attack came, and no answer.

It was depressing. So, on a tender early-spring day of unfolding leaflets, I waylaid Algy. "It's time," I said.

"Time?"

"Algy, it's almost May. You'll be off honeymooning within a month. That is, you will be if I get a situation at the White House tomorrow."

"Ah. I see."

"Otherwise," I spelled it out for him, "there is an envelope containing your shirt-stud and a letter that explains in vivid detail how it came into my possession. Nellie's name is on the envelope."

He gave me a sidelong glance. "Mm. And where do you keep this letter?"

"Algy! How insulting for you to think I would tell you!"

That boyish grin again. No wonder poor Nellie was besotted. "Deepest apologies, dear Bridget."

"In any case," I informed him, "there's no reason for either of us to become anxious, is there? You want Nellie and her fortune. I want voice lessons and revenge for Aunt Mollie. No reason we shouldn't all attain our goals and be happy as canary birds."

"Ah, Bridget, if only the rest of the world were as reasonable as we!"

The next day he informed me that I was to be interviewed by Mrs. Grant in the White House conservatories. "How should I act?" I asked Algy.

"Just make her believe she is a grand lady."

"Lots of curtseying?"

A smile twitched at his mouth. "Yes, and remember to look her straight in the eyes."

The greenhouses sprawled west of the White House, enclosing a delightful tropical world. I was glad Algy did not attend the interview—he was off murmuring sweetnesses to Nellie, no doubt—because his presence might have sent me into fits of giggles and finished the whole business right there. Mrs. Grant was a short, stocky woman, in mourning because of her father's death last year. Her dark hair was just beginning to be streaked with gray. I found her admirable—a St. Louis girl who had become the most proper lady in the land. Even her chief feature I could have accepted calmly if it hadn't been for Algy's naughty comment: she had a squint that caused one of her eyes to roll wildly off in random directions even while the good one studied me carefully. Look her straight in the eyes, indeed! Algy, you cad! I dropped my own lashes modestly and succeeded in murmuring answers to her questions without inappropriate titters. Apparently my air of confusion did not count against me; she expressed her approval of taking me on as assistant in the conservatories, and even suggested that they might soon need people to assist with Nellie's wedding. She smiled kindly at me, and simultaneously at the glass dome of the greenhouse, and sent me away to my new supervisor.

Algy had chosen my work, I decided, to prevent me from discovering his contact. From time to time my tasks took me as far as the basement kitchen of the White House, but for hours on end I was cast away in the alien world of the greenhouses.

Gardeners and maids came frequently; Mrs. Grant almost daily; even Nellie once or twice. But the men I most wanted to observe, though tantalizingly near, kept their distance; an occasional glimpse of one or two of them on the South Portico was the best I could do.

But one day in early May, as I was tending the palms, my dream came true: the Grants arrived to inspect the wedding greenery, and a large group of people came with them. I hid my exultation as I noticed Nellie's brother, the supposedly undisciplined Lieutenant Colonel Fred Grant; the large and genial General Belknap with his voluptuous new wife Puss Belknap; the sleek General Babcock with Nellie and a giggling group of young ladies; and the ferocious General Sherman, who glowered at my ferns as though planning a second march to the sea through their midst.

"The devil take you, Sam, you've got a tropical isle here!" he exclaimed. "It wasn't this lush the last time I peeked in! What did you do, annex Santo Domingo after all?"

The president nodded. "Mrs. G. plans to move the entire state of Florida into the East Room."

"Oh, Ulys, don't tease so!" Mrs. Grant laughed, her good eye beaming at her husband. "Of course weddings must have flowers!"

"And bells," agreed the president, "but must they have bells made of flowers?"

"Bells made of flowers, ropes made of flowers, columns made of flowers!" Sherman was striding among the palms and ferns, lean and nervous, his pitted face animated. I bobbed behind a palm, out of his way. "Why did you bother to redecorate the East Room, Sam? Your new carpets will be buried in this greenery! Ah, we saw enough of jungles in Georgia and Carolina, right, Belknap?"

Belknap gave an immense, good-natured chuckle. "Right, we had plenty of jungle there! And swamps!"

"Swamps, right!" Sherman whirled, gesturing exuberantly. "Spanish moss hanging from your new chandeliers! Rice springing up from the carpet —nice for a wedding, eh? Water moccasins twining around the columns!"

"Copperheads slithering down from the north!" suggested General Babcock. Everyone was laughing.

"Hang you, Bab, what do you know?" Sherman asked Babcock. "You and Sam were sitting about, taking your ease, teaching young Fred to smoke cigars, while Belknap and I were doing all the work, whipping the South."

"Yes, and if we'd stopped besieging Lee, where would you have been?" demanded Lieutenant Colonel Fred hotly, but he was stopped by a smile from his father.

"You must let Cump have his way, Fred," said the president. "We must be indulgent of the elderly."

I glanced fearfully at the fierce Sherman, but this appeared to be an old joke between the two men, for Sherman's mirth was undiminished. He said, "Old or not, I plan to leave my frock-coat at home and come to this wedding dressed as an alligator. With bright yellow kid gloves."

"Oh, Papa," exclaimed one of Nellie's giggling friends to General Sherman, "you must stop teasing!"

"Minnie, dearest, the First Lady of our splendid republic has a great heart and will forgive her humble servant." Sherman clicked his heels and bowed to Mrs. Grant.

"Indeed I will, General Sherman," said the jolly Mrs. Grant, "but you must promise to stop your slanders and give us advice!"

"My humble opinion in great state matters is worthless, but you are welcome to it," said Sherman. "What is the problem?"

"Why, we are to have a bell, as Ulys told you, formed of snowballs and white roses, or perhaps camellias," said Mrs. Grant. "It's been suggested that we have a wreath, with initials. But what initials?"

"Algy's, by all means," said Lieutenant Colonel Fred, "because he has so many!"

"Oh, Fred, hush!" Nellie exclaimed, "or we won"t let you be groomsman!"

"Hurray! Then I won't have to attend this silly affair!"

Nellie gave a little scream and chased Lieutenant Colonel Fred around the ferns so boisterously that I began to fear for the fronds. He might have been last in his class at West Point in discipline, but Nellie wasn't much better today. Nor was the president, who picked up a morsel of clay from one of the pots, rolled it into a little ball, and tossed a bullseye square in his son's forehead.

"Oh, Papa!" Lieutenant Colonel Fred wiped off his face while Nellie jumped up and down, clapping her hands. A girl of simple mind, yes indeed.

Yet I had to admit that in other respects Algy's taste was impeccable. Nellie Grant was a lovely creature, fresh as springtime, the natural heroine of any scene: eighteen years old, with creamy skin, lush dark hair, and smoky eyes that ranged from dark thoughtfulness to a bright sparkle when she laughed, as now. But could Algy bear to live with that unformed, uneducated mind?

Mrs. Belknap asked, "Julia, why not put all the initials in the wreath? His and hers?"

"Why, that's just what I suggested, Puss," Mrs. Grant told her. "But they say it would become so complex that we wouldn't be able to make out the letters."

"Allow me to suggest two wreaths," said General Babcock. "One on each side of the bell."

"Oh, Mama, that's a good idea!" enthused Nellie.

"Yes, let's ask if they can do that! And now, come see the fuschia, Puss," suggested Mrs. Grant.

"Oh, Papa, I almost forgot!" cried Nellie, running to her father. "Tell me, when is a door not a door?"

The president's face softened. "How can that be, Nellie? How can a door not be a door?"

"When it is ajar!"

"Ajar! Oh, that's very good! We must tell your mother!"

Into this idyllic scene came Algy, handsome and sleek as a saber. I noticed Mrs. Grant's welcoming coo, Lieutenant Fred's warm handclasp. Nellie just stood there, rapture shining in those delicious eyes.

"Greetings, one and all!" said Algy; but his gaze spoke only to Nellie. He crossed to the ferns where she stood and caught up her hand to kiss. They were so beautiful, creatures of fantasy: Lancelot and Guinevere, the Duke and

Viola, Romeo and Juliet. Algy and I knew it was fantasy, but the others believed—Nellie enchanted with her storybook romance, her family and friends carried along by her joy. I stood behind the palm in coarse servant's black with my red knuckles and freckles, a gross Caliban on the magic isle.

Then I saw Babcock move to the president's side, sympathy in his glance, and I noted what I should have seen before: the president's kind, determined face had darkened just a shade to worry. Babcock murmured something to him and he nodded; but I wanted to cry out, you're right, Mr. President, don't let her do it!

Of course I didn't cry out. For once I was a proper lady—or at least a proper servant—and tried to remain invisible, humbly snipping dead leaves from plants and listening avidly to the conversations. Unfortunately, no one confessed to arranging Aunt Mollie's death, nor even to having connections in St. Louis, save the president himself, who was telling Sherman and Belknap of the excellent horses he kept on a farm there.

Babcock interrupted them. "We really must settle the Richardson resignation, sir," he said quietly to the president.

"Oh, the devil take Richardson!" exclaimed Sherman.

"The treasury is important even to the army," commented Babcock with a smile.

"Sherman and Belknap prefer to live on the land," said the president. "Look, Bab, you go draft the papers and I'll talk to him again. Right now I want to tell these fellows about my fine old horse, Butcher Boy."

Babcock bowed and left the greenhouse. Watching him, I suddenly became aware of Algy at my elbow. He still held Nellie's hand, but his gaze shone on me kindly. As though from a great distance, he asked, "How are you, Bridget?"

I curtsied. "Quite well, thank you, sir. Though I wonder that General Babcock does not seem as much a general as the other generals."

"Very astute, isn't she, Nellie? General Babcock was only a colonel in the war. But don't underestimate him. He was chosen to make arrangements for the surrender at Appomattox. He's been a most capable assistant to Nellie's father for years."

"That's right," Nellie affirmed, smiling at me with winning sweetness. "And he's ever so nice."

How could I argue with that well-reasoned testimonial? I changed the subject. "Mrs. Belknap's frock is lovely."

"Oh, isn't it?" Nellie enthused. "It cost a thousand dollars!"

Quite a sum for the wife of a glorified soldier with nothing but his government salary. I said, "The triple pillar of the world transformed into a strumpet's fool."

Nellie looked blank and Algy broke in. "Nellie, here's one for your papa," he said. "Why is Ireland like your rich friend Commodore Vanderbilt?"

Nellie giggled. "Like Commodore Vanderbilt? I'm sure I don't know, Algy!"

"Because its capital is always Dublin!"

Nellie squealed with delight and ran to her father. I tossed Algy a look of contempt. "She has not so much brain as ear-wax," I quoted.

He didn't smile but his eyes were laughing. "Good Thersites, come in and rail!"

"Seriously, Algy, it's a pretty wrapping, but can you live with the emptiness inside?"

The elegant Sartoris brows rose. "Ah, Bridget, 'twas cruel fate that your papa was not elected president! But since he was not, I shall have to forage for my Shakespeare in the highways and byways, and make do with the pretty wrapping at home."

"You're a holy martyr, Algy."

"Now, Bridget, be kind, or I shall take your letter home again."

"My what?"

He handed me an envelope. "For you, care of Sir Edward," he said. "From my wife."

"Your wife?" I glanced after Nellie in confusion.

He smiled. "Your cousin Emily in St. Louis. And I was so sure you had invented her, dear Bridget!"

"You'll be a bigamist soon," I said drily.

He laughed and went to join Nellie.

The letter had been opened, and I feared for the future of my quest if Algy had read—as he doubtless had—the letter from my "cousin." But Mr. Fishback was a clever journalist. The letter, a perfect morass of cousinly gossip, spun a credible tale of the supposed Emily's acquaintances and activities in St. Louis. But in the midst of this chaff was a grain of pure wheat: one of the St. Louis characters discussed, a Mr. W. Ring, had recently moved to Washington, "Emily" claimed; and she gave his address on J Street.

I memorized it and burnt the letter that night.

My work increased as the wedding approached, but took one happy turn: in the ever-increasing frenzy, I was occasionally sent into the White House proper. The day before the wedding, as my colleagues polished and swept,

I was sent with a forgotten bouquet to give to a chambermaid in the upstairs family quarters. I risked a detour on my return trip past the president's office down the hall.

It was empty.

I stole in, looking about at the mantel, the handsome shield-back upholstered chairs around the table, the clever clock with built-in calendar and barometer. The scent of aging cigar smoke clung to the room. There was something familiar about the stack of documents on the table. I tiptoed closer, intent on deciphering the topmost, which seemed to concern funds needed for the army, when a step sounded behind me. I whirled to find the president himself frowning at me.

"Here, now, what's this?" he asked.

I made a swift mental calculation and pulled out a silly giggle. "Oh, sir, I was sent with the flowers, and—in short, I made a wrong turn, sir." I peeked at him with merry eyes. "And I have something to ask you, sir."

"To ask me?" He was lighting a fresh cigar, but some amusement had crept into his demeanor in response to mine.

"Yes, sir, if I may be so bold, sir." I gave a gawky shrug. "Why is a victory like a kiss?"

He was delighted that I was not asking for money or favors. "Why, tell me then! Why is a victory like a kiss?"

"Because both are easy to Grant," I told him, and giggled.

He guffawed. "Saucy girl! Easy to Grant! Well, you are right!" He leaned over and kissed me. I giggled again to cover my confusion, and he took it as an invitation to kiss me again. Then, chortling, he turned away and went toward the stairs. "I must tell my wife," he called over his shoulder, and was gone.

And I'd best be gone too, I realized. I was weak with fear. Would he tell Mrs. Grant I had invited his kiss? Worse yet, would he realize why I'd been so interested in the papers on his table?

The papers, you see, had been in the same hand as Aunt Mollie's note.

Puzzling over my next move, I returned to my day's work helping move tropical plants into the recently redecorated East Room for the great nuptial the next day. We worked late, wrestling palms into place and draping greens about the beautiful new gas chandeliers, and I returned wearily to my tiny lodging that night still perplexed by the new answers and questions the day had presented. I missed Aunt Mollie's guidance more than ever. I closed the door behind me and turned up the lamp on the table.

The glow revealed Warty-nose sitting on my cot.

No knife this time. He'd come up in the world. He was holding a sleek Army-issue Colt revolver.

5

He seemed to have a similarly heightened opinion of me. "The place ye're working now is a bit more elegant, me dear."

"Yes, thank you, sir." I tried a curtsey but my legs most vexatiously threatened to collapse. I clutched the edge of the table for support and groped for hopeful signs. There were only two. First, a revolver was not as silent as a knife, and he might therefore be slightly more reluctant to use it. Secondly, he did not seem angry; indeed, the peculiar expression on his face might even have been a grin. Slightly emboldened, I said, "Sir, I would appreciate learning the purpose of your visit."

"Just clearing up yer story, me dear. I've been in St. Louis."

"I see."

"And I worry a bit about someone who says she is not related to her own dear aunt."

"Sir, I gave you the green-ribboned parcel!" I exclaimed.

"Yes, that's in yer favor, me girl. But I also heard in St. Louis that yer aunt did copy work for the whiskey tax collector."

Relief mingled with anxiety. He still thought I was ignorant, and that I had done what he'd asked; but he knew far too much about Aunt Mollie. Hoping my clumsy tongue would move, I said, "Well, then, you know the story."

"I want to know if she made copies of other papers. And what she did with the originals."

"The original must be at her office, don't you think?"

He smirked. "No. The original turned up right here in Washington a few days later."

"Are you sure?" I feigned astonishment.

"My chief is sure. Now, where did it come from?"

I frowned, making a great show of the ignorant niece in deep thought. I had learned something of great importance: Warty-nose's chief, whoever he was, knew the note I'd given Algy. Most probably had seen it himself, and had been convinced to speak to the president in Algy's favor. Therefore, he was endangered by the note; and furthermore, he was able to sway the president even on a matter touching the happiness of his beloved daughter. It all fit: Algy's success, Warty-nose's reappearance, and the papers I'd seen on the president's desk. But who? The savage General Sherman? The punctilious General Babcock? The impulsive Lieutenant Colonel Fred? The expensively wedded General Belknap? Any one of them might have reason to accept money in exchange for easing the tax load on distillers. But I couldn't solve that problem now, not with that Colt poised in Warty-nose's lap.

So I sold Algy. I replaced my thoughtful frown with a *eureka!* look and exclaimed, "That young man! In the boarding-house!"

"Oh?"

"I gave you everything in Aunt Mollie's package, but she had other papers." This was true. "That young man must have taken them!"

"He said he was yer cousin," said Warty-nose, so craftily that I was sure he knew who Algy really was.

I snorted. "He'd seen me on the street. Thought I was pretty and followed me in. Then stole my papers."

Warty-nose nodded. "That fits. There was more than one other paper, ye say? And he took them all?"

"As far as I know."

"And what did ye get in exchange?"

No sense in lying if his chief already knew about Algy and me. I said, "He got me this job, sir."

Warty-nose smiled. "I'm happy to see ye've become an honest woman."

I used my wide-eyed misunderstood-ally look. "I was frightened before, sir."

"And now ye aren't?" He waggled the Colt.

"I must admit, sir, I am. But before, with that blade on my neck . . ." I shuddered at the memory.

He laughed, enjoying the thought of the blade on my neck. And on Aunt Mollie's too? I clenched my hands to keep from showing the surge of rage that welled up within me. This man too would be punished, I swore by Aunt Mollie's ghost, once he'd served my purpose.

He said, "And where are yer aunt's papers now?"

"At Sir Edward Thornton's, I'd say."

"Where that young fellow lives?"

"Yes. Where I worked for a while. Of course I'm not certain, sir, but the young man keeps a box secretly in the cellar."

A crafty look stole into his eyes. "You know where?"

"Behind the pickles and preserves, sir."

"I want you to get it for me."

"This late?"

"So much the better."

He motioned with the muzzle of the Colt, and I led the way into the night. "Your chief must trust you a great deal," I observed companionably as we and the Colt walked through the dark toward Sir Edward's.

"Aye, that he does. We've been together since Petersburg, you see. A long friendship."

"Yes, you soldiers are very loyal to one another, sir," I observed.

We crept into Sir Edward's carriageway and to the back yard. "There's a door to the cellar from the back porch," I explained. "Do you want to come in, or shall I bring it out?"

"Bring it out."

I nodded. "Yes,sir. Here, you can sit on this little wall, sir." I guided him by the dim glimmer of moonlight to the low ledge.

"Why don't I stand next to the door?" he demanded suspiciously.

"Of course, sir, if you wish," I said dubiously. "But I thought, as a soldier, you'd prefer to have a view of the carriage drive. And if anyone comes, you can run into the kitchen garden behind the well."

Warty-nose grabbed my arm, nudged me with the Colt. "There'll be trouble if you try anything," he growled. "Remember, I can always find you." But as I hurried to the porch door, I noticed that he did stay where I had suggested.

I didn't underestimate him. He'd been a soldier in a long and bloody war, and survived. He'd been hand-picked for this job by a military expert, an associate of the great General Grant's. He would kill in an instant if it suited him. But now that he'd told me who his superior was, it was time to settle about Aunt Mollie.

I slipped inside the porch door, left my foolish bustle dress in a heap next to it, and pried the loose bolt from the cellar door. I scurried through the cellar, past the potatoes, shelves of preserves and marmalades, to the coal bin. I smeared my bloomers and camisole and skin with coal dust, then continued to a front corner of the house and out the low window, like a sooty muskrat emerging from its bank, then circled through the shrubbery that bordered the yard, back to the kitchen garden.

Warty-nose was edgy. His Colt ready, he peered alternately at the carriage drive and the door where I had disappeared.

I glided through the shrubs behind him and slammed his skull with a two-quart jar of Algy's favorite ginger marmalade.

He dropped like a stone. I tucked his Colt into the band of my bloomers and heaved him up onto the low wall. His scant hair was sticky with marmalade and with something warmer, so I covered it with his Union soldier's cap. Then I opened the plank top. "All yours, Aunt Mollie," I murmured, and slid him into the well.

I know, I know, but what do you expect a poor cowardly girl to do? Challenge him to a duel?

Feeling queasily akin to the villainous Lady Audley, I closed the well, retrieved my bustle, and went home to prepare for a wedding.

6

Thursday morning, the White House was a frenzy of activity. The wedding was scheduled for eleven in the morning, followed by a reception and wedding breakfast. We had already begun moving plants into the East Room the day before—not only from our greenhouses, but also fresh imports from Florida. Now we banked flowers everywhere: by the fireplaces, arching over the doors, spiraling around the fluted columns that the Grants had installed. The dais under the east window where Algy was to be married was a masterpiece—a canopy of ferns and vines, with the great floral marriage-bell and the two rings with the couple's initials swinging from ropes of smilax on either side. The beauty of sight and scent was almost overwhelming. I was surprised that every bumblebee in Washington was not in attendance.

Obeying orders, I ran about fetching pots, trimming fern fronds, arranging bouquets—in and out from the greenhouses, up and down ladders. Sometimes I was called upon to help with the flowers on the banquet table, where a twenty-six course wedding breakfast would be served: crab gateaus, tongue aspic, little halved snipes broiled on toast, puddings, a splendid white bride's cake.

A time or two I ran upstairs on the pretext of checking the bridesmaids' pink and blue bouquets. Nellie's dress was a glory: white satin with point lace that was twined with white flowers, green leaves, and tiny oranges. The wedding was the celebration of America's dream come true: the lowly tanner's son had become a great general and a beloved president; now he was uniting his family to European noble blood and artistic fame. Every patriotic American should have felt aglow at the rightness of it all. Yes indeed.

By ten o'clock I had been running in and out, upstairs and down, for hours. Bridesmaids and friends were milling about, as well as servants galore. But even though I'd inspected all the rooms from kitchens and greenhouses to bedrooms, I still had not seen my quarry. Perhaps he had not yet arrived; but, just in case, I seized a bouquet of orange blossoms and tuberoses to serve as a pretext and slipped up the office stairs.

The cabinet room was empty; but General Babcock, astoundingly enough, was hard at work in the office next door. I hid behind the connecting door because he was talking to someone about the appointment of a new secretary of the Treasury. When the man had left, he bent happily to his work again.

I squinted through the crack on the hinge side of the door, pulled Warty-nose's revolver from its hiding-place in my bustle, and levelled it at General Babcock's ear.

Then the hall door opened and the president came in. He looked even more glum than usual. "Bab," he said abruptly, "I don't know if I can go through with it!"

General Babcock went over to him. Not wishing to become an inadvertent John Wilkes Booth, I waited. Babcock patted the president's shoulder and said, "Every father is naturally sorry to see a lovely daughter leave the nest."

"You know it's more than that. Young Sartoris is just not sound!"

"It's mere wild oats," Babcock soothed. "With a wife as sweet as Nellie, he'll settle down."

"Perhaps. But I wish they'd wait."

"They're young and eager." Babcock hesitated, then added, "And as I told you, I don't think young Fred realized that his arrangements could look so shady. In the wrong hands, the evidence young Sartoris showed me could ruin Fred's future. He'll be far safer with Sartoris in the family."

What a liar the man was! I'd seen that evidence, had given it to Algy. It tied only one man to the St. Louis briberies, and it wasn't Fred.

But President Grant seemed to have little faith in the son who, after all, had been last in his class in discipline. He sighed, "Why am I forced to choose between my children?"

"But Nellie loves him! And he's well connected," Babcock reminded him. "And fathers aren't always the best judges. Julia's father thought you would never amount to anything, and look at you now!"

"I hope you're right!" The president shook his head in despair.

"By the way, I have a report on Bristow," said Babcock, as though the rest had been preliminaries. "Do you want to look it over? He's far from ideal, but he has no marks against him and he'll quiet your critics."

"You take care of that." The president wandered sadly out again.

Babcock returned to his chair and I raised the revolver again. But I had just realized something very important.

President Grant was a man who enjoyed his beloved family, his fine horses, the glory and the popularity that came with being president of the United States. But he didn't much like the work.

General Babcock, on the other hand, loved it.

By funneling information to the president, by taking on the tasks that Grant least enjoyed, he had seized great power. He controlled government appointments, policies, even swindles like the bribes the St. Louis whiskey distillers were paying to avoid legal taxes. He could decide life or death for those who threatened to expose the corruption to the president.

For Aunt Mollie, he'd chosen death. Algy, better connected, had been paid for silence. On the pretext that young Lieutenant Colonel Fred would otherwise be endangered, Babcock had convinced Grant to sacrifice his daughter.

I found that the muzzle of the revolver had drooped. I was not going to to shoot this man, I realized. He did not deserve a quick, clean soldier's death. He must be stripped of his beloved power and publicly shamed. I slid the revolver back into my bustle and picked up my orange-blossom bouquet. Suddenly I knew what had to be done.

But my thoughts were rudely interrupted by a hard hand gripping my arm. For a wild moment I thought it was Warty-nose, escaped from his watery grave to torment me again. It was almost a relief to see Littimer.

"My master wishes to see you, if you please," he said.

"I'd think your master would have other things on his mind," I grumbled; but despite the respectable *if you please*, refusing to go was not an option. Littimer took me to the room where Algy was waiting for the ceremony to begin. He looked a prince, of course; both illustrious families in his lineage fitted him for great public moments like this. I imagined myself for an instant in Nellie's lace and flowers, sweeping down the grand west staircase and along the marble corridor, placing my hand in Algy's under the beautiful marriage-bell in the East Room. The very thought of such a moment might make one swoon.

But Algy ignored my admiring gaze. "Where was she?" he asked Littimer.

"Eavesdropping on General Babcock," said Littimer.

"I was fixing the bouquets!" I protested, holding out my little bunch of blossoms as proof. I had stuck a little silver banner in the center that said "Love."

Algy took it from me. "I fear I underestimated you, Bridget Mooney," he said.

"I've lived up to our bargain!"

"Yes, yes; and so have I. Let me explain that I had not expected you to pursue your aunt's killer quite so doggedly."

"I know. Proper ladies don't do that sort of thing," I admitted glumly.

He smiled. "Your talents do not lie in being proper, Bridget," he said; and it sounded almost like a compliment.

"Well, what's the problem?" I asked.

"Threefold. First, Sir Edward's servants found the well by the kitchen garden was clogged this morning."

"Oh."

"I had not expected you to take the villainous Lady Audley so thoroughly to heart. Littimer arranged things, of course, but it's rather annoying on one's wedding day. Second, I find you eavesdropping on Babcock."

"No worse than blackmailing him into supporting your marriage, is it? And he's the one who had Aunt Mollie killed."

"How do you know?"

"His handwriting on papers he prepares for the president matches Aunt Mollie's notes, as you knew at first glance. And our pal Warty-nose gave him away. He said he'd met his chief at Petersburg. The other suspects, Sherman and Belknap, were marching through Georgia at the time. Lieutenant Colonel Fred was only fifteen. So Babcock is the one I'm after."

"And you're welcome to him—but not till I have Nellie safe. Which brings us to the third thing. I can't help but remember that you have my shirt stud."

"I won't trouble you about that, Algy."

"But surely you understand that in the light of the discovery in the well, it becomes more ominous. I have this nightmare vision of an overly theatrical scene in the East Room, in which a wronged St. Louis girl flings herself at the president's feet, pleading for the groom to do right by her and make her an honest woman again."

"What a lovely idea!" I said with relish. "But it might work, you see. And I do not wish to marry you!"

"Perhaps not. But I must be certain. Where is the shirt-stud?"

"At my lodgings," I fibbed.

"I think not. Littimer looked there." Algy glanced at the clock ticking on the mantel. "Come, Littimer, let's search her."

They were certainly quick and efficient at stripping the clothes from a girl. Long practice, I imagine. Littimer gagged me and Algy swiftly removed my dress and petticoats. Littimer was going for my bloomers with a not-so-respectable leer when Algy said, "Wait, I think we have something here."

He had found the pocket I'd sewn into my bustle, damn him. I watched helplessly as he pulled forth my most precious possessions, clucking over each of them: the revolver, his own note to Fanny Kemble, a packet of Aunt Mollie's, and the envelope addressed to Nellie Grant.

This last he opened. He sighed with relief when he saw the shirt-stud, then flicked open the letter. The beautiful Sartoris brows rose higher as he read, and he raised my little bouquet to his handsome Kemble nose. When he'd finished his eyes rested for a steamy moment on my blushing near-nakedness. "My, my, Bridget," he said, and cleared his throat. "We seem to have had quite a jolly time. It's a pity I was too drunk to notice."

It's not easy to look disdainful in bloomers, with a gag, but I did my best. Algy turned to Aunt Mollie's papers. "And these—my God, Bridget, you little vixen, you would have had dear old Bab in the palm of your hand! Such corrupt dealings—and in his own penmanship! How grateful he'll be to me for these!"

Littimer said, "Ahem," with a meaningful glance at his respectable hunting-watch. It was a few minutes to eleven.

"Oh, right," said Algy. "Littimer, tie her up and hide her dress, just in case. Release her just before you depart."

"That's all?" Littimer sounded disappointed. "She could fall off a horse, like your brother."

"How many times must I tell you? I do not approve of what happened to my brother!"

Littimer's smooth respectability was a little ruffled. "You're the heir now, sir, begging your pardon. And it did save you from having to become an American."

"Do be quiet, Littimer. This occasion is quite different." Algy held up my things. "Note that our sylph here has been defanged. Besides, at some point in the future, I would like to find out if she really would do all those lovely things for the sake of a shirt-stud."

Littimer shrugged, took me to one of Mrs. Grant's new-built closets, and tied my hands and ankles. I would have struggled more, but the talk of Algy's brother had rather disheartened me. Then Littimer closed the door and I heard them leave.

I sat in the dark, furious, chewing on the gag. In the great melodrama of life, Algy Sartoris clearly wore a big black mustache. Stupid of me ever to think of him as a hero. But then, that's the kind of mistake you make when you're comic relief.

Far away in the great house I heard the Marine Band strike up the "Wedding March." White House servants, whispering excitedly, ran by in the hall outside. The clock in Algy's temporary dressing-room ticked away. Every fifteen minutes, it chimed softly. How many minutes did it take to get married? A proper lady would know. Bridget Mooney could only gnaw at her gag.

It came loose at last. Instantly I turned my attention to my wrists. I had luckily remembered the stories of a fellow actor in St. Louis who had once assisted a magician with his tricks. By proper tensing of the arms while being tied, what looks like a tight bond might be pulled off with the teeth.

The Marine Band was playing again. Algy and Nellie were married.

But the comic subplot was loose again.

I knew I had only minutes before Littimer or even Algy arrived. But I'd remembered something in the closet. I knew Algy wouldn't trust Littimer with those papers; nor could he hide the parcel in his sleek wedding clothing. But back at the tavern he'd fumbled with his stylish top hat before producing the packet he'd taken from me. Sure enough, I found all my belongings tucked into it, together with a bonus of several hundred dollars in a clip. I left Algy a note: "If Babcock hears, Nellie hears, (signed) Sylph" and ran for Nellie's bedroom. You see, I figured Mr. Algernon Sartoris owed me a dress. So I'd help myself to one of Mrs. Algernon Sartoris's.

As I'd expected, Nellie had packed all her New York frocks to take to England, but was leaving behind many others that were still at the height of fashion. Unfortunately I had only just made my selection when I heard footsteps hurrying in the hall outside. I dove under Nellie's bed, pulling my new dress after me, and held my breath, peering through the fringe of the spread.

It was Nellie's maid, and she was only the first of hordes of people who passed through the room—Nellie, of course, and her maids and tittering bridesmaids, and even Mrs. Grant herself, who came in to talk excitedly to Nellie or to the chandelier—it was difficult to tell which. After long ages of giggles, sobs, and pointless remarks, the heroine of the day was bundled into her beautiful brown silk traveling dress and sent out to her fine new husband. The room was empty at last. I heard the bells of the church nearby chiming out "God Save the Queen," and knew everyone was watching Algy bear his prize away. I crawled out and donned the frock.

Another, unexpected, step in the hall. I plunged back under the bed and was astonished to see President Grant enter. He closed the door, wandered over to the bed, buried his face in Nellie's pillow, and burst into uncontrollable sobs.

Now, I ask you, is that proper for a great hero who has seen the fields of slain soldiers at Shiloh? But he was right to grieve for his daughter. In a moment he had me feeling weepy myself. Poor Nellie Grant, the natural heroine, had missed her cue and married a villain.

Still, Mr. President, I argued silently, if you work with weasels like Babcock, bad things do happen.

After a long time, they found him, still sobbing, and took him away solicitously.

And the comic relief? I brushed myself off, tucked my papers into the bodice of Nellie's fine frock, and slipped unobtrusively down the office stairs and out of the White House—a guest leaving late, to anyone who noticed. Since I had Algy's money, I didn't bother to go past my room. There was only one stop to make in Washington, at an address on J Street. Then I lit out straight for Philadelphia and the tutelage and protection of the illustrious Mrs. Fanny Kemble.

I'd given up on being proper; but I still meant to give rich and famous a try.

7

You know the rest of the story. Fishback found an honest member of Grant's cabinet, and together, starting with the papers I'd left at J Street, they assembled evidence that jailed dozens of members of the Whiskey Ring for defrauding the government of millions in uncollected taxes. Grant saved Babcock from jail, but of course dismissed him from the White House. Babcock became a lighthouse inspector. Far from Washington's seats of power, he spent lonely, disgraced, and powerless years on the fringes of the nation he had cheated. In 1884, while attending to official duties in a place called Mosquito Inlet, Florida, his boat went down in a storm and he—like Warty-nose—drowned. The boat, I know, was not at all seaworthy. I remember it well; I had a few days' holiday from my role as Portia in a southern tour of *The Merchant of Venice*, and I just happened to be in Mosquito Inlet that day myself.

I know, I know; but don't you think that by then he'd suffered enough? The quality of mercy, you know.

Nellie Grant Sartoris raised three fine children in England with the kind assistance of Algy's mother; but in every other way the marriage was the miserable failure her father and I had predicted. Algy was soon foraging in the highways and byways, and Nellie excited great sympathy as well as scandal when at last she divorced him. Algy visited me a time or two, for old times' sake; but I didn't really enjoy the encounters, because he'd become so stout and blowzy, and because I couldn't help but be reminded of those moments in Nellie's bedroom, when the heroic general and president of our United States wept for the daughter he'd been forced to sell.

FROM BRIDGET MOONEY'S SCRAPBOOK

THE MIDLAND MONTHLY
February 1897

NELLIE GRANT SARTORIS
AND HER CHILDREN
by Juliette M. Babbitt

Mrs. Nellie Grant Sartoris, even prettier and more attractive than when she left Washington a bride, in May, 1874, has returned with her children to make her home with her mother, Mrs. U.-S. Grant, who bought a handsome house last year on Massachusetts Avenue above Dupont Circle. Mrs. Sartoris' welcome was as sincere as were the regrets which followed her to England, where she remained, save for short visits to her parents, until about two years ago. There her children were born, grew up and received most of their education. She lost her first child when an infant, but has left to her a son and two daughters. Her marriage, as everybody knows, was not the happy one which such a lovely and sweet-tempered woman deserved, and the death of her husband several years ago was a relief to all his relations.

. . . Leighton was genial and charming, and poor little Nelly Grant was there (Mrs. Algernon Sartoris), with three very handsome but rather common youngsters. She is illiterate, lovely, painted, pathetic and separated from a drunken idiot of a husband. The Sartorises don't like her much, but they like her more, I suppose, than they do their disreputable "Algie."

(Henry James writing to Grace Norton Jan. 10, 1888, in *Henry James: Letters*, Volume III 1883- 1895, edited by Leon Edel, Belknap (Harvard), 1980).

After his daughter had left the house on her wedding trip the General was missed. After considerable search he was found sobbing in his daughter's room, with his head buried in her pillow.

(William H. Crook, Executive Clerk to President Grant, in *Memories of the White House*, Little, Brown 1911.)

DEATH SCENE; or,
The Moor of Venice

I know, I know, a proper young lady is not supposed to smoke. But hang it, there'd been so much bother that day, what with Zeb disappearing and the Pinkerton men asking about those burglaries back in St. Louis. When sorrows come, they come not single spies, but in battalions. So don't you think a girl's entitled to a few puffs as a tonic for her nerves?

Besides, I've noticed that in these times it's very difficult to be a proper young lady.

I was standing alone on the back platform of our speeding Pullman car watching the still-leafless Mississippi Valley hills roll by. I blew a last smoke ring into the wind and reckoned it was time to rejoin my colleagues inside. Gathering up the velvet train of my favorite traveling skirt, a lovely emerald green to set off my Titian-red hair, I tossed my cigar onto the tracks and re-entered the car. Instantly, I smelled trouble.

I heard it too. A glorious, resonant Italian voice filled the car, just as it had filled countless theatres on three continents. But this time the words were not Shakespeare's. I stood amazed while the ringing tones listed every Italian curse I had learned over the last four months and added a passel of new ones. The great Salvini was vexed, yes indeed. *"Ladro sudicio!"* he hollered. *"Dannato!"* He was standing in the aisle at the front end of the car, flinging his arms about expressively, almost felling the Italian translator who fluttered about him like a lost chicken, unable to get in a word.

The only person near me was the colored Pullman porter, hovering bright-eyed and mystified by his linen closet, one dark hand tugging nervously at the bill of his cap. So I rustled on into the car and leaned toward the nearest ear. Letitia's pink shell-like ear, as it turned out. "What's wrong?" I asked.

"Ooh! Bridget!" squeaked Letitia. Offstage she worked hard at being a darling little thing and therefore took every opportunity to squeak. "Bridget Mooney, how you startled me!"

"I do apologize, Letty. But tell me what's wrong!"

"Why, I'm sure I don't know! Mr. Salvini just began to, well, to roar!"

Hopeless. How a little goose like Letitia could ever remember Desdemona's lines, I couldn't guess. Keeping my eye on the raging Salvini,

I moved up to the next seat where Charlie Lloyd sat. He played Roderigo. A proper swell indeed with his shining smile, except that offstage he used so much Macassar oil on his hair that he had the look and smell of a gambler. Some said he was one. I asked, "Charlie, what's the matter?"

" 'I understand a fury in his words, But not the words,' " he quoted. "Perhaps he just heard his wife was unfaithful. Perhaps he sat on a tack." Charlie was a great one for inventing stories. But hang it, he was as useless as the dimwitted Letitia. I wished again that young Zeb hadn't disappeared. Zeb was inexperienced, only eighteen, but always willing to give a civil answer.

Across the aisle from the well-oiled Charlie sat old Jack Bowles. Jack was a cheerful codger who tippled too much and couldn't seem to save a penny of his salary. But his white beard and noble demeanor had won him the part of a Venetian senator. He was serious now, his flask capped beside him as he squinted at Salvini. Timing himself carefully, he waited till the Italian tragedian reached the end of a string of colorful words and was drawing breath again. Then, deftly, Jack inserted a shout. "Mr. Salvini, sir! What's the matter?"

The great Italian eyes flashed at us and Salvini burst again into excited useless syllables. But this time his eloquent hands shaped a distinctive crescent in the air. I exclaimed, "Your scimitar?"

"*Sì*, Breedgeetta!" He always had trouble saying 'Bridget'. "*La mia spada! Teef! Dirty teef!*"

"Dirty thief!" echoed the translator, holding up the bag that normally contained Othello's great curved sword. Scuffed and stained, it gaped empty now. My heart sank.

Now, I reckon you must be thinking we'd all taken leave of our senses to attempt such a tour in the first place. Mr. Salvini spoke only Italian. The rest of us onstage with him spoke only English. Pure madness, we all muttered as we signed our contracts, fully expecting our tour to collapse and leave us stranded somewhere like Memphis or Cincinnati. An actor's life is filled with adventure, yes indeed. But for once fortune smiled upon Bridget Mooney, because it turned out that in this case language didn't matter. Mr. Salvini somehow transmitted Shakespeare's passionate hero straight from his heart into ours. Critic after critic proclaimed him the greatest Othello ever seen.

But that scimitar was crucial. Salvini played Othello as a North African, darkening himself to a coppery brown rather than black, and wearing a splendid authentic costume of scarlet tarboosh, white turban, and white burnoose. The first time we saw him in costume Letitia and I tittered to each other that if Moorish men all looked so dashing, it was time to quit the stage and become Moorish ladies. We were accustomed to seeing cool British Othellos reciting in blackface and committing the climactic suicide with a decorous thrust of a dagger into a cool British breast. Not Salvini. His heroic Moor of Venice was transformed before our very eyes into a roaring vengeful beast. I reckon I've never seen such a thrilling death scene! Salvini seized the scimitar, one hand on the hilt and the other grasping the tip of the shining blade, and held the great crescent aloft. Then he slashed his own throat, brutally sawing the blade back and forth with both hands and collapsing at last amidst spasms and hideous gurgles. What a moment! Audiences gasped, and so did I.

Oh, I know, I know, as Iago's wife I wasn't supposed to gasp, I was supposed to be stone-dead already. But it was such a bore to lie there like some old possum while the greatest death scene in the world took place just inches from my nose. So don't you think a girl might take a little peek? Besides, I reckon that just then there wasn't a soul in the house looking at me.

So now, at the news of Mr. Salvini's loss, a groan of unhappiness ran through the company. That authentic, jewel-hilted scimitar was too important to be replaced by mere pasteboard. I asked, "Was it stolen in St. Louis? Or just now?"

Mr. Salvini and his translator chattered together in Italian for a moment. Then the assistant said, "Signor Salvini looked in the bag when we first took our seats, to see if it had been dented when we boarded. He saw it then. Then he placed the bag on top of the other baggage while we got out some drinks." He indicated a heap of Gladstone bags near the front of the car.

"So that means it disappeared in the last hour or so," Jack Bowles said slowly. He uncorked his flask and took a swig.

"But no one has left the car," Charlie pointed out.

"Well, then it must be here somewhere!" Letty exclaimed with surprising logic. We all joined in the search of the car and all its closets. We owed it to Salvini to find the precious blade. Hang it, we owed it to Shakespeare too.

But nothing turned up. "Perhaps it's in someone's bag," suggested Charlie. "Perhaps out the window. Perhaps one of us is a sword swallower!" I returned his smile but couldn't help pondering our chain of misfortunes.

This was the third calamity. The first had occurred after our final St. Louis performance, a matinee. We had only a few minutes before the departure of the train to New Orleans, so we were particularly vexed when the Pinkerton detectives stopped us on the platform as we waited to board our Pullman. They explained that during our performance, the homes of three audience members had been burgled.

"But why are you stopping us?" asked our company manager indignantly. "Our train leaves in eighteen minutes!"

"We must search your things, sir."

"Confound it, this is outrageous!"

Well, of course it was outrageous, but sometimes there's no explaining to gentlemen who aren't show people. Ignoring our protests, whether in English or Italian, they hunted through our trunks while the big station clock ticked ever nearer our doom. I watched them search Charlie and Jack as I waited where our Pullman car would stop, with Letitia and Zeb Adams. Zeb was our all- purpose understudy, a slim dark-eyed young Southerner who had conned every part—yes, even Letitia's and mine, though he made a very rugged-looking sort of female. He was eagerly ready to play any role if illness struck the company, but we were in excellent health. He helped with our trunks and kits cheerfully enough. But he was worried now too, watching that clock. "Will we miss our train?" he fretted.

I shrugged. " 'Like as the waves make towards the pebbled shore, so do our minutes hasten to their end.' "

"Beautiful, Bridget," said Zeb, "but not at all reassuring."

Our desperation increased as the train, rumbling and hissing clouds of smoke and steam, rolled into the station. Ten minutes.

Still, they were efficient, those detectives, sifting quickly through the costumes and personal items we had packed so carefully, and it began to look as though we might be able to board in time after all. Jack Bowles had even capped his flask. Then two of the Pinkerton men approached us. There was no problem until Letitia said, "Bridget is from St. Louis, you know."

Well, have you ever heard of such a goose as Letty? Minutes away from departure and she tries a blame-fool stunt like that! I cast a glare in her direction but she was too busy simpering at Zeb and Charlie.

I gave up trying to shame Letitia. Much as I hated to discuss my family in front of her, I realized that I had to concentrate on satisfying the Pinkerton men. Contradicting Letty would make them suspicious, and the tour might be delayed so long our salaries would all be docked for missing our New Orleans performance. I admitted, "Yes, sir, but this is the first time I've been back here in seven years."

"Do you have family here?"

I smiled the special mournful smile that I used onstage listening to Desdemona's willow song. "Not a real family," I said. "Papa lives here, Ty Mooney. And my Uncle Mike O'Rourke."

From the expression on their faces I could see they knew those two reprobates. Now that Aunt Mollie was no longer watching their accounts, Papa and Uncle Mike were wasting away their lives in barrooms. My short visit with them had been full of mawkish talk about dear departed Aunt Mollie and dear departed Mama, punctuated with requests for a loan. "Neither a borrower nor a lender be," I advised them at last, and went flouncing back to the theatre.

The Pinkerton men didn't seem any more enthusiastic about my relatives than I was. They changed the subject.

"Are you acquainted with Mr. Silas Moore?"

"I've heard of him, of course, sir," I answered cautiously. "Owns a steamboat company, doesn't he?"

"Yes. And Mr. Phineas McCoy?"

"He's also well-known in St. Louis. A railroad fortune."

"But you wouldn't have gone calling in their houses now, would you?"

Was this a trick? I doubted that those rich and proper citizens had even noticed a skinny red-haired little girl ten years ago delivering Aunt Mollie's work to the back door. They certainly wouldn't believe that she'd become a Shakespearean actress. But just in case one of them had remembered, I said, "My aunt did copy work for businesses. I sometimes delivered it. Tradesman's entrance."

The second Pinkerton man leered and said, "That old drunkard Mooney wouldn't be invited in through the front door."

They both had a good chuckle at the thought of Papa in those rich and proper mansions, and I joined in dutifully, then asked, "Are those the houses that were burgled, sir?"

"Yes. And Mr. Healey's too. Mrs. Healey's tiara was taken."

"Oh, gracious!" I exclaimed. Banker Healey would not have recognized me either. I'd been very young. But I remembered that tiara's icy fire. "I heard about that tiara when I was a girl."

"Well, we've all heard about it now," said the detective morosely.

The clock ticked on. "Sir," I said boldly, "we were onstage during the matinee. Not stealing jewels."

They nodded, impressed by my reasoning. "True enough, my girl. But we have to ask. The thief was quite brazen, marching right into the kitchens, his face muffled. Tied up the servants and went straight to the hiding places. One of the kitchen maids said he acted like a stage outlaw. So we had to ask."

Two minutes till the train left. "But we were onstage, sirs," I repeated desperately. "I imagine that the culprit is still right here in St. Louis."

They agreed, and one of them called out to the impatient company that since they'd found nothing in our trunks we could depart. There was a great scramble and heaving of bags and trunks as we fell over each other getting into the Pullman. But at last we were aboard, panting but safely on our way to New Orleans.

Then we realized that in the hubbub about the burglaries we somehow had left young Zeb behind.

He must have run into the station restaurant for a moment, I told myself. He must have thought we'd never make this train. I half expected him to rejoin us in New Orleans, abashed at having missed it. But if he didn't— well, I worried about those burglaries.

You see, there were several things I hadn't mentioned to the Pinkerton men. One was a conversation I'd had on the long trip from Chicago to St. Louis a week or two ago. The five of us who usually sat in the back seats had talked about St. Louis families—and the three who were burgled had been among them. It had started when Jack Bowles had cocked a bushy white eyebrow at me and asked, "So you're a St. Louis girl, Bridget!"

"Yes. But I haven't been back there for a long time. Aunt Mollie brought me East and she passed away there." I avoided mentioning Papa and Uncle Mike whenever possible.

Charlie Lloyd shifted on his seat. His glossy black hair left a smear on the plush upholstery. "Was your Aunt Mollie an actress too?"

"No. But she wanted me to become an actress. She brought me East so I could have proper voice lessons."

"Why, however did she manage that, Bridget?" asked Letitia. I knew what she was hinting. Her family had prospered in the lumber business, and she had many options besides the itinerant life of an actor, yes indeed. She never let us forget, always giving herself airs.

I said, "My aunt was a copyist with a flair for accounts. She helped some of the best St. Louis businesses."

"Rich men?" asked Jack Bowles between swallows.

"Rich for St. Louis," I admitted. "They live in mansions. Their wives wear the latest fashions. And jewels! Mrs. Healey has an emerald tiara that would dazzle your eyes."

"Goodness, Bridget, how did you come to know all these things? Did you read about them in the newspapers?" Letitia was after me again, trying to show that I was a mere guttersnipe.

I put on my most cultivated attitude. Strut about as she might, Letitia knew that I had studied with the great Shakespearean actress Mrs. Fanny Kemble, a far more illustrious tutor than hers. I spoke in my most Kemble-like tones as I told her, "You mustn't think that all copyists are spurned by the prosperous element of society, Letty. Of course we were not invited to grand balls, but we were certainly received into their homes on occasion. Even I, as a child, was received."

Zeb, his dark eyes sparkling, asked eagerly, "Tell us about their mansions, Bridget." He was the fifth son of a Louisiana plantation family, impoverished by the war but fascinated by the gracious things in life. Charlie claimed that he gambled, and Charlie should know. But Zeb was so young and kind-hearted and fond of Shakespeare that he'd become our pet.

"Well, take Mr. Moore, the steamboat man," I said, humoring him. "His mansion is Greek style, with four enormous columns in front and a grand staircase in the hall. He has Sèvres porcelain, and a library full of portraits."

Letty was looking at me with narrowed eyes. I wasn't about to admit that my knowledge of the Moore mansion had been gleaned from glimpses through the windows as I went around to the tradesmen's entrance where I sometimes delivered Aunt Mollie's copy work. After all, I had been inside the house, even if only in the kitchen. In those days I was a skinny chit of a girl, and the jolly cook had taken one look at me and thrust a piece of peach pie into my thin hands. My wide-eyed childish questions about the dazzling mansion had served me well. The servants had bragged about their positions in this grand house, about the porcelain, and more. So now I could say to Letitia, "Behind one of the portraits in the library there's a locked cabinet. That's where Mrs. Moore keeps her jewels."

"Fascinating!" said old Jack Bowles.

"And then there's the McCoys," I said. "Railroad money. A great brick mansion, very modern, built after the war."

"Are the wives beautiful?" asked Charlie, with a wriggle of his dark eyebrows. "Should I go a-wooing?"

"You'd be tarred and feathered, Charlie. Besides, they're not young," I explained, "and they're more than plump, most of them. But they do have stylish dresses and jewelry."

"Oh, Bridget, go call on them, do!" exclaimed Zeb, adding with a twinkle, "Then I can play Iago's wife at last!"

"Vaulting ambition," sniffed Charlie, and we all laughed.

Except Letitia. She asked innocently, "And where does Mrs. McCoy keep her jewels?" She was trying to prove that I'd never visited the mansion. But I had spent a profitable time gossiping in the McCoy kitchen too. Yes indeed. I smiled kindly at Letty and said, "She's much more original than Mrs. Moore. She has a mantel clock with a false base."

Jack Bowles chuckled. "Well, you're certainly on intimate terms with the cream of society in St. Louis!" he said jovially. Letitia tried to hide a pout by looking out the window.

"Do you know other great families in St. Louis?" asked Zeb.

"And do you know where they keep their jewels?" Charlie put in, with a grin to show that he was joking. Charlie had a fine white set of teeth and I always enjoyed seeing him smile. Letitia still sulked, her gaze on the landscape.

I smiled back at Charlie. "Well, there's the banker. Mr. Healey. A section of baseboard in his bedroom opens out to reveal a small compartment. Mrs. Healey's jewels and her emerald tiara are hidden there."

Letitia's head snapped around and triumph sparkled in her eyes. "Ooh, Bridget, I'm shocked!" she squeaked. "In Mr. Healey's bedroom?"

I withered her with a Lady Macbeth glare. Banker Healey was the richest and most proper of them all, yes indeed. "That's what Mrs. Healey told me," I said icily.

Jack Bowles had another question. "And who else is of interest in St. Louis?"

"Well, those people all live in the center of town," I said. "There were also some famous farms nearby. President Grant's, for example." I continued telling them about the town, a little more cautiously after my slip about the Healey house. In fact Mrs. Healey hadn't mentioned the baseboard compartment to me. I'd discovered it myself one afternoon when I was a scrawny fourteen-year-old who looked younger but already hankered after a life on the stage. Mrs. Healey was away visiting her sister, and I was prowling quietly about the room because Mr. Healey had dropped off to sleep after—well, suffice it to say that Aunt Mollie was a very enterprising woman. When she noticed that Banker Healey's eye often roved from his rotund wife toward more youthful females—extremely youthful, one might say—she made a little business arrangement with him that required my presence.

I know, I know, but how do you expect a poor untutored girl to pay for elocution lessons? By cashing in dividends? My Aunt Mollie struck a good bargain with the rich and proper Mr. Healey, and put the money out at six percent so that a few years later it paid for both our tickets east.

But that's by the by.

When the Pinkerton men told us about the burglaries, I of course didn't wish to add to our delay by mentioning the conversation on the train. But now I settled into my seat across from Letitia and pondered. Here was a puzzle worthy of Hawkshaw himself. Unfortunately there wasn't a Hawkshaw to be seen. It was up to me.

Could one of us possibly have taken those jewels? The St. Louis theatre manager had come beaming to us earlier in the week, telling us the names of the local luminaries who would be attending Salvini's great performances. I had thought I was the only one taking any notice of him. But if someone else had listened, had noted that three of the families attending our last matinee kept jewels in hiding-places I'd mentioned, he—or she—would have had time to locate the houses, even study the habits of the servants. Why, I'd taken a constitutional or two myself along the grand avenue where those three pillars of St. Louis society lived. But was it truly possible that one of my colleagues had stolen the jewels?

I settled back into my seat, as far as one can with a bustle, and gazed at the passing hills. The Illinois Central route to New Orleans allows occasional glimpses of the great Mississippi, and I watched the setting sun glint on the majestic waters as I considered Letitia. She could be a greedy little creature, yes indeed. She doubtless coveted the jewels. And there was another point that strongly favored her. The Pinkerton men had been very thorough in their search of our trunks and bags and cloaks. They had even politely inspected the men's pockets. But of course they had not been so brazen as to look closely at the ladies' clothing. I myself have found it very convenient, since bustles first became fashionable, to tuck a few items into a special pocket sewn into the skirt drapery. My jewelry, my most treasured letters, my special Civil War souvenir, my cigars—all can be kept there in snug security, although I'm bound to admit it's not so comfortable to sit down. Letitia could easily have hidden the stolen items, even the tiara, from the Pinkerton men.

I stole a look at her across from me, dozing to the rocking motion of the train. Unfortunately, there was a flaw in my case against Letitia. As Desdemona, she was onstage frequently from the beginning to the end of the play. She didn't have time to go burgle three houses. Besides, she was such a silly ninny I couldn't believe she could even think of a sensible enough plan, much less execute it.

I turned to look across the aisle. Charlie Lloyd, perhaps? He was intelligent enough, and often complained about how difficult it was to make ends meet on an actor's wages. Gambling is not a cheap recreation, and the price of Macassar oil goes up every day. Also, Charlie's character, Roderigo, was not on stage very often in Salvini's version of the play. He might have been able to slip away for two hours or so.

Or consider Jack Bowles. He had need of a secure old age, and even greater need of a bottle. And his opportunity was ample. His venerable Venetian senator was onstage only at the very beginning and very end of the play. And the same was true of young Zeb Adams, whose help was needed chiefly before and after performances.

But the jewels were still in St. Louis, I was sure, because the detectives had searched all three men quite thoroughly. I remembered Zeb, standing next to Letitia and me, rolling his dark eyes at us in mock exasperation as the Pinkerton men pulled his watch and handkerchief and cigars from his pockets. So I was convinced that none of us had done it.

Until Zeb had missed the train.

The train that would take him into his home state of Louisiana.

I wanted to believe that he had innocently gone back into the station, inadvertently missing the departure. But there were other possibilities, and—well, my imaginations were as foul as Vulcan's smithy.

Surely Zeb was not a thief! But he'd listened to my indiscreet conversation on the train. He'd had time to slip away during the matinee while the families—and their burly coachmen—were at the theatre. He could act a stage outlaw as well as Jack or Charlie. He could have stolen the jewels, hidden them someplace so that they were not among his things while the Pinkerton men searched.

And then, unable to recover them in time to board, he'd missed the train.

I leaned forward and touched Letitia's arm, waited for her to jump and squeak, and then asked, "Letty, where did Zeb go when he left us?"

"Dear me, Bridget, I don't know. He was there, and then he wasn't."

"He was there while the Pinkerton men talked to him, and to you."

"And to you. At least—" she put on her prettiest thoughtful look "—at least at the beginning. But I wasn't taking note of him."

She was taking note of what I was telling them about my wretched family, I thought grimly. But I pursued the question. "What about during the announcement, when the detective was telling us we could leave?"

"Well, my skirt caught on something, and I had to adjust it," she said, flipping the pretty rose-pink train to illustrate, "and I thought he was climbing into the Pullman because he was nearest the steps. I thought he would help us board. But he didn't."

"He certainly didn't," I agreed. That was unlike the gallant, charming Zeb. Another horrible possibility was nibbling at my consciousness. Suppose Zeb had hastened into the Pullman prematurely, as Letitia thought, preparing to help us, and instead had stumbled across a clue? In the crush and noisy confusion while we all struggled to board the car at once, it would have been possible for the malefactor to—

My thoughts recoiled. But there was no escaping my own logic.

The scimitar had been stolen after the train was on its way. Therefore the thief was on board.

Zeb was not on board.

Maybe he'd gone into the station restaurant. Or maybe he'd burgled the St. Louis houses, stayed in St. Louis to collect his swag, and a completely different thief on board just happened to choose this moment to take the scimitar. Or maybe—

I was beginning to sound as outlandish as Charlie. I faced it: Poor Zeb was probably not a thief, but a victim. He was probably dead, pushed from the train, his body lying beside the tracks somewhere.

And we were traveling with his killer.

Which of my companions was guilty?

Mind, now, I'm not foolish. Aunt Mollie explained to me many a time that in this wicked world it's best to keep your own counsel until the truth is clear. So I did not pose this interesting question to my companions. I merely watched the darkening valley and pondered. And when a glimmer of the solution occurred to me, I did not leap up shouting "Eureka!" but waited patiently for a distraction.

It came at last in the form of bedtime. The Pullman porter, his eyes sparkling kindly in his dark face, emerged from his closet bearing stacks of bed linens. He went to the front of the car, Mr. Salvini's end, and began to lower the upper bunks to make up the beds. All eyes followed him in this interesting task. I stood up and wandered toward the back platform, glancing into the porter's closet on my way. There was a padded bench bearing his large carpetbag and the stacks of linens he had readied. They were none too clean. Mr. Pullman ought to be ashamed. I picked up the porter's carpetbag and slipped out onto the back platform.

Cold air swirled about me, and ragged wisps of cinder-laden smoke from the speeding train. The great iron wheels clattered against the rails. A half moon grudgingly oozed gray light.

I opened the carpetbag. Inside I glimpsed clothing, yes; but also a great jeweled scimitar, and a smaller drawstring bag. When I untied it I saw a glint of emeralds.

Suddenly a bar of yellow light fell across the platform as the door opened. He'd come sooner than I expected. I whirled, thrusting the carpetbag behind me, and faced him.

The Pullman porter.

"Zeb!" I exclaimed.

"Clever Bridget. However did you guess?" He closed the door and we were alone in the feeble moonlight on the clattering, rocking platform.

"I knew you were not a real porter, Zeb."

"Cruel maid, you cut me to the quick! You insult my abilities as an actor!"

"Not at all, Zeb," I hastened to assure him. "Your acting was excellent. But when I passed by, you smelled of greasepaint. Most porters don't."

"I see."

"And most porters don't dirty the bed linens, because their hands aren't smeared with makeup."

He laughed merrily, like the old Zeb. "Mr. Salvini was right! I am a dirty teef!"

I smiled and continued. "Jack and Charlie also had time during the matinee to steal the jewels. But later, you were the only one standing close enough to Letty to kick your bag of jewels under her skirts when the Pinkerton men came to search you."

"You saw that?" He stepped closer.

"No." I tried to step back but felt the protective rail at the edge of the platform. "But she said her skirts had caught on something, and the platform was bare. It was you, wasn't it, snatching back the jewels and rushing onto the train to hide them anew? But tell me, why did you have to impersonate the porter? Did he see you hide the jewels?"

"Foolish old darkie!" complained Zeb. "I thought I had escaped notice. But as I leapt up the steps, I saw him staring at me. There was no choice. My gambling debts are urgent. So I pushed him into the closet, closed the door behind us, and, well, silenced him."

That got my dander up. This damn Rebel was talking about silencing darkies for the sake of a gambling debt, as though we'd never fought that bloody war. "You made up your skin and put on his uniform," I accused. "And threw him from the train."

"Yes, dear clever Bridget. Just as you must be thrown."

He lunged. I dodged but tripped against the carpetbag. My flailing hand closed over something.

The hilt of the scimitar.

I brandished it before me. Even in the feeble moonlight the great blade shone and the jewels glinted. "Hold, sir!" I exclaimed in my most ringing Kemble tones.

But, hang it, he didn't hold. He lunged at me again and wrenched the hilt from my hand. I saw the gleaming crescent rising high to smite me down.

So I reached into my bustle pocket, drew out my Civil War souvenir Colt, and shot him in the throat.

He slumped to the platform with a gurgle worthy of the great Salvini.

I know, I know, but it's so difficult these days to be a proper young lady. Besides, he hadn't been very sporting either, had he?

I tucked away my revolver, slid the scimitar carefully into his ragged wound because I dislike questions about my Colt, and staggered back into the Pullman. "Help!" I gasped in the tones I use for my own death scene. "Help! Suicide!"

Mr. Salvini was coming down the aisle, perhaps to ask why the porter had not finished making up the beds. He peered out the door onto the back platform, exclaimed, *"Santo cielo! La mia spada!"* and regaled us with another medley of rare Italian words.

Eventually Charlie's fertile imagination supplied a story that satisfied everyone. Young Zeb Adams, Charlie's account went, hoped to save the family plantation from foreclosure, so he'd stolen the jewels. But then, overcome with remorse, he had made himself up as the Moor of Venice and cut his own throat in a death scene as dramatic as Salvini's own. A lovely story, yes indeed. No mention of unhappy details like Pullman porters or gambling debts or attempts to smite innocent young ladies.

Our tour continued to wild acclaim, in city after city. Othello's death scene was even more moving than before.

Of course the jewels were returned to their St. Louis owners, most of them, and we actors shared in the rewards that had been offered. Unfortunately Zeb had already disposed of the emerald tiara, perhaps pawned in St. Louis, as Charlie suggested. But I'm bound to admit that a few years later a very similar piece served as a crown for the much-praised Lady Macbeth I played. The costume was dazzling. Emeralds look absolutely splendid against my red hair.

Oh, I know, I know, Aunt Mollie would scold too. But don't you agree that a rich and proper man like Banker Healey still owed me a trifle or two?

Perhaps he always will.

FROM BRIDGET MOONEY'S SCRAPBOOK

THE NEW YORK TIMES
December 14, 1880

Signor Salvini made his re-entrance upon the stage here last night at Booth's Theatre, and the audience that assembled to greet him was very large and enthusiastic. The actor performed his most famous part, Othello, and he was assisted by a company of American players. As to the effect of this mingling of tongues, it was less incoherent and absurd than one might have supposed it would be, but it was a discordant effect at best, and Mr. John Stetson's ingenious experiment will not, it is to be hoped, be imitated by other managers. If Salvini were a lesser actor than he is, his performance last evening might have seemed at moments ludicrous; but his genius is like a tempestuous wind that neither notes nor dreads obstacles. It is his manner rather than his speech that masters the imagination; the passion of his words rather than their import which fascinates the spectator.

THE ATLANTIC MONTHLY
March 1883

TOMMASO SALVINI
By Henry James

What an immense impression—simply as an impression—the actor makes on the spectator who sees him for the first time as the turbaned and deep-voiced Moor! He gives us his measure as a man; he acquaints us with that luxury of perfect confidence in the physical resources of the actor which is not the most frequent satisfaction of the modern playgoer. His powerful, active, manly frame, his noble, serious, vividly expressive face, his splendid smile, his Italian eye, his superb, voluminous voice, his carriage, his tone, his ease, the assurance he instantly gives that he holds the whole part in his hands and can make of it exactly what he chooses, —all this descends upon the spectator's mind with a richness which immediately converts attention into faith, and expectation into sympathy. He is a magnificent creature, and you are already on his side. His generous temperament is contagious; you find yourself looking at him, not so much as an actor, but as a hero . . . .

THE EIGHTH WONDER OF THE WORLD; or,
Golden Opinions

I scrambled from the stage door, coughing and gasping, heedless of the damage to my beautiful bustled frock. Most miserable hour that e'er time saw! I reckon I'd never been in such a fix. Smoke billowed about me, and sparks rained down. I smelt a dreadful odor and realized that a lock of my unkempt red hair had caught fire. As I knelt to douse it in a puddle of meltwater, I could hear shrieks, thin and terrible against the background roar of the colossal furnace behind me.

The Brooklyn Theatre had caught fire just moments ago, and flames were already lapping at the dark heavens.

The screams behind me tore at my heart, but I stiffened the sinews, summoned up the blood, and crawled gasping along the filthy alley. I heard new cries—the shouts of men on the street ahead, firemen and curiosity seekers who were pouring from nearby saloons and hotels. Legs booted for the December weather pounded by, and lanterns bobbed. When I reached the street I tried to stand but my scorched lungs were unable to sustain me and the world swam as I fell against a post.

Clarity returned only moments later, and I could again hear the screams and shouts and thudding boots on the cold street. Now I was moving swiftly, being carried along by a pair of strong arms belonging to a sturdy fellow of some twenty years. He was wearing a cheap rough laborer's coat but his smile was a treasure of kindliness.

"Feeling better, missy?" he asked solicitously.

"Oh, sir, my gratitude is boundless!" I gasped as elegantly as I could. His face registered sudden respect. Perhaps I should remind you that I had recently been tutored in elocutionary skills by the esteemed English actress Mrs. Fanny Kemble, the greatest of her generation.

"Excuse me, madam," he said in confusion, and for a moment I feared that he would bow and drop me. "You won't take it the wrong way, I hope, but for a moment I thought you were a mere actress."

Pleased that he now thought me a lady, I said, "I remain grateful."

My hearty rescuer had borne me a block away from the inferno, and now paused. "Are you better, madam? I can leave you here with your permission, and go back for another poor soul."

Well, I ask you, would any young lady, weakened by smoke and fear, want to be abandoned on the cold street in front of a dry-goods store? The prospect was so dreadful that I was weighing several desperate and perhaps improper means of clinging to my rough-clad hero when I heard a woman's voice call, "Harry! Harry Supple, is that you?"

"Yes, ma'am," said my young man, turning to a carriage that pulled up beside us.

"Harry, it's a dreadful fire! Is it Dieters Hotel?"

Her voice was educated, and the carriage lanterns gleamed against a shiny painted gig. Well, I reckoned that the well-bred voice and glossy paint signified places far more comfortable than this cold street. I decided to swoon again as Harry Supple answered, "It's the Brooklyn Theatre, ma'am. I was just going back to help the firemen, for I fear there are people dying. But here's this poor lady I rescued with her frock and hair all scorched, and in a faint again, poor thing. A fine lady too."

"Put her in the carriage, Harry," said the lady. "She is well-dressed. I'll take her home. Your strong arms are needed here."

Quickly, Harry placed me in the carriage and vanished into the night. The lady tapped the horse with her whip, for she herself was driving, and we moved rapidly away from the dreadful conflagration. I remained limp, with my eyes closed, but I was aware that the lady drove only a few blocks before halting again, calling for servants to help her carry me in.

I was laid on a bed with smooth sheets, and my face and arms were cleansed with moistened cotton cloths amidst soft exclamations about my scorched hair and frock. Then the lady and her servants began to discuss removing the frock, to attend to my needs more easily. Since a pocket that I had sewn into my bustle contained a few items that I preferred not to reveal to the public, I emitted a little moan and fluttered my eyelashes.

"She's coming round," said the educated lady.

It was my cue to open my eyes and say feebly, "Oh—what lovely place is this? Am I in heaven, and these the Lord's own angels?" Unfortunately the effect I intended was rather ruined by a spasm of coughing that overtook me.

"Poor dear!" said the educated woman briskly. "You have survived your ordeal, and I believe that when you have taken more good fresh air, you will be able to return to your home."

In the lamplight, I saw that she was a strong woman in her thirties with a pug nose, lively features, and a beautiful smile. I said, "Thank you for your kindness, madam," paused to make sure I had no more coughing to do, and added, "Oh—I remember, the fire! The dreadful fire!"

"Yes. What happened?" The lady's face was as filled with curiosity as the maid's.

"Oh, madam, it was so quick!" I replied. "One of the border curtains high above the stage blew against the flame of a border light, and caught instantly. In a few moments the entire theatre was ablaze!"

"How dreadful!"

"Yes—yes, it was. You are so kind to me, madam, in this hour of misfortune. Permit me to introduce myself. I am Miss Mooney, of a landed Irish family, friends to the Kemble and Sartoris families of England."

Oh, I know, I know, we weren't really landed, unless you count the muddy gutters of St. Louis where Papa spent much of his time. But we were Irish, weren't we? And I certainly knew Kembles and Sartorises. I also knew President Grant—in fact, his daughter Nellie had provided me with the lovely frock I was wearing—but his administration had crumbled in such a flurry of frauds and bribery that I did not wish to mention him until I knew more about this household.

The kind lady said, "I am Mrs. Roebling, and it is a pleasure to make your acquaintance, dear Miss Mooney, though I regret the tragic circumstances of our meeting. Were you attending the spectacle tonight?"

In fact, I had been in the spectacle tonight. But looking around the solid respectability of this house, I hesitated to admit it. Laboring folks like Harry Supple were fascinated by those of us in the limelight, and the higher classes, the noble families of England and the wealthy and politically powerful on both sides of the Atlantic, toasted us. The great actress Mrs. Kemble had married into Southern landed gentry, and her sister Mrs. Sartoris, an opera singer, had married an English noble. But between Supple and Sartoris lay a large middle class of respectable burghers, the men who ran the shops and built the bridges of the nation, and many of them looked askance at those in my profession until they became rich enough to view us as their playthings.

Bridges! That was it, bridges! On my way to the ferry, I had seen this fine lady often, talking to the workers who were building the great span over the East River. "Mrs. Roebling," I said, "are you by any chance related to the illustrious man who is constructing the splendid bridge to Brooklyn?"

Mrs. Roebling beamed. "Yes. My husband is the Chief Engineer."

I clasped my hands. "What a noble work it is, Mrs. Roebling! When I crossed the East River on the ferry, it was stirring indeed to see those two great towers rising like anthems to the sky!" It was true—the two giant structures rose from the river and upwards, ever upwards, taller than anything for miles around, except for Trinity Church in Wall Street.

Mrs. Roebling leaned back in the bedside chair and smiled sadly. "They were not built without cost, dear Miss Mooney."

"Oh, yes, I have heard of the dreadful caisson disease that has afflicted the Chief Engineer."

"It is dreadful indeed. These last four years he has suffered so much that he cannot bear to speak to people, nor stir from his room. I write his instructions for him, and carry them to the workmen. And yet despite the pain and exhaustion his mind remains clear."

"That is good news, for I had heard that it affects the mind as well."

Mrs. Roebling scowled. "That is not true, Miss Mooney! Who has been telling you such rubbish?"

"A gentleman admirer of mine. But of course you know best, Mrs. Roebling, and I will endeavor to correct his misapprehension when next I see him."

Mrs. Roebling leaned toward me and asked urgently, "Who is your admirer, Miss Mooney? Who is spreading these rumors? Is it Abram Hewitt, the ironmonger?"

She was so intent, looking at me like a hound at a rabbit hole, that I forgot my own difficulties and sat up on the bed. "Mrs. Roebling, please do not distress yourself! I have no desire to sow dissension between the Chief Engineer and the others devoted to the bridge."

"Dissension aplenty has already been sown!" Mrs. Roebling snorted. She looked me over carefully and sighed. "Ah, well, it cannot be Abram Hewitt. That prim fellow is incapable of behaving in a manner that would lead a lady to describe him as her admirer. Miss Mooney, you would find it difficult to believe the trials we suffer, trying to accomplish what we were chosen to do! The great bridge stands unfinished while the politicians quarrel. This affair with the cable wire—"

Well, that made me prick up my ears, because my admirer was in fact in the wire business. I asked, "What affair with the cable wire?"

"That hypocritical fellow Hewitt is a trustee of the bridge company, as you may know. And he says that those connected with the bridge must not bid on the cable, thus disqualifying my husband's brothers! Yet people believe in his saintliness!"

"You mean Mr. Hewitt has prevented the Roebling wire company from furnishing the wire for the cables?"

"Exactly! Mr. Hewitt said he personally would not bid for the contract.

But he's an ironmonger, his company doesn't manufacture wire! Of course he won't bid personally! His cronies will bid instead!" She looked at me earnestly. "It is not merely the unfairness to my brothers-in-law that distresses me. It is the fear that Mr. Hewitt's friends will provide a slipshod product for my—for our great bridge!"

Well, naturally Mrs. Roebling would think that Roebling wire would build a better bridge. Still, for such a proper lady, she seemed very knowledgeable. I tried to console her. "That is dreadful, Mrs. Roebling. But surely the opportunity to contribute to this marvel of our age will inspire the company to provide only the best wire! Besides, if Mr. Hewitt values his reputation, he will see to it that his friend's product is excellent."

She said darkly, "Mr. Hewitt is one of Tilden's chief supporters."

"Tilden? They say he has just been elected President of the United States! That is—"

"It is still contested," Mrs. Roebling reminded me. "In any case, just now Mr. Hewitt has great power among seekers of patronage. For all his saintly posing, I prefer the corrupt followers of President Useless S. Grant!"

Well, I was relieved that I had not admitted to my acquaintance with the Grant family, and idly smoothed the skirt of the lovely dress Nellie Grant had given me, then gasped in shock. I reckon I've never seen a skirt so ratty-looking. The white muslin flounces were caked with mud and soot, and burn marks streaked the splendid Mandarin yellow foulard.

Mrs. Roebling saw my dismay and exclaimed, "Oh, my dear Miss Mooney, here I've been chattering on about my problems, while you are the one with troubles!"

"My poor frock!" I said. "Besmeared as black as Vulcan!"

She picked up a fold of the skirt and inspected it in the lamplight. "The muslin is easily washed," she declared briskly, and turned to the servant. "As for the foulard—Bessie, didn't you boil up the mixture for scorch marks last week? Onion juice, vinegar, white soap, and fuller's earth? And bring the scissors, so we can repair Miss Mooney's coiffure."

I stood to peek into a glass, and for a moment did not realize that the bedraggled Medusa-like creature reflected there was my usually sprightly self. "Oh, my goodness, what will Lloyd think!" I gasped unthinkingly.

When I'd first noticed the border curtain catching fire, I had roused the other actors. Then I'd lit out for the dressing room to exchange my flimsy theatrical costume for my beloved Nellie Grant dress, with its bustle pocket filled with my souvenirs and with a few bracelets I found lying about, left behind by other actresses who were fleeing the blazing theatre. There had not been time to arrange my hair, and the long auburn tresses looked sorry indeed, burnt and damp and snaky with dirty snow. No wonder Harry Supple had not assumed I was a lady.

Slowly I became aware that Mrs. Roebling was regarding me with great suspicion.

"Mrs. Roebling, what is it?" I asked anxiously, concerned about her sudden change of demeanor.

She asked in a tight voice, "Did you say Lloyd? Is that the name of your admirer, who is maligning my husband's ability?"

"Mrs. Roebling, I know that your husband is able! The proof stands proudly in the East River, poised to link these two great cities!"

"It is Lloyd, then," said Mrs. Roebling. "Mr. J. Lloyd Haigh."

I said feebly, "I am sorry, Mrs. Roebling. He appeared to be honorable in all other matters."

And indeed he did appear honorable, my Lloyd. He was a handsome gentleman of some fifty years, with twinkling honest eyes. He was a fine vocalist, a jolly man who was always ready with a compliment that could make a young lady shiver with pleasure. He was also eager to be of assistance in business matters, and had purchased a few old deeds and papers that Aunt Mollie had bequeathed me, giving me over a thousand dollars for them with the explanation that a gentleman of good reputation could use them to obtain loans from a bank, but that a young lady wouldn't wish to trouble herself to learn about interest and repayment and similar tedious matters. Don't you think that was kind of him? Yes indeed. His generosity had enabled me to take a room in an excellent hotel instead of the dirty inn where the other actors stayed. He spoke often of marriage but I put him off.

"Honorable!" Mrs. Roebling exclaimed. She was combing my unsightly hair and gave the comb an angry and painful jerk to emphasize her point. "Those of us who know something of the wire business are aware of certain underhanded practices by Mr. J. Lloyd Haigh's company! But I fear that is of no interest to the bridge trustees."

I waited until the comb was safely through the next tress before saying, "What you say is shocking, Mrs. Roebling. It is difficult to believe such things of a fine gentleman."

"Oh, yes, he's very persuasive. You aren't the first lady to believe him, and gentlemen are just as gullible. During the bidding, each firm submitted samples of their wire for testing by Colonel Paine with his new device. Mr. Haigh's samples did well. But I suspect Haigh did not manufacture them at his own mill. Instead, he purchased them from a reputable firm, and submitted them as his own."

"Dear me!"

"Of course Mr. Abram Hewitt is trying to assure his success also. Mr. Hewitt cleared out the Tweed ring from the bridge project, only to arrange for his own friends to profit from it. It makes the Chief Engineer so angry! I believe he would have been up and about years ago except for the nervous exhaustion the politicians inspire in him."

"Poor fellow," I said, reflecting that Mrs. Roebling herself must be able to deal with politicians rather skillfully, or a sick man would not still be in charge of the great bridge. "If a member of the public may offer a suggestion, would it be possible for all the wire to be tested before it is used on the bridge?"

"Yes! Indeed, that may be the answer, testing all the wire!" She thought a moment, smiled, and I breathed a sigh of relief for her kinder mood, for she had finished with the comb and was picking up the scissors. "If Haigh's firm is chosen, we could enforce his honesty, couldn't we?" She snipped carefully. "Still, Miss Mooney, if Mr. Haigh mentions matrimony, be sure to inquire about Miss Jennie Hughes before you accept."

"Accept! Goodness, no, I have no intention of marrying anyone! My Aunt Mollie had a little money from her father, and after she married Uncle Mike she wanted to buy a—" I had to feign a fit of coughing, because I almost said "a saloon" "—to buy a pleasant riverside property, but they said a married lady couldn't sign for it, her husband had to sign for it."

"That is true," said Mrs. Roebling, clipping my singed locks into a fringe across my forehead. "A wife cannot enter into a contract, although a single woman can."

"So Uncle Mike signed for the property, and then he mortgaged it, and spent the money. And soon the bank foreclosed and sold Aunt Mollie's property." I didn't tell her that Uncle Mike had lost the money gambling with the sporting men who arrived on the riverboats. The new owner had hired Uncle Mike to work in the saloon, but Aunt Mollie had to take up copying for a trade. From then on she made more private arrangements with bankers, and frequently warned me that for a poor girl marriage was a snare, no different from being a bound servant or a tart, excepting of course in the eyes of the Lord, and the Lord didn't often pay the bills, did He?

Hastily, I added to Mrs. Roebling, "Of course, with a fine husband like the Chief Engineer, marriage is an excellent arrangement."

"Of course," said Mrs. Roebling. "And yet I have heard other stories much like your Aunt Mollie's. Someday we must ask them to change the laws. The difficulty is that we wives have so many duties, we cannot easily spare the time. Meanwhile, you are wise to stay clear of Mr. Haigh. There, Miss Mooney, that is the best we can do with your hair."

"Oh, thank you! It looks quite fashionable," I said, and indeed it appeared much less pitiful and mangy. "You are the kindest lady in the world! And Mr. Harry Supple is one of the kindest men."

"Yes, Harry's a good lad, one of our most trusted riggers. He used to be a sailor, and is good on the wire ropes."

"Do thank him for me, as I was too enfeebled to do so. Now, I have imposed too long on your good graces. My cough is much improved, and my hair is respectable again."

"But your frock, Miss Mooney!"

"I would gladly accept a jar of your mixture to clean scorch marks."

She and Bessie gave me several jars, and an old travelling cape to ward off the winter winds, as my cloak had been abandoned to the blaze. Mrs. Roebling drove me to my fine hotel, saying she would return to the scene of the fire to see if she could help other poor souls.

The next day I rose early, donned the Roebling cape and a feather-trimmed bonnet that dipped low enough in front to hide most of my damaged hair, and hurried to the site of the great fire. The scene was ghastly, and the stench worse. Well over a hundred people had perished, and the firemen were still carrying bodies from the smoldering wreckage. I saw our stage manager, who was delighted that I had survived, but sad to inform me that two of our company had perished, Mr. Murdoch and Mr. Burroughs.

"Oh, no!" The world grew blurry, and I turned and staggered away from the dismal scene. Murdoch and Burroughs were fine boisterous young actors, and we'd had many a jolly hour backstage trading yarns about growing up in St. Louis or Zanesville.

"Bridget, my sweet! Is it you?" cried a gentlemanly baritone.

I turned, and Mr J. Lloyd Haigh, devilishly handsome in his fine dark cape and checked trousers, ran across to me from the door of the Market National Bank and well nigh hugged my head off. "Oh, Bridget, I was sick with worry!" cried my sweet-scented dandy.

I bowed my head against his elegant woollen cape. "Yes, I would not spend another such a night, though 'twere to buy a world of happy days! But please, Lloyd, I can't bear it here any longer!"

Lloyd pulled out a snowy handkerchief and tried to dry my tears. "Now, now, Bridget, you are safe with me! Let us walk by the river. Tell me, did your Aunt Mollie's business papers burn?"

"No, Lloyd, they are safe."

"Good. Bridget, you are the dearest creature in the world!"

Even through my tears, I could feel the heat of his ardent gaze, and I allowed him to steal a kiss in honor of the great emotion we both felt at my narrow escape. Then he led me away from the scene of the calamity. When we reached the streets near the East River we paused to watch the bridge workers. The great towers, solid and yet airy with their handsome Gothic arches, stood proudly against the gray December sky. Thin ladders stretched the entire height of each tower. Near us stood the stone anchorage building, gray and massive, its top platform spiky with derricks. A few wire ropes had been slung from it to the very top of the two great towers, and thence to the New York side far away. Their scarves blowing in the wind, the laborers were laying slats between these first wire ropes, building themselves a narrow footbridge across the sky. I wondered if handsome Harry Supple was one of the nimble figures I saw scurrying high among the wire ropes.

I said, "Lloyd, is it true that your firm might provide the wire for this astonishing bridge?"

"Yes indeed!" He beamed at me. Lloyd had fine teeth and a most engaging smile. "The trustees of the Bridge Company have an excellent opinion of me. That is the most important thing in the world, Bridget, a good opinion. I am fortunate."

Well, I think that riches are more important than good opinion, because generally if a body has money, the good opinion follows along after. As one of Shakespeare's shiftier characters says, "I have bought golden opinions from all sorts of people." But sometimes it's more comfortable not to argue. I said, "It is important indeed. But isn't it true that the Chief Engineer has an interest in a rival firm?"

"Why, what a pert creature you are, my little Bridget, to be so interested in business matters!"

I smiled the way I smiled when I played Juliet, and hoped that my poor hair did not look too bristly in the daylight. "Sir, when a gentleman proposes marriage, of course a young lady is interested in his prospects!"

"Ah, my sweet, of course! Well, my prospects are excellent. Naturally, the Chief Engineer favors his brothers' firm in Trenton. My mill, however, is located here in Brooklyn. Therefore I have the strong support of the editor of the *Brooklyn Eagle*, who is also a trustee of the Bridge Company. I have also another powerful friend among the trustees. Good opinion, Bridget, that is the secret! For when those who hold this good opinion of me gain nationwide power, my prospects will be boundless!"

"You are a supporter of Mr. Tilden, then?"

"A most loyal supporter! And soon my loyalty will be rewarded!" He was glowing with enthusiasm, and I could see that he had reason. If Lloyd helped Tilden's cause, Abram Hewitt and the other Tilden enthusiasts among the trustees would favor giving him the contract, and it would matter little who made the better wire. The Roeblings, I decided, might well lose this skirmish.

"Your loyalty to Tilden is financial also?" I hazarded.

"Naturally. What a lot of questions you ask, you sweet vixen!"

"Then your reward will be financial also!" I clapped my gloved hands and favored him with my sauciest smile.

It was too much for dear Lloyd, who pulled me into the shadowed privacy of the doorway of a saloon that had not yet opened and attempted to steal another kiss. "Yes, my reward will certainly be financial. And more, I hope, when you are my dear wife, and the queen of Brooklyn!"

Sweet-scented though he was, Lloyd was becoming far too ardent for the early morning of a day when I had much to mourn and much to do, seeing as I was out of work again. So, recollecting what Mrs. Roebling had told me, I giggled fetchingly and said, "Mr. Haigh, sir, I have not yet accepted your kind proposal! First I must confer with Miss Jennie Hughes!"

Well, that gave him a turn! His breath sort of hitched, and then he laughed heartily. "That was merely an attempt at blackmail, Bridget, I swear! Scurrilous people told her to say we had wed! I never married Miss Hughes, I never told her I would! She knew I was married already! You mustn't believe silly rumors!"

Hang it, this was worse than I'd expected. I wanted to know more. I laughed heartily too. "That is a great relief, Lloyd! I know it's true that many people do scurrilous deeds for the sake of money. Still, a charge of bigamy is serious!"

"It's false!" he exclaimed, clasping both my hands in his and gazing at me most sincerely. "I'm not a bigamist, I divorced my first wife in Connecticut! Bridget, my sweet, these falsehoods pain me all the more, for now I have met you, my truest love! Your bright eyes, your russet hair, the hint of freckles on the loveliest nose in the nation!"

I smiled demurely while I calculated. If he'd divorced his first wife, there must have been a second one, and not Jennie Hughes, for he said he hadn't married her. That made Jennie the third, at least, who claimed to have married him. I silently thanked Aunt Mollie, and Mrs. Roebling, for saving me from becoming a bigamist's fourth wife, surely a fate worse than death, and twice as ignoble.

I wriggled from Lloyd's embrace back to the street and started for the ferry landing. "Come, Lloyd, let us not be precipitous! A young lady must keep her reputation pure. You yourself have taught me the importance of good opinion. I will consider your kind offer."

"Bridget, I will do anything!" he cried sincerely. "I will go down on bended knee!"

Well, I must admit I like to see a handsome gentleman on bended knee, but gentlemen have other virtues too. I squeezed Lloyd's hand gratefully, and by the time the ferry reached New York he had promised me a new velvet travelling dress in exchange for another of Aunt Mollie's old papers. An emerald green dress, I decided, because green looked splendid with my hair, what there was of it.

Several days later, after much diligent searching, I had only two offers of work, one from a troupe that proposed to tour to Chicago with two Boucicault melodramas, and another from a Water Street dance hall. Since the duties in Water Street included more than dancing, I chose the touring troupe, and bade my Lloyd a tearful farewell, promising that I'd give him my answer soon.

Oh, I know, I know. Lloyd was a goodly apple rotten at the core, and a proper young lady would have snubbed such a dishonorable fellow; but it's so difficult to find honorable men in these times. And even if you find one he may up and get caisson disease, and lounge about moaning in an upstairs room while you build his bridges for him. My skills did not run to engineering, so it seemed prudent to pursue my chosen profession, while selecting my gentleman admirers for their generous hearts. And hang it, Lloyd did offer pretty compliments, and elegant green velvet travelling dresses, and useful business assistance whenever I found one of Aunt Mollie's commercial papers! Besides, when Tilden became president, and Abram Hewitt was running Washington, who could guess what splendors lay ahead for my Lloyd, and for his good friends?

But Tilden did not become president. Clever as he was, Abram Hewitt's skills at bribery were no match for those of the party of Lincoln and Grant, and Rutherford B. Hayes overcame popular defeat to triumph in the electoral college by a majority of one. It was many months before I returned to New York and encountered Mr. J. Lloyd Haigh again, and I expected him to bear signs of his disappointment as I sent in a note to his John Street office. But when he emerged he was his old ebullient self, handsome and wreathed in smiles.

"Bridget Mooney!" he cried. "I am delighted! Delighted!"

"I too, Lloyd!"

"You are the most beautiful creature in the world, Bridget!" He looked at me all hot-eyed. "May I beg the pleasure of escorting you to dinner?"

I carefully deployed my parasol in order to keep his enthusiastic attentions at bay and said, "I had hoped to take a constitutional to see the great bridge. They are calling it the eighth wonder of the world!"

"Of course, my sweet!" He offered his arm and we strolled along to observe the work at the New York anchorage. Atop the great stone box-like structure, workmen with their sleeves rolled up in the June warmth were working with a thick, tautly stretched wire cable that came all the way from Brooklyn, crossing the tops of the towers to this anchorage, looping around an iron horseshoe-shaped holder, and then returning to Brooklyn as it had come. Lloyd explained that it was but one part of the enormous cable that would support the bridge. Working behind the great steel anchor bars, the laborers—one of them was my kindly hero, Harry Supple—attached the cable's horseshoe-shaped holder to a sturdy wire rope that ran over some pulleys back to a great machine. They started the machine. Amidst the ensuing noise and smoke, I saw the machine slowly easing the cable into position so they could attach it to the anchor bars.

Lloyd was observing with interest too. He shouted, "Dangerous operation! If something gave way it would catapult that iron horseshoe across the river, and the cable too! The pull at the hoisting machine is seventy tons!"

I looked at the taut cable stretching all the way to Brooklyn. Seventy tons of tension. "You must be proud to be associated with such an achievement," I shouted.

"Indeed I am!"

"There's such a lot of wire in each cable! It must be very profitable to have such a contract."

"Yes, but—" A cloud flitted across his handsome face.

"But not as profitable as it should be?"

"Hush, little Bridget! It's no concern of yours!"

"The Chief Engineer has set unfair standards?" I hazarded. "Perhaps he is testing the wire?"

"Don't trouble yourself about it, Bridget!"

"I am troubled only for your sake! I worry so, Lloyd!"

I gave him my most anxious look, which put him in a more confiding spirit. "Fear not, I can manage the Chief Engineer, although he is implacable,

Bridget! He has Colonel Paine check every wire, right at my mill. And he substitutes Roebling wire whenever he's allowed. Not in the cables, of course, but do you see the wire rope that attaches the cable to the hoisting machine?"

"The one that runs over the pulleys?"

"Yes. That's Roebling wire." He gestured at a woman's figure on the anchorage, and I recognized Mrs. Roebling in earnest conversation with the assistant engineers. "And he has his wife deliver letters to the bridge trustees, trying to undermine the good opinion I enjoy among them!"

The good opinion, and perhaps the profits too. I said, "Your friends among the trustees will stand by you, surely."

"They will! I have my ways!" He beamed at me. "Fear not, Bridget, my profits are secure!"

"I'm certain they are, Lloyd!" I was tired of hollering and turned my attention to the anchorage. With many groans, the great machine had eased its seventy-ton load into place between two anchor bars. Quickly, the workmen drove in a thick steel pin to fasten it securely to the anchor bars. I must admit, I was impressed at the minds that had conceived this bridge, and the methods of building it, wire by wire and stone by stone. I was impressed also by the workmen. Harry Supple's sturdy forearms glistened in the sun. He had driven in the steel pin that locked the straining cable to the anchor bars. It all made me proud to be a part of this glorious age.

It didn't seem so glorious a few days later. I was in Water Street, reassuring myself that the dance hall would still hire me if the theatre companies did not, when a great cannon-sound boomed and crashed through the air. It was a noise to harrow up the soul. People began to shriek. Several ladies nearby, including some reputed harlots, fell to their knees to pray for forgiveness for their sins. With prickling spine, I hastened toward the great noise. There were shouts that there had been an accident at the bridge, and a crowd was forming at the anchorage. Someone was wounded. I ran to fetch a doctor I knew, then asked various gentlemen in the crowd what had occurred. Some said a cable had snapped; some said a bridge tower had fallen; some agreed with the young ladies in Water Street, and believed it was the Second Coming. There were many reports of falling stones, and of a fifty-foot high splash of water in the East River that had drenched the passengers on the Fulton Ferry.

It was not until the next day that the newspapers pieced together what had happened. While workmen were trying to fasten a new cable to the anchor bars, it had broken away from the machine, shot as though from a catapult toward the Brooklyn shore. It had sheared off a chimney, leaped clean over the great tower, and smashed rowboats before splashing into the middle of the river. Two men working on the anchorage had been wounded, and two killed.

One of the dead was my own dear hero, Harry Supple.

The cause of the accident was the failure, not of the cable wire itself, but of the wire rope that attached it to the hoisting machine. Someone had made sure the reporter knew that the wire that failed had been manufactured by the Roebling company.

The engineers investigated, and issued a report stating their belief that it had accidentally been cut by the sharp iron rim of its own pulley wheel.

Yes, you're right, of course. I knew better too. I vowed by my Aunt Mollie's shade to avenge dear Harry's death. But what could a young lady do? Mr. J. Lloyd Haigh had powerful friends, and no one would choose to believe the observations of a temporarily penniless actress if the esteemed Mr. Haigh denied them. I soon discarded any notion of joining Miss Jennie Hughes and a few of his other wives in publicly attacking his virtue. Many would prefer to believe his protestations of blackmail, and my own spotless reputation might be damaged. Besides, the bridge company trustees doubtless knew the story already, and had granted him the contract despite his nefarious behavior. After all, he had damaged mere ladies, not the gentlemen whose good opinions counted.

My brother, before he was killed by the Rebels, had taught me marksmanship, and the Army-issue Colt revolver I carried in my bustle was well-oiled and reliable. Still, I reckoned there were more fitting ways to deal with a low-down skunk who had so thoughtlessly struck down the flower of heroism with a seventy-ton slingshot. His proudest achievement was the golden opinion others held of him. That would be my target.

I hocked my emerald-green travelling dress—after all, June is too warm for velvet, don't you think?—and accosted a lad, a street urchin of about my height, with the offer to purchase better garments for him if he would allow me to have his. Once he overcame his natural tendency to flee from a lady whose sanity had deserted her, he agreed.

The next day I dressed in the urchin's smelly clothes, tied up my hair to tuck into his soiled cap, and strutted into Mr. J. Lloyd Haigh's mill in South Brooklyn. I spied a foreman who was clearly as Irish as I was. "Me name is Mike O'Rourke, sir," I told him in Papa's best dialect, "just over from the old country, and in need of a job."

"No jobs here, lad," he said kindly. "Try up at the bridge."

"Whisht and haven't I been up there already? Please, sir!"

"This is no work for a boy."

"Sure and I can learn, sir! That gentleman over there—" I indicated the Chief Engineer's assistant, Colonel Paine, who was testing every coil of wire before it was loaded on a flatbed wagon. "He looks at the wire and writes on a paper. That's simple."

My countryman howled with laughter. "Not so simple, lad! We test the wire in many ways. If it's good wire, then we give it a certificate and it may be loaded on. If it's bad wire, it's discarded onto that pile in the yard. Now, would you know good wire from bad? Off with you, now!"

I looked curiously at the flatbed wagon. "What happens to the good wire, sir? Does it go in the bridge?"

"That's right, they drive it straight to the bridge."

"And what happens to the bad wire?"

He glanced at the pile in the yard. "You're a curious puppy, Mike O'Rourke! I suppose they sell it for other purposes."

"What if they send bad wire to the bridge?"

"Well, it won't have a certificate, will it? We caught them one night exchanging bad wire for the good wire they'd stored here overnight. Now the certified wire goes straight to the bridge, no waiting overnight, so they can't switch it, can they?"

Since I myself, a mere female, could think of several ways to switch it, I decided to investigate further. The certificate was clearly the crucial item; Colonel Paine handed it to the teamster. I bade farewell to the Irish foreman, stuck my hands in my pockets, and sauntered off in the direction of the bridge. Not long after, the flat wagon loaded with wire passed me. I followed and soon saw it turn into the yard of another building where rejected wire was stored. Hiding behind the fence, I watched Mr. J. Lloyd Haigh's men unload the good wire onto a second wagon, replace it with rejected wire, and send the flatbed wagon loaded with the bad wire on toward the bridge, together with the certificate belonging to the good wire that had been left behind.

What would they do with the wagonload of good wire, now that it had no certificate? I slithered an arm through the fence and hooked an apple from the lunch pail of one of Lloyd's men. I had scarce finished it when a teamster climbed into the wagon seat and drove the load of good wire toward the gate. I had to run to keep up with the horses, and was near enough to see them turn into the yard of the building where Colonel Paine tested the wire. Sure enough, soon the same good wire was tested again. I was watching the inspector sign another certificate for it when something jerked me back by the collar.

"You're still about?" cried the Irish foreman, not so kindly as before. "Off with you now, little rascal!" He fetched me a whack with his hand so I skedaddled.

Next day, attired in my serviceable black frock, I intercepted Mrs. Roebling as she started for the bridge. "Forgive me, Mrs. Roebling, but I have important information for you."

She did not pause. "Good day, Miss Mooney. I saw you recently with Mr. J. Lloyd Haigh, against my advice. I fear I have no time for any friend of his." She stalked on stonily.

I hastened along after her. "Hear me out, Mrs. Roebling! I know that your assessment of Mr. Haigh is correct! Please count me a friend of the late heroic Harry Supple, not of a man we both know to be a crook!"

She hesitated, still suspicious, but gracious again. "Miss Mooney, I cannot converse at present, because I have urgent engineering specifications for the laborers on the bridge." She gestured to the packet of papers she carried.

"My message is for them also, and for the Chief Engineer, and for the many members of the public who will tread the bridge in future years. The wire Mr. Haigh is delivering to the bridge yard has not in fact been approved by Colonel Paine."

She looked shocked. "Oh, you are mistaken, Miss Mooney! Colonel Paine certifies each load of wire, and it is not accepted at the bridge without a certificate!"

"But does Colonel Paine accompany each load from the mill to the bridge? Does he know that it is driven into a building where Mr. Haigh's men exchange the certified wire for wire he has rejected? Does he see the rejected wire continue to the bridge with his certificate, while the good wire is returned to the mill, there to be tested and certified again? Why, some of that wire has probably been tested a dozen times, and has produced a dozen certificates for Mr. Haigh to use on rejected wire!"

"And all the bad wire worked into the bridge cables!" Mrs. Roebling clapped her hand to her mouth in dismay.

"Do you mean it is too late? That the bridge could collapse, and kill hundreds?" In the back of my mind I heard again the horrid thin shrieks from the burning theatre.

"Well," said Mrs. Roebling, "there is a margin of safety, of course, and if we can add good wire to the cables—some two hundred wires each, or even a hundred and fifty—" An enthusiasm glowed in her eyes as she began to calculate, as though solving the engineering problem was her true joy.

I reminded her, "First, you must get the good wire."

"True, Miss Mooney." She looked dejected again. "We have tried so often to convince the trustees that we should change contractors, to no avail! Mr. Abram Hewitt holds Haigh's mortgage, you know, and as he himself lost so much in the Tilden campaign, he has no wish for Haigh to default on his payments."

So that was the source of the "good opinion" Lloyd enjoyed. I said, "Another difficulty is that we are ladies, Mrs. Roebling, and the trustees will not value our observations as highly as those of men."

"That is true, Miss Mooney. We must get a gentleman—I know. The Chief Engineer will send Colonel Paine himself, with some trusted colleagues, to witness the replacement of the certified wire by the bad wire."

"A good plan! Here, I've written the address on this card. Colonel Paine can hide behind the fence there and observe what is done. He and his colleagues can testify to the trustees, and then you and the Chief Engineer can advise them as to the best engineering solution."

"Yes. Surely even Mr. Hewitt will not agree to a swindle that endangers the public! Will you testify against Mr. Haigh as well?"

"Oh, madam, I am eternally grateful to you for so kindly rescuing me, and would assist you if I could, but I obtained this information in a manner that might compromise my reputation. I truly believe that the testimony of a gentleman like Colonel Paine is more likely to bring the desired result."

Mrs. Roebling's pleasant pug-nosed face hid a shrewd knowledge of the world. "I see, Miss Mooney. I would not wish your reputation harmed by Mr. Haigh's falsehoods, for your sake, and because such an event would damage our case. I am grateful for the information, and will not bring your name into the matter."

In fact, I was concerned with more than my reputation. A great advantage of having Mr. Haigh as an eager suitor, rather than a jaded husband, was his generosity. I feared that if he lost the bridge wire contract he would be as poor as I, and so I hastened to ask my shifty admirer to underwrite two new costumes I would need in order to join a touring production of *Two Roses*.

We struck a bargain for the costumes, Lloyd and I. He agreed to pay the dressmaker's bill in exchange for another of Aunt Mollie's old papers and a dozen kisses, and I departed for Buffalo and Syracuse, fully expecting that he would be disgraced before I returned. But no such thing occurred. When I arrived in New York at the end of August, he still held the wire contract for the great bridge.

I arranged to encounter Mrs. Roebling as she left the bridge yard, and asked if our plan had failed.

"Goodness, no!" she exclaimed. "Dear Miss Mooney, you are concerned because as yet there has been no public notice of this affair. You must be patient—the bridge trustees will make it public at an appropriate time. Meanwhile, the soundness of the bridge is assured. The trustees were at last convinced of Mr. Haigh's duplicity, and have agreed that he must replace all the bad wire not yet worked into the cables, and must add one hundred fifty wires per cable to assure its strength, all at his own expense. Further, our inspectors now accompany the loads of certified wire from Mr. Haigh's mill all the way to the bridge yard. Fear not, Miss Mooney, the great bridge is sound!"

"I am glad to hear it, Mrs. Roebling. Are the trustees convinced at last that Mr. Haigh is a scoundrel?"

"Oh, yes!" She laughed merrily. "Do you know, he had the cheek to tell the trustees that he wasn't anxious about the money it would cost him, he cared only that they should hold a good opinion of him. One of them replied that it was now the unanimous opinion of the trustees that he was a—" her dark eyes sparkled as she looked about to make certain that no one could overhear her before she whispered, "—a damned rascal!"

"How shocking!" I exclaimed. "And at a meeting of gentlemen, too! But aren't you disappointed that Mr. Haigh has not been publicly shamed?"

"When dealing with the politicians among the bridge trustees, compromise is often necessary, especially when the news would shame them too," said Mrs. Roebling philosophically. "Someday they will make Mr. Haigh's fraud public. Meanwhile, it is my job to build the eighth wonder of the world!"

I held Mrs. Roebling in the highest esteem, and soon gained further evidence that her assessment of the situation was accurate. When I next saw Lloyd, his splendid voice and hot eyes were as delightful as ever, but he had begun to pinch pennies and I soon found it more agreeable to cultivate other acquaintances. Besides, don't you think a young lady should avoid too close an association with a man who is about to be publicly shamed?

But as the months wore on, I realized that the bridge trustees were not going to put Lloyd's disgrace in the newspapers. No doubt Mrs. Roebling was correct, and they feared that reporters might not follow their lead in assigning all the blame to Haigh, so their own foolish complicity in allowing his fraud would be exposed. They might call him a rascal in a private meeting, but publicly he still basked in the golden opinion of his colleagues.

So, for dear dead Harry's sake, I took the riskier road.

I donned a black wig and a veiled hat and went to the bank. Two banks, in fact, both favored by my clever Lloyd, the Market National Bank and the Grocers' Bank. I claimed that I was a lady from Baltimore who had been swindled by Mr. Haigh, that in exchange for a consideration he had given me a bank draft signed by C. Sidney Norris and Company and it had proved to be a forgery.

I left both banks in a state of excited confusion, particularly the Grocers' Bank, where the manager had blanched when I mentioned C. Sidney Norris and whispered to his assistant, "Didn't we loan Haigh money on a draft from Norris?"

Quickly, I slipped away and changed from my proper wig and veil to a vulgar red dress, rouged my cheeks and painted my lips, and was lounging against the building across the street from Lloyd's office when the police came for him. I hoped to be an invisible part of the passing crowd, but Lloyd's ardent eyes were sharp and he shrieked when he saw me. "There! There she is! Officer, arrest her! She gave me the forged paper!"

The officer glanced my way and was not impressed. "Not likely, sir. She's a common harlot."

Lloyd jumped up and down pathetically while both officers restrained him. "She did it! She did it!"

I hoisted my skirt an inch and gave them a glimpse of my ankle along with a lewd wink. "And Oi'll do it again if ye want, sir," I said in a low-down accent, "jist as long as ye pay!"

The officer laughed. "Be off with you, duckie!"

I scampered away.

Oh, come now! Surely you aren't surprised to learn that Aunt Mollie's lovely commercial papers were questionable! In the copying trade my aunt had done many jobs of work for bankers, and became quite skillful at various signatures. From time to time she would bring home an extra copy and slip it into a box which she bequeathed to me, and which I'd kept for purely sentimental reasons, although from time to time brute necessity forced me to sell a bank draft or two to a kindly business advisor such as dear Lloyd. Gentlemen like Lloyd are often eager to assist a young lady who is confused by commercial papers, and will purchase them from her so that she will be spared the unpleasantness of banking transactions. Lloyd had paid me a total of two thousand eight hundred fifty-two dollars for Aunt Mollie's commercial papers. Wasn't that kind of him? And then, because no bank would question a gentleman of such golden reputation, he had borrowed a hundred twenty-five thousand dollars on them from the two banks.

The gentlemen at the banks were not amused to see their assets turn to dust. Mr. J. Lloyd Haigh's arrest upon a charge of forgery was prominently featured in the newspapers, along with his matrimonial escapades and, at last, his bridge wire frauds. Trustee Abram Hewitt, of course, was not mentioned.

Lloyd protested vigorously but as the expenses of making good on the bridge contract had nearly bankrupted him, none of those gentlemen whose golden opinions he had bought in earlier days appeared to defend him.

I know, I know, a proper young lady would never do such a low-down thing to a gentleman admirer. But I've well-nigh given up on being proper. Besides, don't you think people should be stopped from marrying so many young ladies and ruining their reputations, and from catapulting handsome heroes to cruel death, and from weakening the cables of the great bridge, which could collapse and kill as many folks as perished in that dreadful Brooklyn Theatre fire? I know those crimes are not as serious as swindling the gentlemen who run banks, but I'm just a foolish Missouri girl with no sense, who hopes never to hear those agonized shrieks again.

Mr. J. Lloyd Haigh was sent to Sing Sing to repent and break rocks. Mrs. Roebling built her bridge and cared for her invalid. My life for the next two years was singularly eventful, and it was not until the spring of 1883, after a run of good luck in St. Louis, that I returned to New York with my friend Hattie and my ten-month-old niece Juliet James. Wearing one of my new Worth dresses from Paris, I called on Mrs. Roebling. We chatted, and I asked her what she would do now that her bridge was finished.

"No more bridges!" she said vehemently. "I have a son to raise, and after that I may study the law." In fact, some years later, I heard that she had earned a diploma from New York University's law program for women. Her essay won a prize. It concerned the unfairness of the law to married women like my Aunt Mollie, who could not own property, while single women could. She thought the gentlemen of the legislature ought to change the law. But they didn't, not for the longest time.

Before we parted, she again expressed her gratitude for my assistance in the matter of the wire fraud, and gave me tickets to the official opening ceremonies for her great bridge.

A wondrous sight it was, and is to this day, Mrs. Roebling's bridge: noble towers pierced by Gothic arches and linked by soaring cables, as graceful and melodious as a song. I reckon I've never seen a finer sight!

Hattie, little Juliet and I joined a vast crowd to watch President Chester Arthur, Governor Grover Cleveland, the Mayor of New York, the Mayor of Brooklyn, and Mr. Abram Hewitt of the spotless reputation, who all gave addresses to honor the opening of the eighth wonder of the world. Mr. Hewitt specifically declared that Mrs. Roebling represented "all that is admirable in human nature, and all that is wonderful in the constructive world of art." But the most enthusiastic applause came when he stated that all the money raised had been "honestly expended."

The Mayor of Brooklyn praised the beauty and stateliness of the bridge. "Not one shall see it," he declared in ringing tones, "and not feel prouder to be a man!"

Yes indeed.

FROM BRIDGET MOONEY'S SCRAPBOOK

THE NEW YORK TIMES
December 6, 1876

A THEATRE BURNED

DESTRUCTIVE FIRE AND PANIC IN BROOKLYN

THE BROOKLYN THEATRE TOTALLY DEMOLISHED
DURING THE PERFORMANCE OF THE "TWO
ORPHANS"—A FIERCE RUSH FOR THE DOORS—
SEVERAL PEOPLE SUPPOSED TO HAVE BEEN
KILLED—HUNDREDS INJURED—GREAT EXCITE-
MENT CAUSED IN THE NEIGHBORHOOD—THE
ADJOINING BUILDINGS SAVED—THE LOSS OVER
$200,000.

The Brooklyn Theatre, situated on Washington Street,
Brooklyn, was completely destroyed by fire last night. The
flames were discovered over the stage in the flies, just as
the curtain rose on the last act of the "Two Orphans." In
less than half an hour after the flames were discovered the
theatre was utterly destroyed. The scene that ensued in the
auditorium when the whole upper part of the stage was seen
to be on fire is simply indescribable. A panic seized the
people, and in the rush for the door hundreds were injured.

𝔅rooklyn 𝔇aily 𝔈agle

WEDNESDAY EVENING, JANUARY 7, 1880.

From Yesterday's Four O'Clock Edition

J. LLOYD HAIGH.

His Arrest upon a Charge of Forgery.

HIS CONNECTION WITH THE BRIDGE— HOW HE ATTEMPTED TO PALM OFF REJECTED CABLE WIRE AND WAS CAUGHT AT IT—HIS MATRIMONIAL EXPERIENCES.

The affairs of the Grocer's Bank touched a new phase yesterday in connection with the paper held on deposit from J. Lloyd Haigh, the wire manufacturer. It will be remembered that last Saturday Mr. S.V. White, the Receiver of the Bank, said the institution was suffering from forged paper in connection with Mr. Haigh's affairs. Yesterday afternoon Mr. Haigh was arrested upon a charge of forgery in the third degree and was locked up in the Tombs.

THE DIRTY LITTLE
COWARD THAT SHOT MR. HOWARD; or,
Such Stuff as Dreams Are Made on

"When he shall die," I quoted to Billy Gashade, "take him and cut him out in little stars,/ And he will make the face of heaven so fine,/ That all the world will be in love with night."

"Juliet! Bridget, you have a contract to play Juliet!"

I nodded smugly. Aunt Mollie would have been so proud! True, it was only Kansas City, but it was Shakespeare, wasn't it? The leading role! And I reckon a girl has to start somewhere, especially when she's been several months without a salary.

The train for Kansas City had left St. Louis at dinnertime. It was September of 1881, and it was soon dark enough that I couldn't see anything in the window except my own freckled but fashionable reflection. I was wearing my sapphire-blue silk shawl and my splendid bronze-colored natural-form dress with its close-fitting straight skirt layered with bows, but no bustle. My auburn hair—well, Irish red if you insist—was knotted loosely in a perfect Jersey Lily style. And, ever hopeful, I'd just spent my last pennies redeeming my emerald tiara from the pawn-broker, because the Kansas City manager had hinted that after Juliet I might play Lady Macbeth. My old Nellie Grant dress would do for Juliet, but Lady Macbeth is royalty, and requires quality costumes. I knew my genuine emerald tiara would ensure success.

Billy Gashade, in the next seat, was a musician I'd met in a show or two, a pleasing fellow except that he still felt Confederate sympathies fifteen years after Appomattox. Since a dirty Rebel had shot my older brother, I wasn't so sympathetic. But Billy cocked an eyebrow at me and pointed out gently that a lot of Rebels had been hurt by Union soldiers too. "And I adore you even so, Bridget Mooney," he declared.

Well, it's difficult to dislike a fellow who adores you, isn't it? Besides, he was right, the Union soldiers were no better. They'd done in my dear Aunt Mollie. I reckon any argument over which side was worse would end in a tie. So I smiled and changed the subject. "Give us some music, Billy."

Billy reached for his banjo. "I'm working on a song about a famous

Missouri lad. Tell me what you think." He strummed his banjo and sang, "Jesse James is a lad who's killed many a man. He robbed the Glendale train. He steals from the rich and he gives to the poor. He has a hand and a heart and a brain."

"Well—" Some said Jesse James was a cruel killer and robber but in these parts he was a great Confederate hero. Missouri had fought for the Union, but it had been a slave state and rebel guerrillas like the James brothers enjoyed great sympathy even now that they were outlawed. I said judiciously, "I like it, Billy, but not everyone will agree that he was a Robin Hood."

"Was?"

"Didn't another outlaw shoot him after the Glendale robbery?"

"Then why is the Governor still offering a reward?"

"Well, alive or dead, it would be more uplifting to sing about good citizens. Besides," I added, "this train goes through Glendale too. A different song might be in better taste."

Billy grinned and sang "Dixie" just to tease me, but he was a charming singer so I let bygones be bygones and sang with him.

As the evening wore on, however, Billy put away his banjo and settled down for a snooze. I hooked a cigar from his jacket pocket and headed for the front platform of the coach to smoke.

Oh, you needn't tell me! I know proper ladies don't do such things. But it had been such a long time since I'd had money for a cigar. Besides, if he'd wanted to be asked, he shouldn't have gone to sleep, should he?

I couldn't move quickly because my fashionable natural-form suit was very snug around the knees. I minced along the aisle toward the door, pleased at the admiring glances from the men and the envious ones from the better-dressed ladies in the car. But suddenly the train lurched, and I fell like a heap of turnips against a plump lady drinking water from her canteen. As I sat up on the floor, apologizing to the dampened lady, I heard screaming brakes and shots and excited hollering from outside. Then the door was flung wide and the conductor burst in. "Ladies and gentlemen, hide your valuables!" he cried. "We've been boarded!"

"Boarded?" cried the plump lady. "You mean bandits?"

But the conductor jumped over me and rushed through without answering. An excited hubbub arose in the car as everyone began removing their watches and money to hide under cushions.

I suddenly regretted the new styles. The secret pocket I'd sewn into last year's bustle had been roomy and easily accessible. Now, the form-fitting lines of my skirt required me to keep my contract and tiara and Colt buttoned into my bloomers, and rather indelicate gestures were needed to determine that all was well. I took advantage of my sprawled position to pretend that I was merely clambering to my feet.

I straightened up at last and found myself eye to eye with an enormous black revolver.

2

Well, hang it, I've never been able to puzzle out what a proper young lady ought to do when confronted with a gun. In my favorite melodramas the guns are usually pointed at someone else, and the young ladies scream prettily and run upstage out of the way, or perhaps swoon. Now, the scream was easy enough, but running was out of the question in my beautiful bronze-colored skirt. Two other ladies in our car had fainted already, so I decided to try a swoon. I collapsed into the aisle once again.

The man holding the revolver was tall and well-built, with nicely cut clothes and a snowy handkerchief tied across his face so we couldn't see his features. I couldn't see much else, either, squinting through my lashes from my recumbent position, except for his handsome cordovan leather boots. "Ladies and gentlemen," he said in a pleasant well-born Missouri voice, "please raise both hands in the air."

The passengers who hadn't swooned hastened to obey him. Two more masked bandits entered the car behind the first. One of them held a pistol to the head of a fellow who, from my lowly point of view, appeared to be the engineer. The new bandits were both scrawnier than the well-built fellow standing at my head. He went on, "As you can see, your engineer's life depends upon your actions. But we have no desire to hurt anyone. Please get out your money and jewelry." He jerked his head. "Collect it, Charley."

The blond bandit stepped over me and passed down the aisle holding out a two-bushel sack for the money and watches of the passengers. When he brought it back, his chief inspected it, shook his head, and said, "Ladies and gentlemen, we must try again." His voice had hardened. "Do you think that I'm a green boy, and won't know that you've been hiding things? I'm Jesse James! Now get out everything!"

The portly man in the first seat held out his palms helplessly. "But I've given you everything!" he exclaimed.

At a nod from the bandit who claimed to be Jesse, blond Charley jerked the man to his feet, struck him on the head with the butt of his gun, tore at his jacket, and came up with a handsome hunting-watch. He dangled it high, then struck the man again, harder. The portly man groaned and sank into the aisle, blood running into his eyes from a gash on his forehead.

All over the car, purses and watches magically reappeared. The second time Charley brought back the bag, it was nearly full.

"Thank you, gentlemen," said the bandit chief in a mild voice. "Now if the ladies would please come out of their fainting spells, we'll be done."

Now, I pride myself on a good swoon. I'd been paid well to lie as though dead for a long scene in *Othello* while the leading man committed a spectacular suicide, and I'd do the same as Juliet. But the bandit in the cordovan boots was not as impressed with my acting as my audiences had been. When I didn't move, he seized the plump lady's canteen and emptied it over my face. I sat up spluttering, water dripping from my Jersey Lily coiffure onto my beautiful sapphire-blue shawl and my bronze-colored dress.

"A pretty recovery." There was a smile in his voice.

"Sir," I said indignantly, "that was not a gentlemanly act!"

The white-masked face looked down a moment. "Alas, my lovely, you are right," he said. "I am driven to knavish deeds." The revolver still held at the ready in his right hand, he knelt and tipped up my damp chin with his left, and for a moment gazed into my eyes. Behind the mask, his own were a penetrating blue, and danced with devilment. He too seemed pleased by what he saw. He murmured, "But then you aren't always a lady, are you, my beauty?" Suddenly, his left hand was reaching under my skirt.

All over the car there were shocked exclamations and shrieks from the ladies. I shrieked too, but I'm bound to admit it wasn't because of the threat to my virtue. My virtue is quite sturdy, thank you, and seldom objects to threats from well-spoken, dashing, blue-eyed fellows. No, I was shrieking because he must have noticed me furtively investigating my nether limbs when he first entered the coach, and now he'd found the secret pockets that held my few possessions. I clutched at them, but he tugged away my bloomers one leg at a time, dropped them into his sack, and handed it back to his henchman.

Charley collected the last items from the other ladies, all of whom had suddenly recovered from their faints. When he brought back the sack for the third time, the cordovan-booted leader nodded, reached into it, and turned to the engineer. "You've been a bully boy. Here's two dollars to buy a drink in the morning. Drink it to Jesse James." He handed the coins to the engineer, took the sack from Charley, and with a jerk of his head signaled the other bandits. Suddenly they were all gone.

And I was right behind them. I might be wet and sputtering, but I needed my things. Luckily the bandit had missed the Bowie knife in my boot. The first thing I did was slit the back seam of my snug, fashionable natural-form skirt.

I know, I know, don't fret! The bows at the back hid most of the damage. And if one is chasing bandits, mincing is not an appropriate gait, is it now?

I tucked the knife back in my boot and leapt through the door to the train platform. Horses were ready beside the tracks; my cordovan-booted friend had already mounted and was spurring his horse up the embankment. As the last outlaw jumped from the platform to his horse, I caught his belt and sprang aboard with him.

"Get off!" he shouted, even as I locked my arms around his waist. The horse leapt into a startled gallop, following the others. The bandit pulled out his revolver, tried to fire, and cursed as he realized it needed reloading. He seized it by the barrel and twisted around to aim a blow at me.

I buried my face against his back to avoid being struck across the nose by the revolver. He smelled sweaty and unwashed. Trying to ignore the stink and the ungentlemanly blows and the jouncing of the horse, I gripped his belt, pulled his second revolver from its holster, cocked it, and jabbed him in the back. I said in my fiercest Lady Macbeth tones, "Knave, I could shoot you right now. But I must see your chief. Let's go!"

He was more attentive with the gun in his scrawny back. He aimed our horse at the fast-moving band disappearing into the hills. It was a long, rough ride, and we were losing ground. But by and by, the other hoofbeats sounded louder, and I rejoiced that we'd catch up after all. So I was astonished when a horse's head appeared at my side, overtaking us from behind. A powerful hand reached forward and twisted my revolver up and out of my grasp. "Pull up, Ed," said a familiar voice.

I tried to slide off the far side of Ed's horse as we halted, but that hand was gripping my wrist now. Ed was quaking and blubbering an apology. His chief laughed. "You're right, Ed, it was stupid. But be off now. It's already settled that Dick and I will count the booty, and we all meet in Kansas City tomorrow night. Go on, I'll attend to the entertaining Miss Mooney." He lifted me smoothly from Ed's horse to his own.

Ed took his gun back and rode away, and in a moment there was nothing but the faint dappled moonlight, the crickets, and the tall bandit chief. The handkerchief was still over his face so I couldn't see anything but those restless blue eyes. Well, all right, the light wasn't good enough to make out the color either, but I remembered. I still remember. Yes indeed.

"Sir, how do you know my name?" I asked.

"It's on your contract, my freckled beauty." He spoke kindly even as he patted my skirt for weapons. He had slender, well-shaped hands, except that the tip of one middle finger was missing. Banditry was not an easy profession, I thought sympathetically. Of course the portly man bleeding on the train had not found things easy, either. The bandit chief placed one arm around my waist and spurred the horse to a trot. "Gee-up, Stonewall!" he said, adding, "Now, Miss Mooney, why did you come?"

"Please, sir, I'm only asking to have my bloomers back."

He laughed. "Surely a famous actress can purchase more!"

"But I need my contract! And my—my—"

"Your little jeweled headpiece? And your Colt revolver?" His voice had hardened again.

I said, "Sir, I'm not rich. Was Billy Gashade wrong, then? Jesse James is not like Robin Hood?"

"Not much. Come along, Miss Mooney, to a comfortable place I know. We must reach an understanding, you and I."

3

After scrawny, inhospitable, stinking Ed, it was a delight to ride with the bandit chief. He smelt of good soap and Macassar oil. 'Twas a pity we'd met in such unfortunate circumstances.

The comfortable place he spoke of turned out to be a large fresh-swept barn. He dismounted by the half-open door and helped me down, then led Stonewall, and me, into the barn. We were greeted by the stamping and snorting of three stabled horses. He hitched Stonewall to a rail and unstrapped the sack of booty. "Would you light the lantern on that post, Miss Mooney?"

Well, I was a little nervous about being seen in the light, because of the seam I'd ripped out, and it turned out I was right because it must have given him a clear peep at my boots. No sooner had I lit the lantern than he dropped his sack, leapt to my side, grabbed my wrists with one hand and jabbed a revolver into my ribs. "Sir!" I complained. "That's not proper!"

"Nor is it proper for ladies to carry knives in their boots!"

"Oh." It was impossible to deny, so I apologized. "I forgot it, sir. I carry it when I travel. For apples and for gentlemen who become too friendly."

"Forgive me, Miss Mooney, but I must be certain you're carrying nothing else. Hold on to this hitching rail and move your feet apart."

Let us glide over the details of the next two minutes. Suffice it to say that at the end I was wearing nothing but my corset and petticoat, and even they had been carefully explored by the bandit chief's nimble fingers. My fine dress and stockings and shawl and boots had all been examined thoroughly and laid neatly aside on the straw. He sniffed Billy's cigar, nodded, and tossed it and my Bowie knife into his sack. He said, "All right, Miss Mooney. Now, my comrade took the southern route but he'll be along in a few moments. It would be best if he didn't see you. You may dress in one of the box stalls."

I picked up my stockings and asked grumpily, "Do you plan to keep my bloomers as a trophy? Will each of your companions receive a strip of muslin?"

"We needn't be that democratic, Miss Mooney." He laughed and pulled my bloomers from the sack. Under them I spotted watches, money, express-company bags, and my contract. He tossed the garment to me.

"Thank you, sir." My bloomers were badly torn and all the pockets were empty. "Though it does seem to me that a gentleman like you could be successful in some other line of business."

He started to answer, then changed the subject. "Tell me, why are you here?"

"I told you, sir! I came to ask you for my things fair and square! And that's more than I can say for the way you and your ruffians took it from me! My contract, my costumes—everything!"

His eyes twinkled. "Not your brave spirit, Miss Mooney."

"Yes, sir, well, I'll swap you that for my things."

He threw his head back and laughed. "No, ma'am! I could never manage *your* spirit! You're the first lady who's ever tried to follow our band."

"I reckon you never stole a theatrical contract before."

"That's true too." He was still chuckling. "Yours is a desperate breed, Miss Mooney. Almost as desperate as mine."

"Well, sir, a poor girl has few paths to fortune. My Aunt Mollie told me never to become entangled with a poor man or I'd always be poor. And the illustrious Mrs. Fanny Kemble advised that a rich one would want me to retire from the stage. And of course I didn't want to be a servant, and probably end on the streets, or in a house of ill repute. No, the stage is best."

He picked up my shawl and ran his fingers over the silk. "You love the stage so much, then?"

"Oh, yes!" Lifting my arm dramatically, I quoted Juliet, "When he shall die,/ Take him and cut him out in little stars,/ And he will make the face of heaven so fine/ That all the world will be in love with night." I clasped my hands, envisioning the applauding crowds and the flowers.

He seemed to be envisioning something too, and cleared his throat. "You want fame, then, Miss Mooney?"

"Yes, sir, of course. And riches. But you've taken my belongings," I reminded him.

"I'm very sorry, Miss Mooney. But my boys have fewer resources than you have. You are rich, truly, with your beauty and your enchanting voice and your sparkling spirit."

It was the kind of talk that could make a girl tingle, but I hadn't come this far to succumb to flattery. I drew myself up as regally as I could in a petticoat, pointed at the sack, and retorted, "Your boys may have fewer resources, but they have more money."

"Well, if ever I need a lady to ride with us, I'll send for you, Miss Mooney."

"Sir! I'm not a bandit!"

The smile was in his voice again. "But we'd be such a bully team! After all, Miss Mooney, you can handle a gun. You can ride. You can playact, that's important. A bandit acts a dozen roles, here tonight, gone tomorrow, as in the theatre. Actors and bandits, we are all spirits, and are melted—how does it go?"

"Melted into air, into thin air," I quoted. "We are such stuff as dreams are made on."

The hands stroking my silk shawl had paused. "Yes. We are such stuff as dreams are made on. You'd enjoy it, Bridget Mooney."

A bully team. He was teasing, I knew. Still, I had a sudden delicious vision of Robin Hood raids on evil bankers and railroad men, thrilling gallops through the night, a secret hideout full of jeweled doors and decanters of wine and dishes of marmalade, a secret bedroom with crimson damask wallpaper and silken sheets and a dashing blue-eyed bandit to keep them rumpled.

But then I could almost hear Aunt Mollie's voice saying, "Lordy me, Bridget, what foolishness!" And of course she was right. Bandits didn't live like that, even if they were rich. Bandits camped outdoors or hid in caves and barns, like this one. Bandits struck men on the head and made them bleed. I sighed and shook my head. "It's not very likely, is it, sir?"

Gently, he touched my hair, his eyes sad. "Not very. And yet—"

Suddenly his head jerked around, and in a blur his hand flashed to his holster and emerged with his revolver. I froze, and in a moment I heard what my alert companion had noted: hoofbeats approaching slowly. I murmured, "I'll be in the stall with the gray horse, sir."

He nodded and tiptoed to the door to peer from the crack. I scooped up my things and scurried into the box stall, closing the plank door behind me. In a moment he said softly, "Good, it's Dick. Do remain silent, Miss Mooney. He's hotheaded at times."

Well, I'm bound to admit, I was vexed! In any well-written melodrama, the playwright would delay the arrival of the henchman until the exciting scene between the kidnapped heroine and the dashing blue-eyed bandit could develop further, at least to the point where she was fighting off his ardent embraces. But in life I seem to be cast in the comic subplot. The horse nuzzled my back as I donned my wretched damp bronze-colored dress. By the time Dick arrived, I was crouching by a crack in the stall door. My equine companion and I both peered out at the lighted barn.

Dick was shorter than my friend, with a round face and the air of a dandy. He led a sorrel horse into the barn. His leader took the reins and patted the horse's nose while Dick stepped eagerly to the sack in the middle of the floor. "It's almost full," he said, squatting by it.

His chief was hitching the sorrel next to his own horse. He'd pulled his mask from his face, but I noticed that he didn't turn toward my stall, and when he joined his dandy friend he sat back in the shadows. "Let's see what we have," he said. He emptied the sack onto the blanket and the two began sorting the items into piles: bills, coins, watches, rings, brooches, handkerchiefs, scarves. Mine was the only tiara. Dick started to pick it up, but his chief's quick hand suddenly rested on his wrist.

"That's for Zee," he said.

"We should pawn it, Slick," Dick objected. Slick! I liked that better than Jesse, which reeked of blood and cruelty. Dick went on, "Are those emeralds real?"

"Not likely. Came with those papers." He nodded at my contract. "Gal's an actress. They're sure to be paste."

Well, did you ever hear such an insult? But dandy Dick nodded and asked, "What would Zee want with it?"

"Well, for Hattie Floyd then."

Dick laughed. He was convinced, as well he might be. I knew the voluptuous Hattie. We'd been girls together back in St. Louis. She had chosen a rather lewd path in life but thanks to my Aunt Mollie's sensible advice had got into a house popular with the higher classes. When I was in St. Louis, I often stopped by for a chat and a giggle, because she was one of the few folks there who didn't natter on about what a drunkard Papa was.

Dick picked up a ring and stroked his mustache. "How's this for the

Widow Bolton?"

Slick rocked back on his fine cordovan heels. "Now, you know my cousin favors her."

"The question is, who does *she* favor?" Dick grinned.

Well, I thought Dick's point well taken, but his chief slammed down a fist. "She's not worth a fight. Do you hear?"

Dick's smile faded. "Yeah, yeah, I hear."

"If you and my cousin get to fighting, this whole band is in trouble. I won't have it. There's enough trouble with all the green hands."

"Yeah, well, there's trouble with the old hands too. All killed now, or in jail like Whiskey-Head Ryan. And your brother hiding in Texas."

There was a pulse of danger in the air. Even the horses felt it and were still. But Slick's voice was mild when he said, "They were courageous comrades in the war, as true as steel, Dick Liddil. I honor them."

"So do I. My brothers fought and died with them too!"

"And Whiskey-Head was talking in his cups about Glendale."

"Yeah, he's a good man when he's sober. Let's count the money."

They bent to their work again, but the excitement of the earlier evening had soured. I'd ripped one corner of my shawl, but I pulled the remnants about me and, under cover of the chinking coins, took my things to the far corner of the box stall. The plank walls of the barn were not tight, and cool night air blew through cracks as wide as my fist. I was glad I hadn't snatched my tiara when he'd turned his back out there, because he would have noticed, and there was no easy way to escape. No, the bandit chief's nobility of soul was still my best chance.

I only wished the man on the train hadn't bled so much.

By and by I heard their voices raised again, and crept back to peer through the crack in the door. Dandy Dick Liddil was saying, "There was more! You know there was more in that safe!"

Slick said, "We don't know that, Dick."

"Well, I know, blast it!" When I saw Dick's hand start for his holster, I clapped a hand over my mouth in dismay. But there was no need for worry, because a flash of dark metal revealed Slick's revolvers already cocked in those quick hands.

"Dick!" he said, and there was such sorrow in his voice that I almost sobbed myself. "We've been through too much together! I rode with your brothers, rest their souls!"

"Yeah." Dick licked his lips, more convinced by the revolvers than by the sentiment. "But— Blast it, Slick, you know I trust you! I just thought there'd be more in the safe, like the Glendale job. More diamonds."

"I thought so too." There was a dangerous edge to my fine friend's voice. "But we were both wrong, weren't we?"

Dick turned his palms up in a gesture of peace. "It's just that the boys will be disappointed. They heard there was ten or twenty thousand in that safe."

"Well, we both counted it. Three thousand. You know how those railroad cheats lie. Maybe they changed it to the next train." He holstered his pistols and picked up a bottle. "Here, drink up and we'll divide the money."

Dick accepted the bottle, loaded half the booty into his saddlebags and led his horse out of the barn. Slick pulled up his mask again and watched him from the door, standing where his busy eyes could also take in my stall. When the hoofbeats died away he opened my door and picked up my ripped shawl. "Miss Mooney, you will forget this night, won't you?"

"Yes sir. But I'd like my—"

"Hurry, now, we're going to Kansas City."

He saddled the little gray horse for me. As we left, I asked casually, "What's the name of this place?"

He was suddenly stern. "I said, forget this. Let's both of us forget."

We rode through a long confusion of trails I could never retrace, reaching the city just as dawn grayed the skies.

I kept hoping, but Slick didn't give back my tiara or my shawl or even my cigar. Nobility of soul, indeed!

He did give me the contract. He rode with me to the stage door, helped me down, and handed it to me along with four silver dollars. Twice as much as he'd given the engineer. He pressed my hand in his, said, "Farewell, my bandit queen. I wish you fame and fortune," and rode away.

Now, is that your idea of Robin Hood? I sat down on a bench by the stage door and had a good cry because my tiara and sapphire-blue shawl were lost, and I'd never find that romantic barn again. And whoever would have thought a bandit would be so blamed proper? I even found myself envying naughty Hattie Floyd.

But by and by I noticed how hungry I was. I hammered on the stage door until the sleepy-eyed doorkeeper opened it, and I wheedled him into sharing his breakfast of tea and biscuits.

4

Romeo and Juliet was a ripping success. In St. Louis we used to think of Kansas City as uncivilized, populated by the crudest of bushwhackers, but it's not so. The people there, though perhaps untutored, were filled with longing for the higher things in life. They thought that Shakespeare was splendid, and that my Juliet was the most glorious creature they'd ever beheld. Opening night they cheered and stamped and tossed bouquets to me. It was all so thrilling I had tears in my eyes. Flowers came to my dressing room too, with little cards from my admirers. "Miss Mooney, I love you dearly, do you love me?" said one. Another, "To Miss Mooney, who beggars description." Or "What light through yonder window breaks? It is the unforgettable Miss Mooney." I rather liked that one. At least he knew which play he'd seen. One overeager fellow wrote, "I am a 'Prosperous Farmer' and when my wife dies who is sickly I would kindly beg to propose marriage to you."

The newspapers were delighted too. Major John Newman Edwards went into ecstasies about my Juliet in the *Sedalia Democrat*, and the Kansas City papers admitted they liked the show too. Sid, the theatre manager, was happy as a pig in clover. The second night he knocked on the ladies' dressing room door before the show. "Your admirer from Sedalia wants to speak to you after the show, Bridget! Will you see him?"

"Of course." In show business one indulges newspapermen.

That night was another triumph, ending with cheers and Rebel yells. I did love Kansas City! Afterward, Major Edwards appeared, a long, tall, shy man, with sad houndlike eyes and a bushy mustache that drooped down to his chin. He escorted me to a private saloon in the St. James Hotel. In the back corner a card game was in progress, the players in shadows around a green baize table lit by a single gas lamp. When we entered the men turned toward us abruptly, hands reaching toward bulges in their jackets. But Major Edwards seemed unperturbed and bowed me to a velvet sofa near the stove. He sat with a little notebook on his bony knees. With a few furtive glances at the neckline of my Nellie Grant dress, he first asked my opinion of Shakespeare and of Kansas City, then said, "Miss Mooney, I understand that you were on the train that was robbed at Blue Cut."

"Yes, sir, I'm sorry to say that was my misfortune."

His sad eyes snapped up from my neckline to my face. "And do you harbor bitter feelings toward the highwaymen?"

I opened my mouth to complain about so-called Robin Hoods who stole things and pistol-whipped passengers, but reconsidered at the memory of blue eyes. I said cautiously, "It is a terrible experience to lose one's precious possessions, sir. But there were gentlemen among the robbers who expressed remorse for having been driven to such desperate actions."

Major Edwards' head bobbed up and down enthusiastically. "Very true,

Miss Mooney," he said. "Many unjust accusations have been leveled against certain heroes of the late war, who were unjustly branded as outlaws and forced to become fugitives. What can a true man do when cruelly hunted, but turn upon his hunters? Don't you agree?"

"Why, yes," I said, astounded by his sudden fluency.

"Good, good." A tiny smile widened until it disappeared into his drooping mustache. "Miss Mooney, do you think you could identify the highwaymen for the law?"

Well, I'd certainly know dandy Dick Liddil, and smelly Ed, and blond Charley, and of course one other. But Major Edwards' talk about outlaw heroes gave me pause. I shrugged, which drew his eyes to my neckline again, and said, "Alas, sir, they were all masked, you see. How could I ever know them again?"

It seemed to be the right answer. Major Edwards said, "Miss Mooney, there is a man, a friend of mine, who would like to make your acquaintance. He is a businessman, highly respected in these parts, and his name is—" here he consulted his notes "—Mr. T. J. Jackson. Would you consent to a meeting with him?"

My mind went back to the big bouquet of roses that sat next to my dressing room mirror. Mr. T. J. Jackson was the one who had sent the pretty quote about Juliet. What light through yonder window breaks? I wanted to leap up and dance on the piano, yes indeed! But instead I said earnestly, "Sir, I would be happy to make Mr. Jackson's acquaintance, since you recommend him."

Major Edwards beamed. He stood up and led me to the card table and, to my astonishment, introduced dandy Mr. Dick Liddil, who kissed my hand moistly. Next came Mr. Ed Miller. Since someone had apparently made Ed bathe for this occasion, I offered my hand to my one-time riding companion and said, "Delighted, sir." Next came Charley Ford, the blond bandit who'd carried the sack on the train, and his smooth-faced younger brother Bob, who looked as though he'd just come from Sunday school. Yes indeed.

Finally Major Edwards said, "Miss Mooney, I'd like to present Mr. T. J. Jackson."

He stood then and leaned into the light. And wasn't he a grand businessman! He had a well-cut suit, a lustrous beard, a warm and ready smile, and those lively blue eyes. I found myself trembling at the thought of his trust in me, and of what the consequences might be. He took my hand and said, "Miss Mooney, let me congratulate you on an unforgettable performance."

"Thank you, sir. I'm delighted to make your acquaintance."

"And I yours. Mattie, sing us a song!"

The others had all been watching him, as though waiting for a cue. Now one of the ladies sat down at the piano, and Dick Liddil began to deal out cards. Slick murmured to me, "Come along, Miss Mooney, let's talk a bit."

"Yes, sir, Mr. Jackson. We do have business to discuss."

He bowed and opened a door. In the back of my mind Aunt Mollie was trying to holler something at me, but I told her to hush and climbed the rose-carpeted stairs to a second-floor room. In the lamplight I could see that there was no crimson damask wallpaper, but the bed and window were hung with gold brocade and the sheets seemed smooth enough. A picture of General Lee graced the wall near me. I pushed aside a tasseled curtain to see that the window gave onto a porch roof, then turned to face Slick.

He had closed the door and was watching me, one hand still on the knob. "Well, Bridget Mooney. I had hopes of forgetting you, but you do hang on a man's mind."

"I found you memorable too, Mr. Jackson."

"Not Mr. Jackson, Bridget! Call me—maybe Tom?"

"Mr. Jackson, sir, if we reach that level of familiarity I shall call you Slick, like a loyal comrade. But now I am speaking to Mr. Jackson the business-man."

"Oh?"

"You have taken a very kind interest in my career, sir. The cheering and newspaper articles are most welcome. I am extremely grateful, but . . ."

"But not grateful enough?" Frowning, he walked toward me. There was a crackle of danger in the room. I was very aware of the pistols under his well-cut coat.

I raised my palm. "I know you are a gentleman, sir, forced by injustice to certain acts not in your true nature." He slowed, and I breathed again. "But as a businessman, sir, you know the importance of reputation, in my profession as in others. 'The purest treasure mortal times afford, is spotless reputation.' "

He grinned. "I do love to hear you talk, Bridget Mooney! Yes, of course I know that acting Shakespeare is not the same as saloon singing. Spotlessness shall be arranged. But since we're discussing business, let me point out that I've entrusted something of great value to you too."

"I know." I put a hand on his arm and looked at his sweet unmasked face: the strong cheekbones, the trim beard, the gentle mouth, the questioning blue eyes. I said, "Five thousand dollars for arrest, five thousand for conviction. I'm honored, sir, at the gift of your trust. I won't betray it.

Ever."

"You wouldn't live if you did," he said matter-of-factly, then smiled. "It's a knavish profession, my lovely, not for the cowardly. But you shall be a queen. Are we agreed?" He picked up my hand and kissed my fingertips.

Part of me was agreed, yes indeed. I wanted to throw myself into his arms and do all sorts of jolly wicked things, but I knew Aunt Mollie would scold. I said, "Well, sir, as a businessman, you are also aware that any business requires certain equipment, certain investments."

"Your equipment is your beauty, your charming voice, your soaring spirit."

"Yes sir. As to my voice, I paid hundreds of dollars for the illustrious Mrs. Kemble's tutelage. As to my beauty, I need proper attire." When he began to protest, I added hastily, "On stage, that is, sir. I'm still speaking to Mr. Jackson the businessman. Mr. Jackson the businessman would not approve of a Lady Macbeth without a crown."

He laughed. "I wondered when you'd get to the cursed tiara!" He reached up to pull a packet from behind the picture of General Lee. "Here it is, sweet Juliet. I kept your blue silk shawl with the torn corner, and your Bowie knife and revolver for sentimental reasons. Here is something in exchange." He took a sparkling ring from the packet and fitted it gently on my third finger. I turned away and drew it down the window-pane. The scratch glittered in the lamplight.

It quite took my breath away. I noticed that it silenced Aunt Mollie for the moment too. She was always a good businesswoman, and perhaps had only been trying to tell me to collect in advance.

He put his hand on my shoulder, the gentlest and deadliest hand in the West. "Are we agreed at last, my bandit queen?"

I turned my head to kiss his fingers, and said, "Remember, you still owe me a cigar."

He laughed and whirled me onto the bed, and he was right, very very right. We were a bully team.

5

It was good times, those next few weeks. Oh, I know you're thinking it was wicked and shameful, and of course it was. In my mind Aunt Mollie stomped around sometimes, telling me how reckless and improper I was being. But hang it, what's a poor girl to do when she's offered riches, and fame, and sweet frolics with a man who thrills her blood? Do you truly expect her to wait for "Prosperous Farmer's" sickly wife to die?

Aunt Mollie didn't have any answers either.

Most days I'd wake up late, and spend the afternoon rehearsing or at the dressmaker's or going to the bank, and the evening as Juliet or Lady Macbeth or Rosalind. Sid was no fool, and though he complained loudly at the terms, he extended my contract. You see, I'd sent Major Edwards's columns to a St. Louis newspaperman named Fishback who owed me a favor—no, it wasn't that way at all! I'll tell you why some other time. Soon the St. Louis papers were talking about "Bridget Mooney, the Bernhardt of Missouri," and other theatres were wooing me. But I had reasons to stay in Kansas City. After the show, I'd join Slick and his friends for a glass of wine, and he'd ask me to recite or sing something. He loved to sing with me, especially hymns, his poor dead father having been a minister. To Slick, outlawed so young, I think I was a dream of the elegant life he should have had amidst well-spoken ladies and gentlemen. But I was a dream he could touch. After the singing, we'd leave the others and— Well, taste and decorum preclude a detailed description. But it was good times, yes indeed.

And yet the sweet blue Kansas City nights were not flawless. The far-off shimmer of danger, like summer lightning, played around the edges of my moon-bright world. Slick always slept with a gun. Not just under his pillow. In his hand. And once when I asked dreamily, "Where was that barn where we first met?" he grabbed my shoulder and snapped, "Forget that night!" So I kept mum about it for a while. And he was often away. I'd heard there was a wife somewhere, poor thing. But most often he took trips with Dick Liddil or one of the others, so that I saw him only two or three nights a week. With most men this would be a decided advantage, but hang it, I had such an appetite for Slick.

When we sang hymns, his favorite verse said, "Must I be carried to the skies on flowery beds of ease,/ While others fought to win the prize and sailed through bloody seas?" He told me what it meant to him. "We must fight on! The North is robbing us of our birthright. We must keep hitting their banks and railroads. We've sworn to be true till and through death, and we must see to it that our brave comrades didn't die in vain." I knew that Major Edwards and other Rebels sympathized. But I wondered, if his comrades hadn't died in vain, did that mean my brother had? Still, I decided to keep mum about my brother too.

That war would never be over for Slick, I feared. He never slept well. Some nights I'd awaken in the wee hours and find him crouching by the window, gun cocked, eyes searching the empty alley. "What is it?" I'd whisper.

"Nothing. Just a dream." And in a moment he'd be back, laughing and friskier than ever.

Major Edwards, and in fact most Rebels in Missouri, worshipped him—or maybe not him, the idea of him. Jesse James's courage in the war, his refusal to bow to Northern law, his ready smile and quick hands and gentlemanly speech and ability to melt into air, into thin air—it was an idea that was easy to love.

But it was hard to live. And behind the romance and the song, I knew that my bandit king still sailed through bloody seas.

Late in September, it got worse. I sidled over to young Bob Ford one evening to ask, "What is it? Why is he in such a mood?"

Bob was a sweet-faced lad, as dazzled by a fine neckline as Major Edwards was. He fidgeted, his hazel eyes shifting in his Sunday-school face. "I can't tell you if he won't, ma'am."

"Bob, please, it might be dangerous for me."

"Or me! He says if three men jump out to shoot him, he can kill them all before he falls. And it's true, I swear!"

I handed him a silver brooch. "Please, Bob!"

Little Bob, though fearful, loved money. He glanced at the door where Slick had just gone storming out and muttered, "It's the Ryan trial, ma'am. Poor Whiskey-Head may be convicted."

I studied the newspapers. The story was that a fellow named Tucker Bassham had been jailed after the James gang's famous Glendale train robbery two years ago. Just recently they'd caught another member of that gang, Whiskey-Head Ryan—I remembered Slick's complaint about Whiskey-Head bragging in his cups. Well, Bassham didn't much like jail, so he decided to turn state's evidence against Whiskey-Head in exchange for his own freedom.

The next night, as Slick stared moodily out through the curtains, I screwed up my courage to ask, "You're worrying about the Ryan trial, aren't you?"

He whirled from the window. "What do you know about it?"

"Well, goodness, Slick, I can read the newspapers! I'm no ninny. And I can tell that you're worrying."

"You're worrying that I'm worrying?" He sounded exasperated. "We'll soon be running in circles! Please, be my sparkling Juliet, speaking beautiful words, shining in the footlights!"

"Thank you, Slick, but that's a rather insubstantial role. And it's difficult to sparkle in this gloom. You can't attend the trial, for reasons we've agreed not to discuss. But I can. I can tell you what happens there."

"I have friends reporting to me."

"Not in beautiful words."

I had my way and rode to the Jackson County Courthouse the next day, dressed in coarse black like any curious rural widow. He was right about friends. I found the courtroom filled with rowdy local Rebels, and most spoke warmly of the James boys and their friends. I'd doubtless been in one of their barns; but I didn't know which. Slick still snapped whenever I asked.

In this company Tucker Bassham was heavily guarded. He was a raw country man, clumsy in speech but very earnest. His story was that Whiskey-Head Ryan had invited him to join the James gang. He'd declined. A few months later Whiskey-Head returned and ordered Bassham to come along to rob the Glendale train. He obeyed out of fear, he said; and I remembered the bleeding man on the train, and believed him.

But Slick saw only a betrayal of the dream. "That traitor Bassham!" He slammed his fist on the card table and Dick Liddil and I jumped. "My old comrades were true as steel!"

"They fought beside you in the war," I protested. "Bassham was only—"

"Bassham's people were brave guerillas too! No, he's a traitor and a sneak!" Slick's eyes shone like ice in the winter sun. He started for the door, beckoning for Dick with a jerk of his head. I realized I'd given the wrong lines. He didn't want judicious Portia; he wanted Lady Macbeth, urging him on. I shivered and retired to my lonely room for the night.

But very late, there came a whisper. "Under the greenwood tree, who loves to lie with me?"

He was in his long dark coat and cordovan boots, leaning over my bed. I giggled. "Slick, are you auditioning for our show?"

"Come!" He slid his smoke-scented coat over my nightdress and led me to the back door. The moon was in the west and I could see in his eyes the same warmth and devilment I remembered from the Blue Cut night. Stonewall stood outside, blowing a little and lightly lathered with exertion. Slick handed me into the saddle and swung up behind me. "Time for a mid-summer night's dream, my lovely!"

"But it's October!" I said feebly.

He spurred Stonewall down the road toward the woods. "I'll keep you warm, under the greenwood tree."

He did, he did indeed; and I rejoiced in the return of my own lighthearted bandit chief.

The next day, the newspapers blared that Tucker Bassham's house had been burned down.

Well, that made me sit down and have a good think. It seemed to me that poor old Tucker Bassham wasn't getting a fair shake. But what could I do about it? I was an artiste, not a sheriff or a marshal. And there were all my pretty rings and brooches, and cheers and bouquets, and good notices in the newspapers, and lovely trysts under the greenwood tree.

But Bassham's raw, earnest face haunted my memory.

He continued to give testimony, though Governor Crittenden had to send in arms to keep order. And Slick grew tight with fury behind his banter and songs. So, when the jury declared Whiskey-Head guilty and Bassham was released, I waited only long enough to be sure Slick wasn't going to want me that night, then put on my traveling cape and borrowed a horse from the ones hitched in front of the saloon. I set off for Jackson County.

I know, I know, Aunt Mollie would have said it was reckless too. But she hadn't seen Tucker Bassham, nor Slick's cold eyes.

Of course I'd never betray Slick, and I knew that Bassham couldn't be allowed to cross Jesse James and then resume a normal life. But suppose he merely disappeared? I'd learned that two of the ladies in the front row at the trial were Bassham's cousins, and that they lived on the road from Kansas City. My plan was to deliver a little packet for them to pass on to Bassham, containing two valuable rings together with the sensible advice to leave Missouri immediately and for a good long time.

The moon was sinking toward the western woods when I turned into the lane that led to the ladies' house. At the side of the lane, I thought I saw a shirt sleeve, and reined in my horse. The sleeve was very still. Everything was very still. Did someone need help? I dismounted, leading the horse, and pushed aside a branch to let the moon shine on a horrid sight.

Something clamped over my mouth.

I could not cry out. My startled horse cavorted, but my captor did not slacken his grip on my mouth until he had quieted the animal and led us both into the nearest woods. He jerked back the hood of my cape and cursed under his breath. "Bridget!"

He released my mouth. Furtively dropping Bassham's little packet and toeing it into the earth, I whispered, "Slick, I wanted to help!"

"Stay out of this! You'll betray us!"

Well, at such a time, those words were hardly music to my ears. I saw I needed a stronger defense. So I sold smelly Ed. I said, "Betrayal? Slick, you've got betrayal all around! Ed Miller whispers that you stole from the Blue Cut booty before you divided it. And Dick Liddil—"

Some people don't like bad news. There was a puff of breeze and Jesse

James's gun butt slammed into the side of my face.

I woke at noon, tucked into my own bed, with a thundering headache and vague recollections of tightly bound hands and feet amidst a nightmare of galloping hoofbeats.

I held up my wrists and saw the red track of rope burns.

Somehow I sat up. The hoofbeats continued. They were inside my head, I realized at last. I was dressed in the clothes I'd worn last night. I lurched to the dressing table, leaned on it with both hands, and blinked into the mirror. My cheek was gashed open over the bone, and a purpling bruise spread above it from temple to eyebrow.

I closed my eyes to avoid the ghastly sight. But a ghastlier one intruded: Tucker Bassham's body in the moonlight last night, with a bullet hole in his earnest forehead.

I felt sicker than an old hound. But I wasn't dead. I clung to that. Killing a woman would betray Jesse's code. Wouldn't it?

Show people are grand, better than family. Sid tut-tutted and declared my wound to be the most spectacular he had encountered in a long career of ministering to tragedians, with the possible exception of a Hamlet he'd hired once, who had foolishly challenged an enraged sow. Sid spent two hours with sticking-plaster and greasepaint, piecing together the remnants of the Bernhardt of Missouri. At the end he gave his handiwork a good squint and decided to dim the footlights as well. I was playing Lady Macbeth that night, and my copper-red costume looked grand in the lower lights. If I had to be a walking target, at least I'd look splendid. Luckily, Jesse did not show himself that night.

Nor the next.

Nor the next.

By mid-November I realized that he was truly gone. Melted into air, into thin air. Through a milkman I finally found Mr. T. J. Jackson's Kansas City home on East Ninth Street. The problem was that Mr. Jackson had moved out a couple of weeks before. A splendid gentleman, the neighbors said, always with a smile and a pleasant word. Yes indeed.

I rented a livery horse and rode the Jackson county hills for a month; but I saw no dashing bandits, no romantic barns. Where was that barn? Things look different by daylight.

I went to see Major Edwards, at the *Sedalia Democrat*. "Mr. Jackson?" he said, and coughed. "I don't know any Mr. Jackson."

"Sir, please, I have very important news for Jesse James."

"Miss Mooney, you don't understand. This is a matter of courage, of fealty till and through death, of honor!"

In fact I did understand because I'm in the dream business too. Just ask "Prosperous Farmer." I said, "Sir, honor and fealty are splendid, you are right. My message has to do with sacred duty." That sounded important, don't you think?

But Major Edwards merely blinked at my neckline. "Miss Mooney, my admiration for your thespian abilities is sincere. Therefore my advice is to play your tragedies on the stage."

"This is not a play, sir! It's real!"

But he wouldn't help. I went back to the theatre. "Prosperous Farmer" and some others remained loyal, but there were fewer Rebel yells now amongst the cheers at the end, and fewer bouquets. For January Sid decided to book in a wonderful attraction with eleven trained dogs instead of the *Twelfth Night* I proposed. "Next year, Bridget," he said with that shifty-eyed look managers get when receipts fall off. Yet my disappointment was softened by my weariness, and anger, and aching for what might have been, and worry about what was coming.

A St. Louis theatre asked me to come do Lady Macbeth in February. I packed up my tiara and lace parasol and new dresses, all made with bustles this time, and went back to St. Louis. There was someone there I should have seen long since.

6

Hattie Floyd had always had a splendidly ample figure. She was a few years older than I was, and I'd been green with envy of her when I was a girl still waiting to fill out. Now, in her thirties, she was blonder, better-dressed, and rounder than ever, and her hugs were like sinking into a sweet-scented featherbed. "What news, Hattie?" I asked.

"I've got a fellow, Bridget!"

"Um—in your line of work, isn't that to be expected?"

"No, no! Jake is news. We're going to get married, soon as we have enough put away for a house."

Well, I was flummoxed. "You're getting married? And he's not rich?"

"Bridget, honey, I've had the opportunity in life to look over quite a few fellows," she said with dignity. "And Jake is the one. We'll settle down and take in my two orphan nephews, just as soon as we have our cottage. Now tell me about you! The papers say you're rich and famous. But honey, is that a scar?"

"Hattie, did you ever know—" I didn't know what name he'd used. "—um, Jesse James?"

She smiled and settled back in her velvet chair. "Ah, Slick. Now there's a fellow can spin a dream for you. He told me I'd be his bandit queen. Though I taught him some sweet games too."

She certainly did. I swallowed, and Hattie's eyes sharpened. "I ask for news of you, and you ask about him. Bridget, what have you been up to?"

"Hattie, please, how can I find him again?"

"You can't! The sheriffs can't, the Governor himself can't." She looked into my eyes and saw how bad things were. She said, "Sometimes I hear rumors. Last fall he was in Kansas City."

"He isn't anymore."

"Oh, Bridget, honey, and I thought you had such a sensible heart!"

I couldn't help sniffling. "And I was just becoming famous! Hattie, he's chopped my life to flinders!"

"Didn't do much for your cheek either, honey."

I've always thought that if my poor dear mama had lived, she would have been like Hattie. I sobbed out the story. All of it. She hugged me and clucked at all the right places, and gave me lots of sound advice; but this time it was all too late. "I'll help you, honey," she said at last. "Remember, time heals."

But time was in no hurry to knit up my raveled sleeve of care. The St. Louis *Macbeth* closed at the end of February, and I found myself unable to accept more work, unable even to laugh. I bailed Papa out of jail a couple of times, but most of the time I moped along the riverbank under slate-colored skies, watching the gray Mississippi slide by like my gray life.

Then, toward the end of March, Hattie summoned me. "Bridget, come meet my cousin's niece. She works in St. Joseph."

I felt a surge of hope when I saw that the cousin's niece's hair was Irish red like mine. But it turned out she'd never met Jesse. Or Slick, or Tom, or any such man.

"The one I know is Bob," she explained. "Hattie said you'd want to hear. She said you're a grand lady now, and you'd pay."

Hattie was beaming at me, so I unpinned the emerald brooch from the lace fichu at my neck and showed it to her cousin's niece. "If it's useful news, this will be yours."

She looked it over with hungry eyes. We red-haired ladies do love emeralds. She said, "This Bob is a pretty-faced little fellow with a big gun. And he has a brother named Charley."

"That's right! Bob and Charley Ford! What did he say?"

"He likes to brag. He says he knows how to get a big reward from Governor Crittenden if he kills somebody."

Well, sometimes a girl can't help it. I burst into tears and Hattie patted my arm while her cousin's niece asked with an anxious glance at my brooch, "Don't cry, darlin'! Should I go on?"

"Yes, yes!" I sniffled. "Who—who's he going to kill?"

"He calls him Slick. He's a murderer." Her Irish eyes were round with awe. "And isn't Bob scared! He says some fellow named Ed accused Slick of holding out diamonds from a robbery. So Slick hunted him down and shot him dead."

Poor smelly Ed! I felt a pang of guilt for accusing him to Jesse in the first place. Oh, I know, I know, it's the wages of sin, and Ed was sinful enough. But if Jesse was shooting everyone he imagined was betraying him—I shivered.

"Where does Bob live?" I asked.

"I don't know," she said. "But I meet him at the Worlds Hotel in St. Joe. And he doesn't use a horse to get there."

She'd earned her brooch. I kissed Hattie, promised to be careful, packed my carpetbag and parasol, and caught the next train to St. Joe. I worried about Jesse the whole way. His band was eroding. His brother had fled to Texas, Ed Miller was dead. Sneaky Bob Ford was thinking about rewards. Was his only remaining friend Dick Liddil?

No, there were the dream-makers. Major Edwards, writing about the outlaw hero, the last stand of the Lost Cause. Or Bridget Mooney with her bandit king. Or Billy Gashade's Robin Hood: "He steals from the rich and he gives to the poor. He has a hand and a heart and a brain." But no soul, Billy, I thought. The rest of us have stolen his soul to use in our own dreams.

The man sitting in the next seat on the train was reading a newspaper. One headline jolted me. Dick Liddil had been arrested in Clay County.

Jesse was down to nothing but dreams.

St. Joseph was a pretty city of soft hills and budding trees. I found my way to the Worlds Hotel, which did not cater to the upper classes. The sour clerk at the desk had never noticed anyone looking like Bob Ford. I went back out in the street to ponder my next move, and saw my long-lost sapphire-blue shawl.

It was around the shoulders of a short pleasant woman dressed in a dark dress and bonnet and leading two children. "Hurry, Mary," she said; and, to the boy, "Come along, Jesse."

No, I didn't swoon. I only do that professionally. Instead I opened my lace-trimmed parasol and strolled along in the same direction, admiring the flowers in order to stay a few steps behind them. I saw that she'd mended the missing corner of my shawl. The three walked to a small, neat house behind the hotel, with a plank fence and a roundtop window over the door. There was a good view in all directions, and some woods nearby—just what Major Edwards's heroic fugitive needed. There was a barn, and Charley Ford was currying a horse in the barnyard. It was Stonewall.

I tilted my parasol to hide my face and hair and walked on to the woods. There was a comfortable log where I could be invisible yet see the house. I waited.

Late in the day, Jesse came out to the barn, then washed his hands at the pump. The little boy came dancing out of the house and Jesse caught him and swung him up in the air. Their laughter drifted down the hill to my brushy hideaway. He put the boy down, drew one of his revolvers, and emptied out the cartridges. He belted the empty gun to the boy's waist. The boy capered around the yard, and Jesse stood there beaming at his little Jesse.

Whose dreams would little Jesse have to live?

They were sweet children. Jesse might not leave them for me, but surely he could provide for us all. How could I convince him? If only he'd told me how to find that other barn near Blue Cut! Finally, I wrote a note.

After a few minutes the woman came to the door and called "Supper's ready!" Jesse scooped up his son and went in.

As soon as the door slammed I scurried up the hill and slipped into the barn. Voices and the clinking of dishes came from the house. I pulled out my note and speared it onto a splinter on Stonewall's stall door. Then I ran back to the woods again, my spine shuddering in anticipation of bullets. I'm a dreadful coward.

But nothing happened till dusk, when Jesse came out to the barn with both Ford brothers. A moment later he ran out and looked around, even squinting at my woods a moment. He'd drawn his revolver. I noticed he didn't turn his back on the Fords. He was good at his job, hang it. It was going to be difficult.

Soon they all rode off towards St. Joe. I waited. The Fords came back before midnight. Not Jesse. He wouldn't be back before Sunday night, I reckoned, because he'd travel in the dark and my note had sent him all the way to that other moonlit barn, near Blue Cut.

Getting back to the Worlds Hotel so late, I had to turn down a large number of ardent proposals from gentlemen on the steps. The bedbugs were unpleasant also; but then, I wasn't in St. Joseph for its cosmopolitan gaiety.

Sunday night, I huddled outside the back corner of the barn, waiting. The woman and her children went to bed early in a back bedroom. The Fords rode away, and returned. The lamps went out. I dozed a little. When at last approaching hoofbeats woke me, the moon was in the west. I didn't want to surprise him if things had gone wrong, so I held my breath as he rode into the yard and swung lightly down from Stonewall.

I could tell from the bounce in his step that he'd fetched them for me. I stepped out slowly, hands up, palms out, for all the world like Lady Macbeth sleepwalking. He dropped the reins and sprang for me. "Bridget, my lovely!" Then I was in his arms again, and there was heyday in my blood. In Jesse's too, I think.

"But Slick, your wife!" I protested feebly.

"She's asleep." But he pushed me into the shadow of the barn door before nuzzling my hair. "Dear Miss Mooney, are you armed?"

"Well, Mr. Jackson—"

"No, no. Mr. Howard. In St. Joe I'm Thomas Howard."

I smiled at him. "No, Mr. Howard, I'm not armed."

Well, of course I was telling the truth! How can you doubt me? There was room for a revolver in my bustle pocket, it's true, but it would have been worse than foolish to bring a weapon to Jesse James's house.

"I must check, all the same," he apologized; but we both were laughing by the time he was done. He said, "Here, help me unsaddle Stonewall. Major Edwards said you had a message about sacred duty. I never dreamed it would be about those diamonds!"

I smiled and didn't correct him. It wasn't yet time to tell him the other news. He asked, "How did you find me?"

"I didn't find you. I found Bob Ford. He talks too much."

Jesse frowned. "He's young. I'd better warn him again."

"Slick, did you get them?"

He hung up the saddle, then reached into his waistcoat and drew out a little bag, made from a scrap of silk knotted at the top. In the moonlight it was silvery. I clapped my hands.

Jesse tucked it back in his waistcoat and began to rub down Stonewall. "Ed Miller thought I stole them, and I had to— And all the time it was Dick, blast him! How did you find out?"

"I saw him reach into the sack, that night in the barn," I said. "You were tying up his horse." I spun him a tale about how Dick had hidden the diamonds outside my stall, but didn't retrieve them because he feared Jesse would discover the betrayal and kill him, as he'd killed Bassham and Ed Miller and all traitors. But after Dick was arrested, I said, he sent word for me to fetch them and pawn them to pay the lawyers.

Jesse led Stonewall to his stall, closed the door, and turned to face me. "But instead you came to me."

"Yes. I came to you. Of course." I gave a tiny shrug.

"Dear Bridget." I could see that Jesse wanted to believe in his loyal bandit queen. Even when you know all about dreams, you want to believe in them. But his next question showed I wasn't out of danger. He asked, "Why didn't you tell me what he'd done?"

"I was frightened, Slick," I said truly. "Look what happened when I told you about Ed Miller."

"Bridget, Bridget." He touched the mark on my cheek, and for an instant we stood in a blaze of reality, two scarred and lonely creatures. Then he cleared his throat and said, "I sent someone to the theatre that next night. To be sure you were all right."

I looked away. That wasn't very polite, but hang it, I still didn't feel like thanking him.

"Bridget, can we be—friends again?"

I smiled sidelong at him. "I'm here, Mr. Howard. And I would not be averse to doing a little business right now."

He glanced at the barn, then at the dark windows of the back bedroom, and smiled impishly. Jesse and I both liked our loving edged with danger. "Why not? I have the front sitting room. She knows not to disturb me when I get in late. Come, my bandit queen!" He led me into the house.

A voice called out, "Who's that?"

"It's Slick, Bob. Go back to sleep." We tiptoed to the front room and he lit a lamp, turning it low, to my relief. It was a plain little room, with a simple bed made up. A rich home would draw suspicion, I realized. I'd been a rare chance for him to flaunt his wealth at a safe distance. He stepped on a chair to adjust a picture on the wall, "The Death of Stonewall Jackson," and I saw him slip something behind it.

Then he took my hand and dropped two diamonds into my palm.

"Why, Mr. Howard!" I whispered, and met his mischievous eyes. "Perhaps you'd like to make certain once again that I'm not carrying a weapon?"

Amidst muffled giggles, he made certain I wasn't. Then I made certain he wasn't—though with one revolver on the bed and two more in a gunbelt hung on the bedpost within easy reach of those nimble fingers, it was a hollow endeavor on my part. Still, I was able to ascertain that he wasn't hiding any of the Blue Cut diamonds in his clothes. After that, other exceedingly pleasant activities ensued that we needn't mention, except to say that some of them involved a feather duster.

We ended exhausted and as happy as either of us was ever likely to be, and dozed a little. There was no hurry to tell him he owed me far more than two diamonds. For now, I was back in his good graces—at least I would be if I left before his wife saw me. He had to try to live her dream too, poor fellow.

So, when jocund day stood tiptoe on the misty mountaintops, we both stirred. The first sunbeams shot cheerfully across the room. Jesse smiled at me and rose to pull on his shirt and trousers. Then he picked up his gunbelt from the bedpost, but before buckling it on he paused, staring at the wall.

I followed his gaze toward the picture of "The Death of Stonewall Jackson." Bright in the morning sun, a blue thread hung from behind the picture frame.

I came scrambling out of bed as he bounded onto a chair, dropped the gunbelt over the back, and reached behind the picture. He withdrew the little bag and stared at it. In the sunlight the cloth that held the diamonds no longer looked silvery. It was a lovely sapphire blue.

"Your shawl!" he exclaimed. "The corner was torn— *You* stole them! Hid them in that crack in the barn wall—"

His back was still to me, but he turned his head, and for an instant I saw in his face the crumbling of his dream of me. Then his eyes glazed cold and cruel as ice. He was quick as ever, glancing down to grab the gunbelt from the chair back, his hand flashing to his pistol. If he'd been wearing the guns, things would have been very different. But in the extra instant fate allotted me, I snatched up the revolver he'd left on the bed and fired.

There was no time to mourn. When Bob and Charley Ford burst in a moment later, guns drawn, I was struggling into my dress. "What happened?" Bob demanded.

I sobbed, "No real lady would do what he asked!"

"You shot— *you* shot him?" exclaimed Charley. Four guns were leveled at me.

In the back of the house a child wailed. The woman's voice, groggy and fearful at once, called out, "What is it?"

"It's all right, Zee, I was just cleaning my gun," Bob called. Then he said to me, "I bet you did it for the reward!"

"No, no!" Of course I would have loved the reward. But an actress can't afford to be hated by half of Missouri, and the diamonds would suffice. I suggested, "Bob, you take the reward!"

"What?"

"Goodness, I don't want it! It would ruin my reputation if people knew I'd been in Jesse James' bedroom! Please, please, for my sake, take the reward!"

They were staring at me. I said, "Look. Here's the gun that shot him. Take it! When his wife gets up, tell her you did it."

Greed was flickering in Bob's eyes. But Charley frowned. "He's not wearing his guns. They'll say we were cowards."

"It's not cowardly, it's good sense!" I said testily. "Do you know a man anywhere who could draw faster than Jesse James?"

"That's true. But he fell from a chair. Why was he on a chair?"

"Hang it, Charley, don't you have an ounce of invention in your head? Say . . . say he took off his coat because it was warm, and he took off his guns because he didn't want anyone to see them through the window. Say he got on the chair to dust the pictures, there's the duster right there! Hang it, say anything!"

I finished buttoning my dress, slipped one of Jesse's pet revolvers into my bustle pocket, and ran to the barn. I saddled Stonewall and lit out for the railroad station while the Fords were still memorizing their lines.

I know, I know. It was sneaky to shoot him when he was unarmed and his back was turned. A proper lady might have waited for him to draw. But I can't quite get the hang of being proper.

Besides, don't you agree it was better for posterity? So there would be no more Tucker Basshams, no more bleeding men on trains. So Jesse's children could grow up to their own dreams. And I needed those diamonds, remember. For all her help I was going to owe Hattie Floyd a cottage, and more.

And posterity needs its dreams too. Admit it, now, doesn't the notion of a bandit king thrill you too? A hero who swears fealty to his comrades till and through death, courageously raids his evil oppressors, romances his ladies with poetic words, kills rather than betray his ideals? Now, the squalid shooting of a pretty woman would have tarnished his name. I provided Jesse with a hero's exit. Legends are fragile, after all—just look at Jesse's brother. Eventually Frank surrendered, was acquitted, and lived on to a bald old age —and do you know a single soul who prefers Frank to our dream of Jesse?

And furthermore—

Oh, I know, I know, you're right. The real reason was, if I hadn't done it, he would have shot me dead. I never claimed to be anything but a dirty little coward.

7

"Let not Caesar's servile minions
Mock the lion thus laid low:
'Twas no foeman's hand that slew him,
'Twas his own that struck the blow."
That's what Major Edwards wrote, keeping the legend alive.

In my profession too, we know a good idea when we see one. "Take him and cut him out in little stars,/ And he will make the face of heaven so fine,/ That all the world will be in love with night." The very week Jesse died, a New York producer announced J. J. McCloskey's new play, *Jesse James, The Bandit King*, and that was only the first of a whole slew of them.

And there was Billy Gashade. It was September again. We were in the waiting room of the St. Louis railroad station. Hattie had said it was time for me to get back to work, so I'd said my tearful good-byes and was in the St. Louis station waiting for the train to New York. Billy was going back to Kansas City. I offered him a cigar and said, "Watch out for bandits, Billy."

"There's not much trouble from them these days," he said. "Do you want to hear my song, Bridget? It's nearly finished."

"Of course."

It was a good song, and he got the story right, most of it, until he got to the chorus. Billy sang, "Jesse had a wife to mourn for his life,/ Two children, they were—"

"Three," I said.

"Three?" Billy's eyebrows crawled up. "Little Jesse, and little Mary, and—?"

"Just get the facts right, Billy," I said crossly. "Three."

Billy nodded and sang again:
"Jesse had a wife to mourn for his life,
Three children, they were brave,
But that dirty little coward that shot Mr. Howard
Has laid poor Jesse in his grave."

Ah, Jesse, Jesse. We sing of you to this day. You were such stuff as dreams are made on.

The trouble was, I was real.

FROM BRIDGET MOONEY'S SCRAPBOOK

This song was made by Billy Gashade,
As soon as the news did arrive,
He said there was no man with the law in his hand
Could take Jesse James when alive.

Jesse had a wife to mourn for his life,
Three children, they were brave,
But the dirty little coward that shot Mister Howard,
Has laid Jesse James in his grave.

THE NEW YORK HERALD

February 6, 1883

THE GREATEST SENSATION OF THE AGE

The original melodramatic and equestrian Drama,

JESSE JAMES

THE BANDIT KING,
INTRODUCING THE ORIGINAL AND ONLY
HORSES IN THE POSSESSION OF JESSE
JAMES AT THE TIME OF HIS DEATH,
BAY RAIDER AND ROAN CHARGER,
the most wonderful animal actors on earth. They
Pick Pockets, Tear Down Bills, Shake Hands With
Friends, Drink at the Bar, &c.

**MATINEES WEDNESDAY AND
SATURDAY.**
Windsor Theatre, Bowery below Canal

THE JERSEY LILY; or,
Make Me Immortal with a Kiss

"**B**low winds! and crack your cheeks!" I reckon Shakespeare was thinking of February in Chicago when he wrote that. I huddled into my deep blue traveling cape with the Langtry hood, hoping I was not going to have to pawn it too. I was out of work, out of money, and pining to get back to my friends and family in St. Louis. But so far, 1883 was not a very encouraging year for an actress who'd been anointed the Bernhardt of Missouri only a few short months ago.

I turned onto Michigan Avenue and saw a throng of people surging about the entrance of a dry-goods store. Curious, and realizing that a crowd would shield me from those notorious winds, I wriggled my way to the front, and heard one excited lady exclaim, "Here she comes!"

Several people looked my way, but the lady cried, "In the store!"

I followed her gesticulating finger. A tall, elegant man leaned out the door of the dry-goods store and said, "Make way, please!" Those of us in the first row obligingly pushed back against those behind us, despite their complaints. The man held the door, nodded to someone inside, and crooked his arm. A dainty gloved hand was placed on it. Proudly he led out the most beautiful woman in the world.

A little gasp of admiration ran through the crowd; and I'm bound to admit, she was indeed a dish for the gods. She was perhaps an inch taller than I, with a figure that was at once full and willowy. She had a queenly bearing that brought harmony to every graceful move. She wore a rich pearl gray suit, a lustrous fur neckpiece, and a beautiful feathered hat with a veil that didn't quite hide her lovely auburn hair nor the sweetly sensuous curve of her lips. She was the Prince of Wales' celebrated mistress, at once royal and scandalous. She was Lillie Langtry, the Jersey Lily herself.

She was also the reason I was stranded penniless in Chicago.

The crowd was not awed for long. As she stepped forward on her escort's arm, a man at the rear sang out, "Hey, Lillie, give us a kiss!" Another cried, "Take off yer veil! Let's see yer face!" There were more shouts and the crowd began to shove me from behind.

The man with Mrs. Langtry scowled and stepped forward confidently, but only a few people gave way. Someone, still shouting about the veil, snatched at it. Suddenly hands were everywhere, tugging at her hat, her gloves, her fur. The neckpiece came off, and the hat was snatched away and dismembered. I glimpsed her eyes, a perfect violet in color but full of consternation now. The man with her was shouting and striking out with his cane at the greedy arms around them. The cries of the throng became wilder. I dodged back into the dry goods store and watched through the window. In a moment a squad of police appeared and began tapping people with their nightsticks. The policemen surrounded Mrs. Langtry and her escort, and bustled them away amidst catcalls from the disappointed crowd.

I studied my reflection in a window to make sure my blue velvet bonnet with pink ostrich plume tips had not been damaged in the fray. Then I adjusted my traveling cloak, which was falling a little askew because I'd had to push it aside hastily when I tucked Mrs. Langtry's fur neckpiece under my bustle.

Why, how can you think such a thing? Of course I planned to return it! But you wouldn't want such an elegant adornment to fall into the hands of one of the ruffians in that crowd, now, would you?

Besides, I reckoned Mrs. Langtry owed me a trip to St. Louis.

She was staying at the Grand Pacific Hotel. I presented myself at the desk half an hour later and explained in my best British accent that I was an old friend of Mrs. Langtry's secretary, Miss Pattison. The clerk was of the opinion that I should leave a note, so I obligingly scribbled something indecipherable onto a card. "I'm only in Chicago for the day," I explained. "Please deliver it soon, or Miss Pattison will be displeased." I wandered over toward the staircase while the clerk rang for a bell boy. It was a simple matter to follow the boy upstairs to the correct floor. In fact, I let him go on alone to Miss Pattison's office, because it was immediately clear that Mrs. Langtry's door was the one surrounded by reporters. Most of them were interviewing a somber police sergeant about the near-riot, but one dark-haired little fellow with small eyes and a snout very like a possum cast a sideways glance in my direction. "You'll never get in, my sweet!"

I looked at him haughtily.

He handed me a card. "Well, if you do, I'll give you fifty dollars to get me in too! Here, I'm William Thorpe."

Of course, I considered the offer; but it seemed unlikely that he had the fifty dollars any more than I did, and my Aunt Mollie always encouraged me to collect all I could in advance. So I presented my own card with a note to the forbidding manservant at the door, and in a few minutes was allowed inside. Jealous whispers sizzled behind me. "Who is she?" "Is she with a newspaper?" "Look at the red hair! Maybe she's a relation!"

Mrs. Langtry was standing in a large rose-and-white room behind the entrance gallery. She appeared surprisingly unflustered for someone who had just been mauled in the streets, but I remembered her reputation for being imperturbable. Her auburn hair, caught in a graceful loop on the nape of her neck, was a shade darker than mine, and her skin was creamy, unfreckled, and unscarred. She looked me over with a trace of puzzlement as the maid announced, "Miss Bridget Mooney, ma'am."

Mrs. Langtry said, "How do you do. Dominic said you were a lady."

"I am; but as yet untitled, alas," I said.

The beautiful lips curved in a small smile. She knew the same was true of herself. "You're saucy. Are you a reporter? A ghastly woman reporter!"

"No! I am not a reporter, ghastly or otherwise. I was tutored by the greatest actress of her time, the illustrious Mrs. Fanny Kemble."

This news did not seem to hearten her. "Oh, I see. You're an actress! And of course you're going to ask for a favor, and of course you don't really know anything about my fur neckpiece. Please, take yourself away right now."

I stood my ground. "You're right, Mrs. Langtry, I'm here to ask a favor of you. But in exchange, I can restore your lovely neckpiece."

She inspected me carefully. "You're blunt, Miss Mooney. I rather like that. Very well, what price are you asking?"

"A job and passage to St. Louis."

"Isn't it possible for someone tutored by the famed Mrs. Kemble to find her own job?"

"Yes indeed, Mrs. Langtry! I was touring as Portia and Ophelia, and doing very well, too, as far as Milwaukee. Last year, as Juliet and Lady Macbeth, I was hailed as 'the Bernhardt of Missouri.' "

"Were you." Her smile was skeptical.

I thrust my rather worn clipping at her, and she arched her eyebrows. "Goodness, you're right!"

"Yes, Mrs. Langtry. I don't lie."

I know, I know, perhaps I exaggerated my honesty just a bit, because it's true that sometimes a girl has to stretch things, so as not to make trouble.

She looked up from the clipping, smiling again. "And just what happened to the profitable Portia and Ophelia after Milwaukee?"

"Our troupe came to Chicago, and was bankrupted. You see, Mrs. Langtry was playing Chicago too."

"Ah." She looked me over again and came to a sudden decision. "Very well, Miss Mooney. You may be an understudy until we reach St. Louis."

"Oh, thank you! Thank you so much, Mrs. Langtry!"

She picked up a pen and, in a large, looping hand, wrote out a little note explaining my new status. "Give this to Charles, fourth door on the right." She picked up the note and tapped her other hand with it. "Now, as to my fur piece—"

I withdrew it from my bustle, smoothed it, and handed it to her with a little curtsy. "I'm much obliged, Mrs. Langtry."

"Yes, you are much obliged, my saucy Miss Mooney!" She smiled. "I could turn you in as a thief, you know."

"Why, Mrs. Langtry! It fell off in the fray, and I merely retrieved it for you!"

She laughed and handed me the note. "No doubt. Be off, Miss Mooney! And if there's any more thieving, I'll toss you off the train myself!"

"Good-bye, Mrs. Langtry, and thank you."

I started for the door. A maid passed me, going in to Mrs. Langtry, carrying a note on a silver salver. A moment later I heard a gasp and the maid's anxious voice, "Madame! Madame, let me help you sit down! There, there!"

I looked back to see Mrs. Langtry sinking white as marble into a chair, sighing, "Thank you, Alice—oh—"

I ran back to her side, pulling out my bottle of smelling salts. "Alice! Get Madame a glass of water!" I exclaimed imperiously.

Alice scurried away while I applied the vial to Mrs. Langtry's perfect nose. She gasped, "Enough—thank you, enough!" A touch of color came back into her cheeks.

I picked up the note, which had fluttered to the floor. It was written in midnight blue ink on cream-colored paper. "Mrs. Langtry," it said, "thank you for your gift. Your niece will continue to enjoy good health and privacy if you bring a similar gift to the harness room of the Southern Hotel stables, St. Louis, at 2:00 a.m. February 6. Bring it in person."

Could it be? Could the perfect Mrs. Langtry be a victim of vilest extortion? My heart went out to her. I knelt beside her chair, folded the note and handed it to her. "Mrs. Langtry, is there any way I can help you?"

"Oh, Miss Mooney, I'm torn in two! This threat to my—my niece—but my every move is watched by the reporters! I do not even have the privacy to send a cable to learn if she is truly threatened! I can only continue to accede to the blackguard's demands!"

"There were earlier demands?"

She took a deep breath, passed a hand over her eyes, and sat up straighter. "I mustn't say anything more. Miss Mooney, please, I was feeling faint. You must disregard what I said."

"Mrs. Langtry, I believe we both understand the ways of this world. I, too, have a little—niece." The violet eyes were alert now, not quite believing. I explained, "I provide her with a home in St. Louis. She is the reason I stooped to this brazen assault on your goodwill."

Mrs. Langtry looked into my eyes and unexpectedly reached out to squeeze my hand. Then she smiled coolly at Alice, who was hastening back with the glass of water. "Thank you, Alice. I am much better—just a dizzy spell. Please help the others at the door. Miss Mooney will stay with me."

I realized that the clamor outside in the corridor had increased. But Lillie Langtry's attention was on me. She said, "Miss Mooney, it is a rare consolation to enjoy such heartfelt understanding from a stranger, when even my husband is ignorant of the truth about my little niece. But you do see that secrecy is the most important service you could perform for me."

"And you for me, Mrs. Langtry."

"Yes, of course."

"But I would help if I could."

"I don't see—oh, Oliver! Whatever is the matter?"

I turned to see a lanky fellow with sandy hair and pale eyes rushing in. "Lillie, I just heard you were attacked by a throng of ne'er-do-wells! How dreadful for you!" He was impeccably British, with a deep theatrical baritone. "What ghastly ruffians they are in this country!"

"It's those same ruffians who buy tickets and pay your salary," she said crisply. "Miss Mooney, may I present my fellow actor, Oliver Coleman?"

He managed to kiss my hand without once taking his eyes from Mrs. Langtry. "But your safety—dearest Lillie, we must protest!"

"Oliver, I am quite capable of deciding for myself what is to be done."

"She is! And you'd better get out now!" came an angry new voice, American this time. A tall, well-built young man was striding in. And I declare, he was a treat to the eye! He had expensive clothes, snow-white linen, a diamond stickpin and gold cuff links. "Oliver, you're upsetting Mrs. Langtry!"

"I am extending my sympathy for her unpleasant experience!" huffed Oliver.

"And I say you should leave her alone!"

"Freddie, Oliver, let us not fuss, please." Mrs. Langtry's voice had a steely undertone. The two men looked at her sheepishly. She continued,

"Miss Mooney, may I present Mr. Fred Gebhard, my—bodyguard?" There was the tiniest twitch at the corner of her lovely mouth.

Of course I recognized his name from the newspapers. I gave him my hand and murmured, "Delighted." And I was delighted, yes indeed. One is always delighted to meet handsome young millionaires, even if they have already been claimed by the most beautiful woman in the world.

"Miss Mooney," he said. "An understudy, I presume? Well, your height is good, and your hair. But I must warn you that Mrs. Langtry has not yet missed a performance." He kissed my hand with warm enthusiasm, despite the dazzle of the present company.

I said, "Of course I am completely at Mrs. Langtry's disposal. But I trust the need for an understudy will never arise, as Mrs. Langtry enjoys glowing good health."

Mrs. Langtry had been looking at me with half-closed eyes ever since Freddie Gebhard had mentioned my height and hair. Surely she, of all women, could not be jealous! But suddenly she said, "On the contrary, my health is fragile just now. Miss Mooney, please remove your bonnet for a moment and come here."

She was standing before a pier mirror. I untied my bonnet strings and joined her. For a moment we studied our images in the tall glass and I began to get an inkling of what she was thinking. My hair, though a shade lighter, was already arranged in the "Jersey Lily" style. And I found myself standing proudly, squaring my shoulders and tilting my chin to a more classic angle. Unfortunately no amount of tilting could get rid of freckles or scars.

Mrs. Langtry nodded slowly. "We're not likely to do better," she mused, and turned back to the two men. "I desperately need a rest," she told them. "Miss Mooney is going to help me. I will rest quietly in my railroad car, and with your help, Miss Mooney shall meet the St. Louis public for me."

Freddie was instantly solicitous. "Lillie, darling, I didn't know! You poor dear!"

Oliver burst in, "Darling Lillie, why didn't you tell me? We can cancel, or—"

"No!" She almost snapped the word. "I am earning lots of lovely money, and don't intend to stop."

I agreed wholeheartedly with her sentiments. But Freddie said, "Money! Lillie, I could—"

"No, Freddie. I know you could, but I wish to do it myself. You and Oliver may both help. You must attend Miss Mooney as a bodyguard, so that the dear people of St. Louis will believe that they are in fact seeing me.

Oliver, you must convince the rest of the troupe to remain silent about the deception. Otherwise there will be no choice but to cut the salaries." She glanced at me and said, "The same is true for you, Miss Mooney, although as the Bernhardt of Missouri you should have no difficulty convincing people that you are an actress."

Well, that was true enough. For all the Jersey Lily's beauty and fame, no one claimed that she could act. "A pretty elocutionist," said the critics.

"Won't your friends recognize you?" Freddie asked me.

"The only roles I've played there in recent days are Lady Macbeth and Iago's wife," I said. "My Juliet was done in Kansas City. Besides, people see what they want to see."

"But Lillie, are you seriously ill?" Freddie turned to her, looking very handsome and concerned. "Did that rabble this morning bring this on?"

She shrugged prettily. "That, and the long strain of bearing with Henrietta Labouchère."

"Henrietta!" Both men snorted in disgust.

I asked, "Should I know who Henrietta is?"

"A termagant!" cried Oliver.

"A jealous virago!" said Freddie.

"She was my drama teacher," Lillie said to me. "And very helpful at first, I daresay. But she became very possessive once we reached these shores. Freddie offered to show me New York when we arrived there, but she wanted me to be rehearsing all the time."

Well, I thought that possibly Henrietta's point was well taken, judging from the reviews; but it did not seem prudent to say so in this company. Oliver said, "She was domineering, and had no talent of her own."

"She was ruling your life!" Freddie declared.

"Yes, we had a falling out," Lillie said mildly. "Now, Oliver and Freddie, do promise to keep our secret from the public! If I can rest for a few days I'll be fine again. Oliver, promise me?" She took his hand and looked into his eyes.

"Oh, yes!" He cleared his throat, and added, "Of course, Lillie. Would that I could do more!"

Freddie was on his knees before her, looking very gallant. "You have my solemn promise too!" he cried.

She took his hand too. "Thank you," she said in a sweet husky voice; and I knew that secrecy was assured more surely than it could have been with scores of legal documents.

I said, "I hope you will pardon my audacity, Mrs. Langtry. But as I understand my assignment, it involves more than the performances in St. Louis. It involves playing Lillie Langtry herself to the press, and on necessary public occasions, until your health is restored."

Lillie understood me. "You want more money."

"My understanding is that in addition to the travel expenses, your producer is paying you sixty-five percent of the gross." Backstage, our troupe had been a-buzz about that amount. Most famous actors were fortunate to earn fifty percent.

"But I must pay the salaries of the company," she pointed out.

I inclined my head in agreement. "Still, while you are resting in your private railroad car, it seems to me that I should receive sixty-five percent of your share."

"Bridget Mooney, that's preposterous!"

"Yes, Mrs. Langtry." I smiled at her. "So is the assignment."

"Well—I suppose it would add to your incentive—"

"That's true too, Mrs. Langtry."

"I'll do it on one condition."

"What's that?"

"That you call me Lillie, Bridget. You are a woman after my own heart!"

We clasped hands warmly, and I said, "Thank you, Lillie. Of course it goes without saying that I will need some of it in advance."

She burst out laughing and said, "Freddie?" Casually, he pulled a hundred dollars from a roll and handed it to me. Don't you agree that millionaires are perfectly splendid?

Then Lillie shooed out Oliver and Freddie and the servants like so many chickens, and the two of us set to work transforming my freckled Irish prettiness into her Jersey beauty. We mixed grease paint to match her creamy coloring. "How did you get this little scar, Bridget?" she asked as she rubbed some onto my cheek.

"My little niece's father was a violent man."

"He must have been a ruffian!"

"No, no, Lillie! He was a gentleman, as near to royalty as we've ever had in Missouri. But from time to time he was violent."

She finished my face and began to darken my lashes. "So you, too, know a prince. A violent one. Does he continue to trouble you?"

"He was killed. Shot by one of his closest friends."

"Oh dear, a violent death too. And did you love him very much, this prince?"

"I loved what he brought me. Riches, excitement, romance."

"Yes," she said. She had stopped working on my face and was studying me with that beautiful violet gaze. "Yes, Bridget, we are alike, you and I. Riches, excitement, romance—those are the things my little niece's father brought me. And he helped conceal her existence from the world and from my drunken, estranged husband, who would raise a scandal if he knew. Tell me, how old is your little niece?"

"Seven months. How old is yours?"

"Not quite two years."

"We'll keep them both safe, Lillie."

Well, we had a good cry together, the imperturbable Lillie and I, and then we finished painting my face. I looked lovely, though you understand I was still not Lillie's twin. But from a distance, wearing a veil and one of her Parisian dresses with some padding in the hips and corset, only a good friend could tell the difference. The most difficult task was learning to move the way Lillie moved. She was at once queenly and lissome, and it was difficult to imitate in a tight-laced, padded corset.

Lillie had a scrapbook of clippings, and I began to study it so I would know her opinions about America, Shakespeare, fashion, beauty tips, and so forth. One opinion was obviously missing. "Suppose they ask about the Prince of Wales?" I asked.

"Oh, Bridget, you must be very, very discreet! The slightest whiff of public scandal, and I will lose his favor."

"I'll do my best. But they may ask."

"Of course they will, they always do! So I become suddenly deaf. I smile encouragingly at some other reporter."

"And if they accuse you of something scandalous?"

"My dear friend Mr. Gladstone pointed out that a public person is frequently attacked and slandered. Never reply to your critics, he said. Never explain. You will only keep alive the controversy."

So I was ready, with the help of Freddie and the troupe, to become Lillie Langtry for the public. But even Freddie and the actors were not aware of the deeper level of our plan. In fact, Lillie would not be resting in the bedroom of her private railroad car, as Freddie and the others would believe. She would remain in Chicago, wearing dark shabby clothes and a black wig. Her faithful servant Alice and I were the only ones who would know that Lillie was not on the train. Thus, safe from Freddie and anyone else who had no right to know about her niece, Lillie could cable her mother on the Isle of Jersey to find out what had happened to the little girl. Lillie would then rejoin us in St. Louis in time to meet the extortionist at the Southern Hotel.

Meanwhile, I would go ahead in splendor, playing Lillie Langtry in addition to Lillie Langtry's roles. I would not have to ride in the coach with the other actors and the common passengers. I would travel in the private railroad car that Lillie's friend Diamond Jim Brady had acquired for her use. It was called *The City of Worcester* and sported a living room, three bedrooms, and a private bath. The best bedroom would be kept locked, and Alice and I, occupying the other bedrooms, would turn away Freddie and the rest of the world, explaining that she needed her rest.

And wasn't it a ripping railroad car! I bounced on the bed, and opened all the cunning little drawers in the cabinetry, and ran the water in the bathroom. Alice watched with an amused smirk. Outside, the February landscape rolled by, rainy and gray, but inside it was all warm luxury.

After a few hours I put on my Langtry padding and paint, as well as a hat with a veil, and went into the next coach. It was filled with Lillie's actors and servants and stagehands. When I appeared, the actress who played Phebe the shepherdess called out, "Miss Lillie! Are you feeling better, then? Oh!" She clapped her little hand to her mouth.

Pleased, I said, "Thank you, Mary, I am better." I kept my voice sweetly modulated, as Lillie did. "I hope to arrange a rehearsal on the Olympic Theatre stage as soon as we reach St. Louis. Would that be agreeable to everyone?"

"Yes, Miss Lillie!" There was a chorus of approval.

Oliver Coleman had done his job well. I smiled at him. "I'll arrange to speak to the reporters soon after we arrive also."

"Are you sure you are well enough, Lillie?" he asked with convincing anxiety.

"If it will increase the receipts, I'm well enough," I said firmly. There were shouts of "Hear, hear!" amongst the actors.

Suddenly, someone in the aisle touched my arm. "Mrs. Langtry," he said. I looked up and saw the possum-like face of the reporter I'd met in the Grand Pacific Hotel in Chicago.

"Yes?" I said distantly. My heart was galloping. He was only two feet away.

"Mrs. Langtry, my—my newspaper is eager to know your opinion of—of Chicago."

"A splendid city, filled with strength and vigor," I replied.

"Vigor?" he asked, and licked his lips. He seemed nervous, almost shy, unlike his chipper self in Chicago, where he'd called me "my sweet." He added, "Are you unhappy about the crowd that destroyed your hat?"

What would Lillie say? I said, "I was sorry to lose the hat, but pleased to see the enthusiasm the people demonstrated."

His small dark eyes were fixed on my mouth with a strange expression. I was worried—my mouth, I thought, was similar to the Jersey Lily's, and required only a small adjustment in the upper lip. Why was the little reporter staring at me so? I said nervously, "Do you have any more questions, sir?"

"Oh. Oh, Mrs. Langtry, it is true! We Americans are enthusiasts. I for one have read everything ever written about you, and crossed the Atlantic to see you cantering in the park with the Prince." He peered soulfully through my veil, and suddenly I recognized the expression and almost laughed out loud. Lovesick! This short marsupial fellow was infatuated with the dazzling Lillie Langtry!

I said kindly, "What is your name, sir?"

"Oh. Thorpe. William Thorpe. Here—here is my card, Mrs. Langtry, if you would be so kind as to accept it." He thrust the card at me with trembling fingers.

Just then Freddie entered the far end of the car, saw me speaking to Thorpe, and came striding up the aisle waving his silver-headed cane. "Sir!" he exclaimed. "You've been told not to have anything to do with Mrs. Langtry!"

William Thorpe flattened himself against one of the seats to let Freddie by. "She—she was kind enough to answer my questions."

"Well, it's over! Mrs. Langtry must conserve her strength!" Freddie offered me his expensively clad elbow and led me firmly out of the coach toward my own.

"Is there a problem with Mr. Thorpe?" I asked him once we were on the platform.

"He's a pest. He's been after Lillie since New York. He buttered up Henrietta for news. He even bribed the hotel staff to let him into my rooms to try to convince me to get him an interview with her. As though I had influence!"

"Well, it's his job, I suppose."

Freddie snorted. "Well, it's my job to protect Lillie from people like him! He has no business in that car!"

"I'll try not to encourage him. But sometimes it's easier to say a few words to newspapermen, so they don't invent their own."

"That's what Lillie says," he admitted grudgingly as he opened the door of *The City of Worcester*. Alice was in the sitting-room section and he added anxiously, "How is she, Alice?"

Alice shook her head sadly. "She needs rest, Mr. Gebhard."

"Blast it! I'd hoped—well, she's right, of course. Do tell her I've been asking." Freddie flopped into one of the overstuffed chairs and stared out at the damp landscape.

"I'm certain she'll send for you when she is able," I soothed him. "She's very fond of you, Freddie."

"Oh, do you think so?" He looked at Lillie's bedroom door, as calf-eyed as little William Thorpe. If he'd known that Lillie was still back in Chicago, he would have run back to her on foot. Poor Lillie was right—she could never send a private cable with so many eager swains attempting to help. Freddie continued, "She is so—not cool, how can I say it? Warm and cool all at once. I would think she cared only for my money—except that she won't accept my help to leave the stage!"

"Well, goodness, Freddie, I wouldn't either! I love the stage! But I wouldn't despise your money. It's one of your attractions. Though you have many others."

"Perhaps." Freddie sighed. "Oh, Bridget, I just don't know if I have a chance or not! She invites me to be her bodyguard—and then locks me out!"

Well, it would have been lovely, and profitable, to take dear Freddie into my arms to console him. But I knew that in the long run Lillie could be a more loyal friend than he, or a more implacable enemy. So I resisted temptation and said, "Freddie, you're still new in her life. Allow her some time. Now tell me what I should say to the reporters, to ensure good receipts."

"I don't know," he said listlessly. "She usually doesn't have to worry about it. Oscar Wilde meets her ship, or someone speaks against her in the U.S. Senate, or Henrietta storms out, or she's mobbed in the streets—there are plenty of headlines. And if news is slow, they print something about the blasted Prince of Wales."

I nodded slowly. Poor Lillie—the merest whiff of the existence of her little niece would be headlined all over America. She was not rich. Her drunken husband had gone bankrupt, but would not give her a divorce, and even with an admirer like Freddie temporarily at her feet, in the long run she had to depend on her own resources. As long as she walked the narrow line between respectability and scandal, people would buy tickets just for a glimpse of her. But with half of society already snubbing her, any indiscretion that tipped the balance—especially if it caused the Prince of Wales to withdraw his friendship—would tumble her into disrepute and ruin.

So I had to be extremely circumspect. But hang it, I had no intention of allowing those receipts to fall off when sixty-five percent of her share was to be mine.

Freddie went moping off, and after a moment I sent Alice for Oliver Coleman. The lanky actor appeared quickly but seemed disappointed that it was I and not the true Lillie who wished to see him.

"She needs her rest," I told him. "Oliver, she trusts you, and I must ask you some questions. First, as an actor, what is your opinion of my impersonation?"

"Not half bad, Bridget! The walk isn't quite right yet, but the voice and appearance are excellent. Now, of course, I'm not saying that you are precisely—uh—"

"Of course not," I said tartly. "Nevertheless, I dare say I am playing Lillie better than Lillie could play me."

Oliver laughed. "I daresay."

"Now, Oliver, you were in England with Lillie. Tell me about Henrietta Labouchère."

"A terrible woman! Lillie is usually so strong. I can only think that she was ill when she fell under her influence."

"Is Mrs. Labouchère vindictive? Is she likely to write threatening letters?"

"I wouldn't be surprised. Has Lillie received such letters?"

"I have no idea, Oliver!" I said blandly. "I am just trying to account for Mrs. Langtry's exhaustion after Henrietta left. Lillie strikes me as a very healthy person."

"As healthy as she is beautiful!" Oliver's eyes looked suspiciously calflike too.

Well, I was beginning to tire of all these men falling at Lillie's feet when she wasn't even there, and I was. I snapped, "Come now, Oliver, time for a lesson! Help me learn to walk the way she walks!"

As we approached St. Louis I drew Alice aside. "We must part for a few days, Alice. I must move into Mrs. Langtry's suite at the Southern Hotel. The troupe has been splendid about supporting my impersonation, but we must continue to deceive them. They must all believe that Mrs. Langtry is here in *The City of Worcester* with you. You must be alert as ever and prepared to turn them away."

"Yes, madam. I'll turn away reporters as well."

"Good, although if we succeed, the reporters will come to me at the hotel. Well, keep the servants with you; I shall make do with Freddie and the hotel staff. Oh, and Alice, I must borrow a cap and apron from you."

I moved into the Southern Hotel, a magnificent edifice that had always been beyond my means. It had a splendid rotunda, and beautifully appointed rooms, and an efficient staff, except that one of them unaccountably lost a bottle of Lillie's scent, and I had to send to Alice for another. But all in all, my aunt Mollie would have approved of the way Mrs. Langtry had arranged her life. She knew how the quality lived, yes indeed.

I set the staff to work organizing a meeting with reporters two hours hence, followed by a rehearsal on the Olympic Theatre stage. Then, as Lillie Langtry, I asked the hotel staff to turn away all callers, pleading the necessity of a nap. But I didn't sleep. Instead, wearing Alice's cap and apron, no make-up, and a low-down Irish accent I'd learned from Papa, I curtsied my way past the unsuspecting guards at the door and went to my friend Hattie's cottage to see my little niece.

She was the dearest little creature ever, my niece. She had blue eyes and two wee teeth and the most cunning little nose and ears. We giggled and cooed at each other. I bounced her on my knees, and rocked her, and she very nearly chewed off the string of Alice's apron. Too soon, it was time to return.

As I rode back, I vowed that if I ever found the skunk that threatened Lillie's niece, I'd make him pay. That's about the lowest, cruellest thing a body can do, threatening a little niece.

The freckled Irish maid went back into Lillie's rooms at the hotel, and half an hour later the creamy-skinned, elegantly appareled Lillie Langtry descended to the rotunda to speak to the reporters, carrying a lily snatched hastily from a large bouquet that had been sent to her rooms. The interview went very much as Lillie and I had rehearsed—most of the questions concerned how she liked Missouri, and I only had to ignore a few about the Prince of Wales. But it occurred to me as the hotel staff escorted me away from the still-eager reporters that nothing exciting had come up. No Henrietta Laboucheres had stormed off, no Oscar Wildes had met the train, no rag-tag crowds had snatched off my hat. We would get pleasant little mentions in the newspapers, but not the kind of attention Lillie usually received. And since the Olympic Theatre management had told us that, while tickets were selling well, there were still many left, something had to be done before tomorrow night's opening.

I paused and indicated to the hotel staff that I wished to speak to Colonel Cunningham, a highly moral reporter for the *Globe-Democrat*. My possum-like admirer William Thorpe and the other reporters cast angry glances at this favored fellow as he hurried to me. I stepped close to him and lowered my voice. "Colonel Cunningham, I must go to rehearsal so I cannot speak now. But I admire your newspaper. Please come to my room tomorrow morning at nine, and we can arrange an interview."

He looked astonished. I smiled sweetly and tapped his chest with my lily. "And don't let anyone stop you, Colonel Cunningham!" Then I turned and glided swiftly away to rehearse.

Afterward Freddie escorted me back to the hotel, but he was clearly eager to pay another vain call on the empty bedroom in *The City of Worcester*, where he thought Lillie rested, so I asked him to visit me early the next morning. Once he'd gone, I became the freckled Irish maid again, and tripped away for a nice chat with Hattie and a lovely nap with my little niece.

I know, you're right, of course. My Aunt Mollie taught me that it was not safe for a young lady to travel the streets of St. Louis at night unprotected. But I can hit a squirrel at thirty yards with my excellent revolver, once the property of Jesse James himself. It was the second-best thing Jesse ever gave me. So you see, I was protected.

Before dawn, I returned to the hotel. I bathed, applied my Jersey Lily greasepaint and Jersey Lily scent, and donned a dazzling peignoir that Lillie had provided. When Freddie arrived he blinked. "Oh, excuse me, Lil—uh, Bri—uh, Lillie. I'll come back later."

"No, no, Freddie!" I smiled warmly. "Do come have breakfast with me. It's been lonely."

"You're a damned attractive woman," he said, coming in with no further ado.

We settled ourselves at the breakfast table in the sitting room, and I'm bound to admit that it made a scene from a lovely dream: flowers, crystal, silver, delicious rolls and marmalade, the most beautiful woman in the world, and the handsomest young millionaire. We discussed Lillie's health, and then Freddie's racing stable, and Freddie himself, and soon he fell under the spell of the flowers and the peignoir and laid his hand over mine. "You are lovely, damn it!" he exclaimed.

And that was the scene Colonel Cunningham saw when he pushed his way past the protesting maid and burst into the sitting room. He halted at the sight of us. "Mrs. Langtry!" he gasped. "What is the explanation of this?"

I donned my cool Lillie gaze. "Colonel Cunningham, please leave us, sir."

"Mr. Gebhard! What is the explanation?"

Freddie exclaimed, "The lady told you to leave us!"

"What am I to say to my readers? Sir, madam, this has every appearance of the vilest immorality!"

Well, that was unfair, don't you think? Freddie was fully and expensively dressed, and my peignoir concealed more than my ball gowns. In any case, we were not the least bit vile. On the contrary, we were ethereally elegant. But Colonel Cunningham was appalled.

Freddie, of course, was becoming angrier by the moment. His beloved Lillie was being insulted, and he could not explain that she was not even present. I laid a restraining hand on his arm and said, "Let us not fuss, Freddie." We listened to Colonel Cunningham rant on for a few minutes, but I refused to answer and managed to keep my sweet, hot-blooded millionaire from boiling over. When the Colonel finally retreated, though, Freddie exploded.

"Damn him!"

"Oh, hush, Freddie. You know that Lillie wouldn't have spoken to him."

"Maybe not. But if he does anything more I'll crack his skull!"

Freddie, at six feet and probably two hundred pounds, might be able to do so, although I knew that Colonel Cunningham, as a military man from Missouri, was sure to carry a pistol. I said, "Do take care, Freddie. Lillie wouldn't want you to be rash."

Colonel Cunningham's blistering attack on Lillie was published that same afternoon. She was immoral, he said. Fred Gebhard was her partner in sin. The citizens of St. Louis should boycott the theatre.

Freddie was furious. I restrained him while I could, but the minute I left for the theatre, he went down to the rotunda to smoke a cigar, or so he claimed. Unfortunately, Colonel Cunningham was there. I'm told that Freddie shouted "Sir! You are an infamous liar!" and advanced on him, waving his stick. Cunningham backed away, one hand slipping into a side pocket in a way anyone from Missouri would find ominous, but Freddie, undaunted, kept shouting and waving his stick until at last the police came and removed Cunningham from the premises. Oh, I do wish I had been there! It must have been a dandy cockfight!

In most respects, Freddie was performing his part well. There was a beautiful lily bouquet in my dressing room. I picked up the note that came with it. "To Lillie," it said, "from your devoted Freddie."

But then I frowned. His note was written in midnight blue ink on cream-colored paper.

The next morning, an emissary from Cunningham arrived to challenge Freddie to a duel.

"No, Freddie," I said. "Absolutely not. We must never respond to criticism. It's Lillie's own rule, and a very good one."

"I want to shoot the infamous liar!" Freddie shouted.

"Of course you do. But if one of you is killed, Lillie's career will be ruined."

"It's already ruined, isn't it? There's going to be a boycott!"

I smiled. "On the contrary, Freddie. The manager tells me that the controversy has created great interest. We're sold out for the run."

My financial difficulties were solved for the time, if I could keep Freddie from the duel. But then a fresh worry presented itself. A cable addressed to Lillie Langtry was delivered to my hotel room. "Dear Lillie, I'm devastated to say that due to the Mississippi flooding, I cannot reach St. Louis in time for our prearranged meeting about the ruby brooch. I hope you and the others can arrange the business without me. The family is safe." It was signed, "Mrs. L.L. Prince."

So it was up to me to meet the extortionist! It was not a comforting thought, because any extortionist who knew Lillie well enough to mention her niece was likely to know her well enough to see through my impersonation. I sat down to have a good think.

Who could it be? According to Lillie, no one knew about her little niece, not Freddie, not even her husband. It seemed impossible that an American could find out without visiting the isle of Jersey. But why would any of her British troupe engage in such cruel extortion? She didn't pay well, but as I well knew, some troupes were paid nothing at all. I wondered about the angry Henrietta; but she had been escorted onto the ship home. I sighed. There were not enough facts to make a good guess.

Last time, Lillie had said, the extortionist had been content with a brooch. This time he wanted Lillie there in person. I found this ominous. A mind cruel enough to threaten a little niece, even falsely, might be cruel enough to consider abduction of Mrs. Langtry herself, for vile enjoyment of her personal charms or for ransom from Freddie or even the Prince of Wales. I realized I would have to be extremely careful.

Just before 2:00 a.m., I tucked the ruby brooch Lillie had mentioned into my bustle pocket, smiled at the porters dozing outside Lillie's door, and glided swiftly along the hall and out to the stables. The night groom snored just inside the door, an empty whiskey bottle on the floor beside him. The stabled horses shifted and stamped as I entered, and I saw that the hasp on the harness room door had been pried off, though the door was closed. I knocked gently; but there was no answer, so I pushed it open. Inside, a small lantern spread a warm glow over the stored saddles and bridles. The room smelled of leather and saddle soap. But no one was there. Was I to leave the brooch without further instructions? Hesitantly I placed it on a bench.

A moment later there was a soft knock and I whirled to face the door. "Come in," I said.

Freddie closed the door behind him and bounded across the room to me. "Lillie! At last! I've waited so long for this moment!"

"Freddie!" I exclaimed. "But—but—" Hang it, he was a millionaire! It wasn't a brooch he wanted from Lillie.

"But what? You told me—" His face fell as he realized who I was. "Oh, damn!"

Whatever else we might have said, we were interrupted by the door bursting open again. A huge revolver appeared, and a man's voice hissed, "Sir! You are a cad! Lillie, I'll save you!"

"Why, thank you, sir, bu—"

The revolver advanced into the room, followed by the possumlike snout and small, shiny eyes of the lovesick reporter, William Thorpe. "Your designs on Lillie are vicious and immoral!" Thorpe said.

"Liar!" Freddie exclaimed. "I wish to marry her!"

He took a step toward Thorpe, and I grabbed his sleeve. "Freddie, don't be rash! He has a gun!"

"And I'll use it!" crowed Thorpe. "I'll rid you of this pest, Lillie!"

I said graciously, "Mr. Thorpe, I thank you for your concern. But Mr. Gebhard and I were merely conversing. If I wish to be rid of him, I myself will ask him to leave."

"No!" He flicked a frantic glance in my direction, but the revolver held steady on my millionaire. "You need me! You have been unable to dissuade him! I'll rescue you, Lillie!"

Well, hang it, this scene was not working. We were reading from three different scripts, it seemed. And though I thought Freddie's version had the most appeal, Thorpe held the pistol, so I switched to his. "Mr. Thorpe, I'm so very glad you came," I said soothingly, stepping toward him. "But you have already rescued me, you see. Do you know what would give me great pleasure, right now?"

"Oh, yes! You are grateful! You wish to—to kiss me! 'Make me immortal with a kiss!' "

From the corner of my eye I saw Freddie's hands clench, but I continued soothingly, "Of course, Mr. Thorpe, that is exactly right! But first I would find it a great pleasure to hold the gun on the despicable Mr. Gebhard myself. Please allow me!"

"No! No, I'm supposed to hold the gun! He's threatened you!"

"You infamous liar!" Freddie burst out unwisely.

William Thorpe smirked. "Lillie can decide who the liar is when she looks in your suitcases and finds the brooch she gave you last time!"

"How do you know what's in my suitcases?" Freddie demanded.

"Hush, Freddie," I said, trying to regain control. "After all, the extortion note was written on your notepaper."

"Yes, yes, yes!" Thorpe cried, delighted at my acuity.

Freddie looked at me in disbelief. "You believe this fellow?"

Thorpe answered gleefully, "I am her rescuer! I know all her problems! I know everything about Lillie!"

"He's visited London to see me canter in the park," I told Freddie. "He's seen the Prince of Wales."

At the mention of the Prince, Freddie's look darkened. So did Thorpe's. Thorpe muttered, "Yes, the Prince of Wales. And Louis Battenburg. And Edward Langtry. All unworthy of you, Lillie! And now this worm of a fellow!" He gestured at Freddie with the revolver.

Freddie was about to explode. "You are the worm, sir! To make such vile innuendos about a virtuous lady!"

"You say virtuous? And are your plans for her virtuous? No, she needs my help, my poor Lillie! You are like all the others! You are trying to drag her into the mud! I've been to the Isle of Jersey, too, and I know—"

Idiotically courageous, Freddie hurled himself at Thorpe. The sound of the gunshot rang through the little room. Freddie fell on top of Thorpe, and blood gushed onto the plank floor. Freddie looked at it, astonished, and then his eyes glazed over.

I sighed, adjusted my bustle, and gave Freddie a good sniff of my smelling salts. "Freddie! Are you all right?"

"I'm—I'm bleeding," he gasped. He struggled to a sitting position, staring at the gaudy red stain on his lovely white shirt.

"It's Thorpe's blood, you silly goose," I said.

"Thorpe's? But he was aiming at me!"

Well, I've never had much ambition to be the leading attraction at a trial, so it seemed best to keep the truth from Freddie. I said, "You must have knocked his arm aside when you tackled him, and he shot himself."

"Oh. Oh, yes, that must have been it!" Freddie seemed pleased with himself.

"It might be best to arrange to dispose of the body, Freddie."

"Yes. You're right. And I'd best rid myself of this clothing too." He stood up to begin his errands.

"And of course, we keep quiet about all this," I reminded him. "You know how Lillie hates fuss."

He looked a trifle disappointed. It would have been a fine story to tell at his club. But he admitted, "Yes, you're right."

"Freddie, why are you here? Did you, too, get a note?"

"Yes. I believed it was from Lillie. It smelled like her."

"I see. So Thorpe sent notes to both of us. He must have been the one who hooked some of Lillie's scent while I was moving into the hotel, to sprinkle on your note. And he must have stolen some of your notepaper when he bribed his way into your rooms in New York. He was quite mad, Freddie, less a reporter than a fanatic admirer. He wanted to show Lillie that you were a despicable cad, and to rescue her from you."

Freddie was puzzled. "But why?"

I shrugged. "So she would be grateful. So she would make him immortal with a kiss. Now, hurry, Freddie. It's up to you to save Lillie from this scandal."

He bustled off to look for his efficient manservant. I picked up the brooch and started out too. Then I paused and looked back at the poor little body on the rug, and blew it a kiss.

I know, I know, he didn't deserve it. He was thoroughly mad and cruel and low, and he'd threatened her little niece, and was about to shoot a perfectly splendid millionaire.

But hang it, I've done foolish things for kisses too. And I'd already made him immortal. Might as well finish the job.

*   *   *

The Jersey Lily left for Memphis at the end of the next week. I stood by the tracks just outside of town, richer by thousands of dollars—enough, perhaps, to become an actor-manager like Lillie, with my very own troupe and one hundred percent after expenses. Lillie had also given me half a dozen Parisian gowns in gratitude for saving Freddie and keeping him out of the duel. It hadn't been hard, really, once I reminded him that he fainted at the sight of blood.

In my arms I held my little niece. The locomotive puffed by us, and the other cars, and finally *The City of Worcester*, shiny and elegant as a jewel. I waved, and my little niece cooed and mimicked me, and I saw the most beautiful woman in the world looking out the window, fluttering her handkerchief at us and then dabbing at her eyes as she rolled away.

FROM BRIDGET MOONEY'S SCRAPBOOK

FROM BRIDGET MOONEY'S SCRAPBOOK

NEW YORK MIRROR

January 27, 1883

Item: Freddie Gebhardt arrived at the Southern Hotel early in the week, and attracted much attention during his stay. He was submitted to much ridicule, and the press had a great deal of fun at his expense. The outcome of an interview with the *Globe-Democrat* was a *rencontre* between Gebhardt and the reporter A. R. Cunningham, who was recently in serious trouble over an affray he was concerned in. No blows were struck; but Cunningham sent Freddie a challenge, which the latter took no notice of. Those who know the newspaperman's vindictive nature say the end is not yet.

THE UNCROWNED KING OF IRELAND; or,
A Most Toad-Spotted Traitor

Lordie, no! I never meant to bring down the British government! And you know that I love Ireland. But you must understand that sometimes a young lady, temporarily penurious, is in need of a new bustled dress in the latest fashion in order to win a role in a play, so that she may acquire the funds necessary to repair the leaking roof of her dear little niece's house. Now suppose that the said young lady suddenly encounters Father Christmas in New York City—to be precise, in the dining-room of the highly respectable Metropolitan Hotel. Hang it, you wouldn't expect her to turn away from the proffered good fortune! On the contrary, I found myself whispering the Bard's words to myself: "Down on thy knees, thank the holy gods!"

The gentleman bore a striking resemblance to St. Nicholas, his bald head fringed with curly silver hair, his round face adorned with bushy whiskers of the same hue. He was neatly attired in a black jacket and brown striped trousers, and a monocle sparkled in one eye. Other observations, however, were less satisfactory. His nose was rather too fleshy and red, his expression rather too mournful, and his Irish brogue rather too slurred as he called for more port wine.

Nevertheless, a quick survey of the dining-room offered me no better prospect. I glanced at the pier mirror nearby to make certain that my auburn hair peeked prettily from beneath my little plumed hat, and adjusted the lilac-flowered cream flounces of my skirt in order to hide the worn velvet trim and an unfortunate wine stain. Then I approached the bewhiskered gentleman with all the elegance I could muster and said, "Sir, I beg your pardon, but I fear that I left my fan behind when I sat at this table earlier today. Have you seen it, perchance?"

I know, I know, my Aunt Mollie would agree with you. She always told me that proper ladies do not mislead gentlemen—and of course the fan was nonexistent. But I have found that gentlemen are usually quite pleased to assist ladies, whether the problem truly exists or not, and that pleasing a gentleman is more profitable on the whole than ignoring him. Even Aunt Mollie approved of profits, for she was an excellent businesswoman.

"I have not seen your fan, dearest madam," my soon-to-be benefactor replied, bouncing eagerly to his feet, though the gallant effect of his action was marred by his having to grasp the back of his chair in order to avoid toppling over. "But may I help you search?"

We spent a moment or two searching under the table for the fan—trimmed with crimped lace, I told him, like the edging of my neckline. Although he did not find the fan, he had certainly memorized my neckline by the time we gave up the search.

"Dear madam," he said with an adoring glance, "might I console you on the loss of your fan by offering you a glass of port wine?"

"That would indeed be most welcome," I declared, sinking into a chair before he could reconsider. "You sound so like my dear papa, sir! He lives here in America now, but he was born in Dublin."

His small, wide-set eyes brightened. "I reside in Dublin. So you are Irish, madam!"

"Irish-American, yes sir. My name is Bridget Mooney. May I inquire to whom I have the pleasure of speaking?"

"I am, uh, Roland Ponsonby, at your service, Miss Mooney." He leaned forward as far as his round belly permitted, adjusted his eyeglass to peer nervously about the dining-room, and murmured, "Are you, or your good father, members of Clan-na-Gael?"

I hesitated. Clan-na-Gael was the Irish-American society that supported the violent Fenians in Ireland, those men of extreme views who fought most outrageously against the British yoke. Only four years earlier they had assassinated the young British Chief Secretary for Ireland, Lord Frederick Cavendish, and his aide as they walked in Dublin's Phoenix Park. The murders had been committed with twelve-inch long surgical knives smuggled in by an Irish-American.

I knew it would be unwise for me to admit to belonging to Clan-na-Gael if Mr. Ponsonby were a spy in the service of the British government. It would be equally unwise to claim to oppose it if he were himself a violent Fenian. I said, "No, sir, but some of my friends are sympathetic."

He pinched his lip nervously. "Tell me, lovely Miss Mooney, would any of your sympathetic friends have a position for an experienced journalist?"

My heart sank. "Are you an immigrant, then, Mr. Ponsonby?" Hang it, a British spy or even a Fenian assassin would be preferable to a penniless newcomer.

His Father Christmas face grew mournful. "If only I could find a position! I came to this land of splendid opportunity, but have found no way out of my pecuniary difficulties, except for unsuitable manual labor on the docks."

I was puzzled by my new acquaintance. Despite his complaints of poverty, I could not give up hope that he might yet provide the funds for a new roof for my little niece. Yet he had given me a false name. Yes, of course I had noticed his hesitation. Roland Ponsonby—I was willing to wager that was not his true name.

"Mr. Ponsonby," I began, for Aunt Mollie always said that it is prudent to appear to take people at their word if one does not yet fully understand a situation, "I can see from your bearing and excellent turn of phrase that you have achieved success in your profession. Pray tell me, what misfortune leads you to seek a position in America?"

"It was that preening blackguard Parnell!"

"Charley Parnell?" I blurted, astonished. Any Irishman would be astonished to hear the hero of the nation so maligned.

"You know him?" Fear flickered in his wine-dimmed eyes.

Know him? Lordie yes! Sweet memories crowded into my head of the Fifth Avenue Hotel on a chilly night just after the New Year in 1880, when some Irish friends introduced me to the tall, slender, regal man known as the "Uncrowned King of Ireland." Parnell's hair and beard were dark, though his complexion was so pale that one was anxious for his health. In public his manner was reserved and intelligent, even aloof, except for the dark eyes that blazed with inner fire. In private—well, we'd got on quite well, yes indeed. At the time I thought him the most intriguing man I had ever met, and the most heroic except for President Grant.

Unfortunately, Charley had left New York almost immediately for a tour of the United States to raise funds for the Irish cause, and then he'd returned to England to serve as an Irish member of Parliament. Although he had sent me appreciative notes, even those had ceased in July of 1880.

So I regarded the self-styled Roland Ponsonby with added interest. He clearly knew the Irish hero, because although most people pronounced his name ParNELL, Charley himself preferred PARnell, and Ponsonby had pronounced it correctly. But how could anyone regard dear Charley as a blackguard? I exclaimed, "I cannot claim a close acquaintance with Mr. Parnell. But surely such a famous man would never offend a gentleman like yourself!"

"Offend? Ah, Miss Mooney, 'tis far worse than that! I was at one time the editor of the finest newspapers in Ireland, the *Irishman*, the *Flag of Ireland*, and the *Shamrock*. At the end of 1880 I found myself in very needy circumstances, and thus when Mr. Parnell offered to buy the newspapers from me I naturally entered into negotiations with him."

"He bought your papers?"

"Yes, and at a scandalously low price, because I naturally assumed that I would continue in the post of editor. After all, I have fought long and hard against the British yoke!"

"I have no doubt of that, Mr. Ponsonby. But surely it was one of Mr. Parnell's underlings who erred!"

"No, it was himself! I have proof!" my Father Christmas declared indignantly, fumbling in his portmanteau. I could see a revolver within, and stealthily drew mine from my bustle pocket. But in a moment he straightened, holding only a pair of letters. "You see, Miss Mooney, in his own hand!"

The first letter, dated June 13, 1881, was addressed to "Richard Pigott." The name "Richard Pigott" suited my new acquaintance far better than "Roland Ponsonby," don't you agree?

I slid my revolver back into its pocket and read the letter, which indeed said in part, "We cannot undertake to provide you with permanent employment on the paper; but, on the other hand, we shall want you to undertake for at least two years not to publish any other paper in England or Ireland."

I looked up at Pigott/Ponsonby. "Lordie, two years is a long time!"

"Yes it is." Morosely, he swallowed some more port.

The second letter, dated three days later, refused a further plea for employment. Both letters were certainly from Charley. His letters to me had been signed, "With numerous kisses to my American princess, C.S.P." Pigott's two were signed more formally, "Chas. S. Parnell," but there was no mistaking the distinctive flourish of the initials. I asked, "But sir, why did you not refuse to sell the papers, if the conditions were so cruel?"

"There was illness in my family." His small eyes were sorrowful. "I had no choice. Parnell destroyed my livelihood and left my children destitute!"

"Why, then he is a blackguard indeed!" I murmured.

I know, I know, the uncrowned King should not be called a blackguard. It's also true that the illness Pigott mentioned doubtless had more to do with his bottle than with his family, and Charley surely had had good reasons for his refusal to employ the man. I soothed poor Pigott as best I could and asked, "Did you use the money from the sale to come to America?"

"No, no, that's long gone."

"Why then, you have cleverly discovered another way to earn your passage here!"

He fumbled in his pocket and showed me a ticket to Ireland on tomorrow's Cunard. "They pay my passage, yes, and my expenses. But unless I find evidence, they will never pay me again."

"What evidence, sir?"

"Oh, it is quite confidential," he said doubtfully.

I signalled the waiter to bring him more port. He accepted the bottle and poured himself another glass. "Perhaps one of my friends can help," I said. "It may require money—"

He looked at me hopefully. "Yes, Mr. Houston—uh, they expect it to cost money."

"Well, sir, if you tell me what is required, I will direct you to it." I gave him the earnest winning look I use when I play Lady Macbeth welcoming King Duncan to her castle. "But you must tell me what we are searching for."

Eager now, he said, "Many gentlemen who oppose Irish home rule believe that Parnell inspired the Phoenix Park murders."

I was shocked. "Why, Mr. Parnell had finally convinced Gladstone himself to back the Irish Home Rule bill! Those murders set back progress on the bill for years!"

He was glum again. "Yes, it is hopeless. I know he was not involved, and he was distressed by the murders. And yet Captain O'Shea and—uh, my employers believe that I can find incriminating letters, perhaps on this side of the Atlantic."

He'd pronounced it O'Shee. I said, "And you led the gentlemen to believe you could?"

"Oh, Miss Mooney, I am in great distress for want of money to support myself and my large family. My son is ill. I knew that finding such letters was not likely, but claiming to search for them gave me the opportunity to look for a position in America. But I have failed in that as well. Oh, do not think ill of me!"

"Think ill of you? On the contrary, Mr. Ponsonby! As for incriminating letters—yes, I can find incriminating letters."

He could hardly believe his ears. "Letters that link Parnell with the murders in Phoenix Park?"

"Precisely," I said. "The existence of such letters is well known in certain circles on this side of the Atlantic."

Well, yes, I must admit that the circles in question were quite limited; limited, in fact, to myself. But sometimes a young lady must stretch the truth a bit if she is ever to get her little niece's roof repaired.

Pigott appeared to be impressed. He said nervously, "Certain circles? Clan-na-Gael? Your friends must be extremely violent men, Miss Mooney!" His little eyes shifted about the dining room, as though my ferocious friends might be hiding in the carved mahogany buffet or among the tasseled draperies.

I reassured him, "My friends will be quite reasonable if you can offer them, let us say, three hundred dollars for their incriminating letters. Can you obtain that?"

"Yes, of course," he said, so readily that I wished I had asked for five hundred. Then he aimed his eyeglass at the crimped lace at my neckline and added nervously, "But I don't wish you to endanger yourself, Miss Mooney! I have become extremely fond of you in our short acquaintance. Perhaps I can accompany you, to keep you safe from these violent men."

"Why, thank you, sir, but I assure you, it is quite unnecessary. I need only a note from you to my friends."

"What should I say?"

"Say that they must furnish the letters to you without delay. Say hesitancy is inexcusable."

He nodded and dashed off the note. Spelling was not his strong point, but it would do. I stood, arranged my lilac-flowered flounces, and bowed to him. "Please occupy yourself with obtaining the money. My friend will be at this address after two hours. Don't arrive too early, Mr. Ponsonby."

I hurried from the hotel, caught the Broadway omnibus, and in a short time was in my lodging house in Water Street, pounding at my neighbor Tim McCarthy's door.

"Bridget, duckie, whatever is the matter?" Tim asked as he opened the door. He was a short, wiry fellow with freckles spattered from chin to bald pate. He was a long-time actor and an excellent dancer, but like myself, unemployed at the moment.

"Loan me money for paper and ink, Tim, and get ready to play a Clan-na-Gael man."

"Clan-na-Gael? No, no, Bridget! Those hotheads have no sense of humor, and might not take kindly to impersonation!"

"True, but there's no need for them to know, and you shall have fifty dollars before the day is done."

"Fifty dollars? Let's begin!" Tim gave a little celebratory hop.

In a few moments we were hard at work, I at my table and he before my mirror, rehearsing ferocious grimaces.

Imagine my surprise half an hour later when there was a great crashing about in the hall outside. I peered through the keyhole. "Lordie, Tim, it's Pigott, come too early! Hide everything! Are you ready? He mustn't see me." I dove under the bed.

Tim put on a Simon Legree sneer and opened the door, growling, "I'm Tim McCarthy. Are you here about the letters?"

Then he jetéed aside with great alacrity. I understood the reason when Mr. Pigott burst into the room, drunkenly waving his revolver in the air.

Pigott plunged toward the bronze plush window curtains and ripped one down as he looked behind them. "Where is Miss Mooney? Have you done away with her, you blackguard?"

To see Father Christmas wearing such a scowl was terrifying, and to see his drunken finger trembling on the trigger was worse. Tim attempted to soothe him while jigging about the room like a rabbit pursued by a hound. "All is well, Mr. Pigott!"

Pigott whirled from the window, his revolver surprisingly steady on Tim. "Pigott? Pigott? Who told you that name?"

Tim paled under his freckles and ducked behind an easy chair. Fortunately, when Pigott moved to keep him in range, one striped trouser leg landed next to the bed. With a quick tug on his ankle I pulled the corpulent fellow off balance and snatched the revolver from his hand as he fell. While Pigott struggled to right himself and find his eyeglass, I removed the bullets, then pushed the gun back out from under the bed with a sign to Tim that all was well. Tim nodded, crossed his arms, and resumed his Clan-na-Gael scowl, though he stayed behind the chair.

Pigott regained his feet, picked up his revolver, and pointed it again at Tim. "Answer me, scoundrel! Who told you that name?"

Tim sneered. Pigott squeezed the trigger, to no avail. Tim said, "We have our ways. Now, do you want the letters or not?"

Pigott stared at the useless revolver and pinched his lip nervously as Tim's words slowly penetrated his port-fogged mind. "Letters?"

"On the table," Tim said.

Pigott glanced at the table. Then he leaned forward, adjusted his eyeglass, and read it out loud: " 'January 9, 1882.' "

"Shortly before the Phoenix Park murders," Tim interjected.

Pigott read, " 'What are these fellows waiting for? This inaction is inexcuseable; our best men are in prison and nothing is being done. Let there be an end to this.' And signed 'Chas. S. Parnell.' " Pigott picked up the letter, squinted at it, sniffed it, and looked at Tim with joy on his face. "I can hardly believe it! The gentlemen who hired me are right! Why, this letter could hardly be better if someone had—"

And suddenly his scowl was back. Tim had not had time to hide everything. Now Pigott reached for the nearby sheet of delicate tissue paper and inspected the "Chas. S. Parnell" traced on it. Then he looked at the "Chas. S. Parnell" signature on the letter. "Is it—it is genuine, isn't it? It looks genuine."

Well, of course it did! How could he even question it? My Aunt Mollie had taught me well. As I have noted already, she was an excellent business-woman, and while doing copy work for a bank had learned that a few additional copies of financial papers were often convenient to have. She had imparted the skill to me. Working from the letters Charley had sent me as well as the two I'd hooked from Pigott, it had been simple to create letters that indicated Charley's instigation and approval of the Phoenix Park assassinations.

Tim said, "I am sure your employers will pay handsomely for the letter. Do you have the three hundred dollars?"

Pigott was not as foolish as I thought. He looked carefully at the tissue paper and said, "I cannot pay that much for a forgery."

Tim shrugged. "Then we will sell them directly to Captain O'Shea and Mr. Houston."

"Wait, wait!" Pigott pinched his lip, inspecting the letter.

"Look at the others," Tim suggested.

Pigott looked. They were, of course, as excellent as the first.

"Five hundred for the lot," said Tim. I nudged him from under the bed. "Oh, yes, one other thing. If the letters are questioned, you must claim first that they are genuine, obtained through the secret societies. We like to publicize our strength. If that fails, you must confess that you forged them. If you connect our name to a forgery, our assassins will find you."

It was Pigott's turn to become pale. But what could he do in the face of the violent Clan-na-Gael? He soon agreed to our terms and departed with the letters. As soon as the door closed Tim and I danced a jig and divided the money. I immediately sent the roof-repair money to my friend Hattie Floyd, who cared for my little niece, and hurried to the dressmaker's for the new frock I required for my *Twelfth-Night* audition.

The next day, I saw Mr. Pigott off on the great Cunard steamship, innocently inquiring if he'd got on well with my friend, and expressing pleasure that he had. Our leavetaking required more time than I had anticipated, for a combination of gratitude for helping him obtain the letters and admiration for my fetching neckline had made him quite amorous.

Finally, after promising to write, I stood on the Cunard pier, fluttering my handkerchief in what I thought was good-bye to Mr. Pigott forever.

Oh, you are concerned about Charley? No, no, he was a clever fellow, and who would believe Pigott's word over his? I was sure Charley would suffer only mild inconvenience. And don't you agree that he deserved mild inconvenience for dropping off correspondence with an excellent young lady? Yes indeed.

So I believed we had reached the happy ending: clumsy Mr. Pigott had departed to collect his money from the mysterious Mr. Houston and Captain O'Shea, the young lady was rejoicing in a beautiful new striped silk visiting dress, and the little niece was rejoicing in a new roof. At the final curtain the audience would go home contented.

But, hang it, life is not so orderly. On my way back to Water Street from the Cunard pier, I noticed a throng of excited people. I joined them and saw with horror that a poor bleeding corpse lay in the shadows of an alleyway near my lodging.

It was Tim McCarthy.

I turned away aghast, but not before I had noted that Tim had been shot at close range in the middle of his freckled forehead.

Clan-na-Gael struck swiftly indeed at those who borrowed their dread name without their consent. I had warned Tim to keep our adventure to himself, but he loved to tell a good story, and was as unreliable in his cups as Pigott himself. As I packed my trunks to move to a safer address, I remembered my friend's cheerful capering, and vowed to find the scoundrel who had so cruelly cut him down.

There were few clues, however, and even the newspapers took no notice of Tim McCarthy's death, as he was a mere unemployed actor. Because I feared asking too many questions of Clan-na-Gael, my own investigation languished too. A year later, I was none the wiser. Then, while touring in the West, I read the news that no less a paper than *The Times* of London had printed a facsimile of a letter that purported to show that Charles Stewart Parnell had approved of the Phoenix Park murders. It was one of my letters!

The Times, of course, was a more formidable opponent than Pigott. Reminded of dear Tim's misfortune, and hoping that Charley would not suffer too much, I followed the papers anxiously for the next few weeks. Clever Charley merely laughed at the letter, and he did not even take action against *The Times* for libel. I hoped nothing would come of the matter.

Mr. Pigott had proven much better than Charley at maintaining a correspondence, and in August unexpectedly began to propose marriage to me.

Now that his wife had finally died, he explained, he would observe a decent mourning, but then he was prepared to offer me his heart, his ready-made family, and his worldly possessions. Naturally I declined, as kindly as I could, because poor Mr. Pigott did not seem to realize that his heart and his family were decided drawbacks to any thought of union, and his worldly possessions, which included more than a few debts, were hardly more attractive. But, with fond memories of his five hundred dollars and of my niece's sound roof, I declined very politely each time he asked, explaining that I was occupied with my stage appearances and could not yet come to England.

Then Charley's situation took a turn for the worse. Despite his contempt for the letters, *The Times* was unrelenting in its accusations. More of the forged letters were published, and the affair became serious when Charley's enemies in Parliament appointed a Special Commission to investigate his connections with the Phoenix Park murders and with other crimes. The handsome hero had already been jailed once, and I was sorry to be the cause of further persecution. So when our fine production of *Camille* closed because of unfair competition from Buffalo Bill's Wild West show, and I returned to my room to find yet another letter from Pigott, I was ready to consider it. Pigott renewed the offer of his hand, stated that his motherless children would adore me, and added that he would be delighted for me to continue my interest in the stage. In fact, he said, he knew the manager of the Alhambra, and could easily arrange an engagement for me there. And he had saved up fifty pounds to help me with expenses if I came.

He also enclosed a steamship ticket to London.

I sat for a long time, tapping the ticket against my teeth.

I had never been to London, but it seemed to me a delightful prospect to play Shakespeare in the land of my illustrious tutor Mrs. Fanny Kemble and of my dear friend Mrs. Langtry.

And surely in London plays did not have to close because of competition from Wild West shows.

My friend Hattie in St. Louis was envious, but I told her I was sure I would prosper and could soon send for her and my little niece. I packed my best frocks and costumes and boarded the great ship, visions of applause from posh British audiences and guineas from posh British managers dancing in my head.

We disembarked at the splendid new Tilbury Docks, and I took a hansom cab to the address in Wardour Street that Pigott had sent. When the driver announced that we had arrived, I began to have misgivings, for the address was that of a public house. But as it appeared to be of the better class, I paid the driver and entered.

A quantity of cigar smoke enhanced the genteel twilight character of the establishment. A servant appeared, a lively-eyed woman with broadening hips and neatly coiffed hair, who, in answer to my enquiry, said, "Mr. Pigott is dining with Captain O'Shea, mum." She gestured toward a table in the far corner where I could dimly make out a handsome swell. His companion had his back to me, but even in the haze of smoke I recognized Mr. Pigott's silvery hair and rotund figure. I followed the servant to the table.

"Why, Caroline, whom have you brought us?" asked the handsome dandy in an elegant British accent. Caroline bobbed a curtsy to him with a simper that told me the two knew each other well.

Pigott exclaimed, "Miss Mooney!" He bounced up to welcome me, and I had to deflect his embrace with my parasol. Full of enthusiasm, he introduced me to handsome Captain O'Shea, a member of Parliament for Ireland. The captain was of middle age, with fine clothing, a fine mustache, and a discontented air. Then Pigott hurried after Caroline to bring me something to drink.

Captain O'Shea said, "My dear Miss Mooney, how pleasant that you are visiting our sceptered isle."

"I am honored to be visiting the land of Shakespeare," I replied. "But is it true that you are a member of Parliament for Ireland?"

"Indeed it is true. I may add that I have the ear of Gladstone himself."

"And naturally you have the ear of Mr. Parnell?"

His handsome visage darkened. "Ah, Parnell, that swine!"

"Why, sir, I thought that Mr. Parnell was your leader!"

"A leader about to go down in ignominy, because of the letters your friends found for us." Captain O'Shea looked gleeful at the prospect. "The newspapers are full of revelations about the Phoenix Park crimes, and a Special Commission of Parliament will begin examining witnesses next month."

I was alarmed. "Sir, I will not be required to give evidence, will I?"

"No, no, don't fret," said the captain benevolently. "Mr. Pigott will give any necessary evidence, correct, Pigott?"

"But sir, Mr. Houston promised me I would never be questioned," said Pigott, putting down our drinks.

"Well, Mr. Houston is too young to realize how much evidence is needed to bring down a scoundrel like Parnell!" said O'Shea.

Pigott nodded morosely. "He is young indeed. Captain O'Shea, don't you agree that, if I must give evidence before a Special Commission, I am justified in requesting additional remuneration?"

O'Shea laughed. "Come, Pigott, old fellow! You are a man of the world. You know that if one does something politically useful, one may have to give evidence."

I was becoming apprehensive about Pigott's request for money. "Mr. Pigott," I said, "it would be very agreeable if you would give me the money for expenses that you promised me, as I will soon need it."

Pigott pinched his lip. "Well, ah, that is—dear creature, I am short of funds just now. But Captain O'Shea has agreed to provide us with a meal, and I have made arrangements for you to stay the night in the Anderton Hotel in Fleet Street."

"And the funds you promised me?"

"I will not rest easy until they are in your pretty hands!"

Well, this was not heartening news, but I consoled myself with thoughts of my upcoming London debut on the stage of the Alhambra Theatre, and turned to other topics. "Captain O'Shea, Mr. Pigott has told me that your aunt is a kind lady of considerable means. I trust that she is in good health?"

"Yes!" snapped O'Shea. "Who's been telling you otherwise?" He glared at Pigott.

"Why, no one, sir! I am only just arrived from America!"

He relaxed, but retained his discontented air. "The old lady is living quite a long time, you see," he said. "She has always favored my wife Katie, who has lived near her in Eltham and cared for her for many years. But my wife's relatives are jealous, and attempt to drive wedges between Aunt Ben and Katie."

"That is sad news indeed," I said. "Bitterness within families is always unfortunate."

He shot me a suspicious glance before he continued. "When Aunt Ben understood their evil plans, she changed her will to favor Katie. So the relatives began to petition the Masters in Lunacy to commit her to an asylum."

"Oh dear!" My hand flew to my mouth in dismay. Could it be that Captain O'Shea's wealth was in jeopardy, and therefore Pigott's, and therefore mine? I said, "If she is judged a lunatic, I suppose the family may overturn the will and Katie will lose the money?"

"Quite." Captain O'Shea leaned back with a satisfied air. "But you see, dear Miss Mooney, as a Member of Parliament I have come to know Gladstone well, and Gladstone's personal physician has certified that, while elderly, Aunt Ben is of sound mind."

"Why, that is excellent news!" I exclaimed.

Captain O'Shea waved at the servant. "Caroline, you minx, bring us some beef stew!"

"Yes sir!" She took down some bowls.

He said, "Excellent woman. Caroline was once our cook in West Brighton. "Now, Miss Mooney, I look forward to seeing you at the Alhambra. What is your specialty?"

"My specialty?"

"On the stage."

"Why, as I said before, I admire Shakespeare. I play Viola, Lady Macbeth, Rosalind—"

I broke off because Captain O'Shea was shaking his head with amusement. "No, no, my dear! We are talking about the Alhambra! It's a music hall!"

"A music hall?" I gasped in horror.

"Can you sing, or dance? I suppose you might recite Lady Macbeth if you make it comical. What do you think, Pigott?"

I was glaring at my would-be Saint Nicholas. He said nervously, "The Alhambra does excellent shows, Miss Mooney!"

Just then Caroline arrived with our steaming bowls of beef stew. "For the handsomest of MP's," she said fetchingly.

O'Shea kissed her rough hand. "Thank you, my mouse."

Caroline turned away, tucking a pound note into her bodice, and her well-feigned look of affection gave way to one of weariness. I liked her better, yes indeed.

Captain O'Shea had turned back to my problem. "Miss Mooney, surely you understand England has a sufficient number of Shakespearean actresses. You couldn't have thought that Mr. Pigott here has enough influence to promise you a role in Shakespeare, in London!"

"Whyever not?" I said, casting a disdainful glance at the squirming Pigott. "He had enough influence to find letters that incriminate Mr. Parnell, didn't he? At great cost to those who provided the letters!"

"Oh, dear Miss Mooney, it is terrible indeed, the end that came to our mutual friend Tim McCarthy!" Pigott said with a stricken look. "Clan-na-Gael are extreme men, and it is difficult to do business with them."

Not half as difficult as it was to do business with Mr. Pigott, don't you agree? Performing in a music hall, indeed! And no expense money in sight! I realized how foolish I had been to trust a man who would betray the hero of the Irish nation. Wise old Shakespeare had a phrase for Pigott: a most toad-spotted traitor! I wanted to toss the bowl of boiling stew right into that Father Christmas face.

But in my head, Aunt Mollie the businesswoman was yammering away, telling me that I shouldn't burn my bridges, that I must at least scoop up the crumbs that were offered. So I ate the stew instead of hurling it, slipped a chunk of bread into my bustle pocket for supper, and accepted the room in the Anderton Hotel.

I allowed Pigott to bring my trunks there, then, pleading exhaustion, dismissed him. When he had gone I slipped out and found my way to the Alhambra Music Hall.

It was a splendid theatre, yes indeed. Situated on Leicester Square, it was built in the Saracenic fashion, with a great dome and Moorish arches ringing the vast auditorium. It was built of the best fireproof materials, because of the conflagration it had suffered in 1882. The crowd was large and enthusiastic, due in part to the bars fitted into many snug corners of the building. If Pigott's taste ran to music halls rather than Shakespeare, he had indeed offered me an excellent opportunity.

But as I watched the performance my heart sank. The artistes were highly skilled. What could I do that was not already being performed on this stage? The poetic turns were excellent, so my Shakespeare would not be needed. There were skilled step-dancers, singers of jolly political songs and of risqué songs, tumblers, equestrians. I had hopes of doing an Irish song but there were two Irish turns already. I do a most amusing impersonation of Lillie Langtry trying to play Rosalind; but as I feared I might have to apply to dear Lillie for funds, it seemed advisable to avoid any actions that might upset her.

I returned to the Anderton Hotel, having much to consider that night.

One thing I considered was that Mr. Pigott had been quite lavish in his sympathy for dear Tim's death. Now, I had never mentioned Tim's death in my letters to Pigott, thinking it too depressing a subject for a man already fearful of Clan-na-Gael. I did not wish him to hesitate if I needed to sell him another letter. And of course the newspapers that recorded every cough of the wealthy and powerful had ignored my friend's demise. How, then, could Pigott have known of it?

I remembered Pigott's revolver and realized I had been searching for dear Tim's murderer on the wrong side of the ocean.

The next morning I rose full of resolve, donned my fine new visiting dress striped in rose, green, and brown and trimmed with Irish guipure lace, and walked forth into the warm August day. It took some time to find Charley, but I learned at last that he was lunching at the Cannon Street Hotel. I lurked outside and when he emerged and climbed into a carriage, I leaped into the next hansom and asked the driver to follow him. We whirled through crowded Holborn and Oxford Streets to Portland Place and Marylebone Road. He alighted at last in a quiet street of old-fashioned Georgian houses known as York Terrace. I paid my driver and followed.

There was no butler. The parlormaid seemed surprised to see a caller, but after a brief hesitation took my card and disappeared, closing a thick door behind her and leaving me to sit in the hall looking at the egg-and-dart moldings of the ceiling. The parlormaid's voice sounded lower through the door, and I could not make out her words. I thought I heard a door slam. At last the parlormaid returned to show me into the room.

As always, Charley was delightful to look upon. He was tall, lean, and pale as ever, but his smile was contented as he greeted me. Then suddenly his brown eyes flashed and he stared at me with burning intensity. "Why—why, it's Bridget!"

"Yes, Charley," I said demurely, and was surprised to see him step back in confusion. I explained, "In view of our long friendship, I come with news about the letters published in *The Times*."

"Yes, yes, so you said in the note." He tapped it with his long, well-shaped fingers. "But however did you find me?"

"I followed you from the Cannon Street Hotel."

"Ah." He nodded. "You Americans are quite resourceful. Do others know I am here?"

Well, when a famed and handsome man is taking pains to discover if he is alone with a lady, she cannot help but be pleased at her prospects. I said, "I came alone, and told no one, because what I have to impart to you is a very private matter."

"Excellent!" He was clearly pleased. "And are you in good health, Bridget?"

"Why, yes, thank you, although I find myself in pecuniary difficulties at the moment."

"I see. Well, here's ten pounds. I hope you enjoy your stay in London." And he reached for the bell-pull to call the maid.

I took the proffered note, but held up my hand in protest. "Charley, wait! I must tell you about the letters!"

"Oh, yes. What about them?" he asked kindly.

"Well, they are forgeries."

"Of course! I know I didn't write them. But there is no sense fighting it. It will only fan the controversy."

"But isn't your career in danger?"

"Yes, but how can we prove they are forgeries before a Special Commission of Parliament? They have accumulated so much false information that our Irish Home Rule bill is threatened, as is Mr. Gladstone's government, because he has backed our bill."

"Why, I am pleased that my information may help save you, and the Home Rule bill, and Mr. Gladstone's government. But you must promise never to mention my name."

"Secrecy will be observed," he said, so easily I suspected that he thought my information would be worthless.

"First, you should subpoena Mr. Richard Pigott, for he forged the letters," I said.

"Pigott? That poor old drunkard? Come, Bridget, it must be someone of higher rank!"

"No sir, it is Pigott. It might be that he is in someone's employ, but I can say nothing of that."

I know, I know, perhaps I should have mentioned Mr. Houston or Captain O'Shea, but I find it more profitable on the whole to avoid offending gentlemen whose wives have rich aunts. Besides, neither of them had shot dear Tim McCarthy.

Charley appeared to be worried about another problem. "But even if it is Pigott, we still cannot prove it."

"Charley, you purchased his newspapers a few years ago."

"Yes. What of it?"

"Well, if you look at the letters you wrote to him at the time, you will see phrases that are repeated in the forged letters."

"Indeed!" Charley's delightful eyes lit up. "I will look at my copies! You are right, that would go far to prove that they are forgeries. But how do you know all this?"

"An American I know, who must remain nameless, assisted him in this work. Charley, there is more."

"More?"

"Mr. Pigott is not very skilled at spelling."

"What of it? He is not very skilled at anything."

"Consider asking him to write the words 'hesitancy' and 'inexcusable' before the Special Commission, and then compare his misspellings to the misspellings in the forged letter."

The door to the back room burst open and a small woman with dark Italian good looks, large passionate eyes, and a rose in her bodice hurried in. For an instant I thought she was a tart, but her elegant silk faille dress and her well-bred voice spoke of the upper classes. One of Charley's sisters, perhaps. With a pretty smile, she exclaimed, "Charley, this is splendid! I must thank this delightful lady, who has come from America to help you."

I realized that the voice I had earlier taken for the parlormaid's had in fact been this lady's, who had left the room and hidden before my entrance. I wondered why.

Charley smiled, caught her hand in his, and said, "Katie, this is Miss Bridget Mooney, a kind American friend. Bridget, this is—yes, let me say my true wife, Katharine."

"Oh, Charley, you shouldn't!" she exclaimed, looking at him in distress.

"Bridget will keep our secret, Queenie," he said fondly, patting her hand, which he still held. "And she has helped me find a defense against the lies in *The Times*."

"Oh, that is true! Thank you! And do call me Katie!"

"I shall," I replied, hiding my indignation behind my sweetest smile. "And you must call me Bridget. But I had not heard of your marriage! May I congratulate you?"

"Thank you," said Charley, exchanging a merry glance with Katie. "But there is good reason you have not heard, Bridget. We beg you to keep silence. Our hearts are pledged, but there are many reasons that we cannot yet become man and wife in public."

"Of course. I won't speak of it," I promised.

"Thank you," Katie said with her charming smile. "It is very difficult. For eight years, we have kept our secret. But it is so good of you to give us weapons to use against the forger and *The Times*. Dear Mr. Gladstone will be pleased as well!"

She and Charley beamed at each other. Having seen enough of these turtledoves, I took my leave. They heaped more gratitude upon me and then called for Esther, who showed me to the door and handed me my parasol.

"Thank you," I said, handing her a coin. "Esther, have you worked here many years?"

"Why, no, mum, Mrs. O'Shea only rented this house in March of last year. And they have other houses, in Eltham and Brockley."

I stood thunderstruck. Eltham. And she'd said "O'Shee." I murmured, "I see. Yes, I see. Thank you, Esther."

Well, did you ever hear of such a cad as Charley? It was truly reprehensible to tantalize a young lady with a delightful evening at the Fifth Avenue Hotel, and to write her lovely sweet notes, and then to forget it all when a dark-haired temptress with a rose in her bodice, a husband, and a rich aunt appeared! He'd called me a princess; he called her "Queenie!" A most toad-spotted traitor, was Charley!

Worst of all, when I kindly reappeared with the information that would save his career, the Irish cause, and the British Government from the attacks of *The Times*, he had cut me off with a mere ten pounds!

What a cad!

I turned into the verdant acres of nearby Regent's Park, pondering what to do.

Should I forge another letter, one without the tell-tale handwriting and misspellings that pointed to Pigott? No, that would not succeed now. With the information I had foolishly given Charley, even genuine letters would be suspect, and Pigott's career would be destroyed; and when I thought of dear Tim's dead freckled face I remembered how much I wanted to destroy Pigott.

But how could I bring down Charley too?

I crossed a bridge over an arm of a pretty lake.

Should I tell Captain O'Shea that Charley and Mrs. O'Shea were living as man and wife? No; on reflection I realized that he already knew. His bitterness against the leader of his own party, and his delight in the thought that Charley's career was about to be ruined, indicated that he knew. But why didn't the captain divorce his adulterous wife, naming Parnell as the guilty party, and ruin Charley's career in that manner? I realized that the captain would happily be rid of Katie, but not of her rich aunt. Captain O'Shea had to remain married or suffer financial ruin.

A well-tended garden filled with late-summer blooms attracted me. A sign said it was in the care of the Royal Botanic Society.

Should I tell the rich aunt about Katie's sinful ways? No; I realized that it would be difficult to make her believe me. Her own relatives, jealous of Katie, had been unable to convince the aunt that her favorite niece did not deserve her support. And even if I succeeded in proving it to her, a rupture with the aunt would hurt not only Katie and Charley, but also Captain O'Shea and all those he supported, such as Pigott and myself.

It seemed hopeless; but at last, amid the fragrant breezes of the Royal Botanic Society's rose garden, I worked out the answer.

It took me a month to arrange everything, and a difficult month it was, because Pigott had no money, dear Lillie Langtry was not available, my illustrious but aged tutor Mrs. Fanny Kemble saw no one, and even the generous

Captain O'Shea was home suffering from gout. I soon had to leave the hotel in Fleet Street and take up cheap lodgings in Whitechapel, a particularly unpleasant place that September, very nearly worse than Pigott's suggestion that I go with him to Ireland.

I told Pigott, "No, dear sir, things are far too unsettled for me to consider marriage to you. But I would like to make one observation, and that is that Captain O'Shea is a true gentleman, worth three of your other employers."

"But he won't even be seen with me, only in dark corners of that public house. And he said I must give evidence, while the others promised it would not be necessary!"

"And who told the truth?" I asked.

Pigott looked unhappily at the subpoena with which he had just been served. "The captain was right," he admitted. "Oh, do marry me, Miss Mooney! My life is in need of some joy!"

"That is not possible just now," I said kindly. "Now, of course the captain was right. He is as true a man as I have ever seen, Mr. Pigott, and if you ever need assistance, turn to him."

"But if I give evidence, they may require me to mention the captain's name! He will be angry with me then!"

"Do be sensible, Mr. Pigott! To begin with, they cannot prove that the letters are forgeries. Could you prove it?"

"No. Only your friend Tim McCarthy could have proven it," he said, cheering up.

"And poor Tim is gone, rest his soul," I reminded him—as though he needed reminding. "So there is no difficulty. And even if difficulties arise, your course of action is clear."

"It is?"

"Of course it is! You will explain how Mr. Houston and *The Times* paid you, but do not mention good Captain O'Shea. Gratitude will then bind him to you, and he will arrange a way out of the dilemma for you."

"Yes, yes, he would do that for me!" Pigott exclaimed. "One way or the other, it will come right."

He little knew how truly he spoke.

I made further arrangements. When Captain O'Shea's gout improved, he reappeared at the public house in Wardour Street. He was surprised when the lively Caroline led me to his table. "Why, how delightful to see you, Miss Mooney! It has been some time, because I have been ill, and there have been demands on my time from my business in Madrid. But pray, where is your fiancé?"

"Sir, we are not engaged. Mr. Pigott tends to exaggerate."

"That he does. Caroline, my minx, bring us some ale," said the good captain. With his mustache and twinkling eyes, he was a most appealing fellow, even if a bit gouty. I didn't see why the greedy Katie O'Shea needed Charley as well.

But when he turned back with that discontented air, I could see that a lady might weary of him. For now, however, I hoped he would be my ally. I said, "Mr. Pigott has gone to Ireland. I must admit, sir, I am sorely disappointed in him."

"What has the rascal done now?" He was twinkling at me now. As Caroline set down our ale, she gave me a considering glance.

"Nothing as yet, sir, but this subpoena has made the man mad."

Captain O'Shea looked alarmed. "He carries a revolver, I know. Is he dangerous?"

"Yes, because he is a coward at heart. The danger now is not from his revolver; it is from what he may tell the Special Commission."

"Why, all he has to do is tell how he obtained the letters," said the captain. "They are so incriminating that Parnell will fall."

"Yes, but you see, Captain, I fear that Mr. Pigott is so weak that under cross-examination he may attempt to shift the attack to his betters."

Captain O'Shea looked worried. "Well, it's true I would prefer not to be mentioned," he said.

"Of course. You have done well to keep the scandal from your wife's aunt. But if it comes out that you helped pay for evidence that could ruin Mr. Parnell, you can no longer expect the newspapers to remain quiet. Katie's aunt will be sure to hear."

Captain O'Shea glared at his ale and said, "It's true. But we must let him testify! The Special Commission needs his proof that the charges against Parnell are sound."

"Why don't you promise Pigott you'll help him escape if necessary? Then if he appears distressed enough to betray anyone, it won't be you, and you can spirit him away before he does too much damage."

O'Shea nodded slowly. "He could be silenced."

Well, I couldn't have phrased it better myself. I nodded. "He could, but not until he has helped expose Mr. Parnell's perfidy."

"True. Oh, how I wish there were an easier way to bring down Parnell! Mr. Gladstone and I favor Home Rule for Ireland, you know. But Parnell's fall carries some risk to the Home Rule bill, and thus to Gladstone and me."

"I trust that Mr. Gladstone will keep Parnell at arm's length. As for bringing him down—well, sir, I realize that it is your kind consideration for your wife's dear aunt that stays you from divorcing the faithless Katie and bringing down Mr. Parnell in that manner. It is an eternal credit to you."

"Yes." O'Shea succeeded in looking both melancholy and proud at the same time. "After Aunt Ben dies, I can divorce Katie. But I fear I will lose the case even so. You see, Parnell is such a weasel, he will claim I abandoned Katie long before he began his perfidious visits to her, and that we were wed in name only. Then Katie will win the action."

"Even so, sir, you can ensure that whether you win or not, Mr. Parnell will lose."

"How?" he asked eagerly.

"You say that Caroline was your cook once?"

"Yes, in West Brighton. She was one who told me that Mr. Parnell was visiting Katie in secret."

"Excellent. Call her to the table, and I will explain."

When things were arranged, Captain O'Shea gratefully gave me enough money for my passage home.

Back in America, I followed the newspapers with great interest. Perhaps you recall how things fell out. In February of 1889, the Special Commission at last called for testimony from Mr. Richard Pigott, who stated that the letters had been owned by an unnamed source in America, and spun quite an interesting tale of secret societies in Paris and New York. The Special Commission was impressed, until Parnell's counsel rose to cross-examine Pigott, and before beginning, asked him to write the words "hesitancy" and "inexcusable." Of course he misspelled them "hesitency" and "inexcuseable." As the testimony went on, and phrases from *The Times*'s letters were seen to be copied from phrases Charley had written to Pigott when buying the papers, the forgeries became glaringly apparent, as did Pigott's guilt.

After the second day of cross-examination, the poor old fellow disappeared from his hotel room. His flight removed all doubt. Charley was innocent.

A week later, news came from Madrid that a traveler staying at the Hotel des Ambassadeurs had died while police were trying to arrest him. The traveler had given the name Roland Ponsonby.

The Madrid police said he had taken a revolver from his portmanteau and shot himself; but I knew that Captain O'Shea, still eager to keep his name out of the affair, was in Madrid on business that same day.

When Ponsonby was identified as Pigott, Charley returned to Parliament for the most triumphant year of his career. Gladstone embraced him, and the

Home Rule bill seemed assured.

Then, in May, rich Aunt Ben died at last. There was much dispute about the will in the courts, and O'Shea finally brought a divorce action against his wife and Charley. The two did not bother to contest it, partly because Aunt Ben was now dead, and partly, I'm sure, because Charley thought O'Shea would not call witnesses if unopposed, and the divorce would be granted quietly and unobtrusively, thus reducing the damage to his soaring career.

But to Charley's surprise, O'Shea did call witnesses—chiefly the servants I myself had instructed. The best was Caroline, who said that while she was the O'Shea's cook in West Brighton, Parnell frequently slept at the house when the captain was away. Several times, when Captain O'Shea arrived home unexpectedly, Charley had slipped out onto the balcony, slid down the rope fire-escape (that was my invention), and then a few minutes later had rung the front door-bell and asked to see Captain O'Shea.

Just as I'd expected, the absurd idea of dignified, aloof Charley scrambling monkey-like down the rope convulsed British and Irish alike. Columnists joked about him, cartoonists ridiculed him. Very soon, a little toy model of a Brighton house was on sale in the market-stalls, complete with a tiny Parnell dangling from the fire-escape. And those in my profession reenacted it gleefully in music halls like the Alhambra.

The Uncrowned King of Ireland had been shot at, jailed by his enemies, insulted, and accused of the Phoenix Park crimes. From these vicissitudes, he had emerged stronger than ever. But now he could not conquer the waves of malicious laughter about a nonexistent fire escape.

Charley fell. Gladstone's government fell. The Irish people did not get their own nation for another thirty years. I was sorry about that. But don't you think it was partly their own fault for electing a most toad-spotted traitor? Yes indeed.

FROM BRIDGET MOONEY'S SCRAPBOOK

THE DAILY TELEGRAPH
SATURDAY, MARCH 2, 1889

SUPPOSED SUICIDE OF PIGOTT.
(Reuter's Agency)

MADRID, March 1.

This afternoon the police went to the Hôtel des Ambassadeurs for the purpose of arresting an Englishman who had arrived there, and who gave the name of Roland Ponsonby.

The officers entered his room and took him into custody, but, taking advantage of a moment when the attention of the custodians was diverted, the man drew a revolver and shot himself in the head. Death was instantaneous. The cause of the arrest is not stated, but it is believed that it was effected under an extradition warrant.

MADRID, March 1 (11:30 p.m.)

It is believed that the so-called Roland Ponsonby was no other than Mr. Richard Pigott.

THE TIMES
Monday November 17, 1890

Caroline Pethers, examined by Mr. Coward, said,—Mr. Parnell never slept in the house when Captain O'Shea was at home, but he did so frequently when Captain O'Shea was away. He slept in a room, used by the captain as a dressing-room, on the third floor.

On one occasion do you remember Captain O'Shea calling when Mr. Parnell was in the drawing-room? Yes; I went up to light the gas. The door was locked. I heard persons in the room, but I could not get in. Mrs. O'Shea said it did not matter about the gas. Captain O'Shea rang the front door bell. My husband answered it. Captain O'Shea went into the dining-room, and then went upstairs, and ten minutes after that Mr. Parnell rang the front door bell and asked to see Captain O'Shea. (Laughter.)

Could he have gone down by the stairs?— No. There was a balcony outside the drawing-room. There were two rope fire-escapes from the window. This happened three or four times.

THE TIMES
Tuesday, November 18, 1890

The *Dundee Advertiser* says:—"The spectacle of Mr. Parnell sneaking in at back doors and out of windows and sliding down fire escapes is contemptible and pitiable. He was the trusted leader of a nation, and he has been false to his trust. Whatever his colleagues and the Irish people may decide about him, his career is closed."

NEW YORK, Nov. 17.

Mr. Eugene Kelly, a prominent New York Irishman and treasurer of the fund which is being raised by the Irish delegates, has declared that, should Mr. Parnell be proved guilty of the charges brought against him by Captain O'Shea, neither the clergy nor laity in America would have anything more to do with him.—*Reuter*

PUT OUT THE LIGHT; or,
The Napoleon of Science

Proper ladies don't frequent low places like Danny Doyle's. But sometimes a girl has reason to lie low for a while, and Danny is known to keep mum when Pinkerton men come asking questions about his clientele. So I was having a bite of Danny's watery Irish stew in a dark corner of his establishment, glumly wondering if my shrunken resources would allow me to leave New York for a short time, since I could not appear on stage even though I'd been hired to play Desdemona. The problem was that the florid gentleman who had taken me to Delmonico's the night before had not been quite as thoroughly inebriated as I'd believed, and was making a silly fuss about the disappearance of his watch and the diamond-studded gold ring he wore on his little finger. He'd posted a Pinkerton man at the stage door, and another was asking questions of all the pawnbrokers and even of my landlady.

"Bridget! Lordy, it's Bridget Mooney!" caroled a happy voice.

I squinted into the smoky dimness and exclaimed, "Mary Ann! What a surprise!"

"Ain't it, though! It must be ten years since I saw you!" She plumped herself down at my table. Mary Ann was even taller than I, with thick hair and sparkling eyes, though her nose was turning rather red from overindulgence in Danny's cheap Irish whiskey, and I could tell from her unfashionable gown that she had not come up in the world as far as I. She said, "My, Bridget, it all comes back! We had good times in those days with Al and his boys, didn't we?"

Well, I'm bound to admit that we had. Al was a most uncommonly bright fellow, of course, and generous-hearted whenever he wasn't short on cash. He loved the theatre and a good lark, and when he and his men built a new dynamo with a pair of four-foot-long upthrust wire-wrapped columns, he'd named it the "Long-legged Mary Ann."

Oh, I know, I know, proper ladies don't know such vulgar terms. But Al Edison was a salty sort, and that dynamo had been crucial to the success of his famous electric light. So don't you think he was doing my tall friend a great honor? Yes indeed. He never named anything after his wives.

Mary Ann was eyeing my visiting dress, striped in rose, green, and brown, and trimmed with black velvet and white guipure lace. She said, "I suppose you're above such things now."

Indeed I was—though if I couldn't think of a way past the Pinkertons, I might soon be driven to desperate measures. I said, "I'm not in that line of work anymore. But I hear Al's doing well now."

"Oh, yes! He has a grand new place in New Jersey. West Orange. Much bigger than the old lab, and he's hiring heaps of men to work for him."

"Well, he's a clever fellow. Is it true that he has a new wife?"

"Little Mina, yes. And a baby. It makes no matter. You know Al, working all the time. Though I hear he's going to take her to the Paris Exposition, and he bought her a grand new mansion called Glenmont. It's just up the hill from his lab, so he can walk to work. Not that he walks back home often." She winked at me. "He still works night and day."

"He probably always will." That had struck me about Al when I'd become acquainted with him ten years before. He loved his work almost as much as we theatre people love ours, and toiled day and night on his projects. Mary Ann and the rest of us could distract him only briefly. "So Al's rich now?" I asked.

"Oh, yes! Though I do hear he has lots of creditors."

"Most rich people do," I explained. "That's one way to become rich, to tell people you'll do something splendid and then borrow money from them."

We had a nice long gabble about rich people we'd known. But after Mary Ann left me, I found myself thinking again of Al, and of how far West Orange was from where the Pinkerton men were searching. And I reckoned the Paris Exposition was even farther.

But I didn't want to approach him in Mary Ann's line of work, because I needed more than a night's shelter from the Pinkertons.

At the rag-pickers I found a shabby black jacket and trousers that fit me, and a man's shirt that had seen better days, being frayed along the edges. I bound up my hair under a cloth cap, tucked my Colt and other special possessions into a knapsack, and boarded the Delaware, Lackawanna and Western Railroad for New Jersey.

Well, of course the clothes weren't very becoming! But young men get better wages than young ladies. And I'd played Portia, and knew how to wear my dagger with the braver grace, and turn two mincing steps into a manly stride, and speak of frays like a fine bragging youth. And don't you reckon a girl's entitled to a disguise every now and then to slip past the

Pinkertons, and to avoid stirring up unpleasant memories—well, unmentionable memories—in the mind of our nation's greatest inventor?

Glenmont was as splendid a place as ever I'd seen, with gables and verandas, stained-glass windows and a conservatory, grand Queen Anne chimneys and a widow's walk on top. The man who built it had embezzled the money from Arnold Constable Inc. When he went to prison, he'd sold it to Edison. Of course, he was a wicked sinful man, but I'm bound to admit he had a pretty taste. The great house sat on a hill amidst lawns and acres of woods, and far across the valley one could see New York City.

But my business lay in the laboratory. I inquired the way of a gardener working on the grounds of Glenmont. He said, "You don't want to go to that laboratory, sir!"

"Why not?"

He looked around and then bent closer. He was a small man with a hawk nose and thin unkempt hair. "That place is full of evil spirits," he informed me, jerking his thumb at an enormous brick building at the foot of the hill. "There's flashes and booms, and glimmerings and groanings, and poor dead creatures carried out by night. Evil spirits, or my name isn't Silas Bell!"

I looked at the brick building he'd indicated. "But hang it, everyone knows that Mr. Edison is doing splendid work!"

"They call him the Wizard of Menlo Park," he reminded me, as though that were proof. "Now, Miz Mina, she's a good churchgoing lady. But Mr. Thomas, he's doing Satan's work. Somebody should stop him, they should."

The laboratory was as grand as the house. It was three stories high, with several smaller buildings lined up on the north side and a tall picket fence marching around the whole. It had a water tower on the roof and a watchman who was in the process of ejecting a man from the building.

"How many times do we have to tell you, Boggs? You're to see Mr. Edison's secretary, Mr. Tate," said the watchman.

"I've seen Mr. Tate eight times, and still no money!" The visitor added an oath and shook his fist at the watchman, and I thought it prudent to shrink back against the outside of the picket fence, so as not to be in the gentlemen's way if they required more room. "It's Mr. Edison I have to see!"

"Mr. Tate," repeated the watchman firmly.

The angry visitor was a tall, burly man with worn blunt hands and a cloth cap like mine. He pointed a finger at the great building. "Two years ago, I built that! And still not paid!"

The watchman was even taller and burlier, and carried a staff besides.

"Now, Mr. Boggs, we've discussed this before," he said in a reasonable tone, lifting the staff. "You know that Mr. Edison is not to be disturbed at work."

Mr. Boggs fell to cursing in a manner so vulgar that I shan't inflict it upon your ears. The watchman forced him out through the gate at last and he stormed away. I approached respectfully and explained that I was applying for work. "See Mr. Tate," said the watchman, and let me pass.

Inside, a placard informed me that Mr. Edison was so occupied with his work that he was constrained to deny himself to visitors. Well, that's not very hospitable, is it? I ignored the placard and walked in with manly stride. I passed a handsome library with a marquetry floor, Smyrna rugs, and bookshelves in alcoves, all brilliantly lit by electric lights, and approached the laboratory.

And wasn't it grand, far more splendid than Menlo Park! Al was doing well, yes indeed! It was a vast reeking humming space filled with noisy mechanical contraptions and peculiar smells. It was lit by the famous glowing lamps of Al's invention. Men, perhaps fifty of them, worked at the contraptions, alone or in small groups, and occasional bursts of laughter could be heard above the hums and clanks. I saw Al standing near the wall, coughing dreadfully, and after a moment's hesitation I approached him. "Sir, please, I want to work here."

"Work?" He turned toward me.

"Oh, I'm sorry, sir," I corrected myself. Now that he'd moved the handkerchief from his face I could see that he wasn't Al at all. His height and manner of carrying himself were similar, and in the dimness I'd mistaken his blond hair for Al's gray. But he was much younger than Al, and much more handsome and blue-eyed.

"Who are you, lad?" He smiled in a drowsy way and sat down on a cot.

"I'm Mike O'Rourke, and I need work, sir." I often borrow my Uncle Mike's name. He borrowed heaps of things from Aunt Mollie and me.

"And I'm Jesse Cheever." He paused to cough and sniff from a little bottle he held. "And I think if you speak to Tate you'll find that we need bottle-washers. We certainly need them in the chemistry department."

Well, I'm bound to admit I have a weakness for handsome men named Jesse, troublesome though they all turn out to be. This one's drowsy blue eyes were quite fetching, and I began to regret my masculine disguise. I smiled at him. "Pleased to make your acquaintance, Mr. Cheever. Can you tell me where to find Mr. Tate?"

He looked around the huge machine shop, frowned, and elbowed a man sleeping on the cot. "Wake up, Lem Symington."

"What is it, Jesse?"

"Where is—" Jesse Cheever interrupted himself with a fit of coughing.

I asked, "Mr. Cheever, sir, would you like a lozenge for your cough?" Those of us in the theatrical trade always keep a supply of throat remedies to hand.

"Dear me, no, Mike O'Rourke! It's not that sort of cough!" He laughed and coughed again.

Lem Symington had amber eyes as shiny as a cat's and hair that stuck out like a scrub-brush from under his hat. He wore a white shirt and dark waist-coat like Jesse's. He sat up on the cot and indicated a closed door nearby. "He's put some of us muckers to work producing chlorine gas," he told me. "It's poison, you know. If it seeps out of its containers it's very distressing to the lungs."

Jesse Cheever sniffed at his bottle again and explained, "This is chloro-form. It's the antidote. But it does make a feller sleepy."

I looked about nervously. "I would think that a famous inventor who can capture electricity in a glass lamp could keep poison gases in their containers."

For some reason Lem Symington frowned ferociously. Jesse Cheever twinkled at me and said, "Hush, O'Rourke, you must never refer to the invention of the electric light in the presence of the inventor of the electric light!"

"Oh, don't rag me, Jesse! That was long ago!" Lem Symington said with irritation. "I wish I'd never told you!"

"Well, it wasn't time wasted. He hired you when you told him you'd come up with it independently," Jesse said.

Lem Symington ignored him and looked at me. "Now, what did you want?"

"I want to find Mr. Tate, sir."

"Oh, yes. He wasn't in the office by the library? Well, I don't see him down here in the machine shop, do you, Jesse?" They both stood and looked about. "He's probably with Al up on the third floor, working on the phono-graph. Or on that photographic thing of Dickson's."

"The kinetoscope," said my handsome Jesse. "Yes, O'Rourke, try the third floor. There are the stairs."

I gathered up my knapsack and started up, looking about as I did. The first two floors, I saw, were devoted to machinery, except for the west end of the building, which housed the library. When I reached the third floor, I entered a large room over the library. Al Edison sat in a clump of men around a strange little machine. He was stouter than when I'd seen him last, and his brown hair was even grayer, but still fell unkempt over his broad thoughtful brow in a manner that inspired reporters to call him "the Napoleon of science." He ignored the conversation around him, probably because he was deaf. He finished adjusting the machine, started its wax cylinder turning, and shouted at a little disc next to the cylinder, "Mary had a brand-new gown, it was too tight by half! Who gives a damn for Mary's lamb, when he can see her calf!"

The men chuckled, then waited nervously as Al adjusted a little arm on the machine and pushed something. The cylinder turned again and a thin little voice proclaimed, "Mary had a brand-new—" The rest was drowned out by applause and cheers. A couple of the men shouted, "Best yet!"

A great flash of light came from behind me. All the men except Al crowded to the door and peered out. "Just a lamp blowing up," said one.

"Glad it's not another accident," replied another.

Al had ignored the commotion, paying attention only to his machine. He reached into one of the boxes on the floor and pulled out a fresh wax cylinder, and fitted it onto the phonograph. "Who's next?" His eye lit on me. "Ah, come here, my lad! Let's see if our machine can stand up to the onslaught of a new voice!"

"Yes sir." I laid down my knapsack and approached the machine. Al started the cylinder turning. I scoured my memory for a man's speech, and perhaps inspired by the explosion of the lamp, I declaimed, "Put out the light, and then put out the light:/ If I quench thee, thou flaming minister,/ I can again thy former light restore,/ Should I repent me; but once put out thy light,/ Thou cunning'st pattern of excelling nature,/ I know not where is that Promethean heat/ That can thy light relume."

"Why, bless you, lad!" Al exclaimed, with a puzzled look at me. "What is your name?" He cocked a hand behind his ear.

"Mike O'Rourke, sir. I hope to find work here."

"Ah." He glanced at my worn clothes. "Well, any man who knows his Shakespeare will be given a chance. Tate will see to it by and by. First let's hear your Othello." He adjusted a screw and lowered his ear to the machine.

My voice emerged, the actual words. "Put out the light, and then put out the light." Can you imagine? It was wizardry indeed! I clapped my hands gleefully. "Oh, sir, what an excellent machine!"

Al held up a finger. My words continued until, "but once put out thy—" Then they disappeared amid sputters and buzzes. Al groaned and said a few words almost as vulgar as Mr. Boggs's.

Put Out the Light

One of the other men squatted by the machine and said, "Wax shavings in the works again!"

Al said, "We need a harder wax, Jonas."

"I have a couple of ideas."

"Well, let's get to work! Ninety-nine percent perspiration, you know!"

They were all ignoring me. I located Mr. Tate, a genial Canadian who served as Al's secretary and business manager. He told me to report to Jonas Aylsworth, the chemist who needed bottles washed. I started for the stairs, glancing back over my shoulder to see Al Edison, lost in thought, pondering his magical machine.

As I started down, a tall, lean gentleman carrying a set of nearly identical photographs of a man with his arms out passed me. I was puzzled and addressed a boy who was on the stairs just behind me. "Who is that man?"

"That's Mr. Dickson the photographer."

"What is he doing?"

"Kinetoscope photographs. They plan to link moving photographs to the phonograph."

"Moving photographs? That's impossible!"

"I've seen them, I have!" said the boy indignantly. "They're little pictures, and they move! Those pictures he's got show Fred Ott waving his arms about."

"What wonderful inventions are coming from this place!"

"That's as may be." He scowled.

"You don't think so?"

He glanced around and beckoned me into a corner by the stairs. "He can be evil, that Mr. Edison."

"Evil? Why, boy—I don't know your name—"

"They call me Kit Herbert."

"My name is Mike O'Rourke. Well, Kit, I'm certain that Mr. Edison isn't evil! He's doing splendid things for all mankind!"

"That's what they all say," said Kit sullenly.

What could the boy mean? I said thoughtfully, "No, not all. I've heard rumors that Mr. Edison is a wizard, doing Satan's work."

"Oh, that old story." Kit sniffed in derision. "Some people don't understand science. They think it's wizardry. But it's just ordinary electricity."

"But Kit, you just said he was evil!"

"Just ordinary evil. Look!" He drew me across to a door and into a room attached to the main building. It was filled with strange machines, huge shafts and turning wheels and a great boiler puffing steam like a locomotive.

Kit pointed at one of the contraptions. "That's a dynamo. It makes electricity."

I squinted at the wire-wrapped columns. "That's a Long-legged Mary Ann?"

Kit burst out laughing. "Don't say that before the ladies! We call it a Long-waisted Mary Ann in public."

"I see."

"And that—" he scowled again as he pointed to a thick horizontal sheet of metal "—well, go stand on that metal plate."

Obediently, I did. Kit, still scowling, said, "If I throw this switch, fourteen hundred volts of electricity will course through you and kill you."

Well, I've seldom been so spry! I leapt about ten feet from the plate and lit out for the other side of the room. "Hang it, Kit, that's not a good joke!" I exclaimed. I remembered the hawk-nosed Silas Bell's dark mutters about poor dead creatures carried out by night.

"It's no joke, you're right!" Kit exclaimed. "They'll do anything for an experiment! They'll put a fellow's dog on that plate and turn on the electricity! They killed fifty dogs and cats, and a calf, and even a horse!"

I felt myself grow clammy. Was Silas Bell right? Was this marvelous laboratory, with its talking machines and moving pictures, in fact a den of Satan? I asked feebly, "Why did they kill your dog?"

"Well, poor old Biff followed me here to work last year. When they had to do an experiment they'd send out a boy to catch a stray. That boy thought Biff was a stray. I didn't see them bring him in. They pushed him onto that plate, and turned on the electricity. Poor old critter. He did get revenge, though."

"How?" I asked, looking about nervously for ghostly Satanic dogs bent on vengeance.

"One of the experimenters tried to nudge him farther onto the plate. But the current was already on and he was shocked too. Wasn't the same for days. At least I know poor old Biff died quickly."

"What is the purpose of these cruel experiments?"

"The State of New York wants a new way to kill people. They want to replace hanging with something more humane. Executioners can turn on death the way we turn on a lamp."

I shuddered. I preferred electricity safely bottled up in the Edison lamps. "But I read somewhere that Mr. Edison was opposed to capital punishment!"

"He is. But he also needs money. He let Mr. Brown take the job, and they invented the electric chair."

I had seen enough of this room. "Kit, I must get to work! I'm happy to have met you, though I'm truly sorry to hear your sad story."

Mr. Aylsworth showed me the bottles that needed washing and I began my chores, but I was boiling with curiosity. What splendid and terrible projects Al Edison had! I understood better why he sometimes spent days and nights at the labs, and why scientists like handsome Jesse Cheever were willing to sacrifice their health to be part of the work here.

Along with his chemist Jonas Aylsworth, Jesse Cheever, Lem Symington, Mr. Dickson, Fred Ott, and assorted others, Al Edison was spending twenty-four hours a day in the lab perfecting the phonograph, napping occasionally on the cots where I'd first seen Jesse and Lem. Mina Edison delivered a nice dinner to him every day, but I noticed he seldom ate anything but the pie.

Then the unpleasantness began.

The first problem was when I was called in to receive my week's wages. Tate said, "Well, O'Rourke, I hope it won't be any inconvenience if I wait till next week to pay you. We're short of cash just now."

"Yes sir, but begging your pardon, I too am short of cash just now."

He frowned. "Well, here's half. That's the best I can do."

I accepted it, but could almost hear that excellent businesswoman Aunt Mollie chiding me because I hadn't insisted on payment in advance. I went straight to Jesse Cheever. "Sir, why is it that a rich man like Mr. Edison can't pay us our wages?"

"Oh, he'll pay us, O'Rourke." Jesse had such a kindly smile! "Al's wealth is tied up in his lighting companies and in this laboratory. But he's selling them to a new company he's forming with some important financiers, Mr. Villard and Mr. J. Pierpont Morgan. They've already incorporated it. Edison General Electric, they'll call it. There's some little problem so they haven't yet signed all the papers. But as soon as they do we'll all have plenty of money, and he may send some of us to the Paris Exposition!"

"How splendid!" I exclaimed, quite caught up in Jesse Cheever's enthusiasm. Plenty of money and the Paris Exposition was precisely what I wanted too.

But the missing wages were only the first problem.

The Pinkerton men arrived that afternoon. Mr. Tate took them around the laboratory, denying the presence of any ladies, and Al agreed with him absentmindedly. I washed bottles with great industry, quaking all the while, until they left with a final suspicious glance around the laboratory. I hoped they had paid Mary Ann well for her information.

And then that night the abusive Mr. Boggs succeeded in getting inside the laboratory, and broke some bottles and lamps before the watchman carried him thrashing and screaming out the door. A little later there was a commotion on the third floor. I ran up the stairs and found the men in turmoil, all crowded around the door of the photography room, even Kit bouncing up and down at the edge of the crowd, trying to see. As I pieced the story together, Mr. Dickson the photographer had come back to his darkroom after a brief absence and stumbled over a body. "Help! They've killed Edison!" he'd cried.

You can imagine my consternation, and my relief when I saw Al standing there, hale and hearty. But then came another blow. Lem Symington uttered an oath and his amber eyes widened. "It's Jesse Cheever!" He hid his face in his hands.

I know not where is that Promethean heat, that can thy light relume. My poor Jesse! The handsomest scientist that ever there was, and the second dear Jesse I'd lost!

"There, there, O'Rourke, pull yourself together," said Al, slapping me on the back.

I remembered that boys weren't supposed to cry, and swallowed my sobs, saying gruffly, "I'm all right, sir." I peeked through the crowd at poor Jesse's body. The back of his blond head was crimson from ear to ear. "He was hit from behind," I blurted. "With a large stick."

"No, no," protested Al. "He merely fell and hit his head. Now, come with me to the chemistry room. We'll find something to revive him."

Now wasn't Al a silly goose to think that? Nothing could revive a man with a horrid wound like Jesse's! His light was quite put out. But men in the inventing trade are dreamers, and love their inventions as though they were children. The electric light, the phonograph, the dynamo, the electric chair, the kinetograph—all were little miracles. His patent medicine, Edison's Polyform, had sold well for years. Perhaps Al truly believed that he could raise the dead.

"Does anyone know who killed him?" I asked after half an hour of Polyform and other evil-smelling concoctions had failed to revive the corpse.

"No one killed him! Holy Moses, who'd want to kill Jesse Cheever?" Al protested. "He fell and hit his head!"

"But sir—"

"O'Rourke, you'll find the inventing business is full of dangers. We're on the edge, the cusp between the known and the unknown, so accidents will happen. We must take courage, and continue to work. That's what our fallen comrade would wish."

Everyone nodded in sober agreement. After all, Al was an uncommonly bright fellow, yes indeed. They summoned the undertakers and went back to work.

Well, Al might dismiss Jesse's death as an accident, but I was certain it had nothing to do with the cusp between the known and the unknown. It had to do with someone fetching Jesse a great whack on the head. And I was also certain that the man who struck him thought he was killing Edison. Jesse had paid a high price for his resemblance to the great inventor.

But who might it be? Al Edison's life was full of projects and incidents and huge sums of money. Mr. Villard and Mr. J. Pierpont Morgan, of course, wanted him alive, because the proposed new company would be almost worthless without him. But great financiers have enemies. Did a rival financier, a Jay Gould or perhaps a Vanderbilt, want to stop the company? Would it be difficult to hire one of us to kill the Napoleon of science? Many of us were disgruntled by half-wages. Lem Symington bore him a grudge having to do with his long-ago invention. Young Kit blamed Al for the death of a beloved dog. Mr. Boggs was a violent man who believed Al owed him money. Even Silas Bell, the Glenmont gardener, believed that Al was in Satan's thrall and would lead us all to perdition if he wasn't stopped. Would they need much more in the way of incentive?

I seemed to be alone in my conviction that a murderer was stalking the laboratory. Still, I vowed to avenge the death of dear Jesse Cheever. And it was important to save Al Edison, even if he was being leather-headed about the situation. His fruitful mind had so much to offer the future. Besides, I wanted to make sure he survived to pay my wages.

That night I didn't leave the lab but pretended that I had many more bottles to wash. The watchman was alert, walking around the building and through it, and the gate in the picket fence was closed. I told him I wasn't able to sleep because I hadn't finished my work. "Mr. Edison affects people that way," he said, and continued his rounds.

Only a few of the men worked at night, most choosing to be home sleeping with their families. But Al always preferred the night. Night is the time of assignations and of goblins, of secrets and of ghosts. Night is the time when ordinary shapes become grotesque and unfamiliar, the very witching time, when churchyards yawn and hell itself breathes out contagion to this world, and anything is possible. I think Al worked best then, freed of the conventional expectations of the daylight hours. We in the theatre business love night too.

Electric lamps still burned here and there in the vast laboratory, making the shadows of machines and work-tables even blacker. Except for the engines in the dynamo room, most of the machinery was silent. A few men were dozing on the cots. I heard Al's voice shouting a song in the phonograph room, "I'll Take You Home Again, Kathleen!" I washed bottles until the watchman passed, then crept to the bottom of the stairs and hid in a black shadow.

A tiny voice was now singing, "I'll take you home again, Kathleen!" Truly, the phonograph was an amazing invention! Silas Bell could well believe it was the work of the devil, yes indeed. But once again, I heard the song disintegrate into sputters.

"Well, let's try Jonas's new concoction," Al said cheerfully. "It should be melted by now."

"Jonas is asleep," someone answered.

"I'll get it while you clean out the works."

Al emerged from the phonograph room and bounced down the stairs. He'd never been very well coordinated and I hoped he wouldn't fall. Still, despite the lateness of the hour, or perhaps because of it, he seemed frisky as young Kit Herbert. And twice as foolish. Someone was trying to kill him, but he wouldn't believe it, and he was walking through the enormous half-abandoned lab as though angels watched over him.

But there were no angels in evidence, not even the watchman, so I left my hiding place and followed him across the building.

He entered the chemistry room, the long room full of bottles and beakers where dear Jesse Cheever had once worked. I recognized Jonas Aylsworth the chemist snoring near the door. Al hurried into the room and over to a crucible where something was bubbling over a gas flame. He began to hum the song and picked up a ladle.

Behind him, another table was laden with the apparatus for other experiments. It was lit from above by an Edison lamp. A bit of shadow holding a staff detached itself from the blackness beneath the table and stretched high. I grabbed for the Colt I usually kept in my bustle and then realized I was not wearing my maiden's attire. I could only hurl myself at the shadow's knees and hope that the great staff would miss Al's gray head when it came crashing down. In fact it hit the crucible and some of the molten contents splashed onto Al's clothing and onto my jacket and trousers as well. "Stop! Stop!" I cried indignantly. But the shadow lurched to his feet and bounded out the window.

Al sat up and looked at the wax still sizzling on the floor. "Holy Moses! What a clumsy oaf that was!"

"Yes sir."

"It would have gone ill with me if you hadn't bumped him, Mike O'Rourke. Thank you."

"Yes sir."

"Who was it?" He cocked a hand behind his ear.

"I'm sorry, sir. He was muffled in a black scarf, and very quick out the window."

"Some thief, I suppose. I must speak sternly to the watchman, and—"

Well, isn't that enough to make you despair? Inventors are such impractical men, unable to see what's as clear as day. I cleared my throat and shouted, "Sir?"

"Yes, my boy?"

"Begging your pardon, sir, but I think he was trying to kill you. I think he thought Jesse Cheever was you, and—"

"Hush, O'Rourke!" Al beckoned me nearer. "You must say nothing of your suspicions. Do you understand? Nothing!"

"But sir, why not?" I spoke into his ear. "A murderer is loose! Your life is in danger!"

"O'Rourke, I am engaged in a very delicate business transaction. News that someone is trying to attack me could endanger years of work. Even the loss of Jonas's new wax in that crucible is a setback."

Well, he was right, of course. Mr. Villard and Mr. J. Pierpont Morgan would be unlikely to give lots of money to Al if they thought he might be killed at any moment. They'd be reluctant too if they thought someone was sabotaging his new inventions. I said into his ear, "Sir, I understand that this news could dim the luster of your proposed new company. But suppose you claim this was merely an accident, and that you are working despite it all—"

Al thought about it and chuckled. "Then Villard and Pierpont Morgan may be more eager to sign! And furthermore, we may be able to trap the villain! Here, O'Rourke, you're the only one who's proven trustworthy. We shall make a plan!"

Jonas Aylsworth had awakened at last and was shuffling toward us, blinking sleepily. "What's happened?"

Al began to yowl. "I'm burnt! The crucible exploded! Ow, ow!" He sounded like a fenceful of alley cats. The men who were not too deeply asleep to hear the ruckus hurried in and crowded around him. They carried him up to Glenmont, where Mina Edison fluttered about exclaiming, "Oh, poor Thomas! Poor Dearie! Now, just let me put this bandage on!"

Of course he couldn't stand much of that kind of treatment, and soon he was back in the lab, his head bundled up in bandages so he looked like a Turk. He called the reporters in. "Edison Burned but Busy" said the headlines. And he was busy. Stubborn as ever, he was still trying to perfect the phonograph.

And foolhardy as ever, he wandered about the lab at night, bandages and all, an easy target. I stayed at the lab again to watch over him.

It grew later and later. One by one, the people working with Al—Lem Symington, Dickson the photographer, Jonas Aylsworth, even vigorous young Kit—stumbled off to take naps. The watchman was yawning. I too dozed on one of the cots, dimly aware of Al singing "I'll Take You Home Again, Kathleen," when I felt a cool breeze on my cheek. I sat up, alert, and realized that a window was open somewhere, letting in the April air. It was the witching time, yes indeed. But all was quiet, except for Al and the phonograph on the third floor, and the clanking and humming of the huge machines in the dynamo room, and the snores of the men who were catching their forty winks.

It was time to take action.

I slipped through the shadows to the dynamo room. No one was there. Quickly, I tiptoed out and threw a lever, then scurried back to the shadows behind the door.

Half the lights in the main building had gone out. Though the snores did not abate, there was faraway cursing from the third floor. I heard Al descending the stairs. In a moment he was in the dynamo room, his head turbaned in bandages. He began to examine the contraption that had stopped.

And, as I'd hoped and dreaded, a muffled figure slipped through the door and closed it behind him. He held a great staff in his hand. As he approached Al from behind, he raised the staff.

I stepped from behind the door and cried, "Hold, sir! I have a gun!"

The muffled figure spun to look at me and my Colt. Ten feet farther on, so did Al. Al shouted, "Holy Moses, don't shoot! A bullet could ricochet and damage the machines!"

Hang it, inventors are so impractical! They've got no more common sense than a pup. I sighed and explained, "Just getting his attention, sir. I don't need to shoot, because if he moves at all, I throw this switch."

The muffled figure looked down at his feet and gasped. He lifted one foot from the electrified plate and I made a show of grasping the switch. "No, O'Rourke, no!" he whimpered, holding himself very still.

"Lem Symington!" I cried, recognizing his voice and scrub-brush hair.

"What in the world are you doing here?"

Al looked just as confounded as I was. "Lem Symington? You're the one who's been trying to kill me?"

"No, no, I—"

"Don't move!" I reminded him. Lem froze again.

"Don't deny it," Al said. "I've seen you trying to strike me twice, and now I recognize you."

I asked, "But Mr. Symington, why did you kill Jesse Cheever? He was your friend!"

Lem bowed his head but didn't answer.

I said, "You mistook him for Mr. Edison, didn't you?"

He still didn't answer.

I said, "I don't understand why you used that wooden staff! You're an inventor. You could have found a clever scientific way to kill Mr. Edison. Electrocution, or poison gas—there are so many ways to die in this laboratory! Why would a clever scientist use an old-fashioned stick? Why, I thought the killer would turn out to be a crude day-laborer, a mason or a gardener or even a watchman!"

A crafty look came into Lem's amber eyes, and I exclaimed, "That's the reason! That's what he wanted us to think!"

Al had been frowning throughout this discussion. Now he said, "Lem, I don't understand why you did it. I've been good to you! There's no better job anywhere for a man of science!"

Lem burst out, "And why would you hire your rival, except from guilt?"

"Rival?" asked Al. "Guilt? What guilt?"

I explained, "He's jealous, Mr. Edison, because he invented some sort of filament, and you became rich and famous from it."

Al looked puzzled. "Many people claimed to invent the electric light. But I invented it first!"

"No you didn't!" Lem shouted. "I did! You heard about it somehow and stole it!"

"I did not!" Al stepped toward him.

"Al, don't go any closer!" I called.

Lem glanced at my hand on the switch but went on shouting at Al. "You stole it! I invented it first!"

"Balderdash! I invented it!"

"Al!" I called again.

But it was too late. Immersed in this silly schoolboy quarrel, the Napoleon of science stepped close, shaking his fist. Lem seized his wrist and looked at me triumphantly.

"Al, you idiot!" I stamped my foot in vexation. "I've a notion to throw this switch!"

The horror of his situation finally penetrated. Al looked at Lem's feet on the electrified plate, then at Lem's hand around his wrist, and finally at the switch I held in my hand. He mentioned a few of Mr. Boggs's favorite words as a look of pure terror invaded his features..

Lem, knowing I couldn't electrocute him without killing Al too, smirked and stepped off the plate, shoving Al to the floor as he did. He lifted the great staff. Al cringed, certain that he'd breathed his last.

Isn't that just like inventors, to forget the practical side of things? I shot Lem in the knee and he crumpled screaming to the floor. Al and I tied him up with electric wire.

"I truly did think of that filament first," Al assured me.

"Of course you did, Mr. Edison. But this yowling fellow loves his invention as much as you love yours."

Al seemed to understand. "Inventions are like sweethearts, or like children," he agreed.

"He loved not wisely, but too well."

"That's true." We started out to find the watchman. "Your marksmanship is excellent. How can I ever thank you?"

"Well, sir, seeing as how you're going anyway, I would very much appreciate a trip to Paris."

He grinned. "Fleeing the Pinkertons, eh? I'm sure a trip to Paris can be arranged, Bridget."

"You know I'm Bridget?" I asked, astounded.

"You looked familiar," he explained. "And the Pinkerton men were asking about you. But I wasn't certain until you called me Al just now, as in those dear old days at Menlo Park."

"I see."

"Besides, few lads can recite *Othello* as well as you."

You see? Didn't I tell you that Al Edison was a most uncommonly bright fellow?

FROM BRIDGET MOONEY'S SCRAPBOOK

The Brooklyn Citizen

November 4, 1888

EDISON'S NEW IDEAS.
HE BELIEVES ELECTRICITY IS THE
COMING POWER

We Must First Discover How to Produce Electricity from Coal Without Wasting Its Energy in Heat. A Look at Edison's Laboratory. He Has Little Faith in Aerial Navigation.

If you meet Edison this morning he has just discovered something, and if you meet him tomorrow he has added a new find in the realm of scientific invention. It is hard to keep up with him. Probably no investigator in the field of science has ever been surrounded by such perfect conditions for prosecuting his researches. This has not always been so, of course, for Thomas Edison has discovered, among other things, the way of making money.

THE NEW YORK TIMES
April 1889

Mr. Edison was discovered with his head and the greater part of his face swathed in bandages, but, although suffering considerable pain, he was hard at work with his experiments. He said that while at work over a crucible early in the week the affair exploded, and some of the molten contents were blown into his face and over his head, giving him several severe burns. Notwithstanding this, he received his visitors cordially, and showed them over his laboratory. Ex-President DeSoto sang and talked into a phonograph, and took the wax cylinder away with him to have the words and music reproduced for the entertainment of friends in Paris.

THE ROSEWOOD COFFIN; or,
The Divine Sarah

"**M**en have died from time to time, and worms have eaten them, but not for love," said Shakespeare. But he was a wise old jake, and I reckon he also knew that love comes in many shapes. Like Jacques and Sarah's.

My dear friend Lillie Langtry introduced us. I hadn't seen her since St. Louis, so when a new tour brought her to New York I called on her. "Bridget!" she exclaimed in her impeccable English. "I plan to attend Sarah's special matinée. Do come share my box! Her son Maurice will accompany us."

Well, of course I wanted to see the famous Sarah Bernhardt! I donned a feathered bonnet that set off my red hair and a bustled dress of French blue velvet trimmed with cascades of blond lace and set off proudly for the Star Theatre.

I know, I know, you're right, of course. My Aunt Mollie would have agreed that a proper lady would not choose to be seen with these two. One could say—indeed, many did say—that Lillie Langtry was a fallen woman, and that Maurice Bernhardt was illegitimate. But Lillie remained the Prince of Wales' favorite, and Maurice was the son of a Belgian prince and a famed mother, and engaged to marry a Polish princess to boot. So don't you think a simple St. Louis girl ought to be proud to be seen with those whom crowned heads did not disdain? Yes indeed. Besides, they both had heaps and heaps of money.

I edged forward in the elegant box seat, trying to look languid instead of eager as I inspected the audience of New York theatrical luminaries in the rows below. Beside me sat Lillie, the most luminous and languid of all. She was leaning back so that the gilded fretwork partition would screen her from the multitudes. Her dress was a lovely green velvet with purple shadows, and she slowly waved her matching fan. Young Maurice Bernhardt stood behind her, a gallant young dandy. They were discussing their respective American tours, in French. Lillie, of course, had spoken French from childhood, but since I'd learned only the little I needed for the stage, it was sometimes difficult for me to follow their conversation. For all its airs, French is a rather silly language, don't you think? They use a long flowery string of words to say simple things, but then smear them all together to sound like one word, so why don't they do it the straightforward way to begin with? But there's no reasoning with foreigners. Sarah Bernhardt was about to perform an entire play in French, even though we were in New York and the play concerned a Russian princess.

But Sarah's son Maurice was courtesy itself and soon leaned closer to include me in the conversation. "Mademoiselle Mooney, you have never viewed *maman* on ze stage, *n'est-ce pas?*"

"I have never had the good fortune to see her. I myself was on tour with Mr. Salvini the first time she was here in New York." I smiled at Maurice. "But of course I heard her praised everywhere. Did Mrs. Langtry tell you that I have had the great honor to be called 'the Bernhardt of Missouri?' "

"Missouri? *C'est charmant!*" Maurice laughed warmly. "I am all ze more pleased to meet such a delightful and capable actress."

Wasn't that charming? You can say what you want about Frenchmen, but you must admit that even in English they have a sweet way with words, although they can't quite pronounce them properly.

The curtain rose and I turned eagerly to the stage. Two men entered and nattered away in French about the dissipated Count Vladimir and about how much the Princess Fédora loved him. I had time to inspect the scenery, which represented Count Vladimir's handsome apartment in St. Petersburg, and to inspect the audience of this special matinée reserved for theatre professionals and given on a Thursday afternoon so that those of us working in shows could attend. I spotted Mr. Frohman, the famous producer, and a number of my fellow actors, many of whom were gazing at our box. No doubt they hoped to observe the renowned Mrs. Langtry, but I made certain they also observed me.

The long conversation on stage was interrupted as the Princess Fédora made her entrance to warm applause. It was my first glimpse of the fabled Sarah Bernhardt. Sarah was a handsome willowy Russian princess, far more youthful than I had anticipated, and her singularly effective gown of lace quite dazzled the eye. Still, I thought, peering through my opera glass, she was far too thin, and her face, though intelligent enough, did not have half the loveliness of the beautiful Lillie Langtry's. Why was she known as "the divine Sarah?"

Then Sarah moved, and spoke, and lordy, I reckon my jaw almost dropped off! She seemed exotic, a creature come from the realm of spirits far away, and yet she seemed a dear friend whom I'd known all my life. I had planned to study her famed tones and gestures, and to incorporate the best into my own performances, but instead I sat transfixed. Oh, she doth teach the torches to burn bright! Her Princess Fédora was graceful as a swan, sinuous as a snake, coquettish as a kitten when she heard her fiancé Count Vladimir returning. And then, what shock when two men entered to tell her they'd brought Vladimir home wounded, what feverish suspense as the princess questioned the men to learn who had shot him, what joy when at last the surgeons flung wide the doors to admit her to her lover's sickroom, what heart-rending horror as she realized he would never again answer her tender cries of "Vladimir!" Princess Fédora began to weep. I began to weep. Never had I felt so humbled by another's genius, nor so proud to be a fellow practitioner of the thespian art. I found myself once again in love with the theatre.

The curtain fell to thunderous applause. Lillie Langtry said, "You appear to be impressed, Bridget."

"Oh, Lillie, I was mesmerized!"

Lillie Langtry, the most beautiful woman in the world, turned her violet eyes to the stage and murmured, "I would gladly exchange my reputed beauty for a tenth of Sarah Bernhardt's genius."

"She is indeed very skillful," I said lamely, for it was true that Lillie's loveliness was unaccompanied by any talent for the stage, her diligent efforts to study the art notwithstanding. Yet I knew that despite my own great talent, after seeing Sarah Bernhardt I could never again take as much pride in my own abilities. She seemed to be pure spirit, sent from the gods. Even her harshest critics admitted that she could plunge emotion like a dagger into the innermost being of the spectator. I had not been so thrilled since I was thirteen back in St. Louis, when I saw the illustrious English actress Mrs. Fanny Kemble on tour and vowed that someday I too would learn to speak correctly and become an actress.

The rest of the play became ever more intense. Sarah Bernhardt's grace was magnetic, and her voice ranged from tender to fierce so delightfully that I decided on the spot to learn more of her otherwise silly language. The play ended with a perfectly splendid death scene in which the vengeful and passionate princess takes poison and dies, writhing beautifully. I applauded until my hands tingled.

Afterward, Maurice escorted Lillie and me backstage through disappointed throngs who were not allowed to see the star. Sarah's dressing-room was filled with her furs and flowers and admirers. A table laden with her jewelry, including a lovely pearl-encrusted belt, was guarded by a small gray-haired woman. In the center of the room sat the great tragedienne, wearing a rich crimson mantle trimmed with fox fur and nuzzling a brindle cat. "Such a precious little tiger," she murmured, and glanced up at her little audience. "Do you know, I rescued her from ze railroad tracks and nursed her, and zen she bit me?" I remembered that in the Franco-Prussian war Sarah had run a hospital for wounded soldiers in her theatre. The cat began to claw at her fur trim and made her laugh. "But no, I do not complain. She is fierce, like ze Princess Fédora!"

Maurice stepped forward and kissed her on both cheeks, the forehead, and the chin. "*Maman, un succès fou!*" he exclaimed.

"Here, *mon cher*, take ze little Princess Fédora." She handed him the cat, then smiled at us all. "Lillie, *bonsoir!*"

Maurice took this as a signal to begin bidding adieu to the other visitors. The little gray-haired woman aided him. But Lillie beckoned me toward Sarah and said, "I would like to present Miss Bridget Mooney, a very clever American actress. She has done me great kindnesses."

Sarah's intelligent eyes inspected me as she held out her hand. "*Enchantée.*"

"Madame Bernhardt, I am truly honored. Today you were the personification of love itself."

Maurice, having got rid of the other visitors, rejoined us. "Mademoiselle Mooney is also called ze Bernhardt of Missouri."

Sarah smiled. "Missouri! Zat is St. Louis, *n'est-ce pas*? Ze land of riverboats and *vaqueros*?"

"Yes, Madame."

"And bandits! A bandit from St. Louis once tried to steal my jewels!"

Well, hang it, I didn't want foreigners to get the wrong idea about Missouri. I curtsied, pulled her pearl-encrusted belt from my bustle pocket, and presented it to her. "Yes, madame, we are particularly proud of our bandits."

The little gray-haired woman gasped, but Sarah laughed merrily. "Lillie, *merci!* Zis young lady bandit is worth meeting. But now—" A shadow darkened her famous face.

With an angry glance at me, the little gray-haired woman fluttered to her side. "*Allons, allons!*"

"*Je viens!*" Sarah took the woman's hand affectionately. "Madame Guérard, she runs my life, and I must go! But first, I must ask ze advice of my dear friend Lillie about Jacques, ze poor darling."

"No doubt he is asking for money," said Lillie.

"Well, yes, but—"

"My advice is to stop being kind to him!"

"*Madame Langtry a raison, maman!*" Maurice exclaimed. Madame Guérard's gray head nodded fiercely in agreement.

"Oh yes, I know," said Sarah, clasping her hands sadly. "He is cruel, yes! He makes me wish to leap from ze great Brooklyn Bridge, to die in ze cold dark waters, to plunge into ze abyss of ze unknown like your Ophelia, maddened by a mad love."

My heart was rent to hear her, and Madame Guérard stroked Sarah's pale brow with worn birdlike hands. But Lillie was not upset. "Poor dear," she said. "I myself would stay away from the man."

"Oh, Lillie, you English have such cold blood! Mademoiselle Mooney, perhaps you understand. Perhaps you have been in love!"

"Yes, Madame Bernhardt. But it was nothing compared to the love for the art of the theatre that you personified today."

"Ze performance went well, *n'est-ce pas?*" Sarah said with satisfaction.

Lillie smiled. "Now that you are feeling better, my dear, we must go and allow you to obey the good Madame Guérard. You have a performance tonight, and so does Miss Mooney."

We took our leave. Driving to tea in Lillie's fine carriage I inquired, "Who is this troublesome Jacques?"

"Monsieur Jacques Aristide Damala is Sarah's husband."

I remembered then. A shock had gone through the theatrical world five years before when we learned that the great Sarah Bernhardt, who'd already had a long string of lovers and was too rich to require any manly protection, had suddenly married an actor, totally unknown and Greek to boot. A few stormy months later he had abandoned her and I'd heard nothing of him since. "He treated her so cruelly!" I observed. "How can she still love him? I would have tossed the fellow out long since!"

"And so would I," responded Lillie. "But we are not the greatest actress in the world. We are not even French."

"I thought they were divorced," I said. It was certainly true that Sarah's list of lovers had continued to lengthen. One of the handsome, strapping actors we'd just seen was rumored to be her current favorite. To all appearances, Jacques Damala had been just one more on the string.

Lillie smiled her luminous smile. "It is difficult to divorce husbands," said the beautiful Mrs. Langtry, who had firsthand knowledge. "And it is expensive to keep them out of one's life. You are wise not to marry, Bridget. Tell me, how is your little niece?"

"Juliet is thriving. She's learning to read, and to dance, and can almost recite the 'quality of mercy' speech. How is your Jeanne-Marie?"

"Thriving too," said Lillie, and we had a splendid tea discussing our clever little nieces.

Because I was appearing on stage myself, I was able to see only one more of Sarah Bernhardt's presentations that year, the famed *La Dame aux Camélias*. Of course you know that play, the most popular of the decade! Audiences flocked to see it, Verdi based *La Traviata* on it, actresses fought like wildcats to play the heroine Marguerite. But Sarah embodied the love-struck courtesan so perfectly that none could compete. I was profoundly moved by her art and spent many hours before my mirror, practicing her finest effects in order to apply them to my own roles.

Two years later, my path again crossed Sarah's. My friend Mr. Thomas Alva Edison requested my assistance with his exhibit of phonographs and electric lighting at the 1889 Paris Exposition. "Of course I'll help, Al," I told Mr. Edison, "if you will permit me to take my little niece Juliet and her nurse. They would so enjoy seeing the splendors of Paris!"

Mr. Edison was a generous man, and besides, he was returning a favor. No, hang it, not that kind of favor, not that time! He agreed to send all three of us.

Paris was full of splendors indeed. There were broad avenues, ancient cathedrals, plane trees and chestnut trees, and best of all a stupendous new thousand-foot tower, lit by my own Mr. Edison's electric lamps, that had been built on the exposition grounds by the exceedingly clever Monsieur Eiffel. But the splendor I most wanted to see was Sarah Bernhardt. The day we arrived I tucked Juliet and Hattie into our rooms at the Hotel Terminus, donned an apple-green dress with a matching parasol, and hurried to the Théâtre des Variétés to see Sarah once again in *La Dame aux Camélias*.

But Sarah, despite her poetic movement and wondrous voice, had somehow lost the magical spark that had entranced me. She said her lines beautifully but her soul seemed elsewhere. I soon realized what the problem was. You see, in New York, Sarah had had two excellent actors in her company to play the leading-man roles. Here in Paris, she had been able to choose from a vast number of skilled actors including those two. So why had she chosen such a dreadful leading man? He spoiled his every scene. Despite her skill, even Sarah could not completely hide her anxiety in those scenes. Surely after tonight she would fire him! The man was handsome enough, with a lovely smile and a sweet little upturned mustache, but he had a gaunt and sickly aspect, and appeared to be inebriated as well. His voice was feeble, and he had so little manly vigor that I dreaded seeing the end. Sarah had a splendid death scene in *La Dame aux Camélias*. As the dying Marguerite, she struggled upright to embrace her lover and murmur her last words. When he released her from the embrace she'd fall back dead. What an electrifying moment it was as the graceful corpse swung back, supported only by the leading man's strong arm! I winced to think of the scene ahead, because there was no strong arm in evidence tonight.

Perhaps I should do more than wince.

The curtain rose for the last act. With sudden resolution, I went outside and hurried to the stage door. A couple of guards attempted to stop me but I used my apple-green parasol to good effect and crept into the wings. The handsome leading man lay sprawled in a chair, waiting for his entrance. I stood by a door in the set. When the actress who played the maid emerged I seized her by the wrist and whispered in my carefully practiced French, "You must catch her!"

"Catch her? Who? Who are you?"

Clearly there was no time for international communication. I snatched off the maid's cap, tossed my shawl over her head, and bound it tight about her mouth. She grunted and fought like a tackled pig as I removed her dark dress and white pinafore and tied her, still thrashing, to a pipe. A couple of stagehands heard the muffled noises and began to chase me, but I hid behind some items of furniture from earlier acts, struggling out of my handsome apple-green dress and into the maid's uniform. With agitated whispers, my pursuers discovered me at last, but I dodged through a door and found myself on stage. They gasped but did not follow.

The leading man was already there. Sarah's sweet, love-struck voice never faltered, but I saw her eyes flash in surprise when the maid who usually waited across the stage came near to arrange the bedclothes quietly behind them, then clumsily dropped a pillow. The actor didn't seem to notice. He scarce had the strength to utter his lines. But Sarah did not compromise. The last exchange played sweetly, and when the moment of death arrived she collapsed, totally limp, totally artistic.

The leading man's feeble hand slipped.

Fortunately, the clumsy maid kicked the dropped pillow under the falling tragedienne's auburn head in the nick of time, then assisted the leading man as he moved the dead Marguerite gently to the bed. The curtain descended to warm applause.

"*Qui*—ah, Mademoiselle Mooney! Ze Missouri bandit!" Sarah exclaimed, as I removed the maid's cap. "I am very angry at you, you know." She looked at the pillow and added grudgingly, "But zen, you saved my poor head, I suppose."

Hang it, what was wrong? I had expected some little token of gratitude from the rich tragedienne. Instead she was scolding me, rather than the stumbling actor who was the author of our difficulties. The answer came when she turned to her leading man and wagged a finger at him. "Jacques, you poor dear, you must get more rest."

So this was Jacques Damala. I was astonished, even more when he glanced at Sarah, then slowly focussed on me and said, "Mademoiselle Mooney? A bandit?" His eyes began to glow, whether from love or fever it was difficult to tell. "Mademoiselle, you are fascination itself!" He managed to bow and kiss my hand, the very soul of gallantry. Yes indeed. Sarah looked at the two of us with a peculiar expression as she gathered the cast for the curtain call. I slipped back into the wings to retrieve my apple-green dress. The hapless maid, though still in her chemise, had been untied by her colleagues, and when she saw me she burst into vehement French. I attempted to explain to her that I had just saved her employer from a dreadful accident, but she appeared to have a greater interest in tearing out my eyes. Her small plump hands were surprisingly strong. The stagehands watched us, chuckling. I was on the verge of resorting to the Bowie knife I keep in my boot when the curtain calls ended and Sarah swept past us on her way backstage. "*Assez, Saryta!* Mademoiselle Mooney, do not let her tear ze costumes!" she commanded. At last Saryta ceased her attack.

Jacques Damala was eying me with frank delight. I realized that the maid's costume had been half pulled off in the fray. Quickly, I snatched my shawl from Saryta and covered myself. Damala said, "Mademoiselle, you are ze most charming bandit I have ever met!"

I kept my eyes on Sarah, who was looking at him oddly. At last she turned to me. "Mademoiselle Mooney, we leave soon on a tour to London. You are not traveling to England?"

"No, madame, I must remain in Paris until September. I am contracted to work at the Exposition for Mr. Edison."

"Ah, Monsieur Edison! A delightful man. He recorded my voice." She glanced at Damala. "Very well, we shall return early in August. Zen, please, come to visit us. We shall be friends!"

I accepted, pleased to be considered a friend by a woman of Sarah's means. Saryta, straightening the maid's costume, pouted. But Damala caught my hand and kissed it. "Yes, mademoiselle, please visit us! It is number fifty-six, boulevard Péreire."

Sarah, Damala, and the others were soon in London, and I heard little of them, except for occasional reviews in London newspapers that expressed shock at Damala's poor performance. Confident that Sarah would soon send him packing, I turned to my own tasks. Most days I worked in the Palace of Machines, an enormous glass-roofed building that enclosed fifteen acres. Inside were countless modern machines, from railway equipment to a strange writing machine from Remington and a most peculiar carriage from Benz that was powered by gasoline instead of horses. But the Edison phonograph exhibit was the most popular of all, and those of us who demonstrated this new marvel were kept busy.

When I had the time I explored the wondrous city with my dear little Juliet and my friend Hattie Floyd. Hattie was deeply suspicious of the French. "It ain't natural to talk like that! A body can't understand a word they say!" But she agreed that their cooking was splendid, and their clothing. Before I hired her as a nurse to my niece, the voluptuous Hattie had done well enough in a rather lewd line of work, eventually joining a house that catered to the best classes in St. Louis. So it was with a professional interest that she inspected the embroidered silk stockings and lace-trimmed chemises in the shops, and pronounced them most effective.

As for young Juliet James, the apple of my eye, she won over the French with ease. At seven, her blue eyes were as quick as her father's and her ear as quick as mine, and soon she was prattling in French to all who would listen: the coachman who drove the clattering omnibus pulled by three giant Percheron horses, the man who tended the carousel at the Rond Point, the baker who gave her cakes. One day I dressed her in a pretty blue frock with a lacy skirt and a big bow at the waist and escorted her up the Eiffel Tower. It took a long time to make the ascent, there being eleven thousand visitors every day, but with recourse to the packet of cakes I had tucked into my bustle pocket, she remained cheerful, especially when the balloonman strolled by and offered her a balloon in the same blue of her dress. When we reached the top platform it was a delight to look out at the cruise boats on the Seine, the cathedrals, the great glittering Palace of Machines where I worked, the exotic pavilions of the French colonies, the horticultural exhibits in the Trocadéro gardens. Juliet clapped her hands. "It's wonderful, Aunt Bridget! *Très jolie!*"

"Of course it is," I told her with a hug, "and if you continue to learn French, in a few years I'll bring you back to see the most wonderful thing in the world."

"What? What?" she demanded, her eyes sparkling.

"I'll take you to see Sarah Bernhardt perform."

That happy summer flew by. Then, early in August, Sarah and her company returned from London. Remembering her invitation, I presented my calling card at the handsome town-house at 56, Boulevard Péreire.

The door was opened by a nervous man with bulging eyes, a fine mustache, and a pencil behind his ear. I handed him my card and asked if madame was in good health. Oh yes, he told me in excited French, she had accepted an engagement to play the Russian princess Fédora at the fashionable Dieppe racemeeting and was deep into plans for the next season. And her son Maurice would soon be a father, so she was thrilled, he said, beaming.

"Et Monsieur Damala?" I asked.

His pop-eyed face darkened, and he whisked away with my card. In a moment Sarah herself appeared in a doorway, as sweetly sensuous as ever in ruffled white silk and beautiful ruby bracelets. "Do come in, Mademoiselle Mooney!" She took my hand and drew me into a lilac-scented salon. There was a small crowd there—Maurice, her sparrowlike companion Madame Guérard, the hollow-cheeked but handsome Jacques Damala, and even my sulky backstage acquaintance Saryta. Maurice and Damala both hastened to kiss my hand, but I was more interested in Sarah's salon.

What a breathtaking room it was! It rose two stories. Above the fronds of the potted palm trees I could see the night sky through a roof of glass. Everything in the room was the height of fashion. The rich red walls were almost hidden behind the beautiful and the exotic: Indian sabers, Mexican silver, Venetian gilded mirrors, daggers from South America, and of course numerous portraits of Sarah. Jacques Damala, who was still holding my hand, pointed out some handsome bas-reliefs. "From my country, Greece," he said proudly. "And zis rug we bought on our recent tour to Turkey."

I murmured my approval as I looked about. Dragon-headed poles supported a richly tasseled silk canopy over the divan. There were heaps of large embroidered silk cushions, furs piled and draped everywhere, and countless aromatic bouquets of flowers. I had never seen a room so beautiful and fashionable! An enormous cage stood in one corner, filled with beautiful birds that cheeped and squawked.

"Jacques, are you tired?" Sarah asked.

"Ze sight of zis fair lady has revived me!" Jacques declared.

Well, hang it, that was taking being French too far, don't you think? I'm as fond of gallantries as the next lady, but not in front of a wife, especially when the wife is as rich as Sarah. Sarah studied us an instant, then laughed merrily. "Let us dance in Mademoiselle Mooney's honor! Pitou!" she called to the pop-eyed man. He left off twirling his mustache, produced a violin, and began to play a waltz. Maurice danced with me, and I congratulated him on his impending fatherhood. But he danced the next dance with his mother, and I found myself in Damala's arms. It was very pleasant, because he was a handsome sweet-smelling fellow and full of compliments despite his occasional stumbles, but he was not nearly as courteous as Maurice, holding me much closer than was strictly necessary. I was obliged to push him away continually as we danced, for fear that Sarah would be offended. At last I told him that I was exhausted and would like to look at the birds.

Damala smiled as I peered through the bars at the birds. "Zey are lovely, aren't zey? Nearly as lovely as you!"

"They are indeed lovely, monsieur," I responded primly.

"In ze old days, Sarah kept her lions in zat cage."

"Lions! Oh, monsieur, that is terrifying! And is it true that she sleeps in a coffin?"

"Yes, sometimes. A beautiful rosewood coffin." He sank onto the divan, hiding his fatigue by patting the cushion next to him. "Come sit with me, mademoiselle!"

I pretended to be entranced by the birds. In fact, I was entranced by Madame Guérard on the far side of the cage, who was hissing something at Saryta and gesturing angrily at Monsieur Damala. Saryta replied indignantly, and Madame Guérard shook her gray head wearily. It was obviously difficult to manage this unwieldy household. She glanced up and almost caught me looking at her through the bars, but I quickly blew a kiss to a toucan in the cage and turned rapturously to Monsieur Damala. "I like birds so much better than lions!"

"So do I, *ma petite*," he responded. "But come, I want you to see zis fabric." Damala was patting the pillow again.

Well, I may be just a simple St. Louis girl, but it didn't seem wise to become entangled with the semi-invalid beloved of the world's greatest and richest actress. I stood as far from him as I could, snatched the indicated pillow, and took it to a brighter light. "Why, monsieur, you are quite right! The embroidered flowers are indeed the very imitation of life!"

Monsieur Damala struggled to his feet and came to stand by my side. "It is lovely indeed," he said, but he was not looking at the embroidery. He was inspecting the Venetian pearl trim at the low rounded neckline of my dress.

"Monsieur, I believe you are very weary from your travels," I said in clear tones. As I had hoped, Sarah heard and stopped dancing with her son.

"Pitou, *tais-toi!*" she commanded, silencing the violinist. "Do pardon me for a moment, Mademoiselle Mooney, I must see if Pitou prepared my husband's chamber properly."

"*Bien sûr!*" the pop-eyed Pitou reassured her. "*Madame, je vous adore!*" He followed her out, protesting his innocence.

"You ignite my heart, dear Mademoiselle," Damala murmured.

I thrust the pillow into his arms and hurried toward the others. "Mademoiselle Saryta, I wish to apologize for—"

Madame Guérard touched my arm and whispered in vehement French not to give Monsieur Damala anything. I looked at her in surprise, then turned back to Saryta. "I apologize," I repeated, "for interrupting your splendid performance."

The young woman looked a trifle sulky but said pleasantly enough, "Oh, I understand. Tante Sarah is grateful to you. Now I too stand near with a pillow when she dies."

"Tante Sarah? Sarah is your aunt?"

"Yes, of course. I am ze daughter of her sister Jeanne."

"Oh, yes, Jeanne Bernhardt." I had heard that Sarah had a sister, a minor actress. "Isn't she in Madame Bernhardt's company as well?"

"She was, before she became—ill."

"I'm sorry to hear that."

"Some people are allowed in ze company even when zey are ill," Saryta said darkly.

I lowered my voice. "You are right, mademoiselle, it is terrible! He makes even Sarah play badly!"

"Zat is nothing new," Saryta said. "He has always upset her. Once, he had some talent for ze stage, but zat was long ago."

"Yes, I understand." I'd known some upsetting men too, like little Juliet's father.

A door opened and Sarah swept back in, surrounded by a lively band of little dogs. Princess Fédora, the brindle cat, streaked past them all and leapt onto a plant stand near the enormous bird cage, where she crouched and eyed the toucan. Pitou waited by the door, twirling his mustache nervously.

Sarah went first to her husband, speaking soothingly in French, urging him to go to his room. This time he didn't object, though he did cross the room to kiss my hand politely before he left. "How I wish I had a nurse as charming as you! Will I see you tomorrow, fascinating creature?"

"Sir, I must work at the exposition," I said coolly.

"You break my heart, *ma petite.*" He shuffled off, supported by the loyal Pitou. Sarah watched them go. As soon as the door closed, she whirled on

Madame Guérard. The marvelous Bernhardt voice rose to berate her with the most beautifully pronounced invectives I have ever heard. Maurice tried in vain to calm his mother. A couple of the little dogs were inspired to join in with frenzied yapping.

With a flourish, Sarah held up a hypodermic syringe.

The gray-haired lady, who appeared to be used to such shenanigans, asked calmly, "*Dans son chambre?*"

"*Oui, sous le lit.*"

Under his bed. As Sarah continued to harangue poor Madame Guérard, I asked Saryta, "Forgive me, mademoiselle, but am I correct that drugs are the source of Monsieur Damala's difficulties?"

"Oh, yes, chiefly ze morphine. Others too. He promises Tante Sarah never to use it again, she allows him to come back, zen he breaks ze promise and she is furious. She screams, she rages, she beats ze pharmacist with her parasol, all for nothing." Saryta looked angry. "Tante Sarah always accuses me, because Maman was also an addict. It is not fair!"

"Of course," I said soothingly. "She should not accuse you. Nor should she accuse poor Madame Guérard." I crossed the Turkish carpet to the enraged tragedienne and begged permission to speak. "It is not Madame Guérard's doing," I explained. "Please observe what I found in Monsieur Damala's pocket while we danced." I held out a little ampoule for a hypodermic syringe.

I did not hold out the handsome hunting watch I'd found next to the ampoule.

Oh, I know, I know, a proper lady doesn't search a gentleman's pockets while waltzing. But then, he hadn't treated me like a proper lady, had he now?

Besides, the rich and brilliant Sarah Bernhardt was very interested in the ampoule. "In his pocket?" she asked.

"Yes, Madame Bernhardt," I said.

"Such a splendid bandit you are!" She seized my hands warmly. "Please, call me Sarah. And I will call you Brigitte, yes?"

"I would be honored."

"Lillie said you had done her a kindness," Sarah said, her eyes luminous. "Brigitte, would you do one for me?"

"Nothing would delight me more."

She scooped up one of the little pug dogs that was yapping at her feet and cuddled it. "Brigitte, my husband is very ill, bedridden much of ze time. Now, perhaps it is your red hair, or perhaps your exotic youth as a Missouri bandit. Whatever ze reason, he appears to fancy you."

"Let me assure you, I have done nothing—"

"Of course not! Do not think that I am jealous!" Tears filled the lovely Bernhardt eyes. "Once I was jealous, oh yes! Once I loved him with an earthly love. I think of how he tortured me, how I suffered, how I begged him to take pity on me, his slave! Every time he took a *petite amie,* I was wounded to ze depths of my soul! But all zat is in ze past. Today, my love is purer, more noble. And I must do everything in my power to save my sweet Jacques! It is a struggle with Death itself!" She drew out a lacy hand-kerchief to dab at her brimming eyes. The pug licked her chin in sympathy.

"But how can I help? Wouldn't it be better to allow poor Monsieur Damala to recover from his satanic habit in a sanatorium?"

"Oh, no! Zat is impossible! Jacques is very weak, very sensitive. He cannot abide confinement in a sanatorium. No, Hamlet, you cannot abide confinement either," she said to the pug, which was wriggling in her arms. She explained, "I found zis little dog imprisoned in a box and starving, poor little thing." She kissed its wrinkled forehead.

I returned to the subject. "Perhaps Monsieur Damala has exerted himself too much on the stage."

"Mademoiselle, ze poor man needs something to live for!" she said seriously. "And what is worthwhile, but ze theatre and ze love?"

For someone who was a genius, Sarah Bernhardt was being a tangle-headed fool, don't you think? No doubt she herself lived for the theatre and for love, since she no longer had to worry about money, but it was clear to me that Jacques Damala did not value the stage enough to care about giving a good performance, and did not value love enough to refrain from romancing a new lady before his wife's very eyes. Worst of all, he did not value Sarah's amazing genius.

Still, I feared that Sarah was not yet ready to hear such truths. I said, "You are most generous to him, Sarah. But how can I help?"

"Help me to nurse him, and to keep zose dreadful ampoules away from him, and to amuse him! He takes no interest in things and sleeps much of ze day. But when you appear, Brigitte, he is ready to dance!" She nuzzled Hamlet the pug's head. "Jacques is so young, only thirty-four. If I cannot save him, I will want to kill myself!" She gazed into space, as though con-templating a tragic and beautiful death. I remembered her obsession with her rosewood coffin and felt a chill. She continued, "So you see, I must save him. Please, help me, Brigitte!"

I was moved by her plea, but this bedridden fellow seemed a hopeless case to me. Then she placed Hamlet on a chair cushion and pulled a glittering ruby bracelet from her arm. "Oh, do not say no, Brigitte, or I will die! It will be worth your while!"

Well, hang it, how could I refuse such a splendid offer? Jacques Damala was a rotter, but she was so determined to save him that I feared she would do violence to herself if he took a turn for the worse. I dreaded the thought of a world without Sarah. And I'm bound to admit that Jacques could be charming, with his little mustache and flowery compliments that could make a young lady's limbs weak. There was also the great advantage that he was too ill to do much beyond talking. Most importantly, if we nursed him back to health he could perform his roles adequately. I even dared hope that he might leave her again so that she could once more work unencumbered at her art.

Besides, Sarah was willing to pay handsomely, and in advance. I studied the flaming depths of the rubies in my new bracelet. It would be perfect the next time I played the rich and wicked Lady Audley. Even my Aunt Mollie, that excellent businesswoman, would have approved.

So every evening, after supping with Hattie and Juliet, I came to the boulevard Péreire. I soon learned that despite the exuberance and apparent freedom in that luxurious townhouse, Jacques Damala was nearly a prisoner. Sarah and her household nursed him so lovingly that he could not escape. Jacques thought I was his *petite amie;* I knew I was one of his jailers. She would not leave him alone with anyone except Pitou, Madame Guérard, or me. The three of us became very efficient at blocking his efforts, although he and his unknown supplier were clever. Drugs arrived with the flowers, the potatoes, the champagne. In a few days we had a large collection of ampoules, and a patient who was despondent and shaky but still wily.

"Dearest Brigitte," he murmured into my ear one rainy evening, "will you do me a great favor?"

"I would be happy to, monsieur."

"A friend of mine has left a book at the shop for me. As I cannot go out, would you bring it to me?"

"With pleasure."

I donned a cloak and went out into the summer storm to the bookseller's where Jacques' packet waited. As I entered, a small man clutching a cape to his neck came striding out. He looked somehow familiar. I fetched the book, and of course I took a peek inside the packet. Wouldn't you? And of course the book had been hollowed out inside, and contained a supply of ampoules. Smiling, I delivered a different book to Jacques, although the poor man's crestfallen look after he'd opened it tugged at my heart.

He walked into the room that held Sarah's rosewood coffin and stood for a moment stroking the gleaming wood. Thunder rumbled outside. In a moment he looked up with his little charming smile. "Dear Brigitte, ze little bandit. Sarah has bribed you too, I see."

"Why, sir, what do you mean?"

"Let us be frank, Brigitte. I cannot buy anything in person because she has bribed all ze pharmacists."

That's a lot more sensible than beating them with parasols, don't you think? But Jacques did not seem to approve. He continued, "She has bribed Pitou and Madame Guérard. She drives my friends from ze house. And now she has bribed you, my last hope."

I realized what had been familiar about the man leaving the bookseller: the hand clutching the cape was Saryta's. You don't forget hands that have tried to claw your eyes out. Sarah would be very interested in this news. But I hesitated because of the despair in Jacques' eyes. "Sarah does it for your own good, sir."

"My own good." He held out a steady hand. "She has succeeded for ze moment, you see. No more trembling, only weariness. She believes I will regain my health, but she lives in a world of illusion. Zis desire will not go. You know zat, Brigitte. You are wise in ze ways of ze world."

I said slowly, "You are cured, Jacques, if you want to be."

"I will never be cured. It brings ze only joy I know." His face was bleak. "Brigitte, you are a woman of intelligence as well as beauty. You must understand!"

"Dear Jacques, I would be happy to help you!" I said, most sincerely. "But I cannot betray the greatest genius of the theatre!"

He stroked the coffin again and murmured so softly I almost did not hear him above the drumming rain, "Zen I must help myself."

I hesitated to tell Sarah about this conversation, because she thought he was better. Later that day, as she donned a ravishingly beautiful rain cloak to go visit Maurice's country house, she patted Jacques on the shoulder and said, "Dear Brigitte, you have done your work well! Jacques is much stronger. He is still disconsolate, but I will make him happy! He is asking me to give him a fine role in *La Tosca* zis fall, and I will, I will!"

There was a dreadful crash of thunder. "But Sarah," I said in dismay, "he is not yet able to sustain a role!"

"Of course I am able!" Jacques said firmly. "It will be a delight to play in *La Tosca!*"

"Why, Brigitte, I am surprised at you," Sarah said. "You know as well as I zat an inner strength comes from ze stage! It is ze best medicine in ze world!"

"Yes, that's true for you and me, but . . ."

"And true for me," said Jacques with a little smile.

Well, I knew what he meant. In the backstage confusion he would have opportunities that would never arise in the well-policed cocoon that Sarah had created for him here.

Sarah nodded, oblivious to the danger. "Of course it's true! And Jacques knows zat my love is pure and constant, and zat he can depend on his Sarah forever!" She kissed him maternally on the forehead.

I looked at them in consternation. I could see long years unrolling before me, bleak and empty of Sarah Bernhardt's art. I thought of my promise to little Juliet, and suddenly understood that Jacques had won. I embraced Sarah with a sob in my voice. "It's true! You save the wounded soldiers, and the poor little pets like Hamlet and Princess Fédora, and your prodigal husband! Never have I known such a warm heart, nor a love as pure as yours! Dearest Sarah, I will always honor that love!" Both of us were overcome with tears at her nobility.

Sarah, dabbing at her eyes, left for Maurice's country house to play her brand-new role of thrilled grandmother.

Jacques Damala listlessly opened the new book I handed him and found it filled to the brim with Saryta's ampoules and a syringe. With blissful countenance he looked up to thank me but I raised a palm for silence and said, "Never again, Jacques. Do we understand each other? Never ever again." He nodded slowly.

Oh, I know, I know, a proper lady would not have given up hope for his recovery. A proper lady would have fought on bravely, like Sarah, struggling against his satanic habit, for his own good.

A proper lady might even have warned a weakened man not to use too much after a period of abstinence. But don't you think he might have done it anyway?

We called the doctors after a few hours, but they were unable to save him.

Sarah was devastated, of course. Maurice brought his mother back to the boulevard Péreire swooning with grief. She threw herself at her dead husband's feet, wailing and swearing to kill herself.

"*Maman, non, maman!*" Maurice was frantic. At last he came to me. "What can we do? She is inconsolable! She will die for love of him!"

Did you ever hear such twaddle? My poor charming Jacques Damala died for love, it is true. He died because he loved morphine. He died because Sarah Bernhardt loved theatre, and because I did too.

I said, "Oh, Maurice, don't be a silly goose! She didn't love him, she loved playing noble wife and nurse. Now, the first thing to do is stop being an audience for this scene." I shooed him into a corner and walked over to Sarah. She was dissolved in tears; but I knew they were not Sarah's tears. They were Marguerite's tears for her lost love, they were Phèdre's tears for Hippolytus, they were Princess Fédora's tears for Count Vladimir. I murmured to her, "Dear Sarah, difficult as it is, you must think of his funeral ceremony. It should be a splendid funeral!"

"Yes. Oh, yes!" She sat up. "He shall have a rosewood coffin, like mine! And ze ceremony shall be splendid. It shall be Greek!"

I added softly, "He will also need a memorial."

"Yes, a memorial! In Père Lachaise cemetery! No, no, better yet in Greece, alongside ze great philosophers!" The shine in Sarah's eyes was made up of enthusiasm as well as tears. "I shall sculpt ze memorial statue myself!"

"I never heard of a truer love! And you will visit him whenever you tour?"

"Yes, Brigitte, yes!"

"Dear Sarah, you will be the noblest widow in the world!"

And she was, she was. The funeral ceremony in her great salon was presided over by the Greek archimandrite and four of his priests. Outside, the most dramatic storm yet blackened the glass roof except when the brief cold glare of lightning silhouetted the jagged palm fronds. Sarah, tearful in black, leaned on Maurice's arm for comfort, watching the glimmering embroidered robes of the priests.

A week and a half later the widow Damala played Princess Fédora in Dieppe. When she entered to find her lover dead, Sarah could not restrain her tears. The audience was thrilled with sympathy to think that she had so recently returned to find her husband a corpse. Sarah wept, and played divinely.

I sighed with relief. Little Juliet would not miss the most wonderful thing in the world.

I'm sure you've heard the rest. Sarah acted brilliantly for another thirty-three years, even after the amputation of a limb. She continued to triumph as Phèdre, Marguerite, La Tosca, Princess Fédora, as well as new roles—Joan of Arc, Cleopatra, Lucretia Borgia, Roxane, Medea. When she tired of women's roles she played men—Lorenzaccio, young Werther, even Hamlet.

The last time she ever appeared on stage, at the age of seventy-eight, she played the title role in a little-known play called *Daniel*. Daniel was a morphine addict.

Sarah was the noblest widow in the world, yes indeed, and always kept green the memory of poor Jacques Damala, who died for love.

FROM BRIDGET MOONEY'S SCRAPBOOK

THE NEW YORK TIMES
March 14, 1887

Peeping from the pink folds of the robe were two pointed red embroidered satin slippers, in which it is presumed the feet of the tragedienne rested. Her hair, which was not brown enough to be called brown and by no means red enough to be called red, and not auburn enough to be called auburn, was not arranged at all. It did what it liked in its own inimitable fluffy way. Sarah Bernhardt was half covered with a huge fur rug, which she dropped occasionally and which looked then like an animal who had condescendingly sacrificed its life for Sarah Bernhardt to walk on.

All round the room were flowers— rich, rare, and fragrant. In fact, it is a wonder that the whole Hoffman House was not perfumed last night, so abundant were the floral tributes, and so odorous also. They were sent by the ladies of the Madison Square Theatre, the Lyceum and the Casino Company, and Mrs. Abbey. They were confined in jars, but their fragrance would brook no interference. It roamed everywhere. Sarah Bernhardt's lissome arms were bare almost to the elbow. They embraced—it seems sacrilege to say it— a cat, a thankless tiger cat.

"Such a precious little animal," she said, smoothing its spotted skin and looking into its big stupid eyes.

Le Temps
August 20, 1889

M. Jacques Damala, le mari de Sarah Bernhardt, est mort subitement, hier matin, d'une congestion cérébrale, dans l'hôtel du boulevard Pereire qu'il habitait avec sa femme.

Depuis plusieurs mois déjà, il était très souffrant, en proie a de fréquents délires occasionnés, dit-on, par le grand abus qu'il faisait de la morphine.

PARTIES UNKNOWN BY THE JURY; or,
The Valour of My Tongue

Please, I beg you! Don't ask me to recount the story of that cruel night in 1892! As Shakespeare says, "On horror's head, horrors accumulate." I have nightmares to this day! Besides, I was not the tragedy's heroine. I'm bound to admit that I was merely the comic relief. Or worse.

But if you insist—

To begin with, my handsome gray bengaline gown with bouffant Parisian-style sleeves was not suited to the night wind that blew chilly as a graveyard into the open door of the railroad car. But the conductor remained adamant. "Madam, you must get off here."

I fluttered my eyelashes at him, doing my best to appear a proper lady, though I feared he had long since realized that I was of the theatrical profession. "But, sir, my family in St. Louis can pay amply when we arrive. Surely you can allow a young lady a few more miles in the middle of the night!"

"Madam, St. Louis is more than a few miles on. The Chesapeake and Ohio is not in the business of giving free rides to St. Louis." So saying, the conductor thrust my small steamer trunk and my Gladstone bag onto the station platform. I leapt from the train and lifted my trunk, attempting to heave it back aboard, but with deafening blasts of steam and screeches of metal on metal, the train began to move. My trunk and I thumped down onto the platform. I shook my fist at the conductor and shouted into the departing clamor of iron and steam, "The worm of conscience still be-gnaw thy soul!"

There was no response. The train disappeared into the blackness. I shivered again and opened my trunk to get out my worn blue traveling cape, my blond wig—far warmer than any hat—and a cigar. I pulled the wig over my red hair, wrapped the cape about me and sat down on my trunk for a smoke and a good think.

Was ever a lady so beset by misfortune? Ticketless, penniless, jobless, hungry, and lonely, I was in sympathy with the perturbed spirits that seemed to ride the frosty March wind. I missed my brother, who had long since died for the Union cause, and my dear Aunt Mollie. I sorrowed that my beloved elocution tutor, the illustrious English actress Mrs. Fanny Kemble, was failing and might soon join them in their heavenly abode. So, too, my famous colleague Edwin Booth was in decline, seldom leaving his grand home on Gramercy Park. I tapped the ash from my cigar and grieved for the passing of a glorious era.

The great Sarah Bernhardt was still alive and well, of course, but that was of limited consolation to me just now, for she too was touring the American provinces and had cut deeply into my troupe's profits whenever our paths crossed. I was hard put to leave enough with my friends in St. Louis to provide for my dear little niece's spring toilette. My troupe had continued to New Orleans, and not having to contend with Bernhardt, our first night there had been reasonably profitable. I had dared to hope again. But disaster had struck. Our handsome leading man, succumbing to the charms of the French Quarter, had drunk himself into such a stupor that the patrons began to stamp and to throw unpleasant objects at us amid shouts demanding their money back. Leaving the drunken Richard in a blinking heap center stage, we scurried for the stage door, only to find the manager's men there before us. We did not escape until they had emptied our pockets completely so that they could reimburse the angry audience. Thus I was forced to board the train in New Orleans in great stealth, and without benefit of ticket.

And now, the Chesapeake and Ohio had struck the crowning blow, removing me from the train and abandoning me heartlessly in the middle of the night! Do you wonder that I felt forlorn? I found myself longing for my dear departed friend Jesse James, who was handy at wreaking revenge on selfish banks and railroads.

I looked about. The few passengers who had alighted by choice had long since left the station, and the ticket master, snug in his office, would most likely chase me from the waiting room. The rails, reflecting the dull gleam of the station lamps, disappeared north and south into the inky Tennessee night. To the west, the great dark Mississippi rolled. A few shacks and piers could be made out along the near shore, but they appeared to be deserted at this hour. To the east, the city of Memphis slept. I remembered spending three days here with dear Mr. Booth's tour five years before, in 1887. Being short of funds, I'd inquired of a kindly Negro letter carrier if there were a way for an honest lady to earn a few pennies to get her dress repaired, and he had introduced me to an ambitious young teacher at the colored school who desired elocution lessons. Aside from these industrious people, who were doubtless fast asleep somewhere in the colored section, I knew no one in Memphis, and remembered it as one of the sleepier river towns.

The ghostly wind rattled through the weeds and fluttered a corner of my cloak. With a last puff on my cigar, I lifted my Gladstone bag and my heavy trunk and hid them under a stack of grain sacks that were awaiting shipment. I headed for town on the slim chance that I might encounter a kindhearted and helpful gentleman still awake.

I picked my way along the pitch-dark street that led away from the river. But when I reached Front Street, the first crossing, I saw lights and several small clusters of gentlemen standing and talking in the street. The Front Street tavern was doing a brisk trade even at this late hour. I paused to pull my rouge from a handy pocket in my bouffant sleeve, applied just a touch to my lips, and went in.

I know, I know, a proper lady would never enter such a low establishment, certainly not at night in a river town. But what do you expect a poor penniless lady to do? It would be many long hours before the pawnshops opened, and I could hardly book a suite at the Ritz.

Fortune smiled upon me immediately. I caught the eye of a blond fellow with a fine mustache waxed into stylish points and a watch fob ornamented with a golden fleur-de-lis. He wore a gunbelt with a small blue-black pistol. He was sitting at a round table with a plate of catfish, a glass of ale, a newspaper, and a notebook before him. As I entered he inspected my blond hair and elegant gray gown with Parisian sleeves, then jumped to his feet most politely. "Good evening, madam," he said.

"Oh, sir, what a joy to encounter a kind face like yours in this hour of my need!"

Several other gentlemen had turned to look at me, a couple of the more inebriated favoring me with loud suggestions that I shall not dignify by repeating. My fair-haired hero scowled at them, then bowed me into a chair at his table. I couldn't help eyeing his dinner plate.

"I would indeed be delighted to assist you, madam," said my new acquaintance, waggling his blond eyebrows at me. "Tell me—but no, I see that you have not yet dined. They prepare a tolerable catfish here."

"Oh, sir, that would be most delightful!" He signalled the innkeeper and I continued, "Allow me to introduce myself. I am Miss Bridget Mooney, of the St. Louis Mooneys."

"Delighted, madam. My name is Reginald Peterson, and I write for the Memphis *Commercial Appeal.*" He indicated the newspaper before him. It featured an editorial vehement on the subject of protecting Southern womanhood.

Well, I wished someone would protect Southern womanhood from the greedy Chesapeake and Ohio, but I didn't think that was what the editorial meant, so I kept mum about it. Instead I said, "I am pleased to make your acquaintance, sir, for I greatly admire your profession."

"Thank you, my dear Miss Mooney. A journalist's calling is to serve society by observing truly. Sometimes even the law fails, and then we must say so and fight for justice." Mr. Peterson smiled at me quite warmly, perhaps impressed by my conversation, perhaps by my rosy lips. I feared it was my lips. Since I did not want our acquaintance to progress so rapidly that I would miss my dinner, I looked about for a conversational topic that might distract him.

"I see that Memphis has its share of ambitious Negroes," I commented, indicating his notebook, which had jottings about a grocery store owned by three of that race.

My diversion succeeded. Mr. Peterson snorted, "More than ambitious! Saturday night a few fine white men were entering the grocery premises and the damn darkies shot at them!"

"How dreadful!" I exclaimed. "No doubt the men wanted only to purchase groceries!"

"Well, in fact—" My well-dressed and well-waxed companion cleared his throat. "But tell me, Miss Mooney, what misfortune brings you to this place?"

Just then the innkeeper arrived with a handsome plate of catfish, which was indeed as delicious as Mr. Peterson had predicted. I applied knife and fork most daintily while recounting a tale of a dreadful pickpocket who had stolen my money and train ticket.

But just as I was delicately approaching the subject of how eternally grateful I would be if he loaned me enough money for train fare, a stout man entered the room. He was wearing two diamond rings and an expensive dark woolen muffler that hid the lower part of his face. This man stopped briefly at several tables, including ours, and said with barely suppressed enthusiasm, "Let's go, Peterson."

"Yes, sir, Mr. Carmack." My new friend leapt to his feet and bowed to me politely. "Please excuse me for a moment, Miss Mooney. My employer calls." He strode swiftly out the door.

Well, did you ever hear of such dreadful manners on the part of a southern gentleman? Fearing that the innkeeper would make unreasonable demands that I pay for my dinner, I snatched up my blue cape and skedaddled out the door after my new acquaintance.

But Mr. Peterson's fine mustache was nowhere to be seen. Instead, many gentlemen were milling about in the middle of Front Street. They had all tied dark cloths about their faces, like Mr. Carmack, who had summoned my new admirer. Not wishing to anger gentlemen with covered faces, I shrank back into the shadows against the tavern wall, thinking that Mr. Peterson was a clever reporter indeed, masking himself in order to observe the activities better.

The men began to move along the street, quite silently. Not knowing what to do, but hoping to find Mr. Peterson when they had finished whatever mysterious business they were about, I stole along behind them, keeping to the shadows.

They did not go far. Soon I heard the ringing of a bell, and an answering voice, "Who's there?"

"I have a prisoner."

"All right. This is the place, and I am always ready to receive them."

I was hiding next to a large shadowy building and was just able to make out the sign: Shelby County Jail. The voice, no doubt the watchman's, had come from inside. In a moment I heard a click of keys and saw the gate swing open. Instantly, three of the masked men pushed inside. I heard the watchman cry out, "What does this mean?" Then the voices were drowned out by the tramping feet of the rest of the mob rushing into the jailyard.

Hang it, this was not the place for a proper lady! I decided to wait no longer for the attractive and just-minded Mr. Peterson. My Aunt Mollie had taught me that too much knowledge about gentlemen's affairs could be dangerous to a lady. Wrapping my cape about me, I slipped away from the jail and peeped into the Front Street tavern to confirm that every gentleman awake was behind a mask at the jail, excepting only the innkeeper, whom I wished to avoid. I turned back toward the river. Now that I had dined properly, a night among the grain sacks might be more easily borne.

Imagine my distress when I reached the railway and saw the very mob of men I had left behind, pouring out of Auction Street onto the rails! I scurried under a porch to hide, because I did not want these gentlemen upset with me. They turned north, marching briskly and silently along the tracks, and driving before them three Negroes, gagged and securely bound. The three must have done something unspeakable to a white lady, I told myself, to so outrage the law-abiding citizenry of Memphis. Otherwise, surely, these kind gentlemen would let the prisoners' cases be tried legally, in court.

In the lantern light, I could see no unspeakable evil in the prisoners' dark eyes. Only fear.

I waited until the secretive army had passed by. At least their activities would be reported, for one of the masked men, I saw, had a watch fob ornamented with a golden fleur-de-lis. Another wore two handsome diamond rings.

Their footsteps rang out loud and dreadful, and slowly receded into the night.

There hadn't been a lynching in Memphis since the war.

After a time, I heard the crackle of a far-off fusillade. My catfish dinner turned a slow somersault within me.

I waited under the porch, but no one returned along the tracks.

Shivering even in my cape, I tiptoed out into the darkness and back to the grain sacks on the station platform. I curled up among them, but could not sleep. I thought no one had seen me watching the mob, and yet I was nervous, and more than nervous. I had supp'd full with horrors.

I know, I know, a proper lady wouldn't fret about the sound of gunshots in the night. A proper lady wouldn't presume to think that gentlemen might be wrong, and that the virtue of white southern womanhood might be as well protected by judges and courtrooms as by midnight abductions of prisoners. A proper lady would be grateful to her protectors. But I'm just a poor foolish girl from Missouri, and never got the hang of thinking like a proper lady, and I couldn't sleep, not with the nightmare memories of dark fearful eyes and the crackle of far-off gunfire.

Shortly before dawn, a freight train pulled into the station. Although I knew I should wait for the pawnshops to open, I couldn't bear to spend another minute in Memphis, and decided to gamble. Taking advantage of the dark, I hauled my trunk and Gladstone bag to a boxcar door, and when the trainmen were occupied with unloading some bales of cotton, I shoved my trunk inside and scrambled up behind it. I found myself amid crates of turnips, beets, and onions. At last, I could doze.

Yes, my Aunt Mollie would agree with you. It was foolish to stow away in an ill-smelling boxcar when the morning would bring the opening of pawnshops, and perhaps even another meeting with kind Mr. Peterson, who might well be as upset as I at what his profession had forced him to observe. But hang it, those nightmares had me plumb scared and worn out, and I wanted to get shut of Memphis.

Alas, this proved to be very difficult. We had traveled a mere fifteen miles north when an overly alert attendant discovered me huddled half asleep among the vegetable crates. He was as heartless as the conductor of the passenger train. Before I could wake up to protest, he had tossed my trunk down the embankment, and I had to leap after it, Gladstone bag in hand, fortunate only in that the train had slowed considerably to round a curve. My bag and I skidded down the stony embankment and fetched up on a narrow road that paralleled the tracks. I stumbled back half a mile to where my trunk lay, hauled my baggage into a willow copse, and gave myself over to sleep, and nightmares.

I woke at noon, ravenously hungry and eager to continue my journey to St. Louis. But my o'er hasty departure from Memphis had left me worse off than before. It was now clear that the Chesapeake and Ohio was not in the mood to provide journeys on credit. I would have to obtain money somehow. Unfortunately, the nearest source of money was back in Memphis, with its pawnshops and Mr. Peterson. Much as I disliked the idea, the prudent thing to do would be to turn back.

But with no money, and with baggage to carry, it required two days to cover those few miles. I was delayed by an episode involving some fresh-baked loaves of bread that someone had carelessly left on the windowsill of a ramshackle house, and also involving two mangy yellow hounds that lurked under a porch nearby. They chased me into the woods, where the heel of my shoe broke off. I didn't want to shoot them as the sound might bring unwanted visitors, so I shinnied up a maple tree where I remained for a miserable night finishing the loaf and pelting the hounds with branches until they lost interest. I was further delayed because, although a few farm wagons were going my direction, even the ones driven by colored men, who are usually compassionate and helpful, did not pause and even increased their speed. I consoled myself by muttering, "A ragged multitude of hinds and peasants, rude and merciless," and trudged on.

At last a rickety mule-drawn wagon filled with baskets of yams and driven by a rotund old Negro woman stopped.

"I reckon I'm gonna be sorry for this," she said in the warm rural accents of the South, "but you're lookin' like you need some help, ma'am."

"Oh, please, could you help? My money and ticket were stolen on the train, and if I could only get back to Memphis—"

"Memphis!" The woman snorted. "I wasn't plannin' to go by that route, ma'am! There's trouble there, heaps of trouble."

I realized then that the colored men who had passed me by feared for their lives if they were caught in the company of a white lady. I clasped my hands in supplication. "Oh, please, if you could take me even part of the way—"

She considered and asked abruptly, "Can you read?"

"Of course!"

"No 'of course' about it, ma'am, if you're born a slave and nobody sends you to school. But my cousin's husband, he says this newspaper has a story 'bout the lynchin', and if you read it to me I s'pose I can swing down as far as the Memphis streetcar line."

I didn't want to read about a lynching, for the mere thought of what I'd seen made me quake, but I had little choice. I heaved my baggage onto the wagon bed and climbed up onto the seat beside her. Bessie, for such proved to be her name, handed me a copy of the Memphis newspaper, and as the mule picked his slow way along many bumpy, bone-rattling miles, I began to read the dreadful story, wondering if Mr. Peterson had written it.

The reporter explained that twenty-seven colored men had been arrested because they had ambushed and shot four deputy sheriffs while the officers were "looking for a Negro for whose arrest they had a warrant." Bessie snorted at that, and I decided that Mr. Peterson, out of delicacy, had not mentioned the true reason. Lynchings, I'd always been told, occurred when fine gentlemen became so incensed at the violation of their virtuous women that they lost their heads and dealt out justice themselves instead of waiting for the courts. This fact was so well known that my friend Phoebe in St. Louis, who'd consorted willingly and frequently with a handsome mulatto stevedore, was easily able to save her reputation when her aunt discovered her emerging from his cabin. Phoebe simply accused him of assault. A lynching party was formed but the young man had very prudently left town. Still, no violated virtue was mentioned here in Memphis.

I read on. The newspaper said that the mob had selected William Stuart, Calvin McDowell, and Theodore Moss as their three victims. This last name jolted me, for the kind letter carrier who'd helped me years before had been Tommie Moss. I prayed that Theodore was not a relative of his. The story said that the three prisoners had been marched to the edge of town. Every detail agreed with what I had seen. Then, "in an open field, near the Wolf River, the Negroes met their doom. For the first time they were allowed to speak. As the gags were removed Moss said: 'If you are going to kill us, turn our faces to the west.' Scarce had he uttered the words when the crack of a revolver was heard, and a ball crashed through his cheek. This was the signal for the work. A volley was poured upon the shivering Negroes and they fell dead."

"Oh, Lord, Lord!" exclaimed my companion. Tears were rolling down her cheeks.

Well, I didn't want to read any more of this terrible story either. Getting away from it was the reason I'd left Memphis in the first place. Pushing the image of the prisoners' frightened dark eyes from my mind, I skipped to the last paragraphs, cleared my throat, and continued. "'The mob turned about after it had completed its terrible work and came toward the town. At the first crossing they scattered, and all disappeared as silently as they had arrived on the scene. Not a trace of any of them can be found this morning.'"

Bessie lashed at the mule with such vigor that I paused to glance at her, but she said only, "Please, go on, ma'am."

I read on about the angry though unarmed assembly of Negroes, and about the equipping of 150 white men with Winchesters to preserve order, and about the verdict of the jury at the inquest: "'We find that the deceased were taken from the Shelby County Jail by a masked mob of men, the men overpowered and taken to an old field and shot to death by parties unknown by the jury.'"

Bessie snorted, "Parties unknown by the jury!"

I said with relief, "That's the end of the story."

"No ma'am, there's more coming, and I'm not goin' into Memphis."

Well, how could I argue with her? I myself was doubly eager to find a pawnshop, or my admirer, and leave the dreadful town where people shot each other with such abandon.

Late in the day our wagon came to a crossroads, and Bessie pulled the mule to a halt. "Here we are, ma'am. I thank you for the reading. I go east here, where I know folks. You go straight ahead, and 'fore long you'll be at the curve of the streetcar line."

My benefactress had been right to be worried. As I hobbled toward the streetcar tracks I saw bands of colored men around a shop that had been nearly destroyed, its windows broken, its door smashed, the sign "People's Grocery" gashed and hanging askew. There were also bands of white men carrying Winchesters, as promised in the newspaper. They were led by men with sheriff's badges.

The setting sun threw slanting rays across the tense faces, and I paused by someone's henhouse to survey the situation. It appeared to be a wary truce, the colored men muttering and occasionally cursing but making no hostile moves, the white ones swaggering about with their rifles, all of them with that dangerous kind of anger men pretend when they are bone-scared. Under ordinary circumstances I might have tripped daintily across to the streetcar tracks, secure in the knowledge that as a proper white lady I would be defended by every rifle there. But nights without sleep, a broken heel, and bucketsfull of road dust had somewhat diminished my ability to appear a proper lady. Thus, when a gunshot blasted through the late rosy light, I leapt into the henhouse, pulling the door closed behind me amid a great flapping and squawking on the part of the usual residents. Ignoring them, I applied my eye to a knothole.

Outside, no one appeared to be hurt, but most of the colored men had taken shelter behind wagons or houses. The men with sheriff's badges were laughing. One shouted something about a coon dance.

The hens quieted in the darkness, and I became aware of another sort of breathing the instant before a taut voice said, "Who's there?"

"A lady! Fear not!" I cried, diving to the floor as I pulled my well-oiled Colt from the hidden pocket in my bouffant sleeve.

"Yes, it is evident that you are a lady." The voice was a lady's too, educated far beyond the usual Southern female's. I could not tell where she was.

I asked, "Pray tell, madam, why are you in this place?"

"Fear of that armed mob," explained the unseen lady. "And you, madam?"

"The same," I replied. "By a series of misfortunes I find myself here in Memphis today."

"I live in Memphis, I regret to say," replied the lady with considerable bitterness. I decided she had no plans to harm me and tucked my Colt back into its pocket as she continued, "I had thought my town had progressed beyond these barbarisms. Such dreadful stories I could tell! 'Hie thee hither/ That I may pour my spirits in thine ear . . .' "

I was curious to know why a well-educated lady would be found in a henhouse in a colored section of town, but as the same question might be asked of me, I did not pursue it, and instead completed her quotation: "'And chastise with the valour of my tongue/ All that impedes thee from the golden round.' "

The lady gasped. "Can it be? Are you—pray, madam, are you Miss Mooney, who came to Memphis four years ago with the famed Mr. Booth, and for three days kindly instructed me in elocution?"

"Ida?" I gasped in turn, realizing my mistake. "Are you Ida Wells?" Amidst the clucking of the hens, I fumbled my way across the straw-strewn floor and embraced her, though I knew my Aunt Mollie would have frowned at such egalitarianism with a colored lady, even one as proper as Ida. I was so delighted to find a friend I couldn't help myself. "Ida, I am so glad to see you! Well, hear you," I amended, as it was still pitch-dark. "You have forgotten none of your lessons! My teacher, the illustrious English actress Mrs. Fannie Kemble, would be delighted with your elocution!"

"Thank you," she said. "Shortly after you and Mr. Booth left, a score of us formed a dramatic organization. We were very much enthused about improving our vocal skills and our knowledge."

"I well remember your enthusiasm. I never have had a student so apt. Your tongue has valour indeed! You could have a great success on the stage!"

"Thank you, but I find that my calling is journalism," she said. "Did you know that I am now part owner and editor of our black newspaper here, the *Free Press?*"

"How splendid!"

"But we meet again in cruel, cruel circumstances. Oh, how I wish I were allowed to buy a pistol, so that I could defend myself!"

Well, remembering the tenseness in her voice a moment ago when she first challenged me in the dark, I was just as glad she hadn't had a pistol then. I said soothingly, "Things are quieter outside now."

"Is it yet dark?"

I returned to the knothole and peered out. "Dusk has fallen," I reported, "and there are fewer men and rifles about. I believe it is safe to emerge."

"Then I will go home," she said. "I must finish my editorial."

"Oh, Ida, may I come with you, just for a few moments? My travels have left me dusty, and I crave a drink of water."

"Of course! You are most welcome, Miss Mooney."

"Bridget," I said firmly, though I knew it wasn't proper.

We slipped out into the twilit town. She looked much as I remembered, a short woman with a lively round face and eyes that telegraphed her emotions, sparkling with enthusiasm or simmering with scorn or anger. Her dress was dark and neat, yet stylish and very proper once she'd brushed off the straws. She exclaimed when she saw my sorry state. Soon we arrived at Ida's neat rented quarters, and she postponed her editorial for a few moments in order to fill the washtubs on her back porch for me and to take my unfortunate shoe to a cobbler across the street. I washed my face and hands and changed into a plain clean frock, then went out to the porch again to launder my road-soiled garments. When Ida returned, I looked up from the washtub to say, "Ida, I am considering bringing an action against the dreadful Chesapeake and Ohio Railroad. If a colored woman succeeded in the courts against them, surely I can too. Please, tell me how you won your case."

"Win? I didn't win," she said crossly.

"What? How can that be? When we last spoke, you had proved in court that they had not honored your first-class ticket, and had sent you to sit in the smoking car instead! The court had awarded you five hundred dollars!"

"Oh, yes, the lower court. I still remember the headlines: 'A Darky Damsel Obtains a Verdict for Damages.' But the railroad appealed to the Tennessee Supreme Court, and they overturned the decision."

"But the railroad didn't honor the ticket it sold you! How could the judges say a jim crow car was first class?"

"How could they not? My dear Miss Mooney—"

"Bridget."

"My dear Bridget, they could not allow the precedent! My case was the first with a colored plaintiff since the repeal of Sumner's Federal Civil Rights Bill. The repeal means that we can no longer go to the Federal courts, and must abide by state decisions. This state does not want justice for my race."

"Oh dear." I rinsed out my muslin underskirt. "It's true, I have never found the law favorable toward those of us who are not rich."

"Rich and white," she agreed. "Oh, Bridget, when I heard the verdict, I wanted to gather my people in my arms and fly far away with them! There is no justice in this land for us."

"But surely it is better than it was!" I protested. "My brother died fighting for the Union side!"

"The war has been over for twenty-seven years," Ida said with dignity, "and despite the sacrifices of people like your brother, there has been so much backsliding since the days of Reconstruction that I have no confidence in the majority of white people. Our hard-won freedom is hollow without justice. At this moment I am so heartsore about the lynching that it is difficult to feel that anything has improved."

"It was terrible indeed," I agreed. I didn't wish to discuss the terrible affair, but I was curious about one point. "Ida, I believe the newspaper left out part of the story. Doesn't lynching spring from gentlemen's unreasoning anger about unspeakable crimes against womanhood? No such crimes were reported."

"I can hardly blame you for thinking that lynching is the product of un-thinking outrage, because that is the story they always give out, and in fact I too believed it until last week," Ida said. She stretched up to pin my washed underskirt onto a clothesline stretched between the porch posts. "But of course there was no such occurrence here, and they lynched Tommie Moss all the same."

"Tommie?" I froze, the soapy bloomers in my hand dripping into the washtub. "Tommie Moss, the kind letter carrier who introduced us? He was lynched?"

"Yes." She nodded, her face a picture of grief in the light that shone out through the kitchen window. "Tommie Moss, the kindest, best-loved man in Memphis, and my dear friend Betty's husband. I am godmother to his little daughter Maurine."

"Oh, Ida!" Once again I embraced her, heedless of the soapsuds and of what Aunt Mollie might think. "But the newspaper didn't mention his name!"

"The white newspapers got the names wrong too. Misspelled Stewart, and called Tommie 'Theodore' Moss."

"But—how did it happen? How did such a kind man come to shoot a white man?"

"He didn't!" Ida explained indignantly. "He did something far more outrageous."

I had met Tommie Moss only briefly, but still found it difficult to imagine him committing outrages. "What did he do?"

"He owned his home. He saved his money. He took McDowell and Stewart as partners and went into the grocery business with the same ambition that a young white man would have had. Tommie was the president of the company. He continued delivering letters during the day while his partners ran the business, and then took care of the books at night."

"I don't understand. That sounds perfectly proper."

A bitter smile twitched at Ida's lips. "Then you do understand. Tommie was an exemplary young man, with a sweet family. He worked industriously. He was succeeding. But you see, the People's Grocery was located across the street from a grocery owned by a white man."

"I see," I said, and I did. Gentlemen everywhere are like that, don't you agree? They're full of manly ideals and heroic aspirations and kindness in their conversation, but their actions are more often inspired by money. "Still, lynching seems an extreme measure, even for a grocer who was losing business."

"They made other attempts first," Ida explained. "At one point the white grocer and another man swore out warrants against Tommie and some others for defending a little colored boy who'd been flogged by a grown white man. But the judge merely fined them and dismissed the case. Then we heard that the vanquished whites were coming Saturday night to clean out the People's Grocery Company."

"Oh dear."

"Tommie consulted a lawyer, who said that since the grocery was outside the city limits, they were beyond police protection, and therefore would be justified in protecting themselves if attacked. That's what the law says."

Well, I could see what was coming, because I've never found that what the law says has very much to do with what happens. As I pinned my bloomers to the line, I grieved for Ida, who had tried to use the law to stop injustice on the part of the wicked Chesapeake and Ohio, and most of all for kind Tommie Moss, who foolishly believed that if he had freedom to buy a grocery, the law also gave him freedom to protect it.

Ida continued, "Tommie's company armed some guards and stationed them in the rear of the store, not to attack, but to repel the threatened attack, as allowed by the law. And that night, as he was doing the books and McDowell was waiting on customers just before closing, they heard gunfire. Their guards had shot at several white men who were sneaking in the back way. Three were wounded, none killed."

"But the newspaper said they were officers with a warrant!"

"No, they were not. The newspapers also said the People's Grocery Company was 'a low dive in which drinking and gambling were carried on: a resort of thieves and thugs.' " Ida's eyes blazed. "That's what the leading white journals called this legitimate business owned by decent black businessmen!"

Could the just-minded Mr. Peterson work for such a newspaper? I said, "So you think the problem was, Tommie was successful."

"That's right, Bridget. Success was Tommie's outrageous crime. Immediately there was a massive police raid on the entire neighborhood. Over a hundred colored men were put in jail on suspicion. They took our weapons, of course, and forbade any sale of arms to Negroes, so we are completely defenseless. The white newspapers said the wounded white men would die, and for two nights colored men guarded the jail. Then the newspapers announced that the wounded were out of danger, and our men thought the crisis was past and left the jail unguarded."

Had my brother died for this? I was thinking that my handsome blond admirer's friends were about as low and cowardly as they came. How could they claim they broke the law in an unreasoning fit of rage if they waited coolly for three days until they could break it in perfect safety?

No, it was clear that they'd lynched Tommie Moss because he would have won in a fair public trial.

I asked, "So none of the wounded men died?"

"None. But of course that was not the issue. The lynchers did not look for the men who had fired the shots. Instead they took the three partners of the People's Grocery Company. Three decent, kind, successful men." Tears sparkled on Ida's dark face, and I found my cheeks wet too.

"I am sorry, I didn't know! The white newspapers reported so many lies," I said, my faith in Mr. Peterson crumbling.

"There is more!" Ida declared, her eyes flashing. She stepped into her kitchen, returned with a copy of the *Commercial Appeal*, and read, " 'McDowell's jaw was entirely shot away and back of his right ear there was a hole large enough to admit a man's fist.' "

I clapped my hands over my ears. "Stop! Ida, please, I can't bear to hear it!"

"Bridget, don't you see, that is the problem!" Ida's eloquent eyes blazed. "How can we ever stop this injustice if white people refuse to notice it? Did Tommie Moss and your brother die in vain?"

Hang it, all I wanted to do was avoid trouble and get myself to St. Louis. But what can a poor girl do, confronted with someone as persuasive as Ida Wells? Her words, like daggers, entered in mine ears, and I could think of no reply. Reluctantly I muttered, "Go on."

Ida read, "His right hand, too, had been half blown away, as if, in defense, he had grabbed the muzzle of a shotgun. Stuart was shot in the mouth and twice in the back of the head. His body was riddled with buckshot. Moss had one ear shot off and several bullet holes in his forehead.' "

Sickened, I moaned, "Oh no!"

Genteel and unstoppable, she read on: " 'As the gags were removed, Moss said, "If you are going to kill us, turn our faces to the west." ' " Her blazing eyes flicked up to my face. "Don't you see, Bridget? The journalist was there! This is an eyewitness account. He knew!"

In the fading hope that my admirer had been a mere observer, I said, "But isn't it true that journalists are often at the scenes of terrible events that they cannot prevent?"

"Even if you cannot prevent the crime, you can work for justice! You can publish the whole truth!"

"Isn't that story true?"

"The facts of the lynching are true. But listen to this: 'Not a trace of any of them can be found this morning.' Bridget, the inquest found that Tommie Moss and McDowell and Stewart were killed by 'parties unknown by the jury.' That's ridiculous! Everyone knows! And yet—no one tells."

Proper ladies don't involve themselves in such matters; but I was overwhelmed by her outraged dignity and sorrow, and blurted out, "Ida, I saw that mob assemble. Mr. Peterson and Mr. Carmack were both there, masked like the others."

As soon as I'd said it, I wanted to call back the words. Wouldn't you?

It was dangerous to know such things, more dangerous still to speak of them. But Ida did not seem shocked. "Yes, a friend said he thought he'd seen them. It's not surprising. Carmack writes hateful editorials. But they won't admit to being there, and they won't identify any of their friends in the newspapers and certainly not in the courts. There will be no justice for Tommie."

In my head Aunt Mollie was in full bray, pointing out that I must avoid the anger of armed, masked gentlemen, and that I'd best get me some money quick and light out for St. Louis, and other sensible businesslike things. But Ida's words batter'd me like roaring cannon-shot. I took a deep breath. "Suppose someone white testified against them?"

Ida looked at me with pity. "If you have any foolish notions about testifying, forget them. You're white, yes, that's a great advantage. But you're a woman, and an outsider, and an actress. They will make your reputation the jest and byword of the street."

She was right, of course. This was not the first time I had faced the dreadful prejudices against those in my profession. I could not help Ida's cause in the courtroom.

I tried again. "Perhaps I could speak to a judge privately, and he could call for official inquiries."

"My dear Bridget, the criminal court judge too was a member of that mob."

"Oh."

"There will be no justice in this case."

I could almost hear Aunt Mollie breathing a sigh of relief as I realized the hopelessness of the situation. I turned sadly back to cleaning my gown and asked, "Ida, can you safely publish this story in your newspaper?"

"Safely? No. But publish it I will," she said firmly. "So much education is needed! Even I believed the lie that lynching occurs because of unreasoning outrage at the violation of an innocent woman. There is much work to do among both races to dispel that lie. But white people don't read my newspaper. I can tell my people the truth, and I will. But Bridget, how can I tell yours?"

That was a difficult problem indeed. Even I, kindhearted as I was, had done my best to avoid noticing these horrors. I said slowly, "Well, they have revealed their weakness with this lynching. As you say, what they fear is not damage to white womanhood, after all. It is not even being shot, for when a man of their own race shoots at them, they allow fair trials to take place. No, what they fear is colored success. Tommie's grocery won your race's patronage, and they killed him. That means they fear the loss of your business."

"So we are not powerless after all. We must use our power. But how?" Ida began to pace up and down the porch, ignoring the flapping garments on the line. "Ah, Oklahoma is opening up. Tommie said, turn our faces to the west. I'll urge my people to move west!" Ida paused in the light from the kitchen window, her small immaculately dressed person erect, her luminous eyes flashing. "There is only one thing left that we can do; save our money and leave behind a cruel town which will neither protect us nor give us a fair and legal trial, but instead murders us in cold blood!"

I applauded. "Ida, that will work! Money always works!"

"I only wish I could make them see the immorality of their actions."

"I fear they are not yet rich enough to be moral."

"Was your brother rich?"

"Well, no, but he was hired by the Northern army."

"The money's northern, even now," Ida pointed out. "Our streetcar line is owned by northern capitalists, although it's run by southern lynchers. Suppose we stop riding the streetcar? We walked before it was built, we can walk again!"

"Good! Withholding patronage from the streetcar may catch the attention of northerners too. And here's another idea!" I exclaimed. "Ida, go on stage! Tell your story, just as you've told it to me. Other white people will be as moved as I if they hear you tell of these outrages. But don't go west. Go north, and speak to the moneyed classes. Southerners look up to those with money!"

"I don't know," Ida said dubiously. "My acquaintance Mr. Fortune is the editor of a New York newspaper, and he tells me that it's difficult to get white people to read it there too. It's like a great stone wall without a door."

"Then talk to those who are richer and more powerful than New Yorkers! Tell your story to the English, Ida!"

"The English?"

"They are rich and powerful and highly moral. Well, most of them," I amended, thinking of my friend Lillie Langtry, but deciding not to mention her, as Ida was so proper that she might be offended. "And furthermore, the English have nothing to lose if your race gets justice in faraway America, so they can afford to be moral. And their opinion carries great weight among influential people in this country."

"But would they listen to a person of my race? To someone who was born a slave? To an American?"

I looked at her short, trimly attired person, her blazing eyes, her face, so vivid in its darkness, and smiled. "The English will find your story mesmerizing, Ida, because you'll tell it in the ringing accents of their own beloved Mrs. Fannie Kemble."

"So learning the rich folks' language can be a weapon too!" Ida bounced to the edge of the porch and raised both hands to the starry sky. "Do you hear, Tommie?" she cried. "We shall have justice yet!"

Well, I reckoned justice would take a while, but there was no need to say that to Ida Wells, who understood the world at least as well as I. She hurried off to write an editorial urging her people to move away from Memphis if they could, and to save their money and avoid the streetcar.

I hurried off, too, to pawn one of my genuine theatrical emerald necklaces before the pawnshops closed, and to purchase a ticket to St. Louis from the reprehensible Chesapeake and Ohio. Then I donned my blond wig and my striped dress trimmed with white guipure lace, screwed my courage to the sticking-place, and made my way to Front Street.

I know, I know, it wasn't proper to return to such low haunts, and it was mighty risky besides, and in the usual run of things I never would have done it. But somehow Ida's words kept ringing in my head and nudging me on.

In the tavern, several of the gentlemen kindly offered their companionship, but I declined firmly and ordered a catfish dinner, which the innkeeper agreed to bring if I first paid for my interrupted dinner of Tuesday night. Presently, who should appear but my acquaintance of the waxed blond mustache.

"Why, Mr. Peterson!" I exclaimed with a shocked flutter of my eyelashes. "What am I to think of you?"

"My dear Miss Mooney! I beg your forgiveness!" He adjusted his gunbelt and dropped to one knee with an extravagant flourish of his hat. A couple of men in the room snickered, but lordie, his blue eyes and golden hair were handsome!

I gave him my prettiest pout. "Sir, it was not gentlemanly to leave a lady for so long."

"You are right, and you have my most fervent apologies. My business took considerably longer than I had anticipated, and I was desolate to think that you awaited me still. It was a matter of honor and of justice."

"It is true, sir, that the moment I first saw you, I took you for a gentleman of honor and justice."

"True, journalists too serve society. When the law is sure to fail, journalists too fight for justice!"

Hang it, how could a lady resist such a touching apology and such a kindly regard for justice? " 'We will solicit heaven and move the gods/ To send down justice for to wreak our wrongs!' " I quoted, and smiled at him. "And when the law is sure to fail, heaven sends down journalists! Please, sir, sit down."

He called for a whiskey and took the other chair at my table with a hopeful glint in his blue eyes. "Thank you, my dear Miss Mooney, for your understanding. It is delightful to meet again."

"It is a pleasure to renew my acquaintance with a man of intellect, who helps society by publishing the truth."

He beamed. Handsome blond gentlemen have little difficulty believing that they also possess intellect. "It is true," he said. "Mr. Carmack and I are devoted to the betterment of society." The golden fleur-de-lis on his watch fob winked at me as he added gallantly, "I must say, the company of a lovely blond lady who knows Shakespeare is pure delight!"

"My dear Mr. Peterson," I said, leaning near so that he could appreciate my Parisian perfume, "I would be very pleased to discuss justice and journalism at greater length, but I find it very close in here, and fear that I may faint. Do you suppose we could take the air for a few moments?"

"An enchanting idea! But it is rather cool, and there is mist on the river," he warned.

"So much the better!" I exclaimed, most sincerely. "Nothing could be more helpful for light-headedness. Let us take a stroll along the riverside."

With a triumphant wink at his fellows, Mr. Peterson downed the rest of his whiskey, peeled a bill from his roll for the innkeeper, and offered me his arm. We made a lovely pair, yes indeed, such a blond and handsome couple! Smiling into each other's eyes, we passed through the tavern door into the night.

Mr. Peterson's friends never saw him again.

The next morning, a redhead once more, I redeemed my emerald necklace from the pawnshop, then collected my baggage and bade farewell to Ida. "Bend every effort to addressing the public," I urged her. "Your splendid voice moves people to action."

"It is not my voice, it is the justice of my cause," she said earnestly. "And you too will tell the truth to those you meet?"

"I will do what I can," I said, and handed her a blue-black pistol. "I hope you never have to use it, Ida. But even the most proper of ladies must occasionally defend herself."

Her expressive eyes glowed with pleasure upon receiving the gun she was forbidden to purchase. "Thank you, Bridget! I too pray that I never have occasion to use it, but I promise you, if I must die by violence, I will take my persecutors with me!"

I know, I know, I shouldn't have given it to her, but she might well need courage, and I only had room in my pocket for one Colt. Besides, I had the feeling that Tommie Moss would be pleased to see one of the guns that killed him in the hands of his crusading friend.

And crusade she did. Within a few weeks, at Ida's urging in the *Free Press,* hundreds of colored people disposed of their property and left town, leaving Memphis businessmen reeling. Six weeks after the lynching, the superintendent of the streetcar company came to the *Free Press* offices and begged Ida to use her influence to get the colored people to ride the streetcars again, because the company's losses were enormous. She naturally refused. In late May, when she was out of town, Mr. Carmack took exception to her editorial that revealed the truth about false accusations like that of my friend Phoebe, and he incited a mob to destroy the office of the *Free Press.*

That didn't stop Ida Wells. She began writing for Mr. Fortune in New York and telling her story to women's clubs and church groups. Through them she met the famed English Quaker Mrs. Impey, editor of *Anti-Caste.* At Mrs. Impey's invitation, Ida was soon in England and Scotland rousing the churches and newspapers there to protest lynching. They raised such a clamor that this nation could no longer ignore the problem. Chastised by the valor of Ida's tongue, Americans of both races formed antilynching societies all over the United States. There were setbacks in Congress due to southern filibusters, but more and more prominent whites publicly opposed lynching, and slowly, mob rule receded.

Justice, I fear, will be slower to arrive.

Or perhaps it arrives in scraps and fragments. Mr. Carmack, who moved to Nashville, was eventually gunned down in the streets there—but that's another story.

As for my admirer with the blond waxed mustache, surely he could have no complaints, for he himself believed that sometimes the law is sure to fail, and for the betterment of society, other means of justice must be found. Who could argue with such estimable sentiments? His corpse washed up near Natchez a couple of weeks after I left. The verdict at the inquest was that he had died at the hands of parties unknown by the jury.

FROM BRIDGET MOONEY'S SCRAPBOOK

THE NEW YORK TIMES
March 10, 1892

In a few minutes the suburbs of the city were reached, and in an open field, near Wolf River, the negroes met their doom. For the first time they were allowed to speak. As the gags were removed Moss said: "If you are going to kill us turn our faces to the west-" Scarcely had he uttered the words when the crack of a revolver was heard, and a ball crashed through his cheek. This was the signal for the work. A volley was poured upon the shivering negroes and they fell dead.

The bodies were taken to Walsh's undertaking establishment at 7:30 o'clock. The place was surrounded by about 200 negroes. They were afraid to talk, but there were mutterings and curses. Word reached the city that the negroes were assembling in large numbers at the curve, and Judge Dubose equipped 150 men with rifles and sent them there to preserve order.

The following jury was impaneled to hold an inquest on the bodies of the lynched negroes: C. McCormack, Isaac M. Simkins, H. J. Parish, A. E. Hewitt, G. H. Guthrie, M. Kehoe, J. Banan, George Holbus, J. M. Peterson.

This verdict was rendered: "We find that the deceased were taken from the Shelby County Jail by a masked mob of men, the men overpowered, and taken to an old field and shot to death by parties unknown by the jury."

THE KING OF COMEDY; or,
A Policeman's Lot Is Not a Happy One

"**M**ost perfidious and drunken monster!" I quoted, rapping Keystone on his nose. "Get away from my whiskey!" The big tabby-striped tomcat flicked his tail at me disdainfully and scampered up to the balcony that ran over our heads at this end of Murphy's Restaurant.

Well, yes, I reckon you're right, it's foolish for an actress on tour to keep a pet. But Keystone had introduced himself to me in a dank and dreadful Philadelphia dressing-room and promptly found and killed a rat that was lurking in the bustle of the dress I'd been about to don. Wouldn't you be grateful? He had a torn ear, a kinky tail, and he amused me because he enjoyed tippling. All in all he rather reminded me of my dear departed papa. Besides, if the divine Sarah Bernhardt could keep cats, dogs, birds, and even lions, shouldn't an American artiste be entitled to a cat?

Murphy's had etched-glass windows and an attractive fretwork railing on the balcony, and passed for a high-class establishment, at least in Northampton. Yes, yes, I know I promised to tell you about Hollywood, and I will. But the story begins in Massachusetts. Besides, in 1898 Hollywood wasn't much more than a few shacks and a pepper tree. Not that Northampton was much better. It didn't even have the pepper tree.

That night, Murphy's was filled with rich and rowdy patrons. In the corner a group of well-dressed men were attempting to sing "A Policeman's Lot Is Not a Happy One," and above us on the balcony a rich fat man and his friends were carousing and beginning to raise angry voices. "I paid you back last week!" said a tall party in stylish peg-top trousers.

"You only paid half, Simon!" The fat man stood and shook a gold-ringed finger at the other.

"Teddy, you're drunk!" said Simon. The fat man turned his back with a stamp of his expensively shod foot.

I was surprised that the stage-door Johnny who was sitting across from me had chosen Murphy's, because he was obviously not as rich as the other patrons. In the ordinary way of things, I would have sent him packing. But Mike Sinnott was so gawky and Irish, and so young, only a year or two older than my dear niece, that I hadn't had the heart to refuse him. Besides, stage-door Johnnies were becoming rarer these days, even though regular use of Cheveuline kept my hair nearly as red as it had been twenty-five years before, when I first trod the boards.

I soon discovered that young Mike had more on his mind than my red hair, or my splendid performance as Beatrice, or my fashionable Parma-violet traveling suit and my pretty bracelets of gold worked into flowery chains. Mike's concern was quite different. "Miss Mooney," he said earnestly, "please tell me how I too can work on the stage!"

He must have noticed the surprised and skeptical look I cast on his horsy face, his long clumsy arms, his scarred hands. "Oh, I know I look like a gorilla!" He spread out one hand for my inspection. "I've had a job at the iron works. You can see how the molten iron splatters and burns. I must get into a better line of work, perhaps as a singer. I have a fine bass voice. Do you want to hear 'Asleep in the Deep'?"

"I believe you," I said hastily. In fact I had great sympathy for a young man who wished to improve his lot in life, because I too had taken to the stage when I realized that a poor girl from Missouri had few other options. Well, yes, she could marry a poor man, or become a tart, or work for a rich man, which usually amounted to the same thing. In any case she would remain poor. The stage, however, promised riches and fame—though the expenses of dressing properly and of providing for my dear niece had somewhat diminished the rewards it occasionally delivered for me. The theatre would be even more difficult for a youngster as clumsy and unrefined as my young admirer. But I didn't have the heart to tell him so. Youth should have its dreams, don't you think? My dear niece dreamed of a lovely tennis gown trimmed with ombré silk.

I said gently, "The first thing you must do, Mike, is leave Northampton."

Mike nodded glumly. A waiter bustled from the swinging door behind us with the lemon meringue pie Mike had ordered. It was an enormous portion, and I saw that I might have to assist him in finishing it. But before I could make this kind offer, an enormous crash jolted us both from our chairs.

The fat carouser had fallen from the balcony overhead and landed on the next table in a great flurry of silverware, broken china, and splashed soup. The gentleman and lady dining there jumped back, exclaiming.

The fat man lay very still, his knee bent at an odd angle. "Mike! Hurry! Find a doctor!" I exclaimed, pulling out my smelling-salts and loosening the fallen gentleman's tight starched collar.

Mike ran for help while a blonde woman who had hastened down the steps from the balcony began to shriek, "Teddy! Darling Teddy! Speak to me! It's your Millicent!" She waded through the wreckage of china and soup toward us, supported by the shorter of the two gentlemen in peg-top trousers who had been arguing with the fat man a moment before. A crowd of waiters and diners began to press around.

"Please, stand back so the poor man can breathe," I said. The unfortunate fellow was in a faint but his pulse was strong, and I yielded my place to the sobbing Millicent and her two friends. All three bent over the fallen Teddy.

Mike soon reappeared at the door, accompanied by a scrawny police officer and an elegant man in an expensive Chesterfield. "I'm Dr. Dove," he announced, clearing his way through the crowd with his walking-stick. He pushed me aside rudely, knelt by the unconscious man, took a gold watch from his pocket to check the pulse, and soon reported that with the prompt application of his patented formula, Dr. Dove's Elixir, to Teddy's cracked skull and broken leg, the plump unfortunate might survive.

The scrawny policeman asked, "Who pushed Mr. O'Brien?"

The taller of the men in peg-top trousers said, "He stumbled, sir."

Millicent looked up tearfully. "That's right! Everyone there is Teddy's friend! Everyone in this restaurant is Teddy's friend! Except—"

All eyes turned to me. "And just who are you, miss?" asked the policeman.

"I'm Bridget Mooney, sir, leading lady of the company now playing the famous French farce *A Flea in Her Ear* and the renowned Shakespearean comedy *Much Ado About Nothing.*"

"An actress, eh?" The scrawny officer snorted. "Well, we all know how actors carry on! I wouldn't be surprised if you turned out to be our villain!"

"Why, sir, I was nowhere near the man!"

"It's true, Officer Teheezel, she was down here!" said an old gentleman with a napkin still tucked under his chin and flecks of pea soup in his otherwise snowy walrus mustache.

Teheezel frowned at him. "Well, did you see anyone else push him?"

"But who would push Teddy?" Millicent asked, gesturing at the two fellows in peg-top trousers. "Sam and Simon are our friends! Teddy just stumbled against the rail and fell!"

"Still, you have to watch out for actors," growled Officer Teheezel. But he stopped inspecting me and instead squinted up at the broken balcony rail. I breathed a sigh of relief.

Then Millicent screamed again. "His watch! His beautiful solid-gold hunting-watch! It's gone! I gave it to him, and it's gone! It says, 'To dear

Teddy O'Brien from your little lambie!'"

Officer Teheezel turned back to me. "Aha!" he cried triumphantly. "There's a gold watch chain up your sleeve!"

"It's a bracelet, sir," I said in exasperation, turning back my lace-trimmed cuff so he could see my golden flowers.

But the scrawny officer didn't pause for logic. "I'll believe my own two eyes, and nothing else!" he cried, fumbling for his billy club as he headed toward me.

Well, now, did you ever hear of anything so unfair? Here I was, an innocent bystander—in fact, a helpful bystander, selflessly furnishing the unhappy victim with my very own smelling salts, a good Samaritan personified, yes indeed! And yet, rather than look for the true villain, this Dogberry of a policeman was about to arrest me! I glanced about for some hero to rescue me. But my young friend Mike had not yet been able to push through the curious crowd and still stood by the front door, and the walrus-mustached fellow was too old and too impressed by Teheezel's billy-club to be of much use. "I'm innocent!" I protested again, and before the policeman could raise his stick, I pushed Mike's lemon meringue pie into his face.

There was a burst of laughter from the onlookers, although a few of the more delicate sensibilities among them tried to muffle their mirth out of respect for the law. Officer Teheezel sputtered as he swiped at the meringue that covered his eyes.

I gasped in horror at what I had done. "Oh, lordy, sir, I'm so sorry! Please, allow me to help you! I'll get something to clean it off!" Shouting for a towel, I whisked through the swinging door into the kitchen, past the startled cooks, and out into the night. I found myself in a dark, malodorous alley behind the restaurant.

A scruffy gray-striped bundle flew out before I could close the door. "You're right, Keystone," I told him. "The company in there is not very refined. Let us depart."

We tiptoed toward the street. As we rounded the corner, we were greeted by a booming laugh. A big man was lumbering toward us, silhouetted against the bright front window of the restaurant. Realizing that he'd seen me in the light from the window, I shrank back against the bricks, terrified until he spoke. "Miss Mooney! You are such a . . ."

"Hush!" I hissed, recognizing Mike. "I need a place to hide!" A shout back in the alley added urgency to my plea. "You know this town. Quick, where can I go?"

"Follow me!" My young admirer brought his voice down to a whisper and led me across a moonlit backyard to another dark alley. When we were out of danger he said, "Miss Mooney, you are a delight! I haven't laughed so hard in months!"

"Mike, you must leave this dreary town. Where are we going now?"

"My mother runs a boarding house, and there's an empty room."

Mrs. Sinnott was a pleasant Irish woman, obviously fond of her big clumsy son, and somehow divining that I was nearer in age to her than to her boy, she soon installed me in a small second-story room. The furnishings were simple, but the room was quite modern, having been outfitted with an electric lamp invented by my dear friend Mr. Edison. A small window provided a view of a moonlit verbena hedge and a bit of the street. Keystone settled himself on the windowsill as lookout while I gave Mike instructions about fetching the trunk I'd left at my boardinghouse near the theatre. He returned in an hour with my belongings and with news. "As I was loading your trunk into the cart, Officer Teheezel arrived!"

"Did he see you?" I asked in alarm.

"No, no. He was going up to see the landlady."

"But you had already given her the little gift?"

"Yes. She promised me she would say nothing about you. Besides, she has nothing to say! I gave her an address on the other side of town." Mike beamed at his own cleverness.

" 'Sir, your wit ambles well,' as Shakespeare says," I told him. As a reward, I opened my trunk and showed him some of my theatrical souvenirs. He was particularly pleased by a small Kinetoscope that dear Mr. Edison had given me.

But I remained worried, and did not have a restful night despite the excellence of Mrs. Sinnott's bed. My dreams were haunted by the specter of the furious Officer Teheezel, wiping meringue from his eyes.

Keystone woke me at first light, demanding breakfast. As I opened the bottle of cream that had come to hand while I hurried out through the Murphy's Restaurant kitchen, I took stock of my unhappy situation. Teheezel, I was certain, would continue to hunt for me, and while he did not appear to be a giant of intellect, he might well learn that I had been with Mike and trace me to this house. Avoiding him during the day would be possible, but in order to earn enough for my niece's tennis gown, I had to play in *A Flea in Her Ear* that night. It is very difficult to hide in full view of hundreds of people. Teheezel struck me as clod enough to arrest a person right on stage, with no regard for the noble, nay, even sacred calling of the theatrical artiste.

I prepared Keystone's breakfast the way he liked it, with a dollop of whiskey, and took the rest of the cream down to Mrs. Sinnott, who served it with our big bowls of Irish oats and then went into the backyard to wash the sheets.

Mike came downstairs, booming out "Asleep in the Deep." "Mike," I said, as much to quiet him as to obtain information, "it seems to me that the best way to escape Teheezel would be to find the missing pocket watch. Who do you think took it?"

In deep thought, Mike had a comical scowl. But he was bright enough. "Most likely one of his friends," he said. "He was arguing with Pincker and Crane."

"The gentlemen in the peg-top trousers, I presume? Do you know them?"

"Not well. Sam Pincker—he's the shorter one—runs a dry-goods store. The tall thin fellow is Simon Crane. His family has some money, but he's known chiefly as a gambler."

"And gamblers do run up debts," I said, remembering my uncle, who had mortgaged my Aunt Mollie's property and lost it to foreclosure because of gambling debts. "What about Millicent?"

"Millicent is his wife. Why would she take it?"

"Perhaps Dr. Dove took it."

"A doctor wouldn't take a patient's watch!"

"He takes their money for Dove's Elixir."

"No, it must be Crane!" Mike insisted. "But—but how can we prove it?"

"Especially to a policeman who believes his own two eyes and nothing else," I said sadly. "Simon Crane may have pawned the watch already. Do you know where these people live?"

"The doctor's office is only two doors from Murphy's Restaurant. The others all live on Prospect, in the best part of town. Say, we can ask at the pawn shops too," Mike said eagerly.

"Yes. Let's go! I'll fetch my walking cape," I responded, and ran up the stairs.

I took the precaution of donning a dark wig and a veiled hat as well, and soon we were walking through the town. We passed two pawnshops. Mike inquired about hunting-watches, but the only ones there were not engraved with messages to Teddy O'Brien. As he emerged from the second shop, crestfallen, I pointed across the street. Simon Crane, in a fresh pair of peg-top trousers, was in deep conversation with a dapper, cigar-smoking man. It was difficult to hear, but Simon appeared to be pleading for something. The other man shrugged and spread his hands in a placating manner, but was clearly shaking his head. Simon Crane turned away despondently.

"Who is the man with the cigar?" I whispered.

"He's the president of the new bank," Mike replied.

"Mr. Crane does not appear to be happy with what the president was telling him," I said, watching as the banker hailed a carriage.

"I bet Crane heads for the pawnshop!" Mike exclaimed. But to his disappointment the man disappeared into a restaurant.

"Well, let's give him time," I suggested, and we walked on to Prospect Street, which boasted large Queen Anne homes painted in cheerful colors. Teddy O'Brien's house was a tasteful mustard-yellow trimmed with Indian red and forest green. Two elegant carriages waited before it. As Mike and I strolled slowly by across the street, three people emerged from the tall front door: Dr. Dove, hat in hand and with a sad expression; Sam Pincker the dry-goods man, equally serious; and Millicent, weeping once again. The doctor said his adieus and departed in one of the carriages. Pincker murmured to Millicent for a few moments. I had time to reflect that, although I had only seen her in distress and therefore thought of her as puffy-faced and red-nosed, Millicent had the type of ample but small-waisted figure that our new hourglass fashions enhance and that gentlemen tend to appreciate. Certainly Mr. Pincker appeared to enjoy the task of comforting her.

"It does not seem to be the ideal time to accost them about the whereabouts of Teddy's watch," I said to Mike.

"Yes, she is upset."

"Perhaps Dr. Dove's Elixir is not helping Teddy."

We returned to Mike's boardinghouse still puzzling over the situation. I ascended to my room and removed the black wig, which was hot and scratchy, for all its effectiveness. Keystone, on his windowsill, had pricked up his raggedy ears at something below. I glanced out too, and was horrified to see Teheezel striding toward the boardinghouse. The policeman was smarter than I'd expected, or angrier. He looked up, spotted me in the window, and began to jump about, waving his billy-club and shouting, "Murderer!"

Clearly, the fellow was berserk. I locked the bedroom door. For good measure I pushed the bed against it, inadvertently knocking over the whiskey bottle in the process. But there was no time to clean it up. I began to jerk the sheets from the bed.

In a moment there was a furious pounding on the door and the key fell out. "Open in the name of the law, you murderer!" cried Teheezel. "Dr.

Dove says that poor Mr. O'Brien has expired from the effects of his fall! I know you're in there! I can see you through the keyhole!"

Well, I reckon I'd never seen a fellow as rude as this officer! I was sorry to hear of Teddy O'Brien's sad fate, but I had no desire to discuss it with Teheezel. I looked out the window. It was a long way down, three bedsheets high at least. Young Mike came into view by the verbena hedge, looking scared. Hastily, I knotted the corners of my sheets and blankets together and anchored them to a steam pipe. But when I opened the window to make my escape, Mike shook his head violently, pointing at the wall below me. I realized that the knocking at the door behind me had stopped. When I leaned out to look down, a ladder almost hit me in the eye.

Officer Teheezel was determined indeed.

"Sir," I called down to him politely, "you don't want to come up here. I'm nursing a sick cat!" I pointed at Keystone.

Teheezel was halfway up. "What's a sick cat got to do with it?"

"He has hydrophobia," I improvised.

That made him pause. "Hydrophobia?"

Unfortunately Keystone chose that moment to trot across the windowsill and jump back into the room. "Doesn't look like hydrophobia to me," Teheezel declared, and climbed higher.

Well, what's a poor girl to do, when beset by such barbarians? I grabbed the top rung of the ladder and pushed. Slowly, it swayed back, gathering speed as it fell. Teheezel gave a holler and tried to jump off, but landed in the verbena shrubbery on his back, like a great blue beetle, arms and legs flailing about to the tune of Mike's laughter. I ran back across the room, shoved the bed away from the door, and sprinted down the back stairs and out into the yard. Mrs. Sinnott, elbow-deep in lather over the wooden washtub, asked, "What in the world is going on?"

"We have had a visit from a rather unrefined representative of the law," I informed her, and ducked behind a garden shed that sat in the back corner of the yard.

Teheezel, now bedecked with bits of verbena, was on his feet again. The officer may have been slow of wit, but he was quick of eye and spotted me. He ran around the shed to meet me. But I am good at such games too, having practiced them with a variety of shopkeepers in my youth in St. Louis, and by dodging from corner to corner of the little structure in a lively fashion, I succeeded in keeping the shed between me and the uniformed enemy of art. Unfortunately the back fence was forbiddingly tall, and I found no loose planks or other means of escape as I ran back and forth. I began to despair for my future. Then I glimpsed Keystone out in the yard peering into Mrs. Sinnott's washtub. He toppled back with surprising clumsiness. Teheezel gasped and uttered an oath as my little tomcat stood up, swaying, suds all over his face and whiskers, and began staggering toward the policeman.

"Hydrophobia!" yelped Teheezel, believing his own two eyes.

Mike jumped onto the porch, and Mrs. Sinnott gave a little scream too and ran to her son. The officer backed away from the tiny agent of death, his billy-club extended toward him, shouting, "Stop in the name of the law!" Of course the cat didn't stop. Teheezel took another step back, tripped, and sat down suddenly in the washtub.

From the safety of the porch, Mike was laughing uncontrollably.

"I'll be back!" swore Teheezel, and raced away, soggy and leaving a trail of flying soapsuds.

I hurried to my dear little rescuer and cleaned his face. "You clever little tom! You deserve a monument!"

Mike stopped laughing. "Miss Mooney! Beware! Perhaps he does have hydrophobia!"

"It's only soapsuds," I informed him.

"But he was stumbling along, like a sick animal!"

"True," I said. "I fear little Keystone imbibed more whiskey than was good for him this morning."

"Whiskey? You mean he's drunk?"

"He's quite a toper, this one."

Mike began to chuckle again. "Whiskey and soapsuds! And did you ever see anything funnier than that policeman?"

"Now, Mike," his mother reminded him sharply, "the officer says he's coming back. Why don't you two go to the police and straighten this out? And take the cat!"

"The police aren't very reasonable," Mike said.

"Quite right," I agreed. "The trouble is that he has too much faith in his own two eyes."

Mike said slowly, "I can think of a way to destroy that faith."

"Mike, if you can do that, I'll say a good word on your behalf to a New York theatre manager I know. Come tell me your idea." I led the way back into the house and up to the room while he explained, and began to think that the clumsy young fellow might have a bright future after all. Mike's idea was excellent, and worked so well with my own plans that I showed him some particularly rare photographs from my collection.

Twenty minutes later I was crouching under the front porch, and just in time, for Teheezel had returned posthaste. He was accompanied by four other policemen, two of them on bicycles, and by a mean-looking fellow with a huge net, probably the dogcatcher. I was glad that Keystone was under the porch with me, concealed in a basket while he slept off his overindulgence. Mike invited the uniformed visitors in. Two minutes later I followed and tiptoed up the stairs.

They were clustered around my locked door. Teheezel was bent over, his eye to the keyhole. "Open the door!" he shouted. "I can see you're in there! I can see—oh, lordy!" He turned a shocked face to his friends.

"What's wrong, Teheezel?"

"Oh, my, how that infernal woman carries on! She has a jumprope, and no—um—"

"No what, Officer Teheezel?" I asked sweetly from the stairs.

Teheezel whirled to look at me and his jaw dropped. "But—but—" He looked through the keyhole again. "But you're in there, jumping rope!"

The officer was indeed a Dogberry, don't you think? I muttered, "This learned constable is too cunning to be understood."

Teheezel, furious, kicked in the door with a great crash, and stared amazed at a completely empty room.

"Teheezel, don't be a looney! She's right there!" cried a more intelligent man, perhaps the dogcatcher. They all started for me. I slid down the bannister and raced out the front door, pausing only to knock over a porch chair so that the policemen all stumbled over it as they poured from the door. Thankful that I was wearing my best lace-trimmed bloomers, I hitched up my skirts, leaped onto the better-looking of the two police bicycles, and lit out in the direction of Murphy's Restaurant. The police followed close behind. It was a terrifying few moments, not only because the officers of the law were so near, but because Northampton's streets were largely ruts and holes, and the bicycle bumped and bucked like an unruly mule. But I reached my haven a few yards ahead of my pursuers, dropped the bicycle, and ran up the steps into Dr. Dove's oak-paneled offices. "Help! Where's the doctor?" I cried to the woman in a stylish shirtwaist who sat at a desk before a display of Dr. Dove's Elixir.

"Would you care to state your business?" she asked, quite properly. But I'd seen her eyes shift to one of the doors when I asked for Dove, and I wrenched it open to see the good doctor, watch in hand, taking the pulse of a young man in shirtsleeves sitting on a table.

"Dr. Dove! Help me, please!" I exclaimed, flinging myself onto the carpet at his feet.

Dr. Dove returned his watch to its pocket, peered down his nose at me, and frowned. "Madam, I don't believe I've had the pleasure," he said stiffly, then looked up in surprise. Four policemen, a dogcatcher, the woman in the shirtwaist, and my young admirer Mike were all trying to squeeze through the door at once.

I sprang to my feet and embraced the doctor. "Please, please help me, Dr. Dove!" I begged.

I know, I know, a proper lady would never embrace a gentleman without first being correctly introduced. But I was in particularly desperate circumstances, don't you agree? And hang it, being proper hadn't yet helped much with Officer Teheezel.

Dr. Dove, I regret to say, was not the heroic type of gentleman. He pulled my hands from his waist and said in a frosty voice, "My dear madam, do not make a spectacle of yourself!"

"But, sir, the officer believes I knocked poor Teddy O'Brien from the balcony, and then pilfered his watch! And of course I didn't. You did!"

Teheezel was staring at the doctor's watch pocket. Dr. Dove laughed. "I fear you are deluded, madam. This watch is my own, of course. I've had it for years."

"May I see it, sir, if you don't mind?" asked Teheezel.

"Of course." Dr. Dove handed over the watch with a condescending smirk at me.

Teheezel inspected it carefully and cleared his throat. "Dr. Dove, sir, is your watch engraved?"

"Yes, with my initials, C.P.D."

"Sir—well, maybe someone else should look too, because I'm having trouble believing my own two eyes today—but sir, this watch is engraved 'To dear Teddy O'Brien from your little lambie!' "

The other officers, the dogcatcher, and even the woman in the shirtwaist confirmed that it was indeed Teddy O'Brien's watch.

Dr. Dove began to sputter. His patient sprang from the table crying, "I knew I should have gone to Dr. Simpson!"

Teheezel drew himself up to his full scrawny height. "Sir, Mr. O'Brien died under your care! This is indeed a dark deed!"

I nudged young Mike in the ribs and led him from the office. "We've done it! I think Teheezel will leave us in peace now."

"Miss Mooney, I thought it was Simon Crane! How did you know Dr. Dove was the one who stole the watch?"

"I saw him fumbling at Teddy O'Brien's watch pocket while he was checking his pulse," I said.

I know, I know, it was a fib. But let's suppose for a moment that I had taken Teddy's watch, and suppose I'd then exchanged it for the one in the doctor's pocket as I begged him for help. In such a case you wouldn't want me to tell an impressionable young man like Mike, now would you? If we destroy the idealism of our youth our nation will founder, indeed it will. And while Dr. Dove had grown wealthy from selling his elixir, he was otherwise not a great ornament to the medical profession. With a better doctor, poor Teddy might have survived.

Besides, I had to think of my niece's tennis gown. I've noticed that a watch with initials is worth more in a pawnshop than a watch with a message from someone's little lambie.

I thought it would be best to introduce a new topic of conversation. "Mike, it was a splendid idea to show Mr. Edison's motion pictures!" I said. He had fitted the peephole of the little Edison Kinetoscope to the keyhole of the bedroom door.

"It's magical!" Mike exclaimed. "I've seen Edison motion pictures at the Kinetoscope parlors, of course. But I didn't know there were programs with young ladies jumping rope, without—um—"

"Mike, Mr. Edison was conducting a scientific investigation, and clothing would have obstructed the observations," I informed him sternly. "Do you remember Mr. Muybridge's famous photographs of Leland Stanford's horse galloping? Well, Mr. Edison is continuing those studies of animal locomotion. In fact, Keystone's locomotion is featured in some of the motion pictures. They dropped him upside down to record how he lands on his feet every time. Except when he's drunk, of course."

"Well, this one is a capital motion picture!" Mike said with an admiring glance. "I can hardly wait to become an actor too!"

"Dear boy, you mustn't expect too much too soon," I warned him. "But I'll do what I can."

What I could do was limited by Mike's gawky appearance, but when the young man arrived in New York, I directed him to a friend who launched Mike's splendid career by giving him his first role on stage. Well, yes, it was only a vaudeville show. And yes, Mike had to play a horse. Well, half a horse. The rear half. But it was a beginning. And when we met for a whiskey after his first show to celebrate, he was full of plans. "Miss Mooney, apart from the low pay, this life is splendid!" he exclaimed. "I don't want to be an opera singer now. It's much more fun to make people laugh. You know, I've been wondering if I could make people laugh with Mr. Edison's clever motion pictures!"

Fifteen years later, that's exactly what he was doing. I next encountered him in California, where I was touring as the proper Lady Bracknell and the not-so-proper Lady Macbeth. I wanted to see one of the fabled motion-picture studios of Hollywood, so one morning I hired an automobile to transport me to the Edendale area. Parasol in hand, I strolled along the length of a strange building with translucent sides and roof. They called this studio the Fun Factory; and in fact, there was laughter mixed with the shouts and curses that issued from within. Suddenly I heard a familiar voice behind me. "Miss Mooney!" boomed a man in a handsome summer suit. "Would you like to hear me sing 'Asleep in the Deep'?"

"Mike! You look splendid!" I exclaimed. He did indeed, with his expensive suit and glowing suntanned complexion. Only the white scars on his hands bore witness to lowlier days in an eastern iron foundry. "Though I should call you Mack now."

"Ah, you know I've changed my name."

I smiled. "I've kept myself informed. They also call you the King of Comedy, and you run this studio, and you've recently become dreadfully rich."

"And here you are, right on cue!" Mack beamed at me amiably. "Miss Mooney, it would be capital if you would take a role in one of my comedies! We're doing a dozen a month, sometimes more. And we always need funny —um, funny mature ladies."

"Why, thank you, Mack. When my tour ends I'll come speak to you."

"But tell me! There's something I've been wondering for fifteen years."

"What's that?"

"I don't understand—if Dr. Dove wanted to steal that watch—how did he cause Teddy O'Brien to fall? He wasn't even in the restaurant!"

"Why, Mack, I thought you too had seen, and were helping protect the true culprit from the clutches of the constabulary!" I exclaimed. "It was the late Keystone, of course. Teddy O'Brien was standing on the balcony pouting, his back to his friends and his glass in his hand for comfort. Keystone jumped onto Teddy's shirtfront, and startled the man so much he stepped through the railing. The cat, of course, landed on his feet."

"But you said 'late.' Do you mean Keystone is no more?"

"Alas, 'tis true. He grew old, and slow, but he died happy, I believe, attempting to imbibe a magnum of champagne."

Mack removed his hat, looking truly stricken. "Dear old tomcat! I'll never forget how he frightened away that police officer! You and he taught me the key to my success: deflating authority is funny."

"Yes indeed. We did rather deflate that policeman, didn't we? I noticed that your comic police chief is named Teheezel, in his honor. But Mack, do I hear correctly that you named your studio after the insignia of the Pennsylvania Railroad?"

"So they say." Mack smiled at me. "But we know the truth, don't we, Miss Mooney?"

I looked up at the big sign and smiled too. Mack Sennett's Keystone Studios, home of Fatty Arbuckle, Mabel Normand, Syd and Charlie Chaplin, and the amazing, incompetent Keystone Kops.

Few cats, or humans, achieve such delightful memorials.

FROM BRIDGET MOONEY'S SCRAPBOOK

CENTURY MAGAZINE

June 1894

EDISON'S INVENTION
OF THE KINETO-PHONOGRAPH

By Antonia and W.K.L. Dickson

. . . This idea, the germ of which came from the little toy called the Zoetrope, and the work of Muybridge, Marié, and others has now been accomplished, so that every change of facial expression can be recorded and reproduced life size. The Kinetoscope is only a small model illustrating the present stage of.progress but with each succeeding month new possibilities are brought into view. . .

— Thomas A. Edison

"Interesting," the judge said. "Pray explain. And remember you are talking to a police judge."

"Well, sir," I said, "I came to New York to be a singer. I am trying to learn to act so I can sing in the Metropolitan Opera House. I am a bass. So—I am now appearing at the Bowery as the hind legs of a horse."

"I should imagine you'd be good at it," the judge said.

King of Comedy, by Mack Sennett as told to
Cameron Shipp, 1954, p. 31.

Renowned Be Thy Grave; Or, The Murderous Miss Mooney by P. M. Carlson is set in Garamond (the text) and Bernhard (the chapter titles and running titles), and printed on 50 pound Glatfelter Supple Opaque acid-free paper. The cover is by Deborah Miller. The first edition is comprised of approximately one thousand copies in trade softcover, notch-bound, and two hundred copies sewn in cloth, signed and numbered by the author. Each of the clothbound copies includes a separate pamphlet, *Farewell the Plumed Troop* by P. M. Carlson. *Renowned Be Thy Grave* was published in April 1998 by Crippen & Landru Publishers, Norfolk, Virginia.